Fate Forged
Bound Magic: Book 1
B.P. Donigan

Fate Forged
Bound Magic Series™
Red Adept Publishing, LLC
104 Bugenfield Court
Garner, NC 27529
http://RedAdeptPublishing.com/

First Print Edition: November 2018

Cover Art by Streetlight Graphics

This is a work of fiction. Names, characters, places, and incidents either are the product of the author's imagination or are used fictitiously, and any resemblance to locales, events, business establishments, or actual persons—living or dead—is entirely coincidental.

Chapter One

T he sweet smell of vanilla and sugar drifted on the crisp night breeze. Inhaling deeply, I surveyed the dark factory across the street as I considered my options. For the past week, the scent of fortune cookies had drenched my waking thoughts and transformed them into nightmares after dark. At first, I'd convinced myself they were just meaningless bad dreams. Then they started happening every night, each one becoming more vivid and real, until I couldn't sleep. Every morning, I woke up screaming and shaking in my bed.

The completely unexplainable pain from the night terrors left me unable to function for hours after I woke. I missed my shifts and under-the-table cash I couldn't afford to lose. I had rent to pay and a life to live. Boston was expensive. If I didn't get a handle on my brain malfunction, it wouldn't be long before I would be sleeping on the streets again. The damn nightmares had finally driven me all the way across town in the middle of the night with a half-formed plan to break into the old factory and prove that they were just bad dreams.

My internet sleuthing had revealed that the warehouse across the street was the only place in New England that baked and distributed the fortune cookies. That meant it was the one chance that whatever the hell was wrong with me didn't require a soft, padded room or an emergency lobotomy.

1

A reasonable person would've probably gotten a brain scan. At a minimum, I should've waited until daylight when the factory opened. But I couldn't take even one more night of the terrible nightmares, and I knew a brain scan wasn't going to explain anything. I wasn't particularly superstitious, but I just couldn't let go of the realness of the nightmares, not to mention the pain in every single dream. Whatever was happening to me was somehow tied to this factory—I knew it in my gut.

I glared at the warehouse. In the nightmares, I was always tied to a chair in a cold basement—the sweet, thick smell of fortune cookies filling my nose. A blond man with pale skin and flat blue eyes asked questions I refused to answer. Then the torture started. Sometimes he didn't even ask questions. He just used knives, fists, and pain. The unimaginable agony of multiple nights of torture had transformed me into a desperate woman willing to do anything for a peaceful night's rest. A little breaking and entering wasn't going to stand between me and stopping the night terrors.

An icy breeze slapped me in the face as I crossed the street and approached the small parking lot on the east side of the building. I pulled my hoodie up and moved toward the warehouse, careful not to draw attention to myself as I threaded through pockets of shadow between the streetlights. After dark, the empty lot transformed into a sea of temporary cardboard shelters. The pungent smell of the homeless camp mingled with the cookies in a toxic, cloying scent. A chorus of coughs, squabbles, and incoherent muttering carried through the night as I picked my way around the sleeping bodies.

Tonight, most were huddled down, buried under whatever they'd scrounged to protect themselves from the cold, pre-fall Boston air. A small knot of men gathered around a glowing metal barrel, their faces hard and eyes glinting under hoods and blankets. I gave them a wide berth. I could defend myself if I had to, but the people weren't really a threat as long as I followed the rules. I wasn't challenging them or drawing attention to myself. It had been a dozen years since I'd slept on the streets, but I knew how to blend in as just another person seeking shelter from the cold.

Checking to make sure I wasn't followed, I adjusted my backpack, pulled my long, braided hair free of my raised hoodie, and slipped into an alley at the side of the factory. I hurried forward, sending rats scampering behind garbage bins, until I reached two smallish windows at ground level. The thick glass windows were clear holdovers from the warehouse's 1900s origins, and they hadn't been covered with bars. It would be a tight fit, but I was tall and slender, with more lean muscle than curves. I could squeeze through.

Squatting, I checked each one. Both were locked with no alarms. Satisfied that the old building had no tricky security, I donkey-kicked my heel through one of the panes. The sound of shattering glass echoed into the quiet night.

My ears ring with the tinkling of broken glass. Zip ties dig into the bloody skin around my wrists as I strain my fingers closer together. Every twist of my numb hands brings me closer to freedom. A relentless chill curls inside my bones from the damp, cold basement.

A shiver runs through me. Everything hurts.

Another blow lands without warning, and air escapes my lungs in a forceful huff. I gasp and double over until only the restraints hold me to the chair.

Pain. My whole world is pain. Tangy, hot liquid coats my tongue, and I realize I've bitten it. The taste and the thick, cloying scent clogging my nostrils makes my empty stomach heave, and I gag. I gulp in air and try to straighten. I won't let them break me.

"Go to hell!" I spit at the blond man looming over me.

His upper lip curls on one side. A twitch of his fingers brings another man toward me with a broken glass bottle.

The vision ended, leaving me on the ground, cradling my head in my fists. Several minutes ticked by while I rocked back and forth, dragging air into my lungs as I tried to manage the pain. The episodes were getting worse, coming more often. I couldn't handle this anymore. I had to know I wasn't making up the visions—that I wasn't going insane. I needed to see the factory basement. I had no idea what I would do then, but at least I would know if I was crazy or not.

I reached through the broken window, unlocked it from the inside, and slipped carefully through. The small storefront had a peeling Formica sales counter stretching along one side of it and shelves lining the walls, full of various fortune-cookie offerings and custom T-shirts.

The thick, sweet scent inside the building made my stomach rumble. I could almost taste the cookies, reminding me that I'd skipped not only my shift at the shelter, but with it, my dinner. My attention snagged on a metal shelf filled with bags of fortune cookies for sale beside the register. I snatched one up and stuffed it in my backpack. I paused, shook my head at how much I'd changed, and tossed a dollar bill on the counter as I passed to the employee side.

Behind the sales counter stood a single door, which led to a tiny back office. Papers littered the surface of a small desk, along with an ancient desktop computer, and behind that was an unmarked door. That had to be the basement. I opened the heavy metal door and found a wooden staircase leading down to a pitch-black floor.

A pulse of fear stopped me, and I paused, chewing on my lower lip. Someone should cue the horror movie soundtrack. Despite my desperate state, I knew going downstairs was a bad idea. Even if I headed down there and found the exact basement from my nightmares, it wouldn't prove anything. It wouldn't necessarily stop the nightmares either. And the sound of the breaking glass could have caught someone's attention earlier—cops could be headed my way at that very moment.

The fear didn't stop me for long. At that point, I would have done anything to make the visions and torture stop. And if I was right, the episodes had something to do with this basement, where the smell of fortune cookies made my mouth water and my insides clench with remembered pain. I pushed my doubts aside. I *needed* to see what was down there in the dark, scary basement from my nightmares.

I reached into my bag and pulled out a flashlight and my knife. The familiar hilt fit perfectly into the well-formed calluses on my hand. The weight and balance of the weapon was comforting. When I was sixteen, I'd found it at a pawn shop and worked for weeks hustling enough cash to buy it. A skinny teenage girl spending most of her nights sleeping on the street needed a knife in her hoodie pouch. It was one of those large utility knives used by World War II vets. The pawn shop guy had called it a Mark 2 Ka-Bar. I'd named it Ripper.

Ripper had a solid seven-inch blade and a long history. When I was old enough, I'd spent countless hours hopping around bars and winning impossible bets. Ripper was my constant companion and, on a few occasions, the only way I'd made it out of some janky situations.

I propped open the door with my backpack and peered into the dark mouth of the basement. I just needed to get down the creepy stairs, see the basement that my nightmares were made of, and get the hell out.

The stair creaked on the first step, and I froze. Sweeping the flashlight from side to side, I tried to chase away the dark edges, but the beam lit only a narrow path in front of me. Shadows lurked all around. The back of my neck tingled. Fear spiraled down my spine as scenes from slasher movies flooded my mind. Every instinct in my body screamed at me to run.

Not excited about the idea of an emergency trip to the hospital, I forced myself to take the stairs slowly, one at a time, until I reached the cold cement floor. A bare light bulb hung in the center of the room over an upended chair. I pulled the string, and light flooded the basement.

Light flares from above. I squint. Swirls of dust float down from the exposed insulation in the ceiling, glowing like fireflies as my eyes adjust to the new brightness.

Fresh fear pounds through my veins. A line of men descends the creaky stairs, their bodies draped in long robes, and my stomach twists in fear. The shadows masking their faces claw a path toward me like demons coming to steal my soul. The men stand shoulder to shoulder in a half-circle in front of me. Their auras flare with violent magic, and the dark glow is tangible around them, like heavy fog lifting from the ground.

The leader steps forward, light reflecting off a full head of blond hair. I stare into his ice-blue eyes.

Blood pounds in my ears, and heat prickles against my skin as I bare my teeth, wishing I had some way to strike out at him. But he has already taken everything from me. I'm powerless and completely at his mercy.

A smile twists across the blond's face. With confident ease, he flicks open a small knife and slices swiftly across his hand, filling his palm with blood as crimson as his aura. Energy pulses within the thick liquid.

I twisted in a full circle, reeling from the vision that overlaid what I currently saw. The stairs were in the same place, and the ceiling had the same exposed insulation. The men in robes stood over by the wall, chanting. A surprising word bounced through my mind: *Magic.*

This isn't real. Magic isn't real.

Another episode pushed through more forcefully.

My stomach throbs. There is a hollow, piercing ache in the center of me. I've lost something important... magic. The magic is gone, and it hurts. In its place, they've left questions I refuse to answer.

Utter terror grips me as I realize that at some point, I will break. They'll wait for my magic to return and start again. They'll rip the life energy from me over and over as I endure round after round of soul-searing pain.

He'll never stop.

I can't. I can't do it again. It's only a matter of time until they break me. And when I tell them what they want to know, not only will I die, everyone I love will too.

Straining my fingers, I pull hard against the sharp plastic zip ties around my wrists. Through swollen eyes, I glare at the circle of men and their leader. I hate him with every ounce of my soul.

Finally, my fingers reach a sigil on the inside of my wrist, and I channel a spark of magic from it. They haven't taken everything yet, the bastards. A small metal charm lands in my palm—an access point to my source.

It's not a lot, but it's enough for what I need to do. Hope flares wild in my chest, and I try not to let it show on my face.

I cast my mind away from my surroundings. Double vision hits, and I see a young woman with long auburn hair, holding—of all things—a mop. Her hair is tied back in a braid, and she dances around a wet linoleum floor, earbuds and an ancient Walkman providing music I can't hear.

She looks happy.

"What the actual hell?" I cried out, my voice shaking.

I saw... me. The woman pushing around a mop at the hospital was *me*. I'd just seen myself through someone else's eyes!

The realization hit me—those were someone else's memories. The torture and murder plaguing my nightmares had happened to a real person. His name popped into my head with complete clarity: *Marcel*. I didn't know how—maybe the name came with the memories. All of the crazy was straining my brain. I had no idea what the hell was going on.

I whipped my gaze around the room with new realization. Tossed carelessly on its side, the chair held no sign of Marcel, the men torturing him, or anything tying my visions to reality. Other than the panic gripping me, everything seemed normal.

"What's happening to me?" *You've lost it, Maeve. You're completely batshit nuts.*

The empty basement had no chance to answer before a vision grasped me again and pulled me under.

The blond grabs a fistful of my hair in his bloody palm and wrenches my head backward. His calm is gone, and menace flies from his lips. "You can't hide anymore."

I gather every bit of magic coiled within me and shove it outward.

An electric storm explodes in the room. Magic power rips through my captors. They scream in agony. Their red-black magic twists away from them, obeying the call toward me.

"No!" the blond yells, lunging forward.

A harsh wail of pain and pleading rips from me. "Remember!"

The blond slices his knife into the flesh of my neck, ending all the pain.

With shaking hands, I scrubbed away the sting of the blade from my neck. The double sense of the vision and my current surroundings sent my heart pounding in a staccato rhythm so fast, it felt as if two organs were beating inside me. Sweat plastered my clothes to my skin as I tried to sort out how I could've possibly been experiencing someone else's memories.

I searched the room, desperate for something to anchor me to reality. This was more than I bargained for. I didn't know how this was even possible. A glint behind the chair caught my attention, and I reached for the small, round piece of metal. It was partially covered in blood, but I resisted the urge to drop it and wipe my hand on my jeans. Rubbing my thumb across the surface, I discovered something etched into the charm—two overlapping triangles, each a mirror image of the other, with their bases looping out to the sides.

My fingers shook. The design matched the tattoo on my arm.

Chapter Two

The bus pulled away from the cobbled sidewalk just outside Downtown Crossing in Boston, leaving behind a cloud of gray exhaust that floated in the cold evening air. Riding around the city for the past hour with the charm squeezed tight in my fist, I'd tried to figure out if I had completely lost my grip on reality. I still wasn't sure.

I forced my fingers to relax. The round face had a hole at the top where a small ring could be placed. I wondered if Marcel had worn it like a necklace or perhaps a bracelet. I had no idea why it had the same symbol as my tattoo. I'd never seen the mark anywhere else. But I also didn't really know where mine had come from. I'd had it since I could remember, and my birth parents weren't around to ask. *Thank God.* I didn't want to meet the type of idiots who tattooed a toddler. Clearly, I'd been better off without them in my life.

The round, smooth metal seemed unusually warm in my hand as I walked through the dark, empty streets of the city just past midnight. I was stalling. I needed to go home and get some sleep before my shifts the next day—I'd already missed two nights at my restaurant gig—but my tiny basement apartment was two buses and a transfer away. Besides, sleep was a distant reality that would definitely end in more nightmares. I headed away from bed and back toward the city, needing space to clear my head.

I walked for a long time, oblivious to everything but my thoughts, until I realized something felt wrong. The back of my neck tingled. I looked up, suddenly aware of my surroundings. The nine-to-fivers were long gone, leaving the dark downtown streets nearly empty. Only a few people were still out and hurrying about their business, bundled against the cool night. No one stood out, but I knew the tingling on my skin wasn't something I should ignore when I was out alone at night. Almost of their own accord, my feet moved faster across the cobbled street, away from the uncomfortable feeling of being watched.

The anxious feeling followed me. I paused and searched the street again. A homeless man snored loudly, curled on the cobblestone entrance to Macy's. A laughing couple ducked into the entrance to the T, no doubt catching one of the last subway trains for the night. No one else was there, which also meant there was no one to call for help.

I'd learned a long time ago to trust my gut. Something felt wrong, and I needed to get off the street.

I picked up my pace. A gap between two buildings lay about fifty feet ahead. I crossed the street and sprinted for the opening. After crouching behind a garbage can, I set my backpack on the ground and pulled out my knife. It'd been a while since I'd had to defend myself, but Ripper and I could handle any trouble.

As I hid out of sight, I counted to ten in my head. Right on cue, a tall man in jeans and a puffy down jacket rounded the corner and walked briskly past the alley. He took two more steps, paused, and doubled back. He scanned up and down the street. Looking. Stalking.

I grimaced. If I were smart, I would stay hidden until he walked away. But I'd never claimed to be particularly intelligent. And I didn't back away from a fight. I wanted to know why this creep was following me. And next time, I wanted him to think twice before he stalked some other girl.

The younger me would have jumped him with the knife right then, but I hesitated. I wasn't sure if the man had really followed me, or if I was in the middle of a complete mental breakdown. I wasn't exactly thinking straight at the moment. The guy could have just been lost and not following me at all.

He paused in front of the alleyway and peered into the dark, right at my hiding spot. "Hello, kitten."

My stomach twisted. I should have listened to my gut. Now my moment of surprise was gone. Trapped in the dead-end alley without an escape route, I stood and gripped Ripper at my side. I didn't wave the knife at the man like an idiot. Instead, I held it loosely in my hand, ready to strike. If he didn't see it coming, all the better.

"Why are you following me?" I demanded.

The man stepped forward into the light of a streetlamp, which illuminated his pale hair. A slow smile spread across his face, but it didn't reach his cold blue eyes.

My knees locked. He had the same blond hair and ice-blue eyes. He was my nightmare come to life—Marcel's murderer.

When I spoke, my voice came out shaky. "Who are you?"

He stepped closer, completely blocking the entrance to the alley. The whites of his eyes *shifted* to yellow—like a wolf's—transforming his entire face from human to predator.

I stumbled backward, holding my knife up between us. "*What* are you?"

Ripper was a big knife and terrible for throwing. I had good aim, but the chances I could hit the blond man with the seven-inch field knife were next to nothing.

Light flared around him, the street lit with an unearthly glow. He lunged.

I didn't have time to act on anything but reflex and slashed Ripper blindly.

The blond dodged and lunged again, grabbing my arm. I pulled back, but he didn't resist as hard as I expected, and I tripped over the uneven, cobbled brick. Flailing, we both landed in a heap of limbs.

My knife struck home, sinking into his neck. I scrambled away on my heels and hands, staring at the blade buried deep in his flesh.

He pulled Ripper out of his neck and threw it on the ground with a clank of metal. Dark blood gushed from the wound and soaked into his collar. I'd hit an artery—he was a dead man.

Holy hell, I just killed him. I'd seen some brutal street fights, but I'd never killed anyone before. I staggered backward in shock.

The man grasped his neck. Red light edged in black flared around him then solidified into a complex pattern of glowing threads, just like Marcel's memory. The man lowered his hand, revealing perfect, unscarred skin. The blood was the only evidence that I had just stabbed him in the neck. The wound was gone.

I stared like an idiot, transfixed on the glowing threads fading around him and the impossibly healed skin above his collar. The man rose to his feet and snarled like an animal. His teeth elongated into fangs as I watched.

I scrambled deeper into the dead-end alley. He stalked forward with bared teeth and murder in his yellow eyes.

My back hit the rough brick wall at the end of the alley. I was trapped, weaponless. Crouching, I pulled myself together and prepared to put up a fight before he took me down. I wasn't going to die cowering in an alley.

"Titus!"

My attacker—Titus—whirled on his heel toward the head of the narrow alley, where a newcomer stood in the shadows. With dark hair and clothing, he blended into the night except for the gleaming sword in his hand. He twisted his wrist, warming the muscles in a slow, casual way.

A blaze of light swallowed Titus again, and a sword appeared in his hand. Without warning, the two men ran at each other as I stared in open-mouthed shock. I couldn't keep up with this nightmare.

Titus's blade slashed through the air. The newcomer pivoted backward and spun, avoiding the weapon's sharp edge by inches. He swung his blade toward Titus's chest in the same movement, but Titus deflected the blow easily.

I flinched at the incredible noise of metal on metal. *Now I know I'm crazy.* Sword fights didn't happen in real life. I rubbed my eyes, but the surreal scene continued.

The newcomer tried to spear Titus through the chest with an impossibly fast lunge. Titus twisted to the side, but a well-timed kick from the other man caught him in the gut, and Titus crashed into the hard brick wall ten feet in front of me.

"No follow-through," the newcomer taunted.

Titus roared and swung his sword like an axe over his head. He swung again and again with powerful blows that crashed against the newcomer's blade and pushed them deeper into the alley, closer and closer to me. Metal rang as they fought, deafening me.

Someone was going to hear them and call the cops.

The newcomer went on the offensive. His strikes were fast and hard, and each one forced Titus to give up the ground he'd just gained. Titus grunted, yelled, and fought each blow, but he couldn't stop the newcomer's lightning-fast strikes. Within a minute, they were both back in the street.

With my eyes glued to the fight, I slid closer to the opening of the alley, ready to make a run for it as soon as I had an opening.

"You're their pawn," Titus called. "You always have been!"

The newcomer responded with a series of blows that drove them farther into the street. Titus blocked each one until the last one caught him on the arm. Blood flowed.

I moved slowly out of the alley and into the open street, edging my way directly behind the fighters. My heart beat hard in my chest. I had a clear exit, but I froze, afraid any movement would draw their attention to me. The light around Titus intensified, like a bloody spotlight shining in his aura. Dark energy sizzled from him, and goose bumps rose across my skin.

Titus threw out his free hand, and a massive ball of energy flew straight toward the newcomer's chest.

The other man dove out of the way, but I had nowhere to go. The ball of energy hit me in the chest. I flew off my feet and landed hard in the middle of the street, sliding on my backside across the ground.

A million pricks of sizzling energy burned across my skin as I lay in a heap, gasping for breath. Everything hurt. It felt as if I'd been hit with a two-by-four. My ears rang. Streetlights swayed in time with the pounding in my head.

Clashing metal rattled through the fog in my brain. After a minute, I forced myself up onto my elbows and blinked through the mental haze. The men fought in the street, circling and striking at expert speeds, ignoring me on the ground a dozen yards away.

By the time my vision cleared, the newcomer glowed with a radiant golden light, contrasting with the darker power from Titus. I shook my head, wondering if I had a concussion.

Run, idiot. I pushed myself unsteadily to my feet and ran for my life.

FIVE MINUTES OF SCARED-as-hell sprinting later, I threw myself through the front door of the Boston Women and Children's Shelter and slammed the deadbolt home. Father Mike often left it open past curfew on cold nights, but a little extra security was in order.

My knees gave, and I landed on the floor, gasping for breath. Safely inside and under the harsh fluorescent lights, I couldn't believe what I had just witnessed. I couldn't believe an actual sword fight had just happened in the streets of Boston. *So much for the police cutting down on crime.* Like a bad dream, I wondered if I had imagined it all—animal eyes and sharp teeth included—until I looked at my right hand coated in Titus's dried blood.

I squeezed my eyes shut and focused on breathing until my thoughts found some kind of order. I'd lost Ripper. Obviously, getting away with my life had been top priority, but losing my knife really sucked. And it would become an even bigger problem if one of those guys ended up facedown on the sidewalk, leaving a body and my knife. My fingerprints were all over it, and I had a record. I did not need cops asking me questions about dead guys with swords.

I didn't know who the men were or why they'd been fighting each other. It seemed as though the newcomer had tried to protect me. But for all I knew, he'd fought Titus for the privilege of killing me first. The whole situation was too messed up to make any sense.

The charm! I searched my pockets and sighed in relief as I pulled it out of my jeans. The evidence of the connection to Marcel felt comfortably solid in my palm. My head ached with all the crazy, and I hugged my knees to my chest.

It took tremendous force of will to drag myself through the shelter instead of straight onto an unoccupied cot, but I needed to talk to Father Mike. During daylight hours, he would have been serving food from the kitchen or talking with the regulars. But given the late hour, I headed for the small office he'd converted from a storage closet.

I found him hunched over a box of donated clothes. The room was just large enough to fit a desk, a single chair, and cleaning supplies stacked haphazardly along the walls. Seeing him immediately calmed me. I'd spent countless hours in the shelter, a lot of them in his office when I'd gotten caught doing something particularly stupid. He must not have had a current problem child because a thin layer of dust coated the floorboards and the single shelf in the corner. The mop and I had been well-acquainted in my day.

As much as he was a paternal figure in my life, he didn't look that old. With dark-brown hair and brown eyes, he had pale skin like me, and his only wrinkles were laugh lines. He could have easily passed for early thirties. Over the past ten years, he looked as if he hadn't aged at all.

As if I were fifteen all over again, I hesitated in the doorway, hoping he could solve all my problems. "Father?"

He looked up with a friendly grin that died as soon as he saw my expression. "What's wrong?"

"I..." Maybe I should have waited until the sun rose. Perhaps this whole thing was an elaborate hoax or another nightmare. I sighed. It was too late for that—whatever the hell was happening to me was real. The blood was evidence of that, and the energy that had hit me in the chest was definitely real enough. I was in deep shit, and I needed help. Father Mike had always been there for me before. I decided to tell him what had happened even if it made me sound crazy.

He rose from the floor, his full attention on me. "What happened?"

I didn't even know where to start. And I really didn't want him to have me committed. "Someone followed me. He should be dead—then his neck healed—and the blood..." I needed to slow down and sound less crazy. "I had these nightmares, but I think they're real. And now I have someone else's memories." I still wasn't making sense. Maybe I was in shock. I flipped my bloody palm over and back again, staring at the dried patches of red.

Father Mike grabbed my shoulder in a grip too tight to be comforting. The pressure pulled me back to the ground, as did his worried gaze. "What do you remember?"

A dark-haired woman with tears streaming down her face stands in front of me. "When you remember where home is, we'll be here for you."

She disappears, and I'm in the middle of a field of grain, surrounded by jagged brown mountains. The sun warms my face as I wipe sweat from my brow with the long sleeve of my shirt. I'm exhausted, but the effort feels good, productive.

I blink, and I'm in a room full of weapons. The smell of metal and oil fills my nostrils, the familiar warmth of exertion pulsing in my chest. My fingers ache to reach out and grab one of the knives.

Then I'm suddenly crouching, hiding in a building, peering through a crack in a plank-board wall to the pasture outside. I stare at a woman who is surrounded by wild white magic. It storms around her, billowing her hair. Her arms rise in front of her as if to stop—

"Stop!" I gasped. Panting, I pushed down Marcel's memories. It was too much.

Father Mike's eyes were wide. "Maeve?"

The foreign memories pounded inside my skull, trying to escape. My control slipped with each episode, and I almost couldn't breathe. "I'm seeing things I don't remember."

The father grabbed my hand. His brow pinched in concern as he waited for me to explain. I focused on his face, while Marcel's memories rammed against my brain.

My voice came out hoarse as I whispered, "I don't know what's wrong with me. This is really happening, but it can't be real."

He guided me to the hard plastic chair. "Do you remember anything else? Any other memories?"

The air in the windowless office felt too heavy. I couldn't get enough oxygen in my lungs, but childlike hope flared hot in my chest. Father Mike believed me. He would help me.

"The blond man—I think his name is Titus—he showed up, and another guy fought him. With swords. Did I mention the swords? And he hit me with magic." A hysterical laugh slipped out before I could swallow it down. "Please don't have me committed. I know magic isn't real—I swear I'm not crazy." I stared up at him. "Am I crazy?"

With a concerned glance at me, the father started opening drawers in his desk, tossing papers out of his way as he searched through them. His frantic behavior dashed my fragile hope back into confusion.

"You're not crazy. But I'm about to shatter your world view. I'm sorry we don't have time to take this slowly." He opened a drawer, slammed it closed, then yanked open the next one. "You'll just have to believe me when I tell you magic *is* real. The people you saw were from another realm called Aeterna, where the magic is deeper."

"What?" My brain couldn't process what he was telling me, as if his sentences were somehow in the wrong order. I understood the individual words, but the meaning didn't make sense. "What are you saying?"

He threw a sympathetic look my way and grabbed a backpack from one of the donation boxes. "They're a civilization of magic users who split from this realm two centuries ago. The history between our people dates back beyond that, but we keep ourselves separate because of the magic."

He paused his frantic movements for a moment, and I stared at him in blank surprise. "What exactly are you saying? Magic is real?"

"How can I explain? Magic exists, but it's only accessible in certain places in this world, and to certain people who are sensitive

to it. There's the surface realm—Earth—where the Mundanes live."
He gestured at the room around us. "No magic. Or very little anyway. But there are also pockets of magic that overlap this realm.
The deeper the pocket, the stronger the magic. Aeterna is a realm in
the center of this world, and it's full of people who use magic every
day."

"You're saying there's another place deeper inside Earth that's
full of magic?" The words coming out of my mouth were making
my brain hurt. I fully expected someone to jump out and tell me I
was being punked.

"It's more like..." He held up his hands, palms facing each other.
"The realms are parallel. There are lots of realms in this planet, and
they exist in tandem with each other. Magic is simply the energy
found in all life —it's a symbiotic relationship."

I glanced around the room, looking for something normal to
keep me afloat, and found a tower of tissue boxes stacked in the corner. Somehow, I was reacting more calmly to this crazy information
than I had any reason to, maybe because I'd already experienced the
magic throwing me flat on my ass. Or maybe after spending several
days questioning my own sanity, any explanation was a relief.

He started stuffing things into the backpack. "Life energy—magic, as it's more commonly known here—is created from all
life," he continued. "Every living thing gives off some amount of energy, and all that is stored in the very core of Earth. It's the source
of all magic."

"I think my brain might explode." I slumped in the chair. It
hurt my sense of reality to think about magic as more than a Vegas
side act, but I couldn't deny what I had just experienced. I'd seen
the magic energy with my own eyes.

I pushed the heels of my hands into my eye sockets. A headache
was starting behind my skull. The pressure of Marcel's memories
pushed in on me, threatening to take control again. "Why didn't

you tell me this before? I don't understand why any of this is happening."

Father Mike stopped his mad rush around the room and sat on the corner of the desk nearest me. He squeezed my shoulder, and a soft, sympathetic frown curved his lips. "The man you described—Titus—is the leader of a group of radicals who kill people to take their life energy. He hopes to amass enough power from their deaths to control this realm—the whole Mundane world. They call themselves the Brotherhood."

I rubbed away the memory of a sharp knife across my neck. Marcel had been a victim of the Brotherhood. They'd killed him to steal his magic. And I'd somehow gotten stuck with his memories. I didn't even know Marcel or how that could have happened. There was no explanation for why any of this had happened to *me* or how Father Mike knew all of this stuff about magic and other realms. I opened my mouth with a million questions, but they all pushed to the front, jumbling together.

Father Mike scooped the backpack off the desk. "I know you have more questions, but we need to leave before they find you."

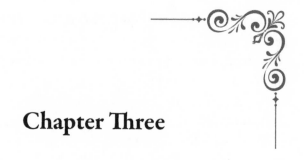

Chapter Three

"None of this makes sense." I tried to stop my brain from spinning. Maybe I wasn't crazy after all, but everything I believed had just flipped on its head and then done three more backflips.

The father squeezed the tops of my arms. "Maeve, I know this is hard to accept. I'll explain everything on the road." He shouldered the backpack. "Right now, we don't have time. We need to get you—" His eyes darted over my shoulder, and he froze.

The newcomer from the alley stood in the doorway. I jumped to my feet.

A frown played across the man's face as he examined both of us, slowly twisting Ripper in his left hand. His long sword was noticeably absent, and he didn't even look as though he'd just fought for his life half an hour ago in an alley *with a freaking sword.* The man took a single step inside the office, and it was hard not to step back automatically from the force of his presence.

He raised his chin at me. "Who is she?"

The father rocked on his feet and licked his lips. "An Earthen child. An orphan with no family." He shifted toward me, subtly positioning himself between me and the newcomer. "And you are?"

The man's brow furrowed. "You may call me Lord Valeron."

Lord Valeron? This guy needed to be brought down a peg. Or ten.

His *Lordly Highness* had dark, road-worn clothing that matched the way his mouth twisted down at the corners. His dark hair was cut military-short, and he was tall, maybe six feet, with broad shoulders, and he was currently blocking the only exit. We wouldn't be getting past him without a fight.

Father Mike's stance had gone rigid. "You're Silas Valeron, the son of Lord Commander Valeron?"

The man's lips pursed a tiny fraction, turning down at the corners. "The same. I wasn't aware of any Harvesters in Boston."

"I'm traveling through on my return to Aeterna," Father Mike said. "Ending my post."

His expression twisted into a suspicious glare. "The leader of the Brotherhood attacked her. Do you know why? Who is she?"

Father Mike glanced at me with wide eyes, silently communicating danger. "I believe she interrupted a Transference ritual, and the spell endowed her with power taken from the Brotherhood, my lord."

My head whipped toward Father Mike. He definitely hadn't mentioned that earlier. I didn't know exactly what he was talking about, but I could figure out the gist of it. And if I had stolen power from this murderous Brotherhood cult, they were not going to just let me slip off quietly. I was so screwed.

His nose wrinkled as he sized me up and apparently found me lacking. "She did this on her own?"

My temper flared. The past few hours had been an emotional rollercoaster, and I'd lost control of just about everything happening in my life. I was beyond done.

I held out my hand. "Give me my knife."

One of his eyebrows arched. He held up Ripper in his open palm. "You should not carry this knife with you all the time."

"Says the guy with a sword," I said, letting my irritation color my voice.

Father Mike cleared his throat. "If I may... Lord Silas is referring to a Tracer spell. It connects a familiar object back to its owner, which is how he followed you from the street." He frowned, possibly because carrying around a knife didn't fit his idea of how I should be living my life.

I ignored the old disagreement and wiggled my extended fingers at Lord Asshole. "My knife?"

Silas jerked his head in a brisk, impatient motion and curled his fingers tight around my knife. "I will escort you both to Aeterna. The Council can determine what to do with her."

I opened my mouth to object, but Father Mike beat me to it. "With respect, Lord Valeron"—he twisted his hands together—"taking Maeve to the Council is not advisable."

Silas's face darkened. "She's not your concern any longer."

"I can take her out of Boston, away from the Brotherhood, where she'll be safe. The Council needn't—"

"She is safe under my protection. The Council will want her."

I snorted loudly. There was no way I was safe with him or his Council.

Silas's irritation shifted to me. "This is not a debate. You *will* return with me."

"I'm not going anywhere with you." I gave him my hard stare. I didn't care if he was hot shit in his world; I wasn't going to let him walk all over me in mine.

Annoyance spread over his face, but he didn't say a thing. He just stared, waiting for me to bow and kiss his ring.

Rage made me itchy. My glare drifted to Ripper, which was still gripped in his left hand.

"Maeve, please be calm." Father Mike's voice was a whisper. "Your magic is unstable right now—"

His warning came too late. Power tingled across my skin. Light flared, and an electric wave of energy rolled through me. I blinked, and threads of white magic danced around the room.

Brilliant golden power flooded the space around Silas a fraction of a second later. With a quickness that spoke of experience, he crouched into a defensive stance. "Her flare!"

Father Mike's hands rose from his sides, palms facing me. "Maeve, you need to stay calm. Just—"

"Stop immediately!" Silas ordered.

He did not get to tell me what to do! He needed to shut his stupid face. Every word out of his mouth pissed me off.

"Mae?" Father Mike drew my attention with the familiar nickname. "I need you to focus. Take a deep breath, okay? You can control this."

The father stepped between Silas and me with a panicked look. A realization cut through my angry haze—I was in danger and making it worse. Father Mike was trying to help me.

Attempting to ignore Lord Asshole, I focused on my breathing. Like unstopping a drain, the energy faded until the glow of magic disappeared. I felt strangely empty as my anger transformed into confusion. "Someone needs to tell me what's going on."

"The Brotherhood cannot get this power back," Silas said, his face hard. "You will return with me to Aeterna immediately."

"Yeah, I don't think so." I tried to keep the anger under control, but if he didn't stop ordering me around, I was going to lose my temper again. "If the Brotherhood is trying to kill me to get whatever the hell is stuck inside me, why should I trust your Council to do any differently?"

He opened his mouth to argue with me then shrugged, either in agreement or a lack of caring; I couldn't tell which. "I give you my word no harm will come to you."

"I don't trust you either."

I expected him to be pissed off and demand that I trust him. But his face remained completely neutral as he said, "That's probably wise."

I narrowed my eyes.

"But," he continued, "you don't have another option. Either the Brotherhood will find you, or the Council will. You can't hide from both."

"I don't give two shits what you think my options are. I can take care of myself, thank you very much."

In two long, aggressive strides, he towered over me, scowling. "I won't let your power fall back into their hands, even if I have to kill you to stop it from happening."

Father Mike laid his hand on my shoulder, breaking our glaring contest, and cleared his throat softly. "My lord, I don't mean to overstep, but if what I have heard about you is true... can you not show mercy to this innocent? She has no part in our world, no understanding of the consequences of her actions."

Silas's perma-scowl twisted into a tight glare. His right hand curled, making me recall the sword he had gripped in the same hand earlier that night.

"The Council will not hesitate to use her," Father Mike continued. "She has no Sect to protect her, no family influence to draw on. The Council will drain the magic from her without hesitation. She's just a child, an innocent who deserves a chance to return to her Mundane life."

Silas stalked to the far side of the room, his back to us.

This whole business was insane. Just days ago, I was making things work on my own. Mopping floors at the hospital and pulling under-the-table shifts at restaurants weren't glamorous, but I didn't owe anyone anything. At the moment, my freedom depended on the mercy of the asshat in front of me. I desperately wished to go back to my normal life before tortured memories, stolen magic, sword fights, and evil Councils.

"What would you have me do?" Silas finally asked. "She has a decided lack of options."

"Take her to a Fate," Father Mike suggested. "If they can remove the magic the Brotherhood transferred to her, the Council doesn't need to know about her, and the Brotherhood will have no reason to harm her."

"An audience with a Fate would require Lord Alaric's blessing." Silas dismissed the idea with a short wave of his hand. "The Council will never allow her to do so if they think the magic she possesses would be lost to them."

"If a Fate can help me," I argued, "I'll deal with this Alaric guy. I just want this nightmare to be over."

Silas guffawed and continued wearing out the linoleum. "You're not ready to 'deal' with Lord Alaric. He'd run you to the post and back."

Lord Asshole was not being helpful.

"However..." Silas stopped pacing and stared at me with a speculative expression. His lips drew into a thin line. "I will take you to the Fate if you agree to a condition."

"What condition?" I asked, my eyes narrowing.

"If we're not able to remove the power, you will submit yourself to the Council for safe keeping in their service."

I frowned. He said the Council would use me for the power trapped inside of me—and that sounded a lot like a lifetime of servitude.

"Taking her into Aeterna is not an option!" Father Mike argued.

"It's her *only* option." Silas paused for a long moment, and his steel-gray eyes bored into mine. "If she does not agree, I will take her to the Council now."

The threat hung in the air for a second, and I had no doubt he was dead serious. He would toss me over his shoulder and drag me off in a heartbeat. *Like the pigheaded caveman he clearly was.*

"The Council will kill her," Father Mike insisted.

"If she agrees to my offer, I'll do my best to prevent that. But yes, they're unpredictable, and I cannot guarantee the outcome if the Fate cannot help her first."

He turned to me, suddenly deciding I could be part of the conversation. "The Council's decision is unknown. But there is no doubt the Brotherhood will kill you. When they find you, they will perform a Transference ritual that will strip the magic from you in what I understand is a painful death. I'm offering you a chance to avoid either outcome."

I remembered Marcel's death at Titus's hands and tried to focus on breathing. So my options were death or certain death. My life kept getting shorter by the minute. I had to get rid of the power stuck inside of me. "If I go with you, you'll swear to protect me from both of them as best you can?"

"I swear it," Silas said solemnly.

There had to be a loophole in his deal somewhere. "Where is this Fate?" I asked.

"The location of the Fate's temple is fluid, but there is one in this realm. It will be difficult, but I can take you to it without alerting the Council."

"Vague much?"

Father Mike placed his hand on my shoulder. "Seeking a Fate will give you time to figure out your options." He searched my face, urging me to agree, but I could tell he wasn't happy with this deal either. "You can't stay here with the Brotherhood after you," he continued. "This is the only way to keep you safe now."

I didn't trust this uptight Lord Silas, and I definitely didn't trust his Aeternal Council. But I *did* trust Father Mike. And honestly, I was flat out of choices. I couldn't stay in Boston with a murderous rebel cult after me, and I couldn't let the evil magic Council snatch me up either.

I studied Silas and wondered what his true motivations were. My world had done a one-eighty in the past twenty-four hours, and now my fate depended on this man. "Why are you willing to help me?"

"Because I can." His face remained completely neutral—a blank mask.

I narrowed my eyes. That wasn't enough.

"Innocents deserve protection," he added.

Maybe so, but he had other motivations I didn't understand. I waited, but he didn't offer any other explanation. My thoughts went to Marcel. Titus had tortured and killed Marcel, and the intensity of his memories threatened to overwhelm me. The Brotherhood had already tried to kill me once, and they would be back. Everything I'd heard about the Council—all of it terrible—meant they would be after me soon too. I had to do something. I needed to get rid of this power and these god-awful memories of torture, and I needed to do it as soon as possible.

"Take me to the Fate," I decided. "I agree to your condition." If I couldn't get rid of the magic, I would figure out a way to deal with the Council later. Possible death was better than certain death.

Silas strode over to me. I locked my knees in place as he towered over me, scowling, all muscle and hard lines. He held out his hand, palm up. When I just stood there, he sighed at my obvious reluctance to touch him. "I'm offering you an oath of protection."

After a beat, I placed my right hand into his. Warm, calloused fingers slid up my forearm, pushing the sleeve of my shirt higher. A bright glow surrounded us, and I caught my breath. I could *see* the golden magic as it wound around us, the pattern of it as clear as handwriting.

The magic bit me in the arm.

"Shit!" I pulled my arm free and gaped at my forearm. A translucent glow faded into my skin, leaving behind a mark of two overlapping circles bisected by thick, curling lines. He'd just tattooed my other arm! "What did you do to me?"

"The Aegis sigil brands you and places you under my protection." His tone implied that I should have been grateful.

"You can't just *brand* people. I'm not a cow!"

Silas and I glared at each other again. Father Mike moved between us, and the blood drained from his face. "I should go with you."

"No," Silas commanded. "Return and report to the Council. They must be informed of the Brotherhood's whereabouts here in Boston. Tell them I remained behind to track Titus."

"What about Maeve?"

"They need not concern themselves with her yet," Silas said. "I will take her to the Fate first."

Father Mike didn't back down. "The Council will not be happy that you're helping her. They've killed people for less. How will you protect Maeve if you're dead?"

Silas bared his teeth. "I'm hard to kill."

He was dangerous—no question—and so far past the point of confident that he was arrogant. I didn't trust him or understand his motives. But I did believe the oath he gave bound him to protect me. I could feel it, like a tether between us. As long as he was alive, I would keep breathing too. I just had to believe he was too damn stubborn to die.

Chapter Four

Father Mike gave me the keys to his Taurus and the backpack. Inside I found several folded maps, a wad of cash, and a passport. I flipped the blue cover open to a picture of me. He'd had this prepared in advance. I had so many burning questions.

"Father, I don't understand what's going on. Why can't you—"

The father glanced over my shoulder at Silas, who circled the car with an intense scrutiny that suggested he'd never been inside one.

"Don't let him take you back to Aeterna," the father whispered.

"I won't," I promised. I jerked my head toward Lord Asshole. "Are you sure this is a good idea?"

"I'm confident he'll keep his oath to protect you. From what I know about his past, he has some issues with the Council, and right now, he's willing to help you for his own reasons. But remember, he has a lot of blood on his hands in the Council's name, and he's loyal to them. If you can't reach the Fate, he won't hesitate to turn you over to the Council. Don't try running either. He'll catch you and consider the oath broken. For now, he's your best protection... until he isn't. Stay with him until I come for you."

That wasn't at all reassuring. "I don't understand any of this," I whispered. A lump welled up in my throat. Even though we were headed for a possible solution, leaving Father Mike seemed like going from bad to worse.

"My dearest Maeve." He pulled me into a hug. "I'll find you as soon as I can. Focus on keeping yourself safe until I'm back, and I can explain everything."

"What are you going to tell the Council?" A terrifying thought occurred to me. "What if they realize you're lying?"

"Don't worry about me. I'm an Aeternal citizen; I have protections." His voice lowered. "Listen, the Council can't learn any more about your powers. Don't access your magic again if you can help it. They'll kill for the power inside you... even with Lord Valeron's oath."

"Don't worry. I couldn't do anything with this, uh, magic even if I wanted to." I stumbled over the word and the idea that the magic was now somehow mine. "That reminds me." I dug into my pocket and handed him the small golden charm I'd found in the basement.

"I found this where they murdered Marcel," I said.

It pulsed with magic in his palm. The father recoiled as if he'd been punched in the face.

"Are you okay, Father?"

He placed Marcel's charm back in my hand and curled my fingers around it. His voice was rough. "Keep this safe and keep it secret. You may need it."

Dread built in my chest. He pulled me into a sudden hug, cutting off any further questions.

"I'm so proud of you," he whispered in my ear. "Be strong, Mae."

I swallowed back my fear before it overwhelmed me. Father Mike was the closest thing I had to family. But with Silas waiting impatiently, we rushed through our goodbyes, and I tried not to get too emotional in front of this stranger I was stuck with. I pulled away with a lump in my throat, clenched the keys in my fist, and headed for the rusty beige Taurus.

"Where to?" I asked, buckling into the driver's seat.

"West," Silas said with a frown.

Rolling my eyes, I reached into my bag and tossed the various maps in his lap. "Can you be more specific?"

He scowled at the papers for a few minutes. "Take Highway 90 West."

I put the car in reverse and grumbled, "The Pike? Are we headed out of state? For how long?"

He narrowed his eyes at me but said nothing.

"Are you going to keep everything top secret, because that's going to get old real fast."

"We have several days' travel ahead of us. I won't tell you more than necessary so you can run off on your own."

I rolled my eyes at him but headed toward Storrow Drive and the unknown destination ahead of us. Spending an unknown number of endless hours trapped in a car with His Highness wouldn't be good for my health. I sighed and reminded myself that I could deal with him for a few days if he could get me to the Fate. After I got rid of the unwanted magic, I could go back to my normal life and forget any of this had ever happened, assholes included.

As we drove, I tried to relax, but it was impossible. Even several hours in, Silas radiated silent menace, and I was hyperaware of his every scowl. Obviously, he didn't want to be on this journey any more than I did, and that bothered me almost as much as the silence in the car.

I turned on the radio and flipped through the stations. Static and country music were the most popular options. I kept twisting the dial until Silas reached over and flicked it off.

"Hey!" I protested.

"That is irritating."

"*You're* irritating!" I cringed at myself. I sounded like a child.

He offered another of his disapproving frowns. The seat was positioned too close to the dash for someone his height, but he hadn't slid it back, even though it forced his knees toward his chin. I chalked it up to karmic justice that we were both uncomfortable.

I wouldn't be able to make it several days in the car with him, and honestly, I would be lucky to make it another hour. My juvenile case file was proof that I didn't do well with authority figures. I drummed my fingers on the wheel, full of anxious energy.

"Would you stop fidgeting?"

"Fine. Then we can talk. I have questions." I needed to do something, anything.

"Talk?"

"Yeah. See, here in Earth, when two people are stuck together for a long period of time, they engage in conversation. First, one person says something, and then the other person responds. You repeat that, and it's called talking."

"You don't like me." His lips pursed as though he found the idea amusing. I wondered if he did, in fact, have a sense of humor. *Buried very, very deep.*

"I'm sure you're used to people falling all over themselves to do what you say, but I'm not one of them."

"I am used to respect," he replied. "Or fear. But I don't know of anyone who finds me... irritating."

So he got his way all the time and thought everyone loved him for it. No wonder he was insufferable.

WE PULLED INTO THE twenty-four seven burger joint four hours and a tank of gas later. The restaurant was empty except for the two bored teenagers behind the counter, playing with their phones. I plopped onto the green vinyl bench and dug into a number one combo meal, complete with fries and a Dr. Pepper.

Silas grimaced at his food. "I have questions." He poked his hamburger with his fingertip.

"Join the club." I stabbed my fries into a too-small paper thimble of ketchup. He hadn't wanted to talk earlier, and I was ready to return the favor.

He opened the top of his cheeseburger and glared at the single pickle and glob of ketchup. "How can you eat this?" he accused. "It looks disgusting, and it smells like..." He leaned in and sniffed at it. "It does not smell good."

I shrugged. "What's not to love? It's greasy and salty." I demonstrated the appropriate attitude by taking a hearty bite of burger.

"Enjoyment of grease and salt must be an evolutionary requisite for an Earthen."

I paused with a bundle of fries halfway to my mouth. I was pretty sure I'd just been insulted. I shoved the greasy, salty fries into my mouth and smacked my lips loudly.

Golden light flashed around Silas, and Ripper appeared in his palm.

I grabbed for it, but he pulled his hand back.

"That's my knife!"

"I believe the Earthen saying is 'Finders, keepers.'"

"Only if you're five years old!" I lowered my voice and looked around the nearly empty restaurant. "And did you do magic in here? Are you crazy?" The sudden flash had been like a lightning bolt inside the building.

"Mundanes can't see pure energy." He indicated the bored teens behind the counter, still absorbed in their phones as he slipped the knife discreetly back to his side. "I propose a trade. Your knife in return for answering my questions."

I folded my arms across my chest and dragged my eyes from Ripper to Silas's face. He watched me with a knowing expression I didn't like at all.

"My knife and a question of my own for every one of yours," I countered.

"Agreed."

He gave in quickly, making me realize I should have bargained for more. Another flash, and Ripper disappeared. "Where did it go? We had a deal!"

"I'll conjure it again when you've fulfilled your end."

I rolled the word conjure around in my head and tried not to think about how crazy this all was. "Is that what you did with your sword?" I hadn't seen it since the street fight. I'd wondered if he had left it behind in Boston.

"Yes. A sword would be conspicuous." He pushed his untouched cheeseburger to the center of the table and folded his arms.

I wished I could "magic up" Ripper any time I needed. "Why do you bother with a sword anyway?"

"That's a second question." He raised one eyebrow smugly. "I've heard in a *conversation* you take turns."

I closed my mouth so I could better grind my teeth together.

"How did you divert the Brotherhood's power to yourself during their Transference ritual?" he asked.

"I didn't."

"Then how—"

"That's a second question," I mimicked. "Why do you use a sword instead of magic? Or a gun?"

His jaw clenched, and he exhaled through his nose before answering. Poking the dragon was stupid, but he'd stolen my knife and refused to talk unless I answered *his* questions first. I wouldn't make it easy for him to get his way.

"I am trained in offensive and defensive use of magic and weaponry," he began. "Use of either depends on the situation and the size of flare you're inclined to make. And even though it's technically two questions—guns are useless against any magic user who can shield worth a shite. An energy-based projectile is more effective, faster, and limited only by the user's own skill."

I got the impression he was trying to overwhelm me with too much information. "What's a flare?"

He started to shake his head.

"That was a clarifying question. Your answer was vague." I leveled a fry at him. "And you know it."

The side of his mouth quirked up. "A flare is comparable to a ripple in water, which others can sense. The more complex the conjuring, the larger the ripple."

His explanation made as much sense as all the other crazy stuff I'd learned about magic.

"How long have you associated with Father Mike?" he asked.

"Why?" I didn't like him asking about the father, not after the way Silas had treated him.

"He seemed... unsettled."

"Well, you have such a calming presence. I can't imagine why he'd be nervous."

He cocked his head at me, apparently impervious to sarcasm.

"I met him nine years ago. I was fifteen." I was also starving, dirty, and homeless. Father Mike had just started his youth outreach program and gave me a safe, warm place to sleep. But Lord Uppity didn't need to know all that. I lobbed another question at him. "Do all of your people do magic?"

"Magic is a generic Earthen term denoting trickery and the things which Mundanes do not understand."

His eyebrow rose haughtily, and I had to bite my tongue to keep from snapping back. I reminded myself that I needed answers more than the very satisfying chance to tell him what an uptight jerkwad he was.

"Fine. Does everyone in your realm have their own *super powers*?" I took a swig of Dr. Pepper and added, "That's not a second question; it's the same one. And I expect you to answer it this time."

"Very well." He leaned back in the booth and crossed his arms. "Most Aeternals use one of two power sources: the familial or the Citizen Source. The Upper Houses of Aeterna each have their own familial source, while the Citizen Source is public."

"Do normal Earth people have the same magic through this Citizen Source?"

"No. There's no magic in Earth," he said. "People without magic are called Mundanes. And the Council provides the Citizen Source for the less powerful Houses of Aeterna, not Mundane Earthens."

His mention of the Council brought back my uncertainty. I stalled, wiping my fingers on a thin paper napkin. I knew very little about the Council except that Father Mike had said not to trust them. As far as I was concerned, they were only slightly better than the Brotherhood in that they weren't actively trying to kill me. *Yet.* "Why does the Council want the Brotherhood's power if they have their own magic?"

"That's another question."

"Look, we could do this all day." An exchange of information question by question would take forever, especially when he was being intentionally vague. I leaned back in the booth and folded my arms over my chest.

His jaw flexed. "Are you breaking our agreement?"

He'd intentionally avoided my question about the Council. His motivations for going against them were suspect, and I was relying on him for a hell of a lot. Even though I'd decided to trust him, an oath to protect me would only get us so far. I had to know *why* he was helping me.

I stared at him, not willing to be the first one to break.

He stared back.

I leaned in and took a giant bite of his hamburger and chewed loudly. Neither of us spoke as I obnoxiously finished the whole thing. He watched without any reaction, his face parked in neutral like a professional poker player. It was a mask, but I couldn't get him to break as he sat watching me chew and smack my lips. Full past the point of comfort, I drummed my fingers on the table. I glanced quickly at the clock on the wall. It was just past eleven in the morning. We had a long day ahead of us, trapped together in the car.

He smirked.

Damn it. "Fine," I said. I would play his game if it got me answers. I needed information more than I needed pride.

"Fine?"

He wanted me to spell out my surrender. *The bastard.*

"Fine. You win. You showed this evolutionarily inferior *Mundane* that you are the boss of all things conversational. I bow down before your infinite superiority. I can't wait to answer your questions." *Okay, that slipped into sarcasm pretty hard.*

"Technically, you're an Earthen, not a Mundane since you obviously have magic."

"Obviously. Or I wouldn't be in this mess."

"Are you always this stubborn?"

"Yep. And that question counts."

I rose and tossed our trash before we headed back to the car. Silas's untouched food was a waste of the limited cash we had, but I let it go without comment. If he decided to starve, that was his problem. While I drove west, I focused on picking my next question. I didn't want to waste a single one. Something didn't add up about his story. I just couldn't figure him out, and I definitely couldn't trust him until I figured out what he had to gain from our arrangement.

A few miles of uninterrupted road zipped by before I picked up the questions again. "Why are you willing to go against your Council?"

He'd made it clear they would want the power inside of me. Father Mike had said Silas worked for them—it sounded as though they might even kill him for disobeying—yet he'd still agreed to help me get rid of the magic.

"That's a difficult question," he said, his eyes on the road.

"I've got nothing but time."

One corner of his mouth twisted. "The Council is weak and desperate. When they can occasionally agree on something, they make bad decisions based on short-term needs. Our people are suffering for it."

I glanced at him out of the corner of my eye. Any good humor had disappeared, and his face was dark and furrowed. He seemed to care deeply about the Council and his people. The whole thing sounded messy and complicated, which solidified my resolve not to get involved with them. I needed to find the Fate before they came after me.

Silas didn't wait before he fired his next question at me. "Tell me everything you know about how the Brotherhood's power transferred to you."

I kept my eyes glued to the road. "That wasn't a question." When he didn't react, I sighed. He might be able to help me figure out what happened if I told him the truth. And with Father Mike headed to Aeterna, I didn't have anyone else to ask. I took a deep breath and decided to trust my gut. "There was a man. Titus. He tortured me, well him—he tortured a man named Marcel. Whatever Titus wanted, Marcel wouldn't give it to him."

The memories threatened to surface again. Marcel's pain and fear were too much. My stomach ached with a hollow feeling that forced me to stop talking and focus on breathing as we sped down the highway. I couldn't lose control again.

Silas's eyes were on me. "You speak as if you experienced it."

"It felt like I was there. I have these memories from him." I wasn't sure how to explain Marcel's memories in my head. I wasn't ready for someone else to think I'd lost my mind. "Marcel was murdered," I whispered, terrified just talking about it would tip me over the edge. "He was a real person... with dreams, a future. I can't help feeling sorry for him." I snuck a peek at Silas, but his face remained unreadable, all sharp angles. "Marcel gathered the power and sort of gave it to me. Everything. I think he knew it would kill him."

I rubbed my hand over my neck, remembering the sense of purpose that had driven Marcel until the end. He'd tried to find me right up until Titus had slit his throat. He'd wanted me to have this power, but I couldn't guess why. Maybe he was searching for someone else, and I got in the way somehow. I had no way to know.

"Titus leads the rebels who call themselves the Brotherhood," Silas volunteered.

I chewed the inside of my lip, thinking back to the fight on the street. "It sounded like Titus knew you."

"Lots of people know me," he said evenly.

I rolled my eyes. "Okay, Mr. Popularity. It seemed personal."

"We have a history." I could tell from his tone I wasn't going to get more out of him, so he surprised me when he kept talking. "The capacity for horrendous acts of violence is universal and usually inflicted on those least able to protect themselves. Marcel will be remembered."

"I don't even know who he was. He might have a family looking for him. God, I don't even know his last name." I swallowed hard, unsure how to respond to Silas's unexpected understanding of my feelings about a complete stranger's murder. He was overbearing and pushy one minute then unusually sympathetic. Even the strange way he spoke, with his slightly formal word choices and strange expressions, intrigued me. I was curious about him, and I wanted to change the subject. "How old are you?" I asked.

One eyebrow rose. "*That's* your question?"

I kept my eyes on the road. "Yep."

He shifted in his seat, stretching his cramped legs as best he could. I took pity on him and told him about the seat adjuster. After he pushed the seat all the way back with a relieved sigh, I reminded him he still hadn't answered my question.

"I am roughly equivalent to a thirty-year-old in terms of an Earthen life span."

"Okay... that's not an actual answer."

"Time in Aeterna is measured differently. Passage of time is not an important measure that we track like Mundanes do. Not to mention, I spend most of my time in other realms, some of which move at different speeds. If I were to track linear progression of time, it would be roughly thirty Earthen years, give or take."

With his thick head of dark-brown hair, strong jaw, and fit, broad shoulders, he appeared to be in the prime of his life. It was the perma-scowl and the air of authority he radiated that made me think he'd had a lot more life experience than me. But he was just five years older.

He met my gaze, and one eyebrow rose. Heat flushed through my face, and I focused my attention back on the highway.

I could feel his eyes on me for a long time before he spoke. "Aeternals are not immortal, but we live longer than Mundanes. Our Healers theorize that the constant influx of magic slows the aging of our cells at a molecular level. Compared to your life span..." He shrugged and let my imminent death roll casually off his shoulders.

"Lucky you," I murmured under my breath. For the first time, I wondered if the magic stuck inside me would make me live longer.

I shelved that thought as quickly as it hit me. Magic had just exponentially shortened my life span, either from the murderous Brotherhood or the unpredictable Aeternal Council. Either way, I wasn't planning to keep it.

A second lane finally opened on the highway. I shifted to the right and accelerated around the car in front of us. "Speaking of dying young, what will happen if the Brotherhood finds me?"

His eyebrows rose slightly.

"Other than my painful and ritualized death, I mean. What do they want to do with all this magic?"

He either forgot to keep score or took pity on me because he answered my second question in a row. "The Brotherhood will need enormous amounts of power to undermine the Council. It appears your Marcel stole a significant amount of the Brotherhood's power with his Transference ritual, and they need it to accomplish their plans."

"Which are what, exactly?"

He grimaced, and his eyes shifted back out the window.

I narrowed my eyes at his sudden interest in the road ahead. "You don't know, do you?" I accused.

He didn't respond.

"Hah! That's perfect, just perfect! You have no idea what you're talking about, do you?"

He turned on me. "I don't know exactly what they plan to do with the magic *after they kill you,* but I'm trying to stop them from getting it in the first place. Unless you irritate me so badly, I end up doing it for them!"

Thick silence filled the car while the miles slipped past. Part of me felt bad for intentionally pissing Silas off, but I just couldn't figure out why he'd offered to help me. I still didn't have any idea what he would gain from our deal since it seemed as though he was going against his bosses' best interests. To top that off, I had no idea why this had happened to me in the first place. I didn't understand the full puzzle yet, and the magic stuck inside me was just one of the missing pieces.

I suddenly wished there were some way to get a hold of Father Mike. I had so many questions I just couldn't trust Silas with. But I had no way to ask the father the questions I so desperately needed answers to while he was in some faraway magical realm.

Silas interrupted my thoughts. "You're an orphan?"

The question came so out of the blue that I paused before answering. "I have no idea who my birth parents were. They gave me up when I was very young."

His brow furrowed. "A child abandoned in Aeterna is unheard of. You don't remember any details about your family?"

I shook my head. "Happens all the time in *this* realm," I said levelly. I was a lifetime past any bitterness about my origins. Being on my own since I could remember had shaped me into the person I was today: independent and tough. I could carry my own no matter what life threw at me.

We sat in silence for a few minutes as we each digested our own thoughts. There was so much I still didn't understand. To start with, I didn't know even the basics about the magic inside me. I felt on the verge of losing control every second.

"Your energy isn't the same color as Titus's," I said. "The patterns he used were different too. Is everyone's magic unique, or—"

Silas's head whipped toward me. His eyebrows were suddenly lost in his hairline. "You can see the individual energy patterns?"

My mind raced as I tried to order my confusion. Apparently, I wasn't supposed to be able to see the patterns in the magic.

Silas took a deep breath. I braced for anger, but his voice was quiet and demanding. "Tell me exactly what you can see." The authority in his voice intimidated me more than if he had yelled.

My eyes locked on the road in front of us, and I wet my lips. Thanks to my slip, that ability wasn't a secret anymore. Father Mike had told me not to show Silas any more of my magic, and obviously that detail about energy patterns was important. *Oops.* What I'd already said couldn't be taken back, so I might as well understand what was going on.

"Titus's magic—energy, whatever—was like a red starburst tinged with black. Yours is more yellow. Golden, like..." I'd almost said "Golden, like the sun," but that would have sounded way too complimentary. He did not need an even bigger ego. "Like pee."

He grunted. "And you can see patterns within the conjuring?"

"The, uh, energy looks like really thin threads of light, all twisted together into complicated patterns. Sometimes they make sense. Sometimes they're sort of thick and layered. Makes my brain feel fuzzy."

Despite his carefully neutral expression, his eyes were bright with surprise.

"Why?" I asked. "Are the patterns important? Do you think that has something to do with why this happened to me?"

My question went unanswered as flashing blue and red lights pulled up behind us.

Chapter Five

The officer swaggered up to our car, one hand resting on her holstered gun. Silas glared into the rearview mirror and watched her approach. His eyes sparked with irritation, and the ever-present scowl had twisted into a near snarl. Instead of a speeding ticket, he would get us arrested if he didn't tone down his attitude.

The officer stopped beside the passenger's side window and lowered her aviator sunglasses. *Officer Radmall,* according to her badge, looked at us over the rims.

"Is there a problem, Officer?" I asked, channeling every cop show I'd ever seen.

She peered into the back seat. "Do you know how fast you were going?"

I glanced at the speedometer. "Um... no? I wasn't paying attention, honestly." *Smooth, real smooth.*

"License and registration, please."

I fished out my ID then dug through the random papers Father Mike kept in the glove box. If Silas gave me a hard time about not paying attention to the speedometer, I would kick him in the teeth.

"Where are you heading"—Radmall examined my license—"Maeve O'Neill from Boston?"

"My brother and I are headed to..." I racked my brain for some place in our general direction and remembered the road sign I'd seen a few miles back. "Buffalo, New York to see some family. We have about a hundred miles left." I clamped my mouth shut and resisted the urge to give her more details. I was a terrible liar.

Not to mention, Silas and I didn't look alike at all. He had dark, nearly black hair, and mine was auburn pushing toward red. His olive skin tone hinted at a multi-ethnic background different from my own, especially with my pale skin from the long Boston winter. I should have said he was a friend or an axe murderer I picked up on the side of the road—basically, anything other than my brother.

"He's adopted," I added suddenly. *Shut the hell up, dummy.*

I prayed she wouldn't ask for his driver's license. I was pretty sure people from magical realms didn't have valid government IDs.

After a long, tense pause, the officer glanced at Silas. "What's your name?"

Little warning bells went off in my head. I'd watched enough cop shows to know that asking for passenger names was not in the standard traffic pullover script.

Silas smiled up at her. "Silas O'Neill."

I blinked in astonishment as his usual grim expression disappeared. The sun glowed on his olive skin. His sharp angles and arrogance softened, and he looked downright trustworthy. *Damn.* If I didn't already know that I could see magic, I would have thought it was some kind of trick.

Officer Radmall grinned back at him, perhaps also mesmerized. I covered up my snort with an unconvincing cough. Silas slid me serious side eye, and I tried to keep my face innocently neutral.

The officer glanced at the registration. "And why are you driving Michael... Smithson's car?" She leveled a cop stare at us over the top of her aviators.

"He's a relative," Silas said. "We're borrowing it."

"Cousin. He's our cousin," I said. *Seriously? Shut up, Maeve.*

"We didn't mean to cause alarm. We can be on our way, Officer." Silas laid the charm on thick, and I had to stop myself from rolling my eyes.

"Stay in the car; I need to run this." She walked back to the cruiser and picked up her radio.

"You are a very poor liar," Silas noted.

"Shut up," I said, my eyes glued to the rearview mirror.

The seconds ticked by into minutes, and unease began to fill me. She was taking too long. My foot hovered over the gas pedal. Another minute passed as I chewed on my thumbnail.

"Something's wrong," I whispered, watching Radmall talking into the radio in her car.

"Five bloody hells," Silas swore. "Stay in the vehicle." Before I could object, he plopped Ripper in my lap and opened his door.

My stomach twisted. I turned in my seat and watched Silas stalk toward the police cruiser, glowing with magic. His hands hung loosely by his sides.

Officer Radmall flung open her door, crouched behind it, and pulled her gun. "Get back in the car!"

Silas continued walking. His hands rose from his sides, palms out.

My heart hammered in my throat. He was going to get shot! I reached for the door handle.

"Stop where you are!" the officer yelled at Silas.

Before I managed to get my door open, Silas rushed the five feet between him and the cruiser, dove toward the open driver's side door, and kicked it into the officer.

She fell backward, and a shot rang out.

I ran outside and found Silas straddling Radmall. She was face-down on the ground, and he had her arms twisted behind her back.

"Are you crazy?" I yelled. "You can't assault a cop!"

Thank God no one was bleeding. I scanned the highway in both directions. The road was empty, but it wouldn't be for long.

Silas's magic flared a brilliant yellow that held its own against the bright sun, filling the air with a complex pattern of woven energy. The streams flowed together in a latticework of magic between him and the officer, and I was momentarily distracted by the beauty of it.

Silas rolled Radmall onto her back, and she struggled against his hold.

"What are you doing?" I demanded. This was a nightmare, an actual living nightmare.

He ignored me and focused on the officer. "Don't fight me. Don't run... and be calm."

She stopped struggling. Silas released her, and she sat up slowly, her face tranquil and placid. I did a literal double take. She wasn't running or fighting back or anything.

"Who did you notify about us?" Silas asked her.

"I called HQ."

"What did they say?"

"Your vehicle has an APB. I'm supposed to wait until a special unit arrives."

"What did you do to her?" I demanded.

"Compulsion spell." Stone-faced, he leaned into the cruiser and grabbed our papers.

I put both hands in my hair and pulled. *This cannot be happening.*

Officer Radmall sat patiently, watching us. I suppressed a shiver.

"We need to leave," he said. "The Brotherhood—"

A burst of pressure hit me in the chest, and I stumbled backward a few feet. Titus materialized between us and our car, flanked by seven beasts. They were the size of small horses but shaped like giant dogs. Tough skin stretched taut over their muscled frames, emphasizing strong, agile bodies. Hairless with mottled gray flesh, they looked like the misshapen hounds of hell. One of them bared oversized flesh-tearing teeth at me.

Silas stepped in front of me. A sword appeared in his hand.

"Give me the girl," Titus snarled.

"Tell me where they are!" Titus snarls in my face.

I can't lift my head from my shoulders. Everything hurts. I'm pretty sure I have a broken rib, and I can only see out of my left eye. I don't know how long I've been tied to this gods-damned chair, but Titus had worked me over every minute of it.

I hiss as Titus pulls my head up by my hair, forcing me to stare into cold blue eyes.

"Tell me now, and I'll let you live."

A manic laugh bubbles up from my chest. It spills out of my cracked, bloody lips in a desperate animal noise of hysteria. There's no way in hell I'll tell him where my people are hiding. They would all die, and he would kill me anyway.

Titus drops my head, and I let it bounce on my neck, too weak to care. "Let's start again."

Hollowness sucked at my insides. Curling over, I clutched my stomach against the pain of the vision. As sudden as flicking on a light switch, magic surrounded me. I could feel everything pulsing with energy—the trees lining the deserted highway, the officer sitting patiently in her cruiser, and the beasts in front of us. Even the air danced with brilliant threads of power. The magic coming from me felt vibrant and full of life, revealing the pattern of every living thing.

Silas rushed forward and swung his sword at the beast closest to us, drawing my dazed attention. The demon animals attacked with a chorus of howls that made my insides shudder, pulling me back to reality, and I clamped my hands over my ears.

Silas slammed his elbow into the animal's head and knocked it into its neighbor, pushing them both out of the way before they could lunge. His sword stabbed between the muscular sheets of its chest, coating the blade in a gush of red blood.

"Back!" Silas yelled at me.

I stumbled a few steps backward, gripping Ripper in my hand.

A third beast leapt from fifteen feet away, its massive body jumping at least five feet in the air as it dove straight toward me. Silas ran forward, dropped to one knee, and sliced into its soft underbelly from neck to navel. The monster shrieked and skidded along the asphalt, stopping at my feet in a bloody, gutted heap.

Silas held the space between us with movements almost too quick to follow, weaving through the beasts with steel. Magic flared around him, made from thousands of threads of light. The energy rose high into the air and spread out to each side of him. Magic flowed with his sword, driving his opponents back as both a shield and a weapon. A fierce, feral smile lit up Silas's face while he moved through the animals, cutting and slashing. Another dropped, headless, and the others backed off momentarily. Silas had downed or severely injured three of them, and their bright-red blood stained his blade and clothes.

The remaining four regrouped and circled, testing for an opening in Silas's defensive perimeter.

Just beyond the demons, I locked eyes on Titus, who watched the fight with teeth bared. He stood back, letting his hounds attack, waiting for his opening. Hatred burned through me, fueled by Marcel's memories of torture. I knew exactly what I needed to do to make the visions stop. I would avenge Marcel's murder and kill Titus. Flipping Ripper in my hand, I shifted around Silas and the magic he wielded and stalked forward.

The beasts twisted to intercept me. Silas moved with them, blocking their advance. I tried again, and everyone did the same dance, stopping me from getting to Titus.

"Stay back!" Silas yelled at me.

I growled in frustration. There was no path around Silas or the animals.

On the other side of the road, a dark red-black fog of power grew around Titus. It built in complex layers, feeding from Titus and the others with him. I stared, mesmerized by the layers and patterns starting to form within the magic.

Marcel's memories threatened to overwhelm me again, but I pushed them down. I couldn't afford to lose myself now. I had to get to Titus, but a wall of teeth and claws separated us.

The spell grew, and the weight of the magic called to me. Before I made a conscious decision to do anything, I reached out with my mind and pulled on the threads of Titus's conjuring. The energy bowed between us. I took a deep breath and drew the magic inward. Like a rubber band stretched from both ends, it broke away from him and snapped to me.

Titus stumbled. His head whipped in my direction as the magic crashed into me, and the fog disappeared. A surge of raw power hit me. I staggered backward under the surprising wave.

A sharp pain jabbed me in the gut. I groaned and hunched over my stomach. Something was wrong with the magic from the spell. It twisted like knives, ripping up my insides, and I screamed in absolute agony. Around me, Silas fought, and the beasts howled. But the terrible fire ripped through my body, blocking out everything except the pain.

Titus stalked forward through the mass of beasts. They moved aside for him, pushing Silas farther away.

The magic hurt so bad. Too weak to move and too sick to use the knife still clutched in my hand, I could barely lift my own head when Titus snarled at me like an animal. He clutched his sword and pushed his way past the beasts, moving toward me. He meant to kill me.

I had one chance. I had to take *all* the magic from Titus, and I hoped it would injure him enough to stop him. I knew it was going to hurt, but I threw my hands out and called the magic.

The beasts between Titus and me died first. They convulsed like dying fish, flopping on the ground in howling agony. I gasped as their magic flooded me. The rush of pure energy burned every pore and cell in my body. The animals' high-pitched screams matched the pain in my skull as I closed my eyes and called all the magic into me.

Less than a dozen feet away, Titus snarled and raised his sword, ready to strike.

Marcel's memories seemed to guide me. I focused on Titus's dark aura—like a small, bloody sunset—and pulled with everything I could.

He stumbled and grabbed his head, then his hands fisted in his blond hair. His body jerked, and he screamed as he struggled to reach me, moving one disjointed limb at a time. The power ripped from him, and his flare faded to a pale crimson, just shy of pink.

The magic slammed into me. I doubled over and fell to the ground.

Unbelievably, Titus forced himself forward with his sword clutched in his hand. He bared his teeth at me.

If he reached me, Ripper wasn't going to cut it against his long sword. I focused everything I had on Titus, and the air shifted with the force of my pull.

Titus flailed as if in mid-seizure. He gritted his teeth in a silent scream until the force of his will could no longer stop me, and he collapsed facedown at my feet.

Then every particle of energy within a forty-foot radius obeyed my call. The beasts beyond Titus also hit the ground, jerking and shrieking. Every bit of the surrounding energy flew to me. It hit me all at once, like a crashing wave of water, crushing me with massive force.

I fell to my knees with a scream, unable to withstand the pressure suffocating me. I couldn't hold it.

Finally, the weight passed through me, and I gasped for breath. I surveyed the damage while pulling in ragged breaths. The beasts lay still on the ground, and Titus lay dead at my feet. The blood-soaked patch of dirt alongside the highway glowed with magic energy. My attention shifted to the downed beasts. One second, they were hideous demons; then the animals shivered with magic, and seven mutilated human bodies lay around me, drenched in blood and drained of magic.

Eight men were dead. The realization hit me with delayed horror. *I killed all these people.*

Fifty feet away, outside the circle of destruction, Silas stared at me, his jaw clenched and nostrils flared wide. Blood covered his shirt and soaked his sword arm. "What have you done?"

Ripper slipped from my fingers onto the ground. I bent over and retched.

Titus moaned and pushed himself to his knees. *How is he still alive?* He scrambled for my knife. I watched him move, unable to respond before he grabbed Ripper and stabbed it into the back of my leg. Pain flamed up my calf, and I screamed. I tried to move away, but Titus fisted my hair and dragged me upward, forcing me to hobble to my feet. He held Ripper's edge tight against my throat, my own blood dripping from the blade. The gash in my calf burned and gushed hot blood onto my jeans.

"Resist me, and you will die," Titus growled in my ear. He positioned me as a shield between him and Silas. His ragged breathing matched my own as he dragged me off the road and toward the police cruiser.

"Let her go, Titus!" Silas yelled, his voice carrying across the death-strewn highway.

"You're fighting a losing battle," Titus called back.

Silas raised the tip of his sword, shifting closer with each step. "We both know you won't kill her," he said. "You need her powers."

"Are you willing to gamble her life on that?" Titus asked with a growl.

Silas shrugged. "You cocked up your Transference. Twice."

Without warning, Titus kicked my wounded leg, and my knees buckled. I cried out and landed hard on my knees next to the officer. Radmall slumped against her steering wheel, unconscious but still breathing. Relief flooded me. I hadn't killed her when I lost control. I latched on to that, letting it comfort me, as if her single spared life could make up for the eight I had stolen.

Titus shifted behind me, pushed the officer back into her seat, and in a sharp downward movement, thrust Ripper into her chest.

"No!" I screamed.

Her eyes popped open. She gasped, a wet gurgling sound escaping from her lungs. Her hands flailed against Titus's grip, while blood blossomed dark and inky across her uniform. Titus ripped the blood-slicked knife from her chest. She jerked, and he buried his palm in her blood. Energy streamed from her into Titus, and his aura flared bright with the black magic.

Her head lolled to the side. She was dead.

The air began to thicken, squeezing my lungs as I fought against Titus's grip, which tightened painfully around me. My stomach lurched as he started to pull us away with magic.

Silas ran toward us. He was half a dozen steps away, but it might as well have been miles.

The part of me that refused to die finally woke up. I threw my elbow into Titus's face with a satisfying crunch. He grabbed me around the waist and punched me in the gut.

Silas rammed into Titus, and I ripped free of Titus's grasp. I landed on my back just as Titus vanished the same way he had appeared.

I looked down and saw Ripper buried in my stomach. Titus hadn't punched me; he'd stabbed me. Pain exploded everywhere, and my vision went black.

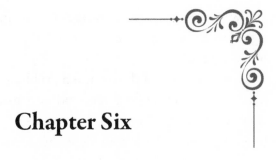

Chapter Six

I awoke in a surprisingly comfortable bed, nestled under a pastel floral comforter. A television with bunny-ear antennas rested atop a small wooden dresser, next to a round mauve lamp. Above the dresser, a generic landscape print in coordinating beiges and soft pinks hung on the wall. I was in a motel room.

The blinds on the single window were closed, but pitch black showed around the edges. A squeal and the clank of ancient plumbing in the wall caught my attention. Someone turned off a shower behind the bathroom door. *Silas.*

The fight resurfaced, and I remembered the terrible pain in my side before I'd blacked out. My hoodie and shirt were both shredded and stiff with dried blood and mud. Pushing aside the tattered fabric, I held my breath as I examined my stomach. But instead of a fresh gash, my wound had healed to a jagged white pucker nearly four inches long. The scar seemed months old. I touched it gingerly with my fingertips and felt no pain. I explored the torn fabric on my calf. The gash was gone, and my skin was smooth and whole. Silas must have healed me with magic the same way Titus had healed his neck in the alley.

It should have relieved me to wake up alive, but my mind went immediately to the people I'd killed. I couldn't even remember how many there had been. Seven? Eight? A sharp pain in my chest replaced the one in my side. I was a mass murderer.

With a lurch of alarm, I thrust my hand into my jeans pocket. I sighed when my fingers closed around Marcel's charm. I hadn't lost it in the fight.

Silas came out of the bathroom, rubbing a towel through wet hair. The fresh scent of shampoo and soap floated across the air. His chest was bare and damp, and jeans were slung low on his hips. The bright light of the bathroom highlighted tattoos covering his arms and upper torso. The left side of his abdomen had a trail of them reaching all the way to his hip, disappearing into the waistband of his pants. Each one was an intricate, layered symbol that flowed into the next. They were almost multi-dimensional.

The muscles of his stomach flexed under naturally tan skin as he bent and pulled a shirt out of a plastic grocery bag on the floor. He threaded his arms through the sleeves, and I saw more markings across his back—scars. They were scattered and random except for a group of four lines that ran parallel across his back like lashes from a whip or claw marks. With broad shoulders that narrowed to a trim and muscular stomach, Silas was built for speed and agility. He had the physique of someone who used his body rather than the too-bulky bodybuilder muscles of a gym rat.

Something fluttered low in my belly. *Get a grip.*

Once he was safely dressed, I sat up on the old bed, and it squeaked.

He spun as fast as a rattlesnake. "You're awake."

"Thanks to your magic healing." I cringed at myself. His abs had apparently melted my brain.

"How do you feel?" He grabbed a water bottle from the plastic bag, twisted it open, and handed it to me.

"Lucky," I said. Without his help, I would be dead.

A pang of guilt hit me. It was wrong to feel lucky when I'd just murdered so many. *All those people, naked and broken on the road. Dead.*

Silas knelt at the side of the bed and pushed the tattered fabric of my shirt aside. His warm fingers examined the wound, moving gently across my skin. I drained the water bottle to cover my shiver. It was not okay to act like a schoolgirl with a crush. A nice body and a little magic healing weren't an excuse for *urges*. I reminded myself that I couldn't trust him, and he would be more than willing to hand me over to the Council if the Fate plan didn't work out.

I searched for something to talk about that didn't involve him touching me. "Did you use all our cash on this motel room?" My tone sounded more accusing than I'd meant it to.

He glanced at me and back at the wound. "You were bleeding to death in the back of the vehicle. I assumed you'd want me to find shelter and save your life."

"Right," I grumbled, feeling sheepish and irritated at the same time.

"If I were an actual Healer, you wouldn't even have a scar."

"You get what you pay for," I said with a small shrug.

He gave me a confused look.

"A scar's not so bad," I clarified. Then because we were being way too nice to each other, I added, "You said the Brotherhood needed me alive to do the ritual thingy. But your friend Titus tried to kill me back there."

"Titus wasn't trying to kill you."

"Someone should tell *him* that."

"He needed a distraction so I wouldn't follow his flare when he skimmed out." He frowned. "It worked."

I chose to ignore his disappointment over saving my life. "Skimmed?"

"It's a way of traveling from one place to another. It takes a high level of magic. More so within Earth. Even I wouldn't attempt it in this realm, yet Titus did it twice."

I sat upright in alarm. "Are you saying he can show up anytime, anywhere?"

"He'd have to track us first. I drove over a hundred miles after I healed you so he couldn't follow the flare. As long as neither of us start manipulating a lot of magic, they shouldn't be able to find us."

I let myself relax against the headboard again.

"It will be some time before he can repeat it," Silas added. "Titus had to steal the life energy from the officer to fuel the second skim."

Officer Radmall. I shuddered at the memory of the thin veins of magic drawing from the woman to Titus like a magnet. Then there'd been a shift of pressure before he pulled the disappearing act.

"Draining life energy requires a blood connection. That spell would get you executed in Aeterna, but without access to the Citizen Source or any magic here in Earth, their only power is likely from sacrificial magic. They'll kill as many Mundanes as they can get away with and store their life energy."

Titus's aura had been black-tinged. The sacrificial magic must have been the cause of the terrible feel of the Brotherhood's powers.

Silas shifted on the bed, his gaze suddenly intent on me. "I've never seen energy pulled out of someone from a distance. I did not know *that* was possible."

I looked away, not sure how to respond.

"How did you do it?" he pressed.

It made me sick to think about the deaths of the beasts, who had actually been people. When I closed my eyes, I saw the events again on a never-ending loop, and my stomach lurched with remembered pain. "I wanted to stop Titus. I was just as surprised as you when... *that* happened."

A ragged breath escaped as I recalled Silas's horrified expression. When I'd killed those people and drained their power, their energy became part of me. I'd stolen it from them just like the Brotherhood had stolen their sacrificial magic. Nausea twisted my stomach.

Silas leaned in. "Tell me what happened." He was so close that the heat of the shower came off his skin. I bit my lip.

I didn't even know what had happened, but I tried to explain as best I could, ignoring his closeness. "I think Marcel's memories taught me how. When they take over, I remember things from his life... it's like he's in my head."

Silas's eyes widened. I swallowed around a dry throat and scooted away from him until my back rested against the faded floral headboard.

I took a drink of the water and tried to explain. "Sometimes his memories sort of bubble up inside me. And his anger. Titus sets me off because of Marcel's hatred toward him. They—the memories—showed me how to take Titus's magic. I lost control and honestly didn't know what I was doing."

Silas's expression got back under control, but I couldn't tell if he believed me.

"I didn't realize they would change back... into people," I finished lamely.

"They were Shifters."

"Shifters?" I realized that at some point we'd managed to stop trading questions. It was a relief just to get answers without bartering for every single one.

"Shifters, Humans, Fae. We're each distinct enough to be our own species." He exhaled and shrugged. "Although very few in Aeterna are only one race anymore. Those particular Shifters were Rakken. The Rakken used to be an elite unit of the Guardians, but Titus has bastardized the concept. He magically altered their Shifter forms, and if he's following the old system, Rakken spend more time in this form than their human ones. It makes them more lethal, but also harder to control."

"How do you know all that? Are you..."

"Am I what?"

"Human?" I suddenly wondered about his perfect physique. Maybe it was some kind of Shifter trait, and he was also one of those demonic beasts.

He laughed out loud, a sharp, sudden sound that made me jump. "Does it matter to you? Would you not have protected yourself against a Human?"

I blinked at him. I had to admit that I would have killed those men regardless of what form they were in. At that moment, I would have done anything to stop Titus and save my own life. The realization didn't make me like myself any better. "I'm a mass murderer either way."

"Your guilt is a good sign. When you stop caring about the deaths on your hands, you should worry for the state of your soul."

"Are you speaking from experience?"

"I've lost count of the deaths I've caused," he said matter-of-factly.

A little spiral of fear curled up my spine.

"Battles, challenges, executions—it blurs together, eventually. More blood than is justifiable across multiple lifetimes. But I still care. Or I tell myself I do." He rubbed his forearm, lost in his own thoughts for a moment. "I am Human, by the way. But I have a brother who is half-Fae and many Shifters I call friends."

We were both silent for a long moment as I pondered the definition of humanity. Maybe I'd lost a little of my humanity for having taken so many lives. But even Silas, who admitted to so much blood on his hands, maintained his own sense of right and wrong. Humanity was complicated.

I twisted my hair back into a quick braid, but the memory of the dead bodies wouldn't pass. "I didn't mean to kill them."

"The Brotherhood are trying to kill *you*." His hand rested briefly on mine, and the intensity of his expression pulled me in. "The way you protected yourself was scary as bloody, fratching hells, but you need not carry guilt for your actions."

He held my gaze. The distance between us seemed to shrink, and I wondered if I had misread him all along. Father Mike had said he was dangerous, an enforcer for the Council's will. But he was also uniquely qualified to understand the guilt I felt. He talked about all the death he had caused then comforted me almost in the same breath.

"This is a lot to take in," I said, gesturing broadly in the air. "Last week, my biggest problem was whether I'd make enough rent each month. I pulled under-the-counter shifts to make ends meet, and volunteered at the shelter to give back when I could. It wasn't glamorous, but I liked my life." I sighed. "I just, I can't believe I'm here, talking about... Shifters... and magic like it's real."

"Magic *is* real," he countered, not unkindly.

I sighed and picked at the label on the water bottle. "Yeah. I figured that one out on my own."

"You truly have no family to... help you? Support you?"

"It's just me. I basically grew up at the shelter. A bunch of foster families before that. Father Mike is the closest thing I have to family."

I wondered if he'd already made it back to the Aeternal Council and made his report. I had no idea how long it took to travel to a magic pocket realm, but I hoped he was working on his promise to find me again. I needed someone I could trust on my side.

"I don't mind, honestly," I said. "I'm perfectly capable of taking care of myself, and I don't need pity because I'm a sad, lonely orphan. My life hasn't been like that."

"I don't pity you," he offered. "It takes strength of character to find your own path."

I swallowed thickly. "More personal experience?"

His mouth twisted wryly. "I have, on occasion, forged my own path. But no, I was talking about you. The way one handles unexpected challenges reveals a lot about their innate character." He was completely focused on me, and the nearness of him suddenly seemed totally overwhelming.

I wrinkled my nose and quoted, "'Life's a bitch, and then you die.'"

He blinked at me then let out a loud laugh. The sudden noise broke the tension building in my chest, and I grinned back.

"And then you die," he agreed. The corners of his eyes wrinkled with rare humor. His face was close, and his hair was damp and tousled from the shower. I had the urge to run my fingers through it.

I swung my feet off the bed. Time to escape to the bathroom.

"What are you doing?" he asked.

"I need a shower. I look like I was dragged through at least a mile of mud." Not to mention the dried blood and shredded clothing stuck to my skin. But mostly, I needed to get away from whatever kept fluttering in my stomach in response to Silas.

His mouth twisted downward. "You need to rest."

"I feel fine." My side didn't hurt, my leg had healed, and I was full of energy. I just needed to get away from temptation.

"You're not tired?" Silas frowned, and I imagined sucking his full lower lip between my teeth.

Stop it.

"Better than ever," I insisted.

"I expected you to be unconscious for longer. Recovery from a healing usually takes hours, sometimes a full day." He glanced at the clock. "It's been less than five hours. Are you feeling any other effects?"

Surely, I'd imagined the way his voice had dropped. *Other side effects? Check.* Shrugging, I focused on a shower. *A cold one.*

His signature grimace crossed his face, but he let me pass. "I purchased you new clothing with the money in your backpack." He pointed at the shopping bag on the floor. "But if you consider it a misappropriation of funds and you'd prefer to go about naked—"

"Shut up." I grabbed the bag of clothes and headed into the bathroom as he laughed at me.

After I showered, I put on the shirt Silas had purchased. It read *Trouble* across the chest in sparkling, cursive letters. His sense of humor left something to be desired.

SILAS INSISTED ON SLEEPING with his back against the motel door while I took the bed. I was secretly relieved. If I had to share the double bed with him, I wasn't sure I would have gotten any sleep, even fully clothed. I'd certainly had my share of boyfriends and wasn't shy about sex, but Silas had me on red alert all the freaking time. It wasn't just his sheer physical presence—although that had somehow leveled up a big, annoying notch—it was his dominating personality, his unexpected humor, and the confident way—

I gave myself a mental slap. *No, bad.* Lord Asshole was not an attractive, interesting man. He was an untrustworthy henchman for people who would kill me if they got their hands on me.

With those types of thoughts rolling around in my stupid head, I slept only a few hours before I woke with a choked gasp. I'd dreamt that I stabbed Ripper into Marcel and stood laughing over him with bloody hands. I stared at the ceiling until my breathing slowed and returned to normal. The sky outside had begun to lighten over the past hour, but it was too early to be up. The bed creaked when I finally gave up on going back to sleep and sat up.

Silas's eyes popped open. He stood in one fluid movement, completely alert.

"I couldn't sleep," I said with a groggy voice. I cleared my throat and tried again. "Sorry, didn't mean to wake you."

"I sleep light."

"I bet." Obviously, Silas hadn't gotten his sword skills from practice lessons. He was clearly more used to action than peace.

He blinked at me before he spoke. "I had a thought."

"Just one?"

He ignored my snark. "You should learn to control your powers."

"I don't plan on keeping them that long." I had no idea where he was going with his thoughts.

"If yesterday is any indication, you are on the verge of losing control at the slightest provocation. Learning how to keep the magic in check would benefit not only you, but also everyone around you."

Welcome back, Lord Asshole. But I had to agree that the fight with the Rakken had been a disaster. Losing control and killing people was not something I wanted to repeat. Reluctantly, I asked, "What do you have in mind?"

"I'm going to teach you a basic conjuring. Every child in Aeterna has mastered it." Silas sat on the edge of the bed. He flared with golden-yellow energy, and a small ball of light appeared in his palm.

"Put that out! You can't use magic! Titus will find us!"

He didn't so much as twitch. "You really know nothing about magic, do you? This level of magic wouldn't register, even if he were standing outside the door."

Annoyance flooded me. "Can't I learn something a little more complicated? I'm not a child."

The orb of energy disappeared. "Guardians work for years to build their abilities, but if you push too quickly, a conjuring will drain your reserves and still demand more." I must not have looked convinced, because he added, "When you have nothing left to give, you die."

I grimaced but didn't argue, because truthfully, I knew nothing about magic. I would just have to start with the basics.

"First, you need to access the magic inside of you. Calm your mind, close your eyes, and focus inward," he said. "Connect with the energy until it fills you."

For the next ten minutes, I tried to calm my mind. Like my earlier experiences, I sensed an ever-present layer of energy around me. But I had no idea how to "connect" with it. My mind drifted to the marks that covered Silas's body, and I wondered if they were decorative or had a deeper magical meaning like the sigil he'd branded on my arm.

His gaze prickled along my skin and caused the inside of my elbow to start itching. I tried not to fidget, but the itch jumped to my bicep. The tickle crawled up to my shoulder. One eye slipped open, and I peeked at him.

He frowned. "Let's try something else."

The little ball of energy glowed in his hand again, and my senses focused on the power it radiated.

"Can you feel the conjuring?" he asked.

I took a deep breath, pulled the orb toward me, and held it in my palm. The magic dissolved into my flesh. A burst of pure energy hit me like a rush of cool, clear water, completely opposite from the terrible blackness of the Brotherhood's magic. I shivered in pleasure.

"Shite!" he swore.

"Was that wrong?" I asked, my voice pitched high in alarm.

His expression went from surprise to narrowed-eyed thoughtfulness. "You absorbed it."

"That was…" I didn't have words for what had just happened. "I feel like I just downed a super-powered mega-energy drink. On steroids."

"That was only a first-level conjuring."

"A what?" I asked.

"Each conjuring takes a different amount of power depending on the level of complexity. That was a basic spell, the lowest possible use of magic."

"Does each spell give you one of those tattoos?" I glanced at the marks just visible along his neckline. Something about the symbols tickled my memory, but when I tried to focus on it, whatever it was slipped away.

His face went completely blank. "You can see the sigils?"

"Is that bad?" I asked.

"Which ones can you see?"

Each of the marks on his skin had a three-dimensional quality, which made them hard to describe since it looked as though two or three layers of patterns were stacked over each other. "There's one on your neck that's shaped from overlapping circles with these smaller, rounded shapes inside. It's kind of layered."

He pointed just above the sigil. "Here?"

"Here." I leaned forward and ran the tip of my finger just under the collar of his shirt and over the mark, curious if I could feel it on his flesh. He stiffened, and his nostrils flared. I lowered my hand into my lap. *Oops. No touching.*

He cleared his throat. "Among my people, only Guardians can see sigils, and only if they have mastered the necessary training."

"Guardians?"

"They are like your police officers—enforcing laws and the will of the Council. We—they—train for years, acquiring combat magic and skill in weaponry. Mastery of the ability to see sigils is required of Second Commanders and above." His eyes rose to the ceiling as he focused. A single mark on his neck glowed with the same golden power that lit his aura. "Do you see another sigil?"

Careful to keep my hands to myself this time, I pointed to the hollow below his ear. "It's glowing."

"Each mark represents a different conjuring the user has mastered. It's interesting that you can see them even if they're not active."

"How many do you have?"

His mouth twisted down at one corner, and his eyes narrowed suspiciously. "I think that's enough for this lesson." His aura of magic disappeared. "It's light outside. We should continue our journey."

I leaned back on my hands. "About that..."

Silas scowled.

"You heard Officer Radmall—the police have an APB out on our car. Titus and the goon squad showed up after she called in our location. Don't you think that's a bit suspicious?"

Silas started pacing. "You're saying the Earth police are working with the Brotherhood?"

"I don't know if they're working together or if maybe Titus has someone on the inside who is giving them information, but it seems likely. Police monitor all the major highways, and after last night... Well, with a dead officer, they're going to be searching for us. We can't just keep driving." I took a deep breath. "If you tell me where we're going—"

He stopped pacing and full-on glared at me.

"Really?" I snapped. "Am I in any position to run off? How would I do that? Where would I hide, Silas?" I rose from the bed and poked him in the chest. "Your oath is the only thing keeping me alive, and I'd be stupid as shit not to know that. You need a new plan besides driving around for days and keeping me in the dark. The way I see it, you can tell me where the Fate is, and I can help

come up with a plan to get us there, or you can get us both killed."
I rested my hands on my hips and stared him down. "Your choice."

Chapter Seven

W e parked the car at the local dive bar just a little after eleven the next night. With some serious skill, and probably a little luck, I had strong-armed Silas into going along with my plan, but he'd grumbled the whole way.

I smoothed my hands over my newly cropped Trouble shirt and took a last glance at my makeup in the visor mirror. A thrift store pair of red heels, my own tight jeans, and too much eyeliner had transformed me into White Trash Barbie.

"We should go in together," Silas complained from the passenger's seat as he eyed the row of Harleys parked in front of the bar door.

"I need them off guard," I replied, already heading off the argument we'd had earlier back at the motel. Silas glaring at everyone in sight wasn't going to attract the right kind of attention for what I had in mind.

The bar door opened, releasing a rowdy burst of laughter and country music into the parking lot. A knot of burly men emerged for a smoke.

"Your plan is reckless and has a low chance of success," Silas said, his eyes on the men.

"I'm still waiting for your genius idea." I'd already told him how I'd spent my twenties winning impossible bar bets. But Silas was a doubting Thomas who didn't have any better ideas. We needed cash, and we needed it fast.

He looked over my outfit. "I don't understand how your ripped shirt is supposed to distract them. And are you trying to fake a bruised eye?"

I re-checked my makeup in the vanity mirror. I'd put it on thick, but it wasn't smudged. Some people apparently didn't appreciate a smoky eye. "Keep digging, Don Juan. Why don't you tell me how big my ass looks while you're at it?"

His eyebrows scrunched. "I—Come again?"

"Just give me ten minutes before you come in." I sighed and stepped out of the car. Before I closed the door, I glanced back at him. "And try not to piss anyone off in there." I smirked and added, "Maybe don't talk."

The over-muscled bouncer didn't even check my ID. He gave me a lingering once-over before letting me through the front door and into a wall of smoke, stale beer, and country twang. There were no other women inside, and I drew appreciative looks from the leather-clad bikers. I smoothed damp palms over my hips, touched Marcel's charm in my pocket for good luck, and worked my way past the stares and a whistle from the bar. I sat down and forced a smile as two guys rushed over, jostling for the chance to buy me a drink.

Thirty minutes and two beers later, I spotted Silas at a table near the back. With his own leather jacket and perma-scowl, he didn't stick out as badly as I'd feared. He raised his beer to me, and I nodded at him before turning to laugh at whatever the guy next to me had just said. "Thanks for the drink," I said, glancing at the clock. *Time to play.*

When I rose from the stool to the grumbles of my companions, Silas's eyes were on me. They traveled over my body, and in the dim bar light, with more than one drink in my system, I could have sworn he looked... interested. I flushed at the unexpected reaction his gaze caused in my body, but his expression disappeared almost as soon as I noticed. I shook my head. Of course he was watching me. We had a plan that depended on what I was about to do next.

I may have put extra swagger in my step as I walked to the pool tables in the back of the bar; it was my turn to show off. My excitement built as I surveyed the rowdy group of dart players tossing back beers and throwing cash around. I leaned against a well-worn jukebox and watched. When one of them finally won and collected his cash, I pushed off the wall.

"You boys ready for some real competition?" I waved the last of Father Mike's cash in front of my face.

Three large, muscled bikers looked me over. One guy openly leered, and slow smiles spread across their faces.

"Wanna play with the big boys, sweetheart?" the creeper drawled.

Within an hour, I had a crowd around me, a pile of cash on the table, and a growing knot in my stomach. The attention made me nervous, but I was so close to getting the money we needed for our plane tickets. If I won this round, we would be all set.

Silas scooted closer, moving slowly through the excited crowd. As much as I hated to admit it, I was a bit relieved. He was my back-up if the bikers turned out to be poor losers.

I focused on the target on the wall and threw my final dart. It landed dead center on the board. The crowd cheered, the losers complained, and money exchanged hands. A biker with a large tattoo of an elaborate cross on his neck glowered at me before he tossed his money onto my pile.

"Okay, okay! Show's over." I laughed, enjoying my moment as I grabbed up handfuls of cash. Silas was an idiot. My plan was awesome. And I couldn't wait to rub it in his face.

Neck Tattoo grabbed my upper arm, roughly stopping my cash collecting. "Nobody throws that good. Double or nothing you're a cheat and you can't do it again."

I pushed down a spike of fear. The guy was big, really big. I couldn't tear my eyes off his thick, roped neck. The giant cross didn't inspire confidence either. As usual, instead of responding to my very reasonable brain telling me to be afraid, I let my mouth do what it wanted. "Sorry, I already took all your cash."

People snickered.

Neck Tattoo slipped out of his leather jacket, revealing a shoulder holster with six throwing knives—three on each side of his ribs with a strap across the back. He unclipped it and laid it on the table. He pulled out one of the knives and slammed it into the wood, where it stuck with a solid *thunk*. Crafted from a single piece of stainless steel, the six-inch double-sided blade curved to its widest point in the middle before tapering back to a sharp point at the tip. It resembled a spade, but it was sharp enough to kill a man. Black cord wrapped around the flat handle. It was a beautiful set and a hell of a lot more expensive than any I'd owned.

Then Neck Tattoo produced a roll of twenties and plopped it on the table. "Double or nothing you're full of shit." He pointed at the knives. "Let's see you do it again with something bigger. Winner takes all."

"The cash plus the knives," I stated.

Surprise flashed across his features, but he recovered quickly. "No problem, sweetheart."

I could walk away without a scene, but the bet included all the cash we would need, plus a full set of gorgeous throwing knives on the line. I couldn't wait to wrap my hands around those knives. My itching fingers pushed my brain to the back seat. "Deal."

I avoided looking in Silas's direction as I pulled the knife out of the table and tested the balance in my hand. I'd spent enough hours practicing with throwing knives to know that it took time to learn the right amount of strength and spin for each blade before the thrower had any accuracy. The bet was risky and probably extremely stupid, but I couldn't help myself. I knew I could win it all.

We agreed to the terms quickly: three throws each, best throw wins everything. Unless he nailed every throw, I would have a little wiggle room to get used to the knives.

Neck Tattoo scanned the growing crowd. I was a stranger, but his reputation with his drinking buddies was at risk. If I won, he wasn't going to be friendly about it.

Silas moved closer, shaking his head, presumably at my poor life choices.

A flurry of side bets settled down as Neck Tattoo lined up for his first throw. He held the knife by the handle, bent his arm back in line with his shoulder, and threw. It hit the outer ring of the board.

The bikers cheered.

It was a good throw, but he'd sacrificed accuracy for force. The strength he had put behind it could have impaled something twice as far, which was good for a fight but bad for target practice. His second throw hit just as hard, but it landed inside the middle ring, closer to the center.

My confidence slipped a bit. He was damn good. Unlike darts, knives weren't easy to throw accurately. The tiniest wobble would throw the much heavier projectile off course, and this guy was getting better, not worse.

He lined up for his third throw. It sank into the board next to the previous one. Three solid throws. His buddies cheered and clapped him on the back. I would have to do better to beat him. I shook the nerves out of my fingers and took a deep breath. I had spent countless hours playing darts for cash and countless more practicing throwing knives for fun. I could do this.

Someone freed the knives from the dartboard and brought them to me. They were heavier than practice knives, meant for incapacitating someone. I wondered if Neck Tattoo might have been ex-military. Not many people carried knives in holsters or threw with his excellent form. I certainly didn't.

I set my stance and took a deep breath. Every throw had to count. I aimed for the bull's-eye, pulled my arm back, and released the knife. It spun toward the target, headed for the center. The hilt slammed into the bull's-eye and dropped with a metallic *clang* against the floor.

The crowd laughed drunkenly. I grimaced and made a point of avoiding Silas's gaze. I didn't need another dose of disapproval.

"Nice throw," Neck Tattoo mocked.

Ignoring the jeers, I flipped the next knife and held it by the tip. I lined up my throw and focused on not over-rotating the knife. The metal blade flashed and landed in the middle ring.

Half the crowd cheered for me, but Neck Tattoo had nothing to add.

I had missed the thrill of something on the line, the anticipation from the crowd. Taking a deep breath, I focused on steadying my nerves. My last throw would have to be perfect to win. *Best shot wins all.* I hefted the third blade, already more comfortable with the weight and balance. I pulled my arm back and steadied my breathing. The rowdy crowd fell away, as did the argument I would soon be having with Silas and even the pressure of winning the bet. All that mattered was the centered feeling between me, the knife, and my target. With a fluid movement, I released the blade.

The final throw landed with a satisfying *thud* in the exact center of the board.

I bowed to the crowd, collecting a few laughs and a lot more grumbles. *Time to go.*

I stuffed the cash into my pockets and reached for the knives.

Neck Tattoo grabbed my arm and pulled me around. His face was scrunched in anger. He grabbed for my cash, and I hit him hard in the throat with the heel of my hand. He doubled over in pain, knocking the knives off the table and onto the floor.

"Cheating bitch!" he coughed, reaching for them.

I swore and reached for the closest knife. The scene was about to get ugly.

Silas appeared from the crowd, kicked the knives out of Neck Tattoo's reach, and pushed me toward the exit all in one movement.

I stared after the beautiful set of blades as they scattered across the wood floor.

Silas gave me another push.

It was a damn shame to lose my prize, but I didn't have a choice. I made it out the front door and ten steps into the parking lot before the angry crowd spilled out behind me. The bouncer was conveniently nowhere to be found—and neither was Silas.

"Who the fuck do you think you are?" Neck Tattoo yelled.

I eyed the distance to the car. It figured Silas would bail when I could actually use his help. I raised my hands, palms up. "Hey, I won the bet fair and square."

"We don't let cheats take our money." He closed the distance between us with angry strides.

"I don't want a fight," I said, backing toward the car. I regretted that I had let Silas talk me into leaving Ripper behind.

"Too late," Neck Tattoo growled, killing my hope of a clean exit. He reached for me.

I ducked, kicked him in the thigh, and swore. I'd shifted my kick in order to keep from spearing him with my heel and tapped his thigh instead of nailing him in the crotch. I kicked off the heels in frustration.

"Back down," Silas commanded, pushing people aside as he made his way through the crowd.

Neck Tattoo lost all interest in me as he faced the bigger threat. He stood several inches shorter than Silas but outweighed him by at least forty pounds of beer belly. He tried to push Silas out of the way. Silas knocked his arms aside and pushed the other man hard enough that he stumbled back from the force.

I kicked the side of Neck Tattoo's knee. I heard a loud *pop* before he fell to the ground, yipping in pain.

Silas looked at me with surprised disbelief. He was a trained fighter with the appropriate height, weight, and skill to take on someone like Neck Tattoo. I, on the other hand, was a slender, five-foot-five woman with anger issues. No one expected me to do anything to take care of the problem, and that was their mistake.

Silas slapped Ripper's hilt into my hand and faced the crowd.

I stared at the knife in surprise. I had truly expected him to insist on doing the fighting. But he'd handed me the knife, fully accepting that I could handle myself. Unless he just wanted me to get the beating he no doubt believed I deserved. Honestly, his motivations were a complete mystery to me.

One of Neck Tattoo's buddies in a bulky leather jacket took the first swing. Silas ducked and, with a precise movement that revealed his experience in hand-to-hand fights, landed a vicious cross-punch to Leather Jacket's jaw. The force of the blow knocked the other man off-balance, and he spun halfway around before he fell to the ground, unconscious.

Two more bikers jumped Silas. A third man with a bandana tied around his head grabbed me by the arm.

I twisted and jabbed Ripper at his face, fully intending to redecorate his features if he didn't let me go. He dodged but couldn't get away from the follow-through kick I slammed into his ribs.

Bandana stumbled backward with the air knocked out of him. I hit him with an open-handed chop to his windpipe. He doubled over, gasping for breath, and I finished the job by sweeping his feet from under him. I flipped my grip on Ripper, ready to react if Bandana decided to get up, but he stayed down, gagging for air.

Silas's own fight took down three of Neck Tattoo's friends. The whole incident took less than ten seconds.

Silas bared his teeth at the others, obviously eager for more. "Anyone else?"

The crowd apparently didn't want to get their asses handed to them. They dragged their buddies back into the bar, including my friend Neck Tattoo with his shattered knee cap, and we made a hasty escape to the car. I left them my shoes as a souvenir.

Once we were safely inside the vehicle, Silas let his anger loose on me. "What in all five sodding hells were you thinking back there? You almost lost your winnings."

"I *didn't* lose. I have excellent throwing skills."

His eyes narrowed. The heat of his anger disappeared, transforming into suspicion. "You *are* surprisingly accurate and steady in a fight. Who trained you in hand-to-hand?"

I shifted in my seat. "No one. I'm not trained in anything."

"You're definitely trained," he insisted. "But I'm not sure of the style. It's reminiscent of the Pri Tai methods but with Earthen mixed-martial influences. Definitely intended for close combat with a weapon."

"Look, I can hold my own in a street fight, but I never studied Pad Thai or whatever."

"It's called Pri Tai, and it's the basis of Guardian combat techniques. And clearly, you have."

"No, I haven't. Scout's honor." I held up my fingers in the universal scout salute.

He didn't seem impressed.

"I told you about the crazy memories I got from Marcel. Maybe I picked up some of his... training?" The idea sounded flimsy, even to me. I was good with a knife—I'd been handling them for over a decade—but even I couldn't explain the way I'd reacted on instinct.

"That's... possible," Silas said, but he didn't sound convinced.

Even if he didn't believe me, I hadn't been trained anywhere but the street school of hard knocks to the head. It was time to distract Silas from his wild theories, especially since he already didn't trust me. "Thanks for kicking ass back there. I'm sorry I cut it so close."

He shook his head as we pulled onto the road. "Dodging a few punches hardly qualifies as *kicking ass*."

"The good news is that thanks to your ability to dodge punches—and my mad skills—we've got enough cash for plane tickets to Alaska. One Fate's Temple, coming up."

Chapter Eight

Silas was borderline rude to me as we boarded the plane and settled into our seats. The perpetual grimace was back.

Watching him fumble with his seat belt, I had an epiphany. "Is this your first time on an airplane?"

"This is a ridiculously Mundane way to travel," he complained, finally managing to latch the buckle.

"It's perfectly safe," I assured him sweetly, tossing him the safety brochure. "Read that. And if we make it up in the air, they'll bring you a snack."

Silas frowned. "If?"

I couldn't contain my snickering, and Silas's exasperated sigh was my reward.

After takeoff and the promised pack of roasted peanuts, which Silas deemed acceptable, the flight attendants started an in-flight movie. They were showing one of those epic box office thrillers full of battles, star-crossed lovers, and general intrigue designed to appeal to everyone.

Right in the middle of an on-scene kiss between the leads, Silas leaned over to me and stage-whispered, "Do you know this is fictional?" His tone was mocking.

"I'm aware of that," I snapped.

"Then why are you emotional?"

"You're making me miss the best part," I hissed.

He stayed quiet for barely a minute. "Do Earthens enjoy these stories?"

I opened my mouth with the intention of giving him a smack-down, but his face was earnest. He seemed curious.

"Don't you have movies in"—I looked around before dropping my voice—"where you come from?"

"No."

Of course not. I pulled out the earbuds, resigned to missing the best part of the movie. He wasn't going to let up. "It's called suspended disbelief." I was proud that I remembered the term from the elective cinematography class I'd taken in high school. At the time, I had signed up because I got to watch movies during class. I'd enjoyed the class and still remembered a lot. "It's when you let yourself believe that something is real so you can experience the emotions of the story."

He glared doubtfully at the little screen. "What is emotional about this?"

I tried to decide if he was mocking me. The actors weren't that bad. "Her family is making her marry this guy she doesn't love, and the man she loves is going off to this battle, where he'll probably die." I frowned. "They never even had a chance."

He sat back in his seat, his face unreadable.

I sighed and turned back to the screen. I didn't know why I expected him to understand. At least the questions stopped. We watched in silence until the big epic battle scene at the end of the movie. The good guys gathered to fight against overwhelming odds with a small chance they might pull it off. The main character was ready to face off with the bad guy when Silas started snorting next to me, holding back laughter.

"What?" I demanded.

"This is ridiculous," he said. "See that archer—the arrows on his back? The first time he bent over, or ran for that matter, those arrows would fall out. It's ludicrous." He folded his arms across his lap, his face smug. "Anyone who's used a bow would know that. And the way he's holding it..." He made a noise of disbelief.

"They're actors. Who cares?" I whispered angrily at him.

"They should at least try to make it realistic. Performers in Aeterna convey their stories much more articulately than these movies."

"Seriously? Give it a rest. The actors are just supposed to look good!"

"That's another thing. I don't understand the Earthen obsession with physical appearance. Why should an attractive face equate to fame and wealth?"

"Says the guy walking around looking like this." I waved my hand around his strong jawline and high cheekbones. Surely, he'd benefited from his rugged good looks all his life.

Silas raised his eyebrows with a smug half-smirk.

I flamed red. *Kill me now.*

"Do you find me attractive?"

"Shut up." I turned back to the screen. Even my ears were burning in shame.

Silas didn't waste the opportunity to embarrass me. He leaned in to whisper in my ear, and I stifled the urge to smack him for also smelling good. "Do you?"

I wanted to tell him he was an ugly bastard, but the words got stuck in my throat. *I could strangle him right now.* "You know what I think about you." I sank enough venom into my voice to make it clear what I meant, but I couldn't meet his eyes.

He laughed, and I avoided looking at him until my face returned to a normal color. The movie finished a while later, but I didn't even notice if the star-crossed lovers ended up together.

THE SUN CHASED AWAY the predawn shadows and bathed the snow-covered Alaskan mountains in millions of icy sparkles. On every side, peaks soared like giants above our heads. Their ridges rose and banked at sharp angles, high above where even the scrappy evergreen trees could survive.

We'd secured a beater of a car in Anchorage for five hundred in cash, leaving us another four hundred for gear and gas. The car was pretty much held together by duct tape, and the heater blew lukewarm air, but it made the ninety-minute drive from the airport to Wasilla. After a quick stop for supplies, we were ready for the two-day trek that Silas assured me would get us to the Fate's temple.

With a hiker's hut a little more than halfway through the journey and a good map to guide us, we didn't have to carry quite as many supplies or a tent. I pulled the thick coat tighter around me and stomped onto the cold, hard ground at the head of the trail.

A tiny bubble of happiness built in my chest. Titus couldn't follow us if we weren't using serious magic, and he would never think to go to this remote mountain range in Alaska when he'd last seen us outside of New York State. The Fate was less than forty-eight hours away, and that meant all my magic problems would be gone soon.

Silas loaded the last of our supplies into his backpack then cinched the waist and chest straps tighter over his down coat, securing the weight evenly across his upper body. He took in the majestic scenery with an assessing gaze. "Let's go."

We hiked for almost three hours, heading steadily uphill along the mountain path. The thin air made breathing difficult. My shoulders were already stiff from the weight of the pack, and my feet were sure to develop blisters by the end of the day. Silas had called this an easy hike, and I wanted to smack him already. The path got rockier, winding past frozen ponds. I glanced up at the sun. All day, misty rain peppered us before clearing out suddenly, leaving only cool mountain air. I considered stripping off a layer or two, but the unpredictable weather left me in a strange state between sweaty and shivering.

"How far do you think we've gone?" I asked.

"About five miles. Should be a little over halfway to the hut. You set a good pace."

I hid my surprise at the unexpected compliment and tucked my water bottle back into the pack. The ground we had already covered was breathtaking. At the bottom of the valley, a wandering river rushed between two steep cliff faces, carving a path around boulders the size of buses. Ahead of us, far into the distance, patches of ice were nestled between impassable valleys, glinting sharply in the falling sun. At least the scenery was worth the effort.

We progressed slowly as the path wound higher and became more treacherous. My legs ached, but with Silas on my tail, my pride wouldn't let me slow down. My feet slipped on loose shale, and I had to scramble up a tremendous incline on all four limbs over what the map aptly identified as Heartbreak Hill. It reminded me of a famous stretch of inclining trail in the Boston Marathon called by the same name. God, I missed that city with its cobbled streets and brick buildings. Alaska was beautiful, but I couldn't wait to get home.

Five hours in, a spectacular sunset spread over the sky, and I paused to catch my breath. Our warm breath frosted in the air as the sun's heat faded. I hoped we found the hiker's hut soon before it got too dark and cold. We would freeze if we had to sleep outside without any shelter.

"My people haven't lived here for thousands of years," Silas whispered, his eyes locked on the distant sun setting over the mountains. "And my source is so far from this realm, I feel as though I'm suffocating. But still... it calls to me." He closed his eyes and lifted his face to the sky. For a moment, with the sun setting across his face, he was serene.

I lifted my face to the horizon. "There is... something." The majestic landscape held the peace of uninterrupted nature, and beyond that, a connection with something bigger than myself. It was more than the agelessness of the mountains, the energy of the river below, the fresh feel of the trees. It was magic and life.

His expression was still soft and relaxed. "Can you feel it too?"

White strands of magic flow around me, dancing through the air in complex patterns.

"Can you feel it?" a woman's voice asks gently.

I reach out for the energy and feel it flex with my call. I pull it into threads and weave them together in a tapestry. The tapestry becomes a shape, which layers into a conjuring. It's effortless, familiar, like breathing.

"The source will always be a part of you," she whispers, "no matter how far you are from home."

As the memory faded, I released a soft breath. It had been a while since I'd had a flashback, but that one had been surprisingly comforting, which was a rarity in Marcel's memories. Before Silas noticed my lapse of awareness, I zipped up my jacket and returned to the trail, eager to get to the hut before it got dark.

We rounded a corner and saw it: a hut roughly the size of my basement apartment back in Boston. Cheery, bright-red paint covered the building. A steeply gabled, Christmas-green metal roof sat on top. The clerk at our supply stop had told us they were brightly painted to make them easy to see in winter, but the intensity of the color still surprised me. From the edge of a hill, the hut had a spectacular view of the whole mountain range and the Little Susitna River at the bottom of the valley.

The inside was clean and dry with two sets of bunk beds on the first floor. A ladder led to the second level and a loft sleeping space.

A small table built out from the wall held some basic supplies and a book for visitors to sign. Silas pulled out our dinner rations, while I flipped through the pages of handwritten notes dating back to the seventies. This particular hike was hard, and apparently out of the way enough, so it didn't take long to flip through the entire book.

The day's exertion caught up to me as I ate my way through beef jerky and pre-cooked beans. Even though I was used to working long hours on my feet, the hike had taken a toll. I would be sore and stiff the next day.

Silas laid out his sleeping bag on one of the bunks and folded himself onto the ground in front of it, his legs crossed.

"What are you doing?" I asked, setting up my own bed.

"I need to reconnect to the source." His magic flared before he closed his eyes. With his hands on his knees and his brow relaxed, he looked as though he were meditating.

I crawled into my sleeping bag and stared, equally fascinated by the gentle patterns of energy around him and his relaxed features. I watched as the magic shifted into complex, multi-layered patterns that flowed around him and formed something almost solid-looking with their golden energy. The gentle buzz of his magic seemed to tickle along my skin, raising goose bumps under my long sleeves. Compared to the simple ball he'd formed earlier in the motel, this conjuring was more complex.

"Join me or stop staring," he said without opening his eyes.

I grunted and turned my back to him, burrowing into my bag. The whistling night wind lulled me to sleep.

I WOKE UP SCREAMING.

Silas leapt out of his bunk, disheveled and ready for a fight. His magic flared, and the sword appeared in his hand as he scanned the little cabin for a target.

"It's okay! I'm okay," I gasped from my bunk. "It was just a bad dream."

The sword tip lowered to the floor as he stared at me. "Fratch, Maeve!" he huffed. "I thought we were under gods-damned attack!"

I flopped onto my back and exhaled, willing my heart to slow down. The nightmare wasn't one of the visions, but it had seemed real enough. Father Mike had been facing down an entire pack of Rakken, but he hadn't screamed or tried to run. He hadn't even tried to protect himself. He'd stood his ground, focused on protecting *me*.

Silas surprised me when he plopped down on the edge of my bunk. He ran his now-empty hands through his hair and exhaled through his teeth. "Do you remember any details?"

"You want to know about my nightmare?" I asked. "Why?" I didn't mean to sound suspicious, but I couldn't for the life of me figure out why he would want to know about it.

The dawning light in the cabin was just enough to see by, and his expression seemed contemplative. He was quiet for a long moment before he spoke. "For my first assignment as a newly minted Guardian, they dispatched the entire legion into a realm called Krittesh. It was..." He paused, searching for a word. "Chaos. Lesser demons rarely cooperate long enough to form coalitions, but one group managed to band together and cause serious damage. They raided the organized settlements, murdering the residents and stealing their supplies." He grimaced as if remembering something particularly nasty. "They tortured for enjoyment. Women, children... whether or not they surrendered. It didn't matter. We followed their trail of destruction for days." His shoulders lifted as he drew in a long breath. "I'll spare you the details. We were betrayed, and I lost a friend."

I sat up on one elbow, my nightmare forgotten. "That sounds awful."

"At the time, I believed I was fine. I buried myself in training and wrapped myself up in righteous anger. When I started having dreams, I simply rationed my sleeping. I let the fear and the anger stew, not realizing how deeply I had been affected by the events." He shrugged. "Another Guardian in my legion, Thessaly, helped me deal with the fallout. I couldn't move forward until I'd dealt with the past."

He looked at me pointedly, but I didn't know what I was supposed to say.

"You said the visions feel as if you are living Marcel's memories," he continued. "You're experiencing the torture he endured. That kind of fear and pain sitting inside of you always manifests outward."

"Look, I'm sorry that happened to you. But I'm not—I'm fine." My throat got tight, remembering all the torture Marcel had endured. "This was just a regular nightmare. It happens."

"Have you ever killed someone before?"

I stared at him. Finally, I managed to shake my head.

He pushed off from my bunk and returned to his own. "You need to confide in someone. It doesn't have to be me."

I lay back on my bed for a long while, unable to fall back asleep as the sun grew brighter by degrees. He may have been right, but I had more pressing issues I needed to deal with before my nightmares, like the small detail of staying alive. If I wanted to keep breathing for much longer, I needed the Fate to get the magic out of me.

When the sun finally peeked over the horizon, we packed our things and got an early start. On the trail, Silas led the way, and I followed, grateful for a more relaxed pace than the day before. We planned to hike up to Mint Glacier, traverse across the expansive ice sheet, and up to the highest peak, where the Fate's temple was supposed to be.

The frigid air stung my lungs with each breath. As I predicted, my whole body was stiff. Carrying the heavy pack had left me with tired shoulders and legs. After about a mile, my thighs burned from the constant uphill climb, but I forced myself to push through the discomfort. Silas consulted our map and his compass and adjusted our course yet again. Almost an hour later, we reached the last pass and stood at the edge of a cliff overlooking the glacier. The cold air numbed my face as I toed to the ledge and peered down a thirty-foot drop to the ice below. The flat, massive surface of Mint Glacier stretched as far as I could see.

My stomach twisted. I scooted back and breathed through my nose.

Silas called me back to the cliff's edge and pulled out a rope. "Take off your pack and tie this around your waist. I'll hold it and guide you down."

I gave him a skeptical scowl.

He gave me a wide, challenging smile. "Scared?"

"How will you get down after I get to the bottom with the rope?" I asked.

"I'll lower the packs and then climb down after you. I don't need the rope."

Of course he didn't.

Silas twisted the rope expertly into a makeshift harness then helped me into the loops and tied it around my waist. Being that close to him made me uncomfortable, and I silently cursed his confidence and the way he smelled crisp and clean after two days of hiking. I wondered if it was some kind of magic trick. He secured his end of the rope to a large boulder then looped it around his waist.

"Face me, kneel down here, and ease your foot over the edge," he instructed.

With my stomach clenching, I inched closer to the ledge and searched blindly for a foothold. If he slipped, I was dead. Forcing myself to remain calm, I stretched my foot into open air.

"Left," Silas said.

"Yours or mine?" I cast my foot out blindly.

"Mine."

Scowling, I switched feet. If not falling to my death required good communication between Silas and me, I might as well just throw myself off the cliff.

I very slowly worked my way downward, and fifteen teeth-clenching minutes later, I exhaled with relief when my feet hit the ground again. Silas lowered our packs, and when they reached the ground, I untied them and wound the rope in a loop. As Silas descended without a guide or rope, he hit the same footholds I had and made it down in half the time.

"You're insane," I said with conviction.

He smiled at me, his eyes bright and carefree. I laughed at his boyish enthusiasm. He nodded toward the nearest peak looming above us. "The temple should be on that crest. But first, we have to traverse the glacier."

The sales clerk in Wasilla had outfitted us with spiked contraptions called crampons that slipped over our shoes. They were a safety measure against crevasses, which were deep cracks hidden beneath brittle ice caps. We put on the special footwear and secured the rope ends around our waists. I felt a bit like a dog on a leash. With everything secure, Silas took the lead and headed out over the flat, expansive sheet of ice between us and the Fate.

The metal teeth of the crampons pierced the top layer of thin, crunchy snow before biting into the sheet of ice beneath. I let Silas lead. He walked a dozen feet ahead, and our footsteps echoed with sharp, metallic snicks along the glacier. Small gusts of wind kicked up snow over the smooth, glassy surface as we progressed slowly forward. I watched the little flurries, distracted by their swirling patterns. An eagle soared high above us, its wings spread wide. I couldn't imagine anything more gorgeous and serene than this.

The rope tied between us jerked, and I flew off my feet. I fell flat on my back and shot across the ice, arms and legs thrashing. The rope dragged me, feet first, along the slick surface. My spiked shoes shredded the ice. Stinging shards of snow flew into my face, blinding me.

Finally, I caught a foothold. The crampons on my heels dug in, and I jerked to a stop. The rope bit into my waist, stealing my breath. Pain shot through my torso. My snow-crusted boots were inches from a jagged crack in the ice. The rope was pulled taut between my legs and over the ledge a few feet away, where Silas dangled inside the crevasse.

I couldn't breathe. The rope was too tight. I gasped and strained against it.

"I can't get a handhold!" Silas yelled from below, his voice echoing off the walls of ice.

My entire body trembled, unable to breathe properly. I pulled with all my strength, but I couldn't ease the pressure of his weight against the rope.

"I'm going to swing to the ledge," he called. "Hang on!"

I braced myself a second before the rope jerked to the side. My insides squeezed, and I gasped in pain. His weight pulled my butt off the ground, and one of my spiked heels slipped.

The rope swung again and pulled me into a squat. The crampons carved through ice as I jerked toward the edge. The crevasse loomed just feet away.

"I'm slipping!" I yelled.

"Don't move!"

I was almost vertical. "I'm being pulled in! Silas!" I gasped, desperate for air.

"I'm going to cut the rope!"

"You'll fall!" My mind raced. There had to be a way to get him out.

"Get to the temple," he ordered.

"Wait!"

The rope tugged sharply. I pitched toward the jagged break in the ice. The weight on the rope disappeared, and I fell backward, landing on my butt. "Silas!" I scrambled to my hands and knees and peered over the ledge. The other end of the rope dangled loosely above a thousand feet of air that narrowed into a dark, impenetrable crevasse.

I screamed his name and listened as it echoed off the walls of ice.

Silas was gone.

Chapter Nine

I crawled away from the ledge, unable to process what had just happened. *He cut the rope.*

I screamed his name into the crevasse. Dry heaves wracked my body, and bile rose in my throat. My brain wasn't able to catch up. It stuck on one thought. *He's gone. He cut the rope so I wouldn't be dragged in with him, and he fell. He's gone!*

I plopped back down on my butt and stared up into the serene blue sky. Hot tears streaked down my face and over my chin.

How did this happen? One minute, we were walking along the flat sheet of ice, and it was peaceful. Then...

"He's gone," I said. The words voiced aloud made my panic rise. I was alone, and Silas was gone. The stupid, arrogant jerk had sacrificed his life to keep me from falling into the crevasse.

A wave of magical pressure hit me from behind, almost knocking me over. I twisted and saw a mound of clothing lying fifty feet behind me. I blinked. "Silas!"

He lay faceup and unmoving. The large pack was still strapped to his back. I rushed to him, but the rope dragged, and my feet got tangled in it. I stumbled. My legs couldn't move fast enough.

Finally, I dropped to my knees and grabbed his face between my hands. "Silas? Silas!"

All tension had disappeared from his face, and he looked so peaceful.

Fear flashed through me. *Is he...* I held my breath and listened for his breathing. My heart drummed in my ears, drowning out everything else.

His face scrunched into a small scowl.

I exhaled the breath that had caught in my lungs, and a burst of inappropriate laughter spilled out. The roller coaster of emotions was too much. I dropped my forehead onto his chest, and the laughter transformed into hysterical tears. My hysteria soaked into Silas's jacket as I banged my fists on my thighs. My life was never meant to be so insane. Just *days* ago, my greatest fears had been making rent and living up to Father Mike's expectations. He worried I wasn't eating enough vegetables, for crying out loud.

When the tears slowed and my thinking cleared, I sat back on my heels.

Silas must have used his magic to skim out of the crevasse and knocked himself out in the process. He'd said he didn't have access to as much magic while he was in our realm. Remembering that a spell could kill if it drew too much magic, I wondered how close to death he'd just come. Then I remembered what he'd said about flares. If the Brotherhood could follow his magic flare, we had to get away from the glacier as quickly as possible.

I shook him. "Silas!"

His chest rose and fell in a steady rhythm, but he didn't stir. I contemplated something I'd wanted to do since I met him—I slapped him across the face. Pink flushed across his cheek, but his eyes remained stubbornly closed.

Shit. I had no choice but to drag him off the glacier.

After a few minutes of thinking, I took off my backpack and heaved Silas onto his side. I slid my pack under his lower half, using the severed rope around his waist to lash it to him. With his own pack still strapped to his back, the two packs together made a crude sled. The bags would get shredded, but it was the best I could do.

Tired and sore, I untied the rope from around my own waist and made a large loop to pull the sled with.

My entire body was bruised, and exhaustion threatened to send me face first into the ice. But we couldn't stay on the glacier. Silas's trick with skimming had probably caused a big flare of magic, and he'd said that Titus could track that. If the Brotherhood showed up while Silas was unconscious, they would kill us both. The mountain range with the Fate's temple was so close. We had come so far! I just had to get us to the temple and get the damn magic out before they found us. I would get us there, even if I had to drag Silas's unconscious butt up that mountain.

Grunting with effort, I pulled on the sled. My lungs burned, and my back ached. His weight dragged behind me, plowing a path through the thin layer of snow on top of the flat, icy surface. Every step took a force of will to keep putting one foot in front of the other. And still, we were barely moving. I plodded along methodically, ignoring the possibility of another crevasse. I had no choice but to go forward. The sun set quicker than I'd anticipated, and the temperature plummeted. I had no idea how much farther the glacier stretched, when Silas would wake up, or if the Brotherhood would appear in the next second. The uncertainty drove me forward until the temperamental skies opened and poured rain on us.

My layers of clothing were soaked instantly. I gritted my teeth and swore at the sky. When the rain stopped abruptly a few minutes later, I was wet and frozen. Wind howled across the wide expanse of ice. My teeth started to chatter. Silas shivered on the sled, his lips tinged blue. We needed shelter. I looked up at the mountain peak that still seemed no closer than it had an hour ago. Staying where we were wasn't going to solve anything, so I kept pulling.

Another half hour later, we reached an expansive boulder field. My determination crashed. It would be impossible to pull Silas through it. I'd come all this way only to be blocked by rocks. I couldn't drag Silas any farther. I scanned the rocky field and spotted several large boulders forming a small cave about fifteen yards away. It would be big enough to fit us both, and we desperately needed shelter, warmth, and rest.

I untied Silas from the packs and tried to wake him again. When that didn't work, I attempted to lift him. My aching body almost collapsed as I dragged him by his armpits over the snow and toward the mound of boulders. I willed my legs to keep moving, begging my frozen body not to give out. After I spent an eternity crossing the field, I laid Silas carefully on the ice-hard ground outside the cave and went back for our supplies.

When I returned, Silas was convulsing with shivers. His naturally olive skin had turned pale and waxy. Our soaked clothes had to come off, or we were both going to die of hypothermia. With frozen fingers, I unpacked our sleeping bags and zipped them together. Tugging at his jacket until I was out of breath, I finally managed to get it off of him. With my hands on my knees, I panted and considered the number of wet layers he was wearing—it would be impossible to take them all off and dress him in dry ones. Damn it, if he died of hypothermia, I would kick his ass.

I fumbled through our packs for a few minutes in search of a lighter and something flammable before I realized that a campfire out on this open field would be a disaster. If the Brotherhood followed Silas's flare, I would literally be setting up a beacon to our hiding spot.

Instead, I dug Ripper out of my pack and sliced through Silas's wet shirt. My fingers were clumsy and numb, and I thanked God his fleece-lined snow pants and the fatigues underneath were easier to slice through than jeans. Even still, the knife kept slipping from my stiff fingers, and I nearly stabbed him several times. I readjusted my grip and worked the blade through the rest of his clothes with uncoordinated, jerking motions. The wind howled across his exposed flesh, wracking us both with chills. Shivering and grunting, I rolled him onto the makeshift bed made from our conjoined sleeping bags, shoved dry clothing into the bottom, and dragged the whole bundle into the cave.

The freezing air sucked all heat from me as I shed my own wet clothes and maneuvered into the sleeping bag, completely and utterly exhausted as I zipped us in together. Skin-to-skin contact would get us both warm. Our bodies trembled in unison as I rubbed my hands roughly over his arms and chest, trying to create heat. His teeth chattered behind blue lips until eventually, his shuddering slowed and finally stopped.

I fell into a deep, exhausted sleep.

Blinking, I woke up disoriented. My eyes adjusted to the small amount of light seeping through cracks between the boulders. Everything was quiet except for our breathing. Overnight, our combined body heat had returned, warming the little cave.

Silas slept next to me. His arm and half his chest were a heavy weight pinning me to the ground. Between the weight and the warmth, I was sweltering inside the sleeping bag.

Now that we weren't dead, I realized we were waking up naked. Embarrassment flooded me. I wasn't ashamed of my body or anything, but being naked with Silas was not a good idea, not when I'd been fighting off *urges* the day before. I needed to get dressed before he woke up. Slowly, I reached over him for the zipper, praying I wouldn't wake him.

His eyes jerked open, and I froze. He blinked twice. A small frown crimped the corners of his lips.

I snickered at his priceless expression. Confused Silas looked kind of adorable.

His eyes flicked to my bare skin, and we both froze. "Why are we nude?" he asked in a low voice that sent shivers up my spine.

I bit my lower lip to keep from doing something totally, completely stupid. "It rained, and hypothermia, and your lips turned blue." I cleared my throat and tried again. "I dragged your unconscious butt across a glacier after your stupid stunt nearly gave us both hypothermia."

"You were supposed to keep moving," he said, untangling his limbs from mine. I held very still as his firm torso slid against mine. He hovered over me, lifting his body so we weren't touching. His biceps flexed on either side of my head. His eyes lowered to my lips.

I forgot all the perfectly reasonable and important reasons why I shouldn't get tangled up with him. An entirely inappropriate thrill shot through me. "You could say thank you."

"Why don't you ever listen to me?" His eyes were on fire. I didn't know if he was angry or turned on. Maybe both.

I wanted to run my fingers over the muscles of his chest. My insides twisted as a slow tingle spread in my belly. I ached to kiss him until his scowl disappeared for good. "You don't get to tell me what to do."

His voice dropped to a low growl, and his head dipped toward mine. "You're entirely too stubborn."

I put my palm on his chest, fingers splayed. I meant to push him away, but my hand drifted across his chest, feeling the hard muscle there as he held himself above me. "I'm not one of your little soldiers."

He lowered to his elbows, closing the distance between our bodies. His face was inches from mine. "You couldn't follow orders if your life depended on it."

My brain short-circuited, and I gripped his hair, pulling him down to my mouth.

He kissed me back hard. As he pinned me with his weight, the evidence of his desire fueled the flames inside me. Our verbal sparring became physical as our mouths fought for dominance. He gripped the back of my head and held me exactly where I wanted to be. My tongue teased his lips, and he deepened the kiss. He kissed like he fought—passionately and with skill.

When our lips separated, his mouth traveled down the side of my neck. I slid the tips of my fingers over the tattoos along his back, fascinated with the contrast of soft skin over hard muscle. The symbols continued all the way down his side, twisting with the curve of his muscles as far as I could see. I had the sudden urge to go exploring for more.

"You're determined to get yourself killed," he said as his mouth moved to the base of my neck. He nipped at the sensitive skin before his mouth traveled across my collarbone.

"You're a control freak," I said, grinding my hips against him.

His hand slid between my legs, and I moaned. Then my brain caught up. "Jesus Christ!"

"Not my name," he murmured against my skin.

His lips traveled to my breast, and I lost coherent thought for several seconds.

"Silas!" I yanked at his hair.

He hissed and pulled back.

In a moment of sanity that wouldn't last long if I didn't act immediately, I pushed him away. His eyes were dilated, and in the shadowy dark of our little shelter, they looked almost black.

"This is a bad idea," I said. There were so many reasons not to have sex with Silas. But God, I wanted more. And obviously, he did too. The air seemed to crackle as we stared at each other.

A sudden flare of power shifted the air around us in a familiar pull that seemed to spear me straight through my stomach. *Skimming.*

We both froze, alert to every noise outside our little cave.

Silas motioned for me to stay quiet and reached for the packs at the entrance to our shelter.

Clothes. I need clothes. Fear snaked up my spine as I dug for the clothing I'd shoved into the bottom of our bags and tossed stuff at Silas.

He maneuvered into his clothing and slipped silently out of the cave. Just as I finished dressing, his head popped back in. His voice was barely audible over the whistling of the wind against the rocks. "Hurry. We need to move."

We ran through the field, crouching low between the gigantic boulders, our tattered packs on our backs. Silas scouted behind us, while I moved as quickly and quietly as I could, but we didn't see anything. Still, I didn't question what we'd both experienced—someone had skimmed onto the mountain, near enough that I had sensed the impact of their flare.

In a dozen yards, we reached the end of the field and the base of another mountain range. A ten-foot cliff face rose above us.

"Silas!" I whispered frantically. "I can't climb this without a rope."

He glanced behind us. "We don't have time to find another path. Put your hands and feet where I do. You'll be fine."

Don't look down. Don't look down. With my heart pounding, I placed my sweaty hands exactly where he had put his and gripped the rock, hyperfocused on each movement and not on the drop below me. At the very top, several inches beyond my grasp, I reached for the final foothold. His longer legs spanned the distance with ease, but I couldn't stretch that far. He reached back over the ledge and offered me his hand. I took it, expecting a small boost to the foothold. He pulled me straight to the top, and I landed on my feet next to him with a little yelp. He steadied me with his hand against the small of my back, and our gazes caught.

Heat pooled in my stomach as I remembered the feel of his hard body on mine. His eyes lowered to my lips for a moment before he stepped back and scanned the path ahead.

Focus, Maeve. I surveyed the cliff top. Another hiker's hut sat a short distance away. Like the last one, a bright shade of green clashed with red trim along the sloped metal roof. It was a safe oasis in the middle of the snow. "Let's go to the hut."

"This way," Silas said at the same time, pointing toward the west and the ridge he'd chosen. "The elevation will give us a vantage point to scout for the Brotherhood's position. We'll have to avoid them if we want to get to the temple. I'm not sure we'll be able to take the most direct route any longer."

Getting stranded out in the open would be a death sentence, which increased my desire to curl up in the little cabin and hide. But that was stupid. We were being chased, and we couldn't stop moving until we found the Fate's temple, wherever it was.

We climbed the ridge to the west, moving as stealthily as possible. Every crunch of snow made me flinch as I imagined it echoing back to the Brotherhood. Silas reached the summit first and lowered to his belly. I caught up a minute later, trying to ignore the nauseating flip of my stomach as we climbed higher and higher. The range became a dead end—a huge drop surrounded us on three sides. But the height did give us the view of the entire valley below.

We stood over an endless expanse of peaks and valleys. Hundreds of ranges spread before us, but no path seemed any more promising than the next, and no mystical road signs pointed to the temple. Disappointment weighed me down. We had come so far but were no closer to our goal. Below us, Mint Glacier glinted in the distance. It was strange that something so beautiful had almost killed us.

Silas's mouth pulled into a thin line. He pointed at dark shapes loping along the glacier. I squinted at them in the distance. My stomach plummeted as I counted ten distinct shapes, each moving on four legs.

"More Shifters?"

"Shifters includes anyone who can change to another form. These are Rakken." He scowled as he peered at the beasts. "They'll track our scent, and they're close." He grimaced. "Fratch. I told you to keep moving."

"If I kept going, you'd be dead! Last night, I dragged your stupid ass across a glacier and saved you from hypothermia. Would it kill you to show a little gratitude?"

His brow furrowed in anger. "You were supposed to get to the Fate's temple."

A shrill shriek echoed through the valley, and I cringed. Only something excited to eat us would make that kind of noise. We watched as the Rakken in the lead found our little cave, and the others rushed over to sniff it out. They all took up the call, building into a frenzy of screeches and howls until my ears rang with their high-pitched calls.

"We have to get off this ridge before they cut us off," Silas said.

I scooted away from the edge and scrambled back toward the path we'd just ascended, the sound of the Rakkens' screams making me cover my ears as I ran.

The noise ended abruptly.

"They have our trail," he said.

"Can they get up that last cliff face?" It had been almost impossible for me to climb; surely a four-legged animal couldn't scale it.

"They'll claw their way up."

I so didn't want to know that. I wasn't sure what was worse, hearing their frenzied, shit-in-my-pants howls or knowing they were approaching silently with claws that could sink into rock.

We descended back down the little western summit and once again stood at the intersection of the ridge and the hut. To the north, the Rakken were closing in on us. The south held the endless maze of mountains. With the Rakken chasing us, we wouldn't be able to hide for long. Our only choice was the east. I looked up past the radiant green hut to the east range.

I blinked and focused back on the hut. The little building almost glowed in the sun. I squinted at it, closed one eye, then switched to the other.

Silas glared into the distant south, probably calculating our survival odds in the twisting, unknown mountains.

The hut still glowed.

"The hut," I whispered.

"We'll head south," he said, his eyes never wavering. "It's our best chance to lose them, maybe double back..."

"We have to go to the hut." The magic was impossible *not* to see. The cabin radiated with energy.

"We can't stop here."

"It's glowing." Arguing with him was a waste of time we couldn't afford. I sprinted for the little building and threw open the door. Like the other cabin, bunk beds lined two cabin walls with emergency supplies stacked neatly on a shelf between them.

I glared at the plain wood walls, willing them to shimmer with energy. *Nothing. No magical Fate's temple anywhere.* My shoulders drooped with sudden and intense disappointment.

Silas entered behind me and scowled with furrowed brows. The sour feeling in my stomach perfectly matched his expression.

"I've seen Rakken take their prey alive," he said. "They tear into the soft organs first, drawing out death while they eat you. I'd like to avoid that if you're agreeable."

A grimace spread across my face. I refused to believe our only option was to hide in the mountains and hope the organ-eating, clawed demon dogs didn't find us.

"But..." The cabin was identical to the other one, except that I had seen it glowing with magic from the outside. The Fate *had* to be there. It was the only explanation. "It's glowing with energy. The magic—"

"Now." He pulled me outside.

I turned back to the cabin once more, and it hit me. The building stood at least two stories high like the last hut, but there was only one floor inside.

The second story was missing.

I rushed past Silas back inside. He swore in a language I didn't recognize and stalked after me, snow crunching harshly under his boots. I threw the door open and scanned the room again, my heart pounding with every wasted second. My gaze went to the ceiling, where I searched the wooden planks for an opening. Along the edge of one wall, two jagged lines were barely visible, running with the grooves of the wood. Three feet separated the parallel seams. I could have stared at them all night and thought they were cracks in the ceiling, but the opening would be wide enough to fit a person.

"There! Do you see that?" I demanded.

The sharp wail of claws on stone pierced the air with sickening closeness. The Rakken were climbing the cliff face.

"Give me a hand." I tossed my pack on the ground and dug out Ripper.

Silas hesitated.

"You're wasting time! If I'm wrong, we'll know in a second. Lift me up, Silas."

His eyes narrowed, but he wrapped his arms around my legs and hoisted me up on his shoulder. I pushed against the ceiling then pried Ripper between the cracks. The wood loosened and swung upward on silent hinges.

I pulled myself through the ceiling into the attic.

Triumph filled me. The space was at least four times bigger than what should have been able to physically fit inside the cabin, and a radiant white glow lit it from within. The ceiling soared ten feet above, supported by arched beams carved with overlapping geometric patterns. Around the secret entrance, the floors melted from the rough wood of the cabin into smooth white stone. At the far end of the space in the center sat the only furnishing in the room—an ornate, high-backed chair.

I knelt on the smooth stone floor and motioned for Silas to come up.

He took off his pack, jumped, and pulled himself through the opening. "Fate's balls!"

"I really need to teach you better swear words," I said, my eyes on our impossible surroundings. I'd expected some kind of grand Roman edifice but had gotten a hiker's hut instead. But far from disappointing, the sheer amount of power radiating from the room thrummed inside my chest, confirming that this could only be one thing. We'd found the Fate's temple.

Chapter Ten

Inside the Fate's temple, patterns of magic wove through everything, emitting a brightness that overwhelmed my senses. It was more than physical light. The weight of the magic seemed tangible. It was like being able to see the individual pieces of matter that created everything in the universe.

Silas stood next to me, an equal measure of shock and awe on his face as we took it all in. I rose first, still gripping Ripper, and headed toward the only item in the room—the empty white chair. The back of it was taller than me and curved in a winged arch to the highest point. The gilded wood frame had carvings in a similar design to the arches on the ceiling. I bent closer to inspect the symbols, when a familiar magical pressure sucked at the air around me.

I leapt backward and stifled a gasp when a child appeared in the chair. I couldn't tell the child's gender as I stared at its long, straight blond hair and smooth, round face. Its eyes were too piercing for the baby face it wore. My skin crawled.

Determined not to threaten the powerful being that might be my only chance to live through this nightmare, I forced myself to lower Ripper. "Are you the Fate?"

The child smiled, and my stomach flipped.

"Don't be fooled by its appearance," Silas said, pulling me back. "It's not a child."

No shit, Sherlock.

We waited in silence while the Fate's gaze penetrated my soul.

"You are of Earth," the Fate finally said, surprising me with a strong feminine voice that belonged to a much older person. She cocked her head to the side and examined me. "And of Aeterna."

I bit the inside of my cheek, wondering what the Fate could have possibly meant by that doublespeak, while Silas went rigid beside me. I was definitely of Earth. The Aeterna part must have meant the magic trapped inside of me.

"The lost shall be found," she said.

The Fate waved her fingers casually, and I gasped at the sense of being connected to something infinitely more powerful than myself. Without warning, the room glowed with millions of streams of magic energy. Each strand intertwined with the next until the strength of it grew brighter than any light I had ever imagined, bathing us in a surreal glow.

Silas's skin glowed with the intricate markings of the sigils tattooed over his skin. The layered designs I had seen on his skin radiated magic, subtly moving in layers to create a stunning, interconnected web of archaic tattoos across his body, outlining him with golden energy. He flipped his arms over and back. Finally, he looked up at the Fate with wide eyes as he surveyed the amount of power that flowed from her.

Like a small sun, the power emanating from the Fate lit the air with clear, bright energy. The veins of magic wound toward her, so bright the aura of energy directly around her hurt to look at. I felt as if I were staring into the sun. The immense power was beyond my comprehension.

"What is this?" Silas asked, staring at his glowing sigils.

The Fate's eyes slid to him. "Silas. Son of House Valeron: The Eternal Might." Her voice was low and hypnotic. "Death's Fury."

Silas glared, and his shoulders tensed. He looked ready for a fight.

"You were destined for more," she stated as if that made perfect sense. "Fate forged by magic's light."

"I'm not here to discuss *fate*." He practically spat the last word.

"We know your heart's desire."

The room flared with energy so powerful, I could see the patterns behind my eyelids when I blinked. The air around us blurred into the shimmering image of a beautiful woman I'd never seen before. Her long blond hair spilled over a golden dress that was fitted to her slender body. A delicate circlet of woven gold sat on her brow. She had petite features and full, defined lips, but the expression on her face was indescribably sad.

The woman in the vision stood under a large flowering tree beside a man whose face I couldn't see. From the tense set of his shoulders and what I could see of his jaw, I guessed it was Silas. He was dressed in gleaming metal armor. Ornamental golden filigree accented his chest and the tops of his shoulders. A gold cloak ran across one shoulder and draped over his back. The woman held a small bundle in her arms—a baby? She reached across the space to hand it to him.

"Stop!" Silas ordered.

The vision disappeared, and the Fate sat silently with her child's eyes and a smooth, expressionless face.

I shivered.

Silas's face had gone dark, and his entire body was rigid. The muscles in his jaw flexed tight under his skin. Whatever that vision meant to him had shattered the exacting control with which he usually held himself.

"Return to Aeterna, and all will be unbound," the Fate finally said. "We can restore your rightful destiny: Prime of House Valeron, Commander of the Guardians."

I didn't know exactly what those titles meant, but based on the slack-jawed surprise etched all over Silas's normally stoic features, the Fate had offered him something big.

"How is that possible?" he asked.

The Fate shrugged in an expression more cunning than a child her age should have made. She creeped me out. I wanted to tell Silas not to trust any promises she made.

"Prophecy will be interpreted and... *reinterpreted*," she said. "What is lost can be restored."

The air between us blurred and shifted into a shimmering, opaque pool of energy. A rectangular doorway appeared. It was twice as high as a normal door and domed at the top, wide enough for two people to fit side by side. The surface wavered as if rippled by a slight breeze.

The Fate held out her hand in an invitation to walk through. "Your new fate awaits."

Silas tensed.

Panic flared inside of me at the thought of him leaving me with the creepy Fate and an unknown future.

His eyes narrowed. "No. I won't break my oath to Maeve. And I won't be a puppet to a Fate."

The Fate gave him a small, secretive grin. If it was a test, I couldn't tell if Silas had passed or failed. My heart ached for him even as relief flooded me. I didn't know the extent of what he'd just given up, but the Fate had called it his heart's desire. Making him choose between that and his oath to me was cruel.

"Can you reverse the Transference?" I asked, drawing the Fate's attention away from Silas.

"What has passed is here now and will come again."

Okay, Yoda. "Can you remove the magic inside of me?" My throat grew tight. I'd risked everything to find the Fate, and her answer would determine my future.

"You will only lose your powers to death."

"What?" My heart skipped a beat as I digested her words. I'd suspected I would have to bargain or maybe endure some ritual, but I hadn't really considered the possibility that it wasn't possible for the magic to be removed.

"You must restore the balance of power," she continued.

"What does that even mean?" Removing the magic would kill me. *I'll never be normal again.*

"A life exchanged for yours, Maeve O'Neill of Earth. Your moments are filled with death."

My heart lurched and restarted, thudding hard in my ears. A terrible sinking feeling settled in my gut. *Marcel.* He had died to transfer his power to me. *A life exchanged for mine.*

A thunderous explosion rocked the room. I stumbled forward and caught myself on the chair. The room rocked violently again, and inhuman shrieks pierced the air.

"The Rakken!" I yelled.

"We're trapped up here," Silas said, moving back toward the closed trapdoor in the floor.

The Fate sat motionless, her eyes glowing with power. She didn't react as another boom shifted the floor under our feet. The shrieking grew louder like claws scraping on a chalkboard. I clapped my hands over my ears to keep my brain from melting. With a flare of magic, Silas's sword appeared in his hand, and he strode toward the opening.

The trapdoor slammed open with such force, it tore off its hinges. A Rakken clawed its way up through the hole just before Silas reached it, leaving enormous gashes in the stone floor.

The second one through received a vicious kick in the head from Silas's boot and went crashing down onto the others below, blocking their path momentarily.

Silas grinned and swirled the sword, twisting his body and loos-
ening his muscles as he faced the Rakken that made it through.
With a stunning burst of speed, the beast leapt, and Silas slashed
at its forelimbs before pivoting out of the path of its razor-sharp
claws. The thick gray skin of the hairless beast seemed as strong as
armor, and the shallow wound didn't slow it down. It made another lunge at Silas, who twisted and sliced again, keeping himself between the Rakken and where I stood by the Fate. This time, thick
crimson blood welled on the Rakken's chest, reminding me that
this was a person with greater than animal intelligence.

As they fought and parried, that intelligent monster kept Silas
away from the trapdoor long enough for five more of its companions to jump through. Titus came through the hole with three
more Rakken at his heels. All nine Rakken, and the man who controlled them, blocked any chance of escape in the previously expansive space.

Titus didn't pause to say hello before he threw a sharp wave of
red-black magic straight at us.

Silas and I dove in opposite directions. I hit the ground and
rolled. The magic slammed into the floor, shattering the stone.
Shards sprayed around me, and I flung my arms over my face.

A Rakken lunged with its jaws unhinged. I rolled again, and
its double row of jagged teeth gnashed inches from my leg. It pivoted and dove toward me, digging its claws into the marble floor.
I scrambled to my feet, and it sprang again, claws extended. I
dropped flat on my back and thrust Ripper upward with all my
strength. Ripper's short blade pierced into the Rakken's throat only
a few inches deep, not far enough to do considerable damage. The
beast landed on me, its giant paws crushing me into the floor.
Claws dug into the tops of my shoulders, and I screamed.

I gripped the knife with two hands and dug through the tough
flesh of its neck. It shrieked and dug its claws in deeper. Finally, Rip-

per broke through the thick hide, and warm blood gushed over my arm. I pushed the blade deeper and twisted it. Seconds later, the enormous beast collapsed on top of my lower body. The smell of its rotten breath made me gag. I pushed frantically against its heavy weight. Crushed under its oversized body, I heaved with everything I had but couldn't get loose.

Across the room, Silas had turned six of the remaining Rakken into headless heaps of corded, hairless flesh, their necks cauterized as if sliced through by a lightsaber. The bodies started to waver as the last of their magic left them, and I deliberately looked away.

Silas stepped over the beheaded Rakken and ran toward me, his attention locked on my struggle to free myself from the Rakken's dead weight before another one ate me. With his help, I finally managed to push the dead carcass off my legs and wiggle free.

Flanked by the last two Rakken, Titus cast a sizzling orb of dark magic at Silas's back from across the room.

Too late to yell out a warning and propelled by instinct, I lunged forward and caught it like a baseball. Surprised, I held it between my hands. The power was amazing, like a tornado trapped inside a glass ball. The strands of magic twisted as I rolled it between my fingers, examining the layers inside. The desire to absorb it itched desperately inside me, but I remembered the way the tainted magic had made me sick and forced myself to resist. With a deep, primal hatred, my gaze lifted to Titus's snarling face. He would pay for all the pain and death he'd inflicted.

I dashed forward and hurled the magic back at him.

He dove out of the way, and the energy slammed into the Rakken beside him. The unintended target released an animalistic wail as it flew backward and crashed into the far wall.

In an explosion of speed, the last Rakken lunged across the room, its giant jaws snapping. I skittered backward, out of its reach.

"Take her alive!" Titus yelled.

The air shifted. The Rakken growled and swiped massive paws at me, pushing me backward and farther away from Silas, who was still dodging attacks from Titus's magic.

A pair of arms wrapped around me from behind, pinning my hands to my sides and pressing my back against his chest. I slammed my head backward and missed the unknown man's face by about six inches. Twisting in his arms, I angled the knife still gripped in my hand and tried to stab his thigh.

The Rakken in front of me *shifted* into the shape of a man and tore Ripper from my hand. He pressed the sharp blade against my throat, and I froze. I was trapped between the two men. They snarled in my face, looking ready to eat me despite the lack of sharp Rakken teeth.

"Silas!" Titus bellowed his name like a curse.

My captors held me tight. The blade dug into my neck. I couldn't even talk without getting sliced. Suddenly, it all seemed too real, too dangerous. I had no business being in this fight armed only with my tiny field knife and my anger. Silas had said they needed me alive, but the Fate's proclamation had changed everything. The Brotherhood would have to kill me to get the magic out of me, and I had no guarantees that they wouldn't do it right then.

Silas tensed and raised the tip of his sword at Titus.

Oh shit, he was going to fight. There was no way he could get across the room and take out my attackers before they sliced my throat. My entire body tensed.

Titus opened his mouth and... froze. His mouth hung open, silent and completely unmoving. As far as I could tell, he wasn't even breathing.

The temple radiated with raw power, burning with the combined light of a hundred suns. Pure white light surrounded me. Each of our attackers stalled in mid-movement, their weapons raised, and dark magic surrounding them.

Silas gave me the same bewildered look that must have been plastered on my face. He slowly lowered his sword. The Fate was still nowhere to be seen, but that much magic power could only have come from her.

"That's... super creepy," I said slowly.

"Can you get free?" he whispered.

It took me a second to realize I needed to move. With a wary glance at the frozen man holding the knife to my throat, I very carefully worked Ripper loose from his grip. I didn't want to move too quickly and somehow break the spell, but at the same time, I didn't know how long they would remain frozen. My heart pounded in my throat as I twisted against the arms wrapped tightly around my shoulders and waist, but there was no give in his grip.

The childlike Fate appeared in front of me, startling me so violently that I jerked in the man's grasp. If the knife had still been there, I would have slit my own throat.

"Death's Fate is set this hour," the Fate stated.

My stomach twisted, and suddenly, I stood on the far side of the room, behind the Fate's throne. Silas stood beside me with a matching look of surprise. Behind us, a new doorway of energy rippled.

Everyone unfroze at the same moment.

The Fate stood in the middle of the tangled mass of violence with Titus, his men, and the mutilated bodies of Rakken that had shifted back to human.

The surviving men lurched, momentarily confused as they realized we had disappeared from their grasps. Titus's head whipped toward us just as Silas dragged me backward toward the Fate's doorway. My stomach pulled in all directions as we entered the outer edges of its magic reach.

Titus bellowed and shoved his sword through the Fate's stomach.

She stared at me as blood gushed from her abdomen, and Earth fell away.

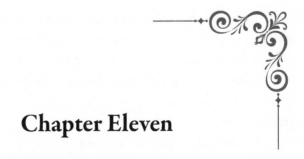

Chapter Eleven

My lungs burned, and my stomach sloshed violently. I bent over my knees and stared between my feet, trying to catch my breath. Traveling through the Fate's doorway felt like being squeezed through a ketchup bottle.

I gripped Ripper with white knuckles coated in blood. "Is she dead?"

Silas's brow crinkled. "The Fate?"

"Titus stabbed her," I said with more calm than I felt. I took a deep breath and willed my stomach to settle as I took in our surroundings. The round room was completely devoid of furnishings. The gray stone walls and floor reminded me of a stark prison cell but with better lighting. The room had no doors and no windows. The only things of interest in the room were the stone pillars we'd traveled through when we entered the Fate's doorway.

"No." He shrugged. "The Fates manifest in different temporal forms. It isn't permanent."

Relief washed over me. The Fate was creepy as hell, but she had tried to help us. Not to mention, I just didn't need any more deaths on my hands. "What did she say about 'Death's Fate'?"

Silas's face twisted into a grimace. "Fates and their blasted piece of shite prophecies."

"Prophecy?" I tried to straighten and managed to almost fall on my face. A new pain flashed up my calf.

"Are you hurt?" Silas crouched next to me, blood staining his shirt. Insistent fingers loosened my grip on Ripper. I let him take it, and the knife disappeared in a flare of his magic.

I rolled up my pant leg, inspecting a long, shallow cut on my calf. "It's just a scratch." It stung like crazy, but it wasn't an emergency. "Where are we?"

He took a deep breath that seemed to fill his entire body. The golden energy in his aura became a slightly brighter shade. "Aeterna. Portals from every realm come through this facility. New arrivals are detained here until approved for entry."

Every nerve in my body sparked with fear. I was in Aeterna, the Council's realm.

"You're hyperventilating," Silas said. "Calm yourself. The Brotherhood can't attack you here."

"I have to get out of here!" I spun toward the Fate's doorway just behind us. The pale glow of magic began to fade from within the two pillars. "No!" I lunged for it, but I was too late.

I stumbled through the structure to the other side of the room. The gate was closed. I scanned the structure, desperate for an escape path. The runes on the columns, which had radiated a soft white glow of magic when we came through, faded to nothing.

I searched the room, but there was no escape.

"Turn it back on," I demanded.

"I can't do that," Silas responded.

"Take me back," I commanded. "The Council—Shit! I can't be here." Terror welled up and wrapped its claws around my throat. I'd lived through Titus's attacks, the Rakken, and even hypothermia, but it was all for nothing. The Fate had told me the only way to get the power out of me was to kill me. I stood in a realm ruled by even more powerful people who would kill for the power stuck inside me, and I was never going to return to my old life. Father Mike had told me to do everything I could not to go to Aeterna, yet I'd come like a lamb to the slaughter. It was too damn much. The fear burned so strong, Marcel's memories started to surface again.

I spun around, searching for some way to get out of this impossible situation. "I have to—Where's my knife? I need Ripper!"

Silas grasped my shoulders and forced me to stop. "Maeve! Be calm."

"They're going to kill me!"

"You're safe. I swore to protect you, and I always keep my word."

"Then get me a goddamned way out of here!"

White magic flared around me, and I gasped at the sudden pressure of the magic escaping me. The memories were taking over. "Not again!"

Silas pulled me against his chest, and his mouth pressed down on mine. It was a desperate, aggressive kiss. Held too tight in his arms, my panic flared brighter for a split second. Then the pressure behind his lips softened, and his arms wrapped around my back. I relaxed into his hold, and we were really kissing.

A new kind of tension built between us. I leaned into him and hooked my arms around his shoulders. Heat blazed through my body. For one perfect moment, all the fear and uncertainty faded to the background.

"Uh, thanks," I mumbled as I pulled back. His distraction had worked. A small bubble of calm blossomed inside my panic, and the frantic magical energy came back under control. With Silas's help, maybe it was possible for me to make it out alive. The calm grew into hope as I scanned his confident face. I had no choice but to face the Council, but I wasn't alone.

His face went suddenly hard. "Fratch. I can't do this."

My brain was fuzzy. "What?"

"Sex is one thing." He waved his hand between us. "And I *will* do everything I can with the Council, but I can't give you more. I'm not... I can't give you anything more."

My heart flipped over. "I don't understand. I'm not asking you for anything. I—"

A door slid open in the wall to our left, and a crisply uniformed man entered and bowed toward Silas with his fist over his heart. He spoke, but the words were completely foreign to me.

Silas responded.

"What are you saying?" I whispered.

Silas held up his hand, and the man stopped talking. "You can't understand him?"

I shook my head, totally confused.

Silas said something, and the man responded. Silas's lips pursed. "That is... interesting."

"What's going on?"

Silas's power flared, and the man flinched almost imperceptibly, his eyes on Silas's flare.

"Aeternals get a translation sigil at birth. Without it, you won't be able to understand anyone here, nor will they understand your native tongue."

I held out my arm. "Give me the sigil then."

One of his eyebrows rose. "I've been told it's rude to brand someone like an animal."

I resisted the urge to roll my eyes. "You have my permission this time."

His warm hand cupped the side of my neck, and I tensed. The cool rush of his magic flowed through me followed by the quick sting of the spell. It wasn't nearly as bad as receiving the Aegis sigil that bonded us together. This seemed lighter, less powerful than the mark he'd given me back in Boston.

"Say something, Centurion," Silas said.

"My lord?" the man responded, looking between us in utter confusion.

Silas raised an eyebrow, and I nodded.

"Good. Continue, Centurion."

The man's eyes shifted between Silas's bloody shirt and my grime-covered clothes before he spoke again. He swallowed. "The Council requests that you and your guest present yourselves immediately, my lord."

My heart clenched. The Council already knew about me.

"My guest is injured. I'm taking her to House Valeron."

The man thumped his fist to his chest and bowed out of the doorway. Silas strode past him with me in tow and led us to an outer atrium made of the same thick, drab stone. The room was circular, with six identical doors spaced evenly along the walls. In the exact center of the room stood a large stone platform. As we approached, it lit with clear energy. I paused in front of it, unsure.

"It's called a port," Silas explained. "A short-distance portal to take us up to the surface."

The cut on my leg started to throb, and I couldn't slow the furious beating of my heart. This was my last chance to make a run for it. I glanced behind me toward the portal room. The Fate's doorway was back there, but it was closed. I didn't know how to make it work again.

"It's completely safe," he added, misinterpreting my hesitation. "Like a Mundane elevator."

I took a deep breath. I was terrified by the Council and more confused than ever about Silas. I didn't know what I wanted from him. I wasn't looking for *more* from anyone. And deciphering his feelings for me made my head spin. I couldn't tell if he wanted to protect me, have sex with me, or if he just wished I would disappear out of his life altogether. But despite all that, I still believed in his oath to protect me. I could feel the sincerity of that promise embedded in the sigil on my skin.

I'd run out of time, and I had to face the consequences of my deal. The Fate had failed, and now the Council was the only thing keeping me out of Titus's hands, unless they decided to kill me themselves.

I stepped up onto the port.

We emerged on another platform, and I managed to reorient myself more quickly. The shorter-distance port had less of a kick than the Fate's portal that had sent us between realms.

The stone courtyard was a wide, circular space with a confusing meld of classic architecture and technology. Red-stone columns reached into the sky, connecting into arches at their peaks. Between columns, the open-air archways allowed for multiple entry points into the rounded courtyard.

A cloudless blue sky stretched in the distance, giving me the impression we were high in the air. Floating. Dozens of people milled about the courtyard, and each one glowed with magic. I stared in open fascination at the variety of clothing and features. A few people were dressed like us in jeans, and some others wore jewel-toned saris. One woman wore a long black hijab. With wide eyes, I took in the whole confusing scene. A man close to me was a good foot shorter than an average-sized person and had mottled green skin. An equally short woman walked next to him, and I noticed with alarm that her eyes were bright orange. They both glowed with sky-blue magic, but they were the ones staring openly at us. I couldn't blame them. We were covered in blood, Silas's shirt was torn to shreds, and I limped alongside him, reeking of Rakken innards.

"For fratch sake, they sent an *escort,*" Silas said with a growl.

I followed his gaze to the source of his ire. A group of five soldiers in leather armor marched toward us, sending people scooting out of their path. They glowed with bright-red energy. I tensed, recognizing the same color of magic that Titus had, but even from a distance, I could tell it was different in these men. Their power didn't fade to black at the edges. Pure red, the color of fresh blood, ringed each of the soldiers approaching us.

The leader of the group stopped before us and executed a formal salute. His head was shaved on each side, sporting a small knot of dark hair on top. "My lord, the Council welcomes you and bids you to attend them at the Centre."

"What is your name, Legatis?"

"First Legatis Landas, my lord"—he dipped his head slightly—"of House Crispin."

"First Legatis Landas, I'm honored at this thoughtful reception from the Council." Silas's tone scorched the words.

The Legatis's Adam's apple bobbed. "We've been ordered to assist you," he said.

"I wasn't aware I needed *assistance*."

The Guardians shifted on their feet, looking anywhere but at us.

"Where is Commander Corin?" Silas demanded.

Landas bowed his head again. "The Commander has other matters at hand, my lord."

Silas considered him silently for a moment, and Legatis Landas shifted on his heels.

"Very well," Silas said slowly, "take us to the Lower City."

Landas's brow scrunched in confusion. "My lord?"

"My guest will need to use the ports."

"Of course, my lord." Legatis Landas gave me a curious once-over, and I glanced down at my own blood-soaked clothing. At least Silas wasn't any cleaner. I would have hated to be the only one covered in gore for a meeting with the most powerful magic Council in the whole world.

Silas offered me his arm, but the gesture didn't feel gentlemanly as much as possessive. Silas's demeanor had shifted to formal, clearly placing me under his protection. The gesture made me nervous in more ways than one. Hesitantly, I rested my hand in the crook of his elbow, and his jaw flexed. We started walking, and the soldiers fell into step around us. I was hyperaware of Silas at my side, his hip at my waist, and my hand touching his arm.

He had insisted there couldn't be anything "more" between us. A small defensive part of me wanted to tell him that I wasn't trying to get anything from him, *thank you very much*. But the other part ached for so much more than a few interrupted kisses. The tension between the warring desires made his nearness even more overwhelming. But he'd made it clear he didn't want anything more from me, despite what seemed like mutual interest, and I had to respect that. I tried not to touch him more than absolutely necessary, shuffling quickly to keep up with his long, confident strides.

We walked across the courtyard to a group of sleek silver vehicles hovering two feet off the ground. They were smaller than cars and tapered at both ends. Each one glowed with faint, almost clear energy. One of the guards waved his hand over the center vehicle, and an opening appeared in the side. A rounded bench curved along the walls of the pod, creating padded seats that faced each other. Silas and I sat, and the door closed again, sealing us inside the softly lit gray interior. A softly glowing panel on one wall displayed scrolling information in a language I couldn't read. We glided forward, but without windows, I had no idea where we were headed.

"What's going on?" I asked.

Silas's mouth tightened into a flat line of anger. "I don't know yet. Being summoned to the Council is not good, though."

"Are we, like, under arrest?"

His brow furrowed. "I don't know."

We descended to a lower surface, and my stomach lurched. When we slowed to a stop, the opening reappeared, and we emerged in a city square nestled between squat stone buildings. With carved red-stone columns, the Grecian-inspired stone architecture seemed similar to the courtyard from above, but older and worn down. And it was crowded. All around us, people jostled each other as they rushed about their business. A buzz of conversation floated in the air. Our group received open stares and some whispers as people noticed us. This time, I heard Silas's name echo on their lips and started to suspect the talk wasn't just due to our bloody, torn clothing.

On the far end of the plaza, a raised platform held fifteen ringed stone ports. Eight of them glowed with colorless energy. The guards escorted us past a line of people waiting to use the ports. Regardless of gender, most were dressed in similar styles of tunics and leggings, sporting shaved heads with long hair on top or draped over one shoulder. Most people had identical markings on their skin. Four rows of parallel lines ran from behind each person's left ear and twisted into graceful geometric patterns down the side of the neck. The symbols weren't glowing with power, and I couldn't tell if they were fashion statements or magic like the sigils on Silas's skin. I was too afraid to ask Silas with the Guardians so close in case I was the only one who could see the symbols.

Silas gestured with his chin toward the dark circles embedded in the platform. "Why are some of the ports down?"

"The Council has rationed all nonessential use of magic during the energy shortage," Landas said.

Silas's eyes narrowed. "Wait here," he ordered the guards. Without further explanation, he pulled us off course and guided me toward a row of uniform buildings on the side of the square. He moved quickly, forcing me to take two steps for every one of his.

We entered a single-room store full of all kinds of weapons. I took it all in with awe, inhaling the rich smell of leather and oiled metal. Velvet-draped display pedestals placed strategically throughout the space featured collections of short swords, daggers, and double-sided knives. They even had a selection of fist knives with T-style handles designed for close combat.

"What are you doing?" I demanded.

"We must be quick. The Guardians will soon remember they don't have to follow my orders." Silas strode to a tall counter at the back of the store. "Jarvin, where are you?"

A middle-aged man with a bare, broad chest appeared behind the desk. He glowed with blue energy, highlighting the same geometric symbol on one side of his neck. Shiny black hair fell past his shoulders as he bowed from the waist. "Lord Valeron! It's an honor to see you again."

The Guardians arrived and hovered anxiously outside.

Silas's voice lowered to barely a whisper. "Thank the gods you're here. Find my brother and tell him I have an important guest with me. We've been summoned to the Council."

Jarvin's lips thinned as he surveyed me and then the guards outside. "They *summoned* you, my lord?"

"Have him meet me at the Centre," Silas continued. "Inform Commander Corin as well."

Legatis Landas entered the store, and his eyes narrowed. Silas scowled at him. If Silas's instructions to Jarvin were going to stay secret, he needed a cover.

A thin, short knife on display caught my eye. "I like this one," I said, pointing to the nearest display case. Designed beautifully and ergonomically, the knife would be good for throwing.

Jarvin took my cue without pause. He moved out from around the counter. The marking on his neck lit with energy as he waved his palm in front of the case, and the wall of shimmering energy dissipated. He collected the knife and handed it to me with both hands, along with a small bow. "A beautiful knife for a beautiful lady."

The blade was expertly cast from black metal. I didn't have to pretend very hard to admire it even while my mind spun. Even though the Fate had said removing the magic would kill me, the Council wouldn't hesitate to try. Silas would do his best, but I needed a backup plan, and I needed it quick.

I handed the knife back to Jarvin. "The workmanship is amazing," I said sincerely.

He bowed again, and a pleased grin lit his face.

Landas stepped forward, making his presence felt. "My lord, we must continue."

Silas held out his elbow again, and I looped my arm through his. To Jarvin, he said, "We'll take it. Detail it as we discussed."

"Silas, I don't have the money for a knife like that!"

He didn't even glance at me. "Detail it as we discussed and send it to House Valeron."

Jarvin bowed again. "It is an honor to serve House Valeron, my lord. I will see to it personally, exactly as you requested."

The guards escorted us out of the store and back to the raised platform. As we walked past the line of people, I heard Silas's name whispered up and down the line, but he strode stoically ahead, ignoring the stares.

The Council was waiting.

Chapter Twelve

All the guards, along with Silas and me, skimmed to a ring of four ports located just outside the Council Centre. My stomach didn't revolt over the shorter trip, which meant I'd oriented myself faster than before. The valley below was surrounded by tall rusty-red mountains, penning in a mass of dense urban landscaping.

Silas had said the portal beneath the center courtyard held the only access point back to Earth, and I had to fight the panic down when I realized how far away it was. Escape was getting harder by the minute. The courtyard floated like a giant disc above a sprawling Lower City, casting its shadow across the entire valley. Delicate walkways stretched from the courtyard like a spiderweb, connecting it to buildings built into the mountain faces. An entire Upper City floated in the sky. On the ground, the Lower City nestled in its shadow.

Carved directly into the red mountain's stone face nearest us, one building loomed bigger than the rest—the Council Centre. Large buttresses supported open-air walkways that wrapped around the outside, connecting airy breezeways. Delicate, twisting spires topped golden domes, stretching far into the sky. Wispy clouds surrounded the entire building, giving it the appearance of a floating castle.

"This is the only access to the Council Centre," Silas said, pointing to a double-wide set of stairs leading up and into the mountain. "Direct skimming is blocked."

The cut on my calf burned as I panted up to the top with our group. After conquering way more stairs than anyone should have to endure, we encountered a long stone hallway stretching in front of us. Guardians lined the walls in black-as-night uniforms, staring at us as we marched deeper into the mountain. Double doors the size of castle gates dominated the end of the long hall. Two men stood outside. One was the size of a professional football player. He had a shaved head and wore the black uniform of the Guardians. I'm sure they were meant to be utilitarian, but the severe tailoring emphasized the massive bulk of the man.

The second, normal-sized man leaned casually against the wall until he saw us. He was dressed in a sleeveless tunic that fell to his thighs and split at the hip. The cut of the garment accentuated his lean, muscular arms. His long hair was shaved on one side and pulled into a tight bun on top of his head.

A mischievous sparkle lit his gray eyes as he bent to kiss my hand. "My lady, it's a pleasure to meet you."

He had to be Silas's brother. They had the same facial features, but where Silas had dark coloring and was serious to the point of brooding, this man was blond and sported an easy smile. He flashed it at me, showing off a set of perfect white teeth. I got the distinct impression that he would be fun in bed.

He smirked as if he'd heard my thoughts, and I blushed like a teenage girl.

Silas was tight-lipped as he introduced us. "This is my bond-brother, Lord Stephan, Prime of House Valeron."

Stephan's eyes flicked to Silas's bloody shirt. "Have you been having fun without me, brother?"

"You have enough fun for the both of us," Silas said with a disapproving frown that only an older brother could pull off.

Stephan released my hand and winked at me. "He never has any fun."

I decided I liked Silas's brother.

"Stephan is an Empath," Silas said.

Shock hit me. I backtracked through my emotions and blushed bright red.

Stephan grinned. "Don't worry, love. Your feelings are safe with me."

The other man addressed Silas, his voice a deep baritone. "Should I call a Healer for you, my lord?"

Silas grasped forearms with the man. "It will keep. Lady Maeve, this is Commander Corin."

Corin's dark, almost true black skin at first masked the fact that his face was covered in tattoos. The designs were complex and almost delicate but not lit with energy like the markings I had seen on Silas's body. I couldn't tell until Corin accessed his magic, but I suspected they were actual ink tattoos.

Corin's nostrils flared. "Your wound is bleeding."

I took an involuntary step back as he bared his teeth. They were human-looking enough, but his expression made me confident that an animal lurked just below Commander Corin's skin.

Stephan's hand landed lightly on my shoulder, and calm filled me. *So, the Empath can manipulate my feelings. Just perfect.* Silas had said his brother was half Fae, and contrasting with Silas's golden-yellow aura, the flare of Stephan's magic was a lovely seafoam green—a stunning mix of blue and yellow. I wondered if a full Fae would project a blue flare.

Silas growled at Corin. The sound was so animalistic, my attention snapped to him. "I don't have time for a challenge right now."

"Even the Humans won't fail to notice the blood on your clothing." Corin jerked his head at one of the Guardians waiting against the walls, and the man jogged forward.

His nostrils flared as he stopped in front of Corin and Silas. "Yes, Commander?"

"Give Lord Valeron your shirt and fetch a Healer."

The man didn't hesitate as he whipped his shirt off, bowed, and retreated out of the room. At the same time, Silas took his own shirt off, revealing three deep gashes curving from his back to his front. I sucked air between my teeth. That had to hurt.

Corin growled low under his breath, and I could feel it rumbling in my chest. I froze, afraid he would shift into a ravenous animal right in front of us.

A woman approached in a swirl of blue robes that matched her magic aura. Her no-nonsense expression focused on Silas's wound. "My lord, you asked for a Healer?"

The bloody shirt in his hand disintegrated in a flash of magic. He nodded toward me. "The lady has a wound on her right calf."

"Jesus, Silas, I'll be fine. Let her heal you first."

He scowled at me as he spoke to the Healer. "Heal her."

Stephan and the woman considered me with speculative expressions. The woman's attention seemed to be on my various possible injuries, but Stephan's expression was more curious. Despite his friendly demeanor, he had a keen perception behind his gray eyes. He seemed to be considering the implications of my presence in a way that made me nervous.

"Do I have your consent, my lady?" the Healer asked.

Nodding at the Healer, I internally cursed Silas's stubbornness. Sky-blue magic flowed around her, building into a lace-like pattern of intricate magic. She knelt in front of me and ran her hands from my knee down my leg. Her fingers paused, and the wound on my calf warmed under her touch.

When she finished, I flexed my leg, twisting my ankle in a circle. "Thank you," I said, sincerely amazed.

Her eyes widened a fraction, surprising me with what seemed like an edge of panic. "There is no debt," she said with a quick glance at Silas. "It is my pleasure to serve." She bowed to Silas. "My lord?"

With his consent, she placed her hands on the row of wounds just below his ribs. He grimaced as she glowed with energy, and another spell began to weave through the air. I watched it in fascination.

Stephan cleared his throat. "Lord Councilor Elias called an open session as soon as you returned. He sent transports to Lower Aeterna to bring citizens in."

"Why would he do that?" Silas asked, his face tight with a mixture of either pain or annoyance. "Is something happening in Lower Aeterna?"

"He always has at least three plans in motion," Stephan said. "I suspect you're about to walk into one of them."

Corin shrugged slightly. "He wants an audience. Whatever he's doing, he wants everyone to know about it."

The Healer finished, leaving no trace of the claw marks on Silas's skin. As Silas had said, not even a scar remained. I was impressed. It made me wonder about the other scars on his back. He must have chosen to keep them—perhaps they happened in battle. I also noticed several old scars on the inside of his forearm, running parallel to each other. They were spaced deliberately apart, perhaps from a blade, but they seemed almost decorative. He finished dressing, and my curiosity had to take a back seat.

The Healer bowed and left without a word.

"I can handle him," Silas asserted. "I've done it before."

"And what about your... ah, guest?" Stephan asked.

I was suddenly aware that lots of eyes were on me. The expressions on the faces around us made it clear everyone was speculating about who I was and what Silas was doing with me. He hadn't bothered to really explain anything about me or what the Council wanted me for, increasing the mystery.

"Bring her up to speed on the basics, brother," Silas said. He started to turn away, lowering his voice to speak with Corin.

I grabbed him by the arm before he could get away. "Basics?" I dropped my voice to a harsh whisper, which I hoped only Silas could hear. "We are so far beyond basics here! How am I supposed to convince the Council they don't want to kill me with the *basics*? We need a plan, Silas."

"I don't have time to teach you everything you'd need to know to negotiate with the Council. Stephan will go over basic etiquette. Your part involves not offending anyone. Let me do the talking... and maybe don't speak."

I didn't find his dig very funny. My panic escalated.

"You need to know about the Council members," Stephan said, interrupting my rapidly growing fear.

"Fine." I huffed, resigned to letting Silas do the talking while I crammed more supernatural details into my brain. I suspected there was a maximum capacity for the amount of crazy someone could absorb, and I was pretty confident I'd maxed out already.

"The leader of the Council is Lord Councilor Elias of House Marius. He is Human, and he'll make the final decisions." He frowned at Silas's back. "Whatever that might be about exactly—after input from the other Councilors. The other Human representative is Lord Alaric of House Certus."

My ears perked up. Silas had said earlier that Alaric controlled access to the Fates. He'd also implied that Alaric would be difficult to deal with.

"Treat them both as you would an Earthen dignitary," Stephan continued. "Speak when spoken to. Add Lord to everything you say. Try not to ask questions, and let Silas answer if possible."

"I'm happy not to talk to them at all. That's easy so far."

"The rest is harder. The Fae—Lady Treva and Lord Nuada of House d'Nali—will be difficult to appease. If you can avoid addressing them, that would be best. And do not thank them. Putting yourself in the debt of a Fae is tricky. You saw how the Healer reacted."

"Okay..." So that was why the woman had reacted so strangely, and it confirmed my theory about the Fae's magic being shades of blue. Humans had yellow flares, and Shifters had red. That included Titus and the Rakken—I suppressed a shiver—but their stolen red magic was tinged with oily black. I was starting to figure some things out.

"That leaves the Shifters. Lord Nero and Lady Octavia are fond of Silas, so they may not be as hostile to you. But they respect strength, so try not to appear weak. Or too aggressive either. You don't want to be a threat."

Great, that doesn't sound complicated at all. "Will they attack me?" I suddenly wished for Ripper back.

He flashed me an amused, but kind, smile. "Not likely. But try not to ask questions," he reminded me.

"Ready?" Silas asked behind my shoulder, making me jump.

The giant doors opened, and Silas moved toward them. "One more thing," Silas said, pausing to turn back. "Under no circumstances should you access your magic."

"Why can't I—"

"Just do as you're told for once," he commanded.

I glared at his back as we walked through the doors, with Stephan and Commander Corin following close behind. It wasn't as if I could control the crazy magic. It came over me at the worst times. The only thing of consequence I'd managed was absorbing Titus's magic—and that had been a life-or-death situation. I reminded myself that I was walking into another one of those and braced myself.

My first impression of the inner chamber was that it was small, but only because of the sheer number of people packed into the tiered seats. Multi-hued energy emanated from so many magic users, it was like staring into the sun and trying not to blink. The room fell eerily silent when we entered.

Silas strode confidently into the auditorium, watched by hundreds of people. I followed him past rows and rows of staring Aeternals and down into the belly of the chamber. We stopped in front of a rounded platform built three feet off the ground. The raised dais where they sat formed a gilded half-circle. The other half of the circle was carved into the wall behind the Councilors, with golden spikes forming a glowing sun. The overall effect placed the Councilors as the radiating power of the center of the universe.

The Councilors sat in pairs, wearing long white robes. The six men and six women each glowed with pure red, blue, or yellow energy, and the combined power of their magic was like a physical presence in the room. Their auras mingled together at the edge of the circle, forming white magic. *White, like mine.*

"Lord Silas of House Valeron, the Council greets you," the man in the center chair said loudly. He was a handsome man with chocolate-brown hair and intelligent blue eyes. Somewhere in his mid-thirties, like Silas, the color of his golden energy reflected his humanity.

"Lord Councilor Elias of House Marius, I greet you," Silas replied flatly. "What does the Council require?"

At his tone, a few of the Councilors shifted in their seats.

Elias's eyes locked on me. "We wish to discuss your delayed return. But I suspect it has something to do with this lovely guest you've brought before us. You may introduce her."

"This is Lady Maeve of the House O'Neill, an Earthen," Silas said.

Elias's sudden smile was way too friendly, like a shark's. "The Council greets you, Lady Maeve of House O'Neill."

I was too overwhelmed to think of the appropriate thing to say. Everything Stephan had explained got jumbled in my brain. I wished Silas and I had talked through a strategy. I had no idea what he was planning, and I was out of my depth.

Elias raised his hand, quieting the murmurs of the crowd. A man to his left leaned over and whispered in his ear. The man's yellow flare meant he was the other Human Councilor, Lord Alaric of House... something. He tossed back long blond hair and glared at us over a strong, hawkish brow.

"Since you are not presenting us a severed head, we must assume you *still* haven't found the traitors." Alaric's voice was dripping with dry disapproval. "And yet you returned with this Earthen?"

Silas scanned my face and frowned as though weighing his options before he addressed the Councilors again. "Lady Maeve is a descendent of the Lost Sect. To secure her trust, I bound her as my Aegis and vowed to take her to a Fate. I hoped she would lead me to the others."

Wait, what?

The room exploded into surprised chatter. The Guardians waiting around the perimeter of the dais drew their weapons and stepped in unison toward me.

Holy shit. What the hell is the Lost Sect?

"Did you find them?" a man seated to the left of Alaric demanded. Shaved hair on both sides of his head accentuated pointed ears and a slender, sloped nose. His blue aura indicated that he had to be the Fae representative, Lord Nuada d'Nali.

"Where are the defectors hiding?" the Shifter woman, Lady Octavia, asked on the heels of the previous question.

I stared back while she sized me up with a wrinkled nose and an angry scowl.

"What are you doing?" I hissed at Silas. He'd just linked me to a group of *defectors!* He was trying to get me killed.

Elias's golden magic flared, and a dome of energy flowed down around us, surrounding the Council and the two of us in a silent bubble. The noise from the crowd disappeared. Elias leaned forward in his seat, his gaze intent. "Where did you find her?"

"In Boston. She has no idea of her true heritage," Silas continued. "She's been orphaned—abandoned by her people."

I stared at Silas in utter shock. I had no idea what he was talking about, but he seemed to be doing a damn good job of feeding me to the sharks.

"Look," I interrupted, "I have no idea what this Lost Sect is, but I can promise you I'm not one of them."

Silas finally glanced at me, and he didn't look happy that I'd spoken up for myself.

"The magic isn't even mine!"

No one seemed convinced. Elias scowled in confusion. "What does she mean?" he asked Silas.

Silas waved his hand, dismissing my argument. "She can see the patterns of magic within a conjuring." Silas paused, gathering everyone's attention. "And her flare is white."

Every single one of the Councilors sat forward in their seats, their eyes locked on the space around me as though waiting for my aura to manifest right then.

Elias rubbed his fingers across his lower lip. "Well, that is interesting indeed."

I held up my hands. Silas had taken the little bits he'd learned about me and twisted them. The Council didn't know the whole picture, and his story about me being part of some group of defectors would get me killed. "No, no! You don't understand. I have someone else's magic stuck inside me. His name was Marcel, and the Brotherhood murdered him for his powers. There was a... a spell that got all messed up." *Shit, what is the name of that spell?* "A Transference! Maybe Marcel was part of this group, but I'm not! I don't want anything to do with this mess."

The Councilors stared at me with greedy eyes.

"What Transference?" Alaric demanded.

Lord Councilor Elias frowned, and I got the impression the other man had spoken out of turn. Alaric leaned over and whispered in Elias's ear again.

"The Council recognizes the Lord Magister's right to inquiry," Elias said.

Alaric's head tilted haughtily. "What do you mean, the Transference got 'messed up'?"

The whole Council stared me down, intent on the blood in the water. Silas's face was tight, and he shook his head slightly. I swallowed thickly. Silas was clearly trying to get me killed, or he was a complete idiot who might get me accidentally killed. Either way, it was time for Plan B. I had to convince the Council I wasn't one of the defectors. I couldn't let them believe I was a member of this Lost Sect.

"The Brotherhood tried a Transference to steal Marcel's powers." I willed them to believe me. "But somehow, he turned it around. Marcel stole power from the Brotherhood and transferred it all to me."

Alaric's eyes widened. "How is that possible? I've never heard of such a thing."

"I don't know!" My heart beat so fast in my chest, I could barely breathe. Adrenaline pumped through my veins until my vision seemed to vibrate with each frantic beat of my heart. I was starting to lose my grip on the tightly coiled energy inside of me.

"How much power do you have?" Alaric asked.

"How much power do you have?" Titus muses.

I don't give him the satisfaction of a response. His men have tied me to a chair. The talisman they've placed around my neck is blocking my magic, and all of my focus is wrapped around it. They'll have to remove the pendant before they begin, and I might have a few seconds to react.

I'll show him how much power I have when I rip him apart.

Titus's magic flares. "You can't hide them, Marcel."

Then I see the knife in his hand. The men behind him start chanting louder, and the energy of their conjuring builds.

Titus approaches me.

With my heart pounding, I fight against the restraints. They dig into the skin around my bleeding wrists. I jerk like a hooked fish, and the chair screeches against the cement floor.

Titus grabs the crook of my elbow, pinning my bound arm against the chair, and draws the knife down the length of my forearm. My hoarse scream sounds weak even to my own ears, and black tunnels close around my vision. The pain is too much. I can't black out. I can't black out.

Titus retreats long enough to draw the blade across his own palm. I sway in my seat.

The medallion is lifted off my neck like a weight from my chest. I inhale, shocked at the sudden warmth of magic. It saturates me to my bones, cradling me like a cocoon.

I reach for it, but their dark magic hits me like a wall of ice, ripping away the warmth.

"You'll never find them!" I yelled.

Every member of the Council flinched at my harsh outcry. I clamped my mouth shut, appalled at my outburst. Those had been Marcel's last words in the vision, and I'd just screamed them at the Council.

"Your guest will speak to the Council with proper respect," said the Shifter I guessed to be Lord Nero. He bared his teeth at me, and the Guardians on the ground edged closer, ready for a fight.

I tensed, prepared to dodge an attack. *Shit! Get a hold of yourself, Maeve.* I didn't want to lose myself in another vision. I had to calm down.

Silas glared at me, his jaw tight and his nostrils flared. He didn't say anything, but the disapproving expression helped pull me back into my own head. I gritted my teeth, making an effort to rein in my anger. After losing control and killing those Shifters on the side of the highway, it would have been a disaster to give in to the rage boiling beneath my skin and use my magic in front of the Council.

"I've already questioned her," Silas said. "She has no memory of her heritage, no family, and no idea how to use the powers transferred to her by the Brotherhood's last victim."

Alaric spoke up again. "So you cannot lead us to the Lost Sect? You have no knowledge of them?"

"I'm not..."

Every single Councilor stared at me with intense concentration. They all wanted me to be someone I wasn't so they could use me. They wanted to steal my magic, and my life, for their politics.

Finally, I looked at Silas. His intense expression urged me to go along with his claims. But he'd played me to earn my trust, all so he could tell the Council my secrets. He was one of them, just like Father Mike had warned me. I squared my shoulders. "No. I can't. I'm not one of them."

Elias raised his hand, drawing everyone's attention. "Then she is of no use to us," he said with finality.

I exhaled in relief. They believed me.

"Proceed with a Transference and collect the misplaced powers within her for the Citizen Source."

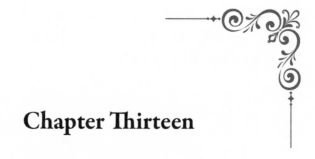

Chapter Thirteen

By the time I realized I had said all the wrong things, I had a Guardian on each side, grabbing me by the arms.

I twisted toward Silas. "Do something!" Maybe he'd been trying to protect me after all, but he'd dug me a hole instead. He wasn't supposed to let this happen.

Silas tensed and took a half step toward the dais. "If she is a *descendent* of the Lost Sect, her abilities are worth more than any raw power you could transfer out of her. With training, she could learn to absorb magic at greater levels than any Harvester in Aeterna. I've already seen her call magic from a great distance. She's a greater asset to the Council alive."

"The stolen magic is an asset that can be leveraged immediately, without risk," Lady Treva countered. The Fae Councilor's long blond hair fell in braids on either side of her neck. It should have made her appear childish, but she conveyed authority through the power of her stare.

"This woman came before the Council, seeking help," Silas insisted. "She is an *innocent*, deserving of the Council's protection."

Elias held up his hand. The Councilors quieted as he stroked his index finger across his lower lip and considered Silas and me for almost a full minute.

I bit the inside of my cheek to keep from speaking. I'd screwed everything up. Silas had been trying to establish the value of keeping me alive, and they seemed to be reconsidering the Transference.

I stared at the Lord Councilor and waited for him to decide my fate.

Finally, Elias said, "For the good of our citizens, we cannot afford to lose this opportunity. If she cannot lead us to the others, then we have but one option. We will take every precaution to spare her life, but the Transference will go forward."

I stared at him, numb with shock. The room around me began to spin slowly as I digested my death sentence. My breathing was too fast and shallow. The room was too crowded. So many faces stared at me, whispering and speculating behind the wall of magic separating us.

A dizzy array of energy and color all blurred together. I had to get out of there. I couldn't just stand there and let them take me. I wouldn't go down without a fight.

"If the Council won't see reason," Silas said, recovering faster than I could, "I invoke the right of House Valeron to grant her sanctuary as an Aegis under my protection, according to the law of Aeterna, set forth by my forebears."

My attention refocused on Silas, and air caught in my lungs.

"Your Aegis?" Alaric sputtered. His face turned an unhealthy shade of red.

Silas glared at him, a clear challenge in the set of his shoulders. "Yes. She bears the Valeron sigil."

Alaric opened and closed his mouth, not just once, but two times. Anger built into white splotches against the red of his cheeks. "You can't do that!"

Elias leaned forward in his chair and stared intently at Silas. "You cannot invoke privileges you relinquished when you refused to take your family's seat on the Council. You ceded your title as Prime of your House. Without your family's seat, you cannot keep your vow of protection."

Elias's words rang in my ears, and it slowly dawned on me that Silas couldn't protect me, no matter what he had vowed. He'd promised me safety, but he had no way to guarantee it. Oath or not, the Council would kill me.

Silas's jaw clenched. His face contorted before it settled back into a blank mask. When he spoke, his voice was level, flat. "You'd have me abandon the hunt for the Brotherhood to take the seat? I am close to finding them. We know where Titus—"

"You've wasted too much time chasing the Brotherhood across Earth without any results," Elias said more firmly. "The search within Earth can continue without you. You are required here."

"You can't force me into this," Silas said through clenched teeth.

"As you wish." Elias waved his hand in my direction, and the guards on either side started dragging me backward.

I could feel the magic prickling on the surface of my skin. I was about to lose control. "Silas!"

"If I take the Council seat, will you honor the bond and the sanctuary claim?"

"That would be your privilege as a member of this Council," Elias said with an eagerness that made me think he anticipated Silas's response.

"My bond-brother has been declared Prime of House Valeron," Silas said. "I would not strip him of that *honor*." The way he stressed the last word made it clear what he really believed. "He will take the seat as the representative of our House."

"No!" Alaric exclaimed. "You can't have it both ways. Lord Stephan is not eligible to take the Council seat."

"Agreed," Elias said. "Your bond-brother is not a Guardian and cannot take their representative's seat, as you well know, Lord Silas. And since only a House Prime can take a Council seat, you must reclaim your Guardian position *and* House status to take the seat yourself."

Silas's jaw flexed, and his hands curled at his sides as he stared at Elias and Alaric. After a very long, tense moment, he spoke. "Very well."

Elias nodded at the guards at my side, who released me. The staggering relief that hit me almost dropped me onto the floor.

Silas's magic flared. His hands flexed at his sides, and suddenly, he was gripping his sword.

I grabbed his arm. "Have you lost your ever-loving mind?" He was going to get us both killed.

We locked gazes. He turned the sword around and held it out hilt first to Elias. "I accept your offer."

Elias smirked at me as if I were a misbehaving child. He accepted the sword and laid it flat across his lap. "Lady Maeve will be a guest of the Council until we can confirm her origins and her usefulness. In exchange, Lord Silas will take his family seat. Are we in agreement?"

The other Councilors agreed one by one. Alaric leaned back in his seat, his face still red and his narrowed eyes locked on Silas. He didn't say anything else because he was already outvoted.

Elias and Silas waited expectantly for my response. I had no idea what they intended to do to verify my origins, but for the moment, Silas's deal meant that I would live another day. And that meant I had more time to get myself out of this mess. My heart beat in my throat, but I nodded. "I have nothing to hide."

The dome of energy unraveled and shivered to the ground. The noise of the crowd buzzed in my ears until Elias held up his hand, quieting them. His voice carried across the room, confident and official. "The Council welcomes *Lord Commander* Silas, Prime of House Valeron, to its ranks."

Applause broke out, and Silas's name echoed from a hundred different voices around the room. Silas stood with his back to the crowd, so they didn't see the scowl that took over his already tight expression. The Councilors retreated to an opening at the back of the platform. A few gave long, curious glances my way before disappearing. Lady Octavia, the Shifter female, locked gazes with me in obvious challenge. I held her stare for a long second before I worried about challenging her and dropped my eyes.

The noise in the room grew louder as people lingered, speculating over what had just happened in excited tones. We'd put on quite a show. And I'd put myself in the Council's hands, which was exactly what Father Mike had told me not to do.

The Lord Councilor reemerged onto the main floor and stopped in front of us, his floor-length white robe swirling dramatically around his legs. "Appoint your Second this night, Lord Commander," Elias said. "No more avoiding your life here, or our agreement is void."

Silas folded his arms across his chest. "I understand."

"And a word of advice—Lord Certus is not your enemy. You've extracted your revenge; now I suggest you focus on keeping Aria happy. Fulfill your mating bond."

Silas turned away without responding. I stared at his back, trying to decipher what I'd just heard. *Mating bond?*

Elias took my hand between both of his. "I suspect we will be seeing one another very soon. I so look forward to spending time with you, my lady." The words were loaded with meaning.

I tried to control my shaking hands. He'd suggested killing me with no more thought than ordering himself a sandwich. I didn't want to be on his radar at all.

He left, and with the room nearly empty, I quickly found Silas speaking with Stephan next to the dais. I didn't know him well, but Silas's brother didn't seem upset at losing his title. I couldn't hear them, but from Stephan's expression, he seemed to be trying to calm Silas down.

The brothers clasped forearms before Stephan glanced over Silas's shoulder and said something. Silas turned with a frown.

"What the hell is the Lost Sect?" I demanded instantly. "And why didn't you tell me about them before?"

His mouth went tight. "You didn't need to know."

"Like hell I didn't! You just accused me of being one of them and almost got me killed."

One of Silas's eyebrows arched in that irritatingly superior way he had. He crooked his fingers at someone behind me. "You're overreacting," he stated.

"You knew since the moment you saw my flare, didn't you? You saw my white magic, and you did whatever it took to get your claws on it."

His jaw clenched, confirming my suspicion.

"You only swore to protect me because you thought I would lead you to this Lost Sect." I lowered my voice to a harsh whisper. "You tried to have sex with me so I'd trust you—all just so you could drop me in the Council's lap!"

"You're making no sense. I could have taken you to the Council at any point! I was trying to protect you, but as usual, you wouldn't listen." Silas's voice came out in a low growl. "The Council had to believe you were more valuable to them alive, and linking you to the Lost Sect was the best way to do that."

"Are you crazy? Setting me up as part of some group they've been hunting down is the stupidest plan I've ever heard. As soon as they figure out I can't control this magic, I'm dead! You were supposed to protect me from them."

His nostrils flared in anger. "I kept my word. I took you to the Fate, and I've gone out of my way to keep you alive. Time to live up to your end of our oath. The goodwill of the Council is your best protection now."

A man spoke behind me. "If you'll come with us, my lady?"

Legatis Landas stood behind me with two other Guardians. His smug expression made me want to smack him. A spike of panic overtook me as my situation sank in. Elias had called me a guest of the Council, but I was obviously a prisoner until they decided what they were going to do with me. They wanted me to use the magic abilities I'd inherited from Marcel, but I had no idea how to do that. If I couldn't convince the Council I was more valuable to them alive...

I turned back to ask Silas where they were taking me, but he and Stephan were nowhere to be seen inside the hall. Silas had left me without a word of explanation. Hurt and panic flared. I had no choice but to follow Landas to whatever prison cell awaited me.

The Guardians escorted me up a narrow staircase cleverly hidden behind the raised dais. Sandwiched between two guards, I followed Landas, twisting through several guarded hallways. We walked in silence until we reached a solid section of wall with a doorframe carved into the stone.

Landas laid his palm on the frame, and his aura flared a pale red. The stone wall melted away, and he stepped back to let me enter. "If you require anything, you can use the communication panel inside."

"What if I want to leave?"

"We will bring you anything you require, my lady." His eyes darkened, and I wondered what he shifted into. I bet there weren't a lot of bunny rabbits among the Shifters.

"I want to talk to Silas—Lord Silas. Lord Commander. Whatever." I would drag answers out of him if I had to.

He didn't move. "I will relay your request."

I looked past Landas and down the long, guarded hallway. Beyond that were two sets of ports to get down to the surface, none of which I could use. Even if I were able to make it all the way back to the portal to Earth, I wouldn't have been able to use it without help. There were no exits, no matter how badly I wanted to turn and run.

I made the only choice I had left and entered my prison with as much dignity as I could muster.

The door solidified behind me, and I was alone. I counted to ten and placed my palm on the solid wall to see if it would open. *Nothing.* I tried to clear my mind and access the power trapped inside of me, but I couldn't control it. The magic was present but faint, completely useless. I was trapped. Exhaling, I surveyed the inside of my prison. The plush sitting room held a velvety-blue overstuffed sofa and side chair. A simple wooden table sat on top of a thick rug covering the red stone floor. Without any windows, the chamber's only light source filtered from a grid-like spell embedded in the ceiling. The room was elegant but sturdy.

I walked into the adjacent room and noted a round stone table and four oversized dining chairs. On the opposite side, through an open doorway, was a large bedroom drowning in blue fabric. When I walked in, another lighting spell activated in the ceiling, startling me. I needed to get used to seeing magic blending in with technology.

A small bathroom completed the suite.

The place was better than a dank cell, but it was still a prison. I walked back to the middle room and pulled open the thick blue draperies to reveal a large picture window.

In the valley below, the City Centre glowed against the night sky. A jumble of streets and lights spanned the entire window. That deep inside the mountain, there was no way I was looking out over the city. Slowly, I reached my finger toward the window. The image of the city bowed and rippled with the slight touch of my forefinger. Despair and homesickness hit me, and I blinked back tears.

Numbly, I walked through each room again and replayed everything that had happened since I'd arrived in Aeterna. I had believed Silas would help me navigate this mess, but now I wasn't sure. Technically, he'd fulfilled his duty to keep me alive, but it seemed as though he'd washed his hands of me. Every kindness he'd shown me was suspect. He'd only been trying to get information on this Lost Sect. Then again, he clearly hadn't wanted to take the seat on the Council, and he'd done it anyway. Just as he'd said, he had fulfilled his end of our bargain by taking me to the Fate rather than dragging me to Aeterna when we'd first met. It was the stupid Fate who had sent us into the hands of the Council, not Silas.

I was so confused. Then I remembered our kiss, and I flushed with embarrassment. No wonder he'd pushed me away. Elias had mentioned a mating bond to someone named Aria. I wasn't stupid. I could put two and two together. Silas was married to another woman. The stream of curse words in my head would have made Father Mike blush. Thank God nothing more had happened in that sleeping bag.

My current situation was not looking good. I had all this power, but so far, all I could do was relive Marcel's memories and steal other people's magic. *Sometimes.* Because I didn't even know how I'd done that. I briefly considered an attempt at stealing magic from one of my guards but decided against it. Even if I could figure out how to do it, there was no way I could get myself through the ports, across the city, and through the portal to Earth.

No, I was stuck in Aeterna for the moment. If the Council decided I was a threat, there was no way I could stop them from killing me. I had to figure out how to use the magic trapped inside me to convince the Council I was useful to them alive. If I could buy myself some time, maybe I could figure out a way home. I could even find Father Mike—maybe he was still in Aeterna. And while I did all of that, I needed to figure out how to fight back with Marcel's magic if I couldn't convince the Council.

Determined, I padded back to the sitting room. Sinking down onto the thick rug, I rolled Marcel's charm between my fingers as I focused on breathing. Folding my legs yoga-style, I closed my eyes and tried to concentrate on the power inside me. The magic was a ball of energy inside my gut, connecting me to... something bigger. I just needed to get the power on the outside, where I could do something with it—like scorch off Silas's irritating eyebrows.

Focus.

I took a deep breath and tried to clear my mind. I had accessed the power before; I just needed to do it again. The power was there—yet far away. It was like trying to grab something on the other side of a window. I could sense it, but I couldn't get to it. I needed to figure out a way to shatter the barrier between me and the magic.

I ground my teeth. *This is hopeless.*

A three-toned chime rang through the room. I popped to my feet as the door to the suite shimmered and disappeared. A Guardian wrapped in a bright-blue aura bowed slightly in front of me. She was tall, but lithe and graceful in a way that her brown, boy-cut hair and severely tailored uniform couldn't hide. When she straightened, I noticed delicately pointed ears and lavender eyes, confirming her Fae heritage. Unless I was misjudging, she was only a few years older than me.

"My name is Thessaly d'Vente. Lord Valeron asked me to watch over you."

A little burst of butterflies fluttered in my stomach. I recognized that name; she was Silas's friend. Maybe I wasn't being abandoned. Maybe Silas had just sent me an ally. "I'm Maeve." I stuck out my hand to the Fae woman. "Nice to meet you, Thessaly."

"If we're being informal, you may call me Tessa." She gripped my forearm in a strong hold that almost left a bruise, and smiled. She stepped farther inside, and five people in brown tunics entered from the hallway, their arms loaded with supplies. They dispersed around the apartment.

"What is all this?" I asked, waving my hand at the people fluffing pillows and placing trays of food and drinks on tables throughout the suite. One of them placed a vase full of fresh flowers on a side table. I glared at the blooms. *Seriously*?

"The Council wishes you to be comfortable during your stay." Her tone stayed perfectly neutral, but the expression on her face was just shy of an eye roll.

"I need to talk to Silas."

"He received your request, my lady. He sent me."

"Sonofabitch!" I should have known better. "Silas needs his ass kicked." I would have been happy to be the one to do it.

She bit her lip and stifled a laugh.

"I don't see why that's funny," I said, my hands on my hips.

"Shall I summon him? Perhaps you'd like to challenge him to a fight?"

I sighed. Confronting Silas right then would not have been a good idea, not when I had such confused emotions. I needed to calm down.

The people bustling around us each had a double set of those parallel markings glowing with energy on both sides of their necks. They cleaned and stocked the suite, glowing with pale, clear power that seemed strangely translucent. I'd seen the same clear power in the ports in the Lower City.

"What's wrong with their magic?" I blurted. Then I clamped my mouth shut. I had a very bad habit of letting my tongue move faster than my brain, and the day had been long and taxing.

Tessa grimaced. "These servants are Barrens, born without a natural connection to magic."

Once the room had been stocked to their satisfaction, the servants left silently. Only a man with shoulder-length brown hair remained behind, standing by Tessa's left shoulder, his eyes glued to the ground unobtrusively. Despite being huge, both in height and muscle mass, his entire demeanor screamed submissive. Plainly dressed in a brown tunic-style shirt and pants, his most obvious feature was a wide band of sigils wrapping around each wrist, dark against his pale skin.

"Don't all Aeternals have magic?" I asked Tessa.

Everything I had seen in Aeterna functioned with magic. A person couldn't even open a door without it. I certainly couldn't.

She hummed in agreement and picked up a glass from a silver tray. The amber liquid inside bubbled gently. "It's a problem. They drain our resources more than other citizens. Most Houses can't afford the energy it takes to sustain a Barren. They almost always choose termination at birth."

Shocked, I examined the man closer. He still hadn't met my eyes, and his gaze remained locked on our feet. This conversation about—people like him—suddenly seemed so... inappropriate. We were discussing him as if he weren't there, and I felt really uneasy about what my questions had started.

She waved her hand, dismissing my surprise. "In the last century, Barrens have been kept by the Council. The Barren receive special sigils to access the Citizen Source, and therefore, they serve to offset their drain on the public resources."

Everything finally clicked in my brain. The marks on their necks, the plain clothing, and submissive posture—all those people were slaves. My eyes flicked to the man standing behind Tessa. He didn't have the same parallel rows of marks on the sides of his neck, which I realized gave Aeternals access to their public energy pool—the Citizen Source. Each Barren had two sets of sigils, perhaps to compensate for having no magic of their own. I wondered if the man behind Tessa had been born a Barren, but I didn't dare ask such a potentially personal question.

Tessa noticed my stare. "This man is a Traiten. He is yours for the duration of your stay."

The man didn't react as Tessa spoke about him.

"A what?" I asked.

"Traiten. He has been assigned as your personal servant. You may use him how you see fit." Her face stayed completely neutral, reminding me of that blank mask Silas got whenever he was determined not to show what he was thinking. I noticed that Tessa hadn't looked at the Traiten even once. She'd been ignoring his presence in a way that seemed strangely intentional. "Whatever you need, he will provide. He'll fetch your food, send and receive messages, provide personal entertainment, whatever you need. He'll obey your direct command, provided it doesn't cause harm."

Personal entertainment? My mouth opened in shock.

"Would you prefer a female?"

I opened and closed my mouth without sound as I searched for an appropriate response. Using the Traiten was wrong on so many levels. A furious anger built inside of me, threatening to lash out at Tessa, my only potential ally.

"Traiten, tell the Lord Magister that Lady Maeve prefers a female companion this evening. You can receive another assignment."

The markings around his wrists flared with energy. "Yes, Legatis," he said in a low baritone before he bowed and moved toward the door.

"Wait!" I called.

He turned, and we made eye contact for the first time. He had the kind of boy-next-door looks that made me think he would be a great friend. His dark-brown eyes were full of intelligence, and in another life, they might have sparked with a good sense of humor.

I was so angry, shaky sounds came out of my throat. "This is slavery. How could you do this to someone?"

"A Traiten sentence is a punishment for a crime," Tessa defended, her delicate features set with harsh disapproval. "They must repay their debt to society."

My head jerked side to side. I refused to accept slavery as an acceptable punishment for any crime. "What's your name?" I asked the man.

"I am Traiten," he replied without meeting my gaze.

What am I getting myself into? Nausea roiled in my stomach. No one should be treated like that.

"I want him to stay," I said to Tessa.

"As you wish." Tessa's expression was neutral, but she seemed concerned. "Send him away when you're done with him. I'll be on guard outside this night." With that, she bowed her head and left.

Chapter Fourteen

I plopped down on the sofa and buried my hands in my face. The Traiten's eyes were on me from across the room. The Council had made me their prisoner, and now I'd tied someone else's fate to my own. I needed to stop reacting and come up with a plan.

"Could you not stare at me? I'm tired of being gawked at today," I murmured through my fingers.

The markings around the man's wrists flared, and he looked away. Tessa had said he was required to obey me, and I realized that the marks on his wrists were the magical insurance that he would do everything I said, literally.

"Shit, I'm sorry," I said. "You can look at me if you want to."

His eyes drifted back to me warily. I was really screwing this up.

"Why don't you sit down if you want to?" I was pleased when the Traiten sigils didn't flare again. I didn't want to be a puppet master.

He sat stiffly on the edge of the overstuffed chair.

"Could I just order you not to follow any of my commands? That would be a lot easier."

"If you wish," he said.

"Would that make it so you wouldn't have to do whatever I say?"

His mouth twisted down at the corners. "I would most likely be reassigned. My free will won't be returned until the Traiten sentence ends."

"How long is that exactly?"

"One hundred anni."

"How long is an anni?"

He mentally calculated before answering. "An *annis* is almost one of Earth's years."

"You're a slave for a hundred years? That's insane! Did you kill the Pope?"

He flinched. "Murder is an executable crime."

"Sorry, that's not what I meant. What did you..." I wanted to avoid a direct command and not participate in this barbaric form of absolute slavery, but I needed to know if he was dangerous. "Can I ask you what you did to get such a harsh sentence? You don't have to answer if you don't want to."

"I accepted a bribe." He grimaced as a second sigil glowed on his neck with a faint red aura. It was small but incredibly complex. Something about it seemed familiar.

"That seems harsh," I said more to myself than to him.

He wrung his hands before he dropped them into his lap. "The Council voted to strip my magic." He shuddered slightly. "Being a Traiten is better than death. There's an end to my sentence, even if I can never be a Guardian again."

"You're a Guardian?" I was surprised, although given the size of him, I probably shouldn't have been.

His jaw flexed. "I was."

He clearly didn't want to talk about it, but my curiosity was burning. The whole Traiten thing made no sense. Uncomfortably aware he was at my mercy, I decided to change the subject.

"What is that mark for?" I asked, pointing to the sigil I'd seen on his neck. Something about it kept tugging at my mind. It wasn't like any of Silas's magical tattoos.

His jaw tightened, etching the lines around his mouth deeper. "I don't know what you're referring to."

The mark glowed again.

I pointed. "It just did it again!"

He frowned, and I lowered my finger. A terrible idea occurred to me. Maybe he really couldn't see the sigil, and I was, once again, giving away my unique abilities. I really needed to call it quits for the day and get some sleep. My brain might melt at any second. But I was stuck with this man, and I needed to figure out what to do with him. I didn't want him to get in trouble.

"My lady, may I serve you in some way?"

I sighed and put my head in my hands again. "What's your name? I refuse to call you Traiten every time I want to talk to you."

The damn marks around his wrists flared again. "I was called by Atticus."

"Atticus. Okay, that's a start. I'm Maeve. I'd appreciate if you stopped calling me 'my lady' because I'm not. And I'll do my best not to order you around while we're stuck together." I held out my hand. "Deal?"

Slowly, he reached out and gripped my forearm with a solid hold that made the muscles in his forearm bulge.

We were making progress.

The door chimed, and Atticus jumped out of his chair as if it were on fire. He took one look at the man standing in the hall and bowed low at the waist.

From the hallway, Tessa announced, "Lord Magister Alaric of House Certus for the Lady Maeve of House O'Neill."

My adrenaline kicked into overdrive yet again. I wasn't expecting to have to deal with the Council again so soon. I wasn't ready to show them what I could—or more accurately, couldn't—do with the magic they so desperately wanted.

Alaric entered the room without being invited, sweeping into the suite with his white robe billowing dramatically behind him. Atticus moved out of his way and melted into the background. Tessa slipped inside with a pinched look between her brows as she stared at Alaric's back. The room suddenly seemed very crowded.

"My lady, may I join you?" Without waiting for an answer, Alaric swept the fabric from behind him, folded it over his arm, and lowered himself into the seat Atticus had just vacated.

I grimaced and didn't bother hiding it. I was too tired to deal with more political games. If he felt unwelcome, then he'd read my mood correctly.

"I came to see if you've settled comfortably. I hope the accommodations are satisfactory." He looked quickly at Atticus then smiled at me like a gracious host. So, he was the one who had assigned me a Traiten slave. And he thought I would be grateful to him for it.

I frowned. I wasn't buying the nice-guy act. He had pushed hard for the Transference, even knowing it might kill me. I folded my arms across my chest. "No matter how you dress it up, the door still locks on the outside."

His pleasant demeanor slipped a fraction. "You are a guest of the Council. I'd be happy to show you around the Council Centre myself if you would like."

"I think I've seen enough of the Council today." It was probably too much to hope that he'd picked up on the double meaning behind my words.

Tessa's eyes widened, but Alaric didn't even pause. "Perhaps you would like something to eat then," he offered.

"I'm not hungry."

"Traiten!" His loud command startled both Atticus and me. "Fetch the Lady some food from the central culina. By foot."

The sigils on Atticus's wrists flared, and I ground my teeth. Atticus bowed behind Alaric's back and left to fetch the food I didn't want.

"And you—Guardian. Surely you have someone to report to?"

"No, my lord," Tessa responded coolly. "I've been assigned to guard Lady Maeve."

Alaric gave her a long look. "Very well, you may wait outside."

"Lord Silas charged me with her safety. I—"

"The lady is in no danger from me." His tone implied a slight offense.

Tessa opened her mouth.

"Go tattle to Lord Silas if you must," Alaric said. "Until then, Lady Maeve and I must have words in private."

"I'll be just outside the door, my lady. Just raise your voice if you need anything." Tessa bowed slightly before she slipped back outside and the door sealed behind her.

"I'm afraid I may have been too harsh upon our first encounter, Lady Maeve." He leaned forward in his chair, earnestness painted on his expression. "In truth, I've come to make amends."

"What do you mean?"

"Truly, I did not know the Fate had divined that the Transference would kill you. It's an archaic spell that we have not practiced for many centuries. Upon further consideration, I realized that your only example of the implementation of the ritual has been... extreme. What the Brotherhood do is an abomination." He folded his hands in his lap. "They use the Transference to drain life completely from their victims, which is why we banned the spell in the first place. It's dangerous in the wrong hands. But it is possible to remove only a portion of someone's magic." He paused until I looked into his eyes. "I won't lie and say it would be pleasant, but I'm confident we could remove the excess power from you. I merely want to find the best solution to your present situation."

"The best solution for the Council, you mean."

"For everyone," he said with a sweep of his hand. "But we have agreed to forestall the Transference, thanks to the seating of our new Lord Commander." He smiled. I didn't know him very well, but his smile looked too tight around the edges. "I want to offer you an alternative."

"What alternative?"

"If you are truly a descendent of the Lost Sect, then you possess the ability to absorb energy. There are rumors they could also transfer that energy to others."

My mind immediately went to the power I accidentally absorbed from Titus. Everything I'd done was out of my control. I couldn't possibly make it happen again. On top of that, I'd never transferred the energy *to* someone else. I bit my lip. If I could learn to transfer out Marcel's magic, then the Council wouldn't have any reason to force the Transference.

But I had no idea if the abilities I'd inherited from Marcel worked that way. And even if I were a descendent of the Lost Sect—I was an orphan after all, so I had to consider the possibility—I knew nothing about their abilities and had no one to teach me how to use them. I needed more information, but I definitely couldn't trust Alaric with my questions.

He leaned forward, his eyes intense. "Transfer the power, and the Council will have no reason to keep you against your will."

"And if I'm not a descendent of the Lost Sect? If it isn't possible?"

"If it *were* possible, I'm certain we could come to an arrangement that would allow you to return to your previous life."

He was attempting to bribe me with my freedom. And I was so, so tempted to try. But even if I *could* transfer the power, they would never let me go. If their reaction to my potential heritage was any clue, they would never give up someone who could get them more power.

"And who are you lining up to accept the power?" I asked.

"I would take that risk, my lady," he said with a gracious bow of his head. "The power locked inside you is too valuable to lie idle. It must be put to the benefit of Aeterna."

That would also make him a very powerful magic user.

The door chimed, and Tessa entered, carrying a gold platter loaded with food.

Alaric frowned. "Where is the Traiten?"

Tessa smiled sharply. "I sent him to Lord Valeron."

Alaric's expression lost any pretense of pleasantness as Tessa set the tray on the table and moved to the back of the room. I shifted in my seat. Tessa really didn't trust Alaric.

Nothing on the platter seemed particularly edible. Brown cheese squares lay along one side, and there were colorful vegetables and tough-skinned fruits. I pretended to examine the assortment, thinking furiously.

"I'll think about your offer," I said to Alaric when I couldn't come up with anything better.

He was quiet, waiting for me to say more. For once, I kept my mouth shut.

"Then I bid you gods' eve, my lady."

Tessa nodded solemnly at me and slipped out the door with him.

When the door sealed behind them, I slumped onto the sofa. I had just enough time to think about dragging myself to the shower before the door pinged again and Atticus entered.

I sighed and resigned myself to never being alone again. "You hungry?" I asked Atticus.

His startled gaze drifted to the platter. "You want me to eat with you?"

"If you're hungry," I said with deliberate care, "help yourself."

He sat down on the edge of the chair Alaric had just vacated. After a moment, he must have decided I was sincere and picked up a strange-looking root. He chewed on it as he stared at me.

I rested my head on the back of the sofa and rubbed my eyes. My brain spun. I was exhausted and filthy. I just wanted a shower and a bed to sleep in for the next year.

"You are unlike anyone I have ever met... Maeve."

I grinned when he used my name. And considering whom I was being compared to, I considered that a compliment.

"You seem distressed," Atticus said. "Can I assist in some way?"

I paused before I turned him down out of habit. As a former Guardian and an Aeternal, he was my best source of information. He had to know more than I did. I sat up with renewed energy. "What do you know about the Lost Sect?"

His eyes went round. "Are the rumors true?"

"I don't know. What are the rumors?"

He swallowed the last of his root and eyed the platter again. I picked up something purplish and tapered like a carrot, hoping he would keep talking if I ate with him. I bit into it, expecting a crunch, but it was spongy and slightly bitter. *Gross.*

Encouraged, Atticus bit into something roughly shaped like a potato. He downed the juicy flesh inside in two bites. "The Lost Sect were the original Harvesters," he said, grabbing another potato fruit. "Today, anyone with a lick of harvesting talent is assigned to gather energy for the Citizen Source, mostly from the radiant energy of other realms, but they have only a fraction of the Lost Sect's natural abilities. They were powerful. Aeterna lost centuries of learning and training, and our most powerful Harvesters, when the entire Sect defected. Without them, we cannot access power from Earth any longer. Over time, we have depleted our reserves of magic, leaving us with an energy crisis."

Silas had been concerned about the ports that were shut down. That must have been part of the rationing.

"The rumors say the Lost Sect wanted the Council to stop taking power from Earth. They believed consistently drawing from the radiant energy of Mundanes stunted their natural development, but when the Council refused, they disappeared overnight, taking with them the ability to access the Earthen Source. No one has been able to track them down. Without their abilities, we're all tied to the post."

I liked that he was straightforward with what information he knew. He wasn't playing games like everyone else in this stupid realm. And there was a comforting calm around him that I really needed in my life right then. "What happened after that?"

He popped two squares of the brown cheese into his mouth. "It's been almost four decades, and no one has heard anything from them. They're gone. Some say the Council found them all and killed them. Others believe they're hiding within Earth. And now you'd be hard pressed to find any information on the original Harvesters. It's like they were erased from our history. Lost."

If the Council thought I was a link to find the Lost Sect, and these original Harvesters really were as powerful as Atticus said, then the Council would need a lot of convincing to believe I wasn't one of them. On one hand, I understood why Silas believed it, but I didn't have a single ounce of my own magic before the botched Transference spell. If I were a descendent of those people, it was logical that I would have at least some magic of my own. I was one hundred percent Mundane without any natural magic abilities, and I liked it that way.

But Marcel's powers were a different story. A lot of what Silas had theorized made sense. I *could* use the magic differently than anyone else in Aeterna—like seeing the patterns within the spells. I *had* absorbed power from other people, just like those defected

Harvesters. And the amount of magic locked inside me—evidenced by my white flare—was testament that Marcel might have been one of them.

I needed to learn how to control those abilities and use them to escape before the Council decided I was exactly what they needed to cure their energy crisis. Dead or alive, they were never going to let me go. "The Council must be desperate to stop the energy crisis," I mused aloud.

Atticus clucked his tongue. "They're equally desperate to find the Lost Sect and force them to return. They have an entire legion of Guardians secretly searching for them before we run out of magic in the Citizen Source."

"The Citizen Source... that's what the Barrens use, right?"

"Yes, and the Lower Houses who don't have enough familial power to draw upon. It's a shared power source from the Council, and most of Aeterna depends upon it for their daily use. Without the Citizen Source, our civilization could not function."

I sighed with frustration. "I have the opposite problem. All this magic inside of me, but I can't figure out how to even access it."

He shrugged. "I could show you how I access magic."

Now that was a loophole I hadn't considered. Atticus was a slave, but even a slave had to use magic to serve. And he was a former Guardian too. Ideas started forming in my head.

"That would be great. If you show me how you do it, I can practice."

A red aura surrounded him, and I flinched, immediately on edge. He was a Shifter, like the Rakken.

"Is all well?" he asked, his eyes rounded with concern.

I took a deep breath and tried to remember that I'd decided I trusted him a minute ago. And his magic wasn't tinged in the black of stolen energy. "What do you shift into?" I asked slowly.

"I belong to the wolf clan." His head tilted to the side in a way that suddenly seemed dog-like to me.

I swallowed and tried not to show my fear. But I trusted my gut. Corin was a Shifter, and Silas trusted him. Just like everyone else, Shifters made the decision to be good or bad people.

Atticus held his palm open, and a small sphere of power floated above it. "First, I'll show you how to pull the energy into the physical manifestation you desire."

I could see the threads of power feeding the orb he held. The energy crackled like tiny sparks of lightning, luring me in. I concentrated on it, and the little ball of energy flew to my palm.

Atticus jumped out of his seat, knocking the platter of food onto the ground with a crash. "You *are* from the Lost Sect!"

"Shhh! Don't freak out!"

The red magic sizzled on my hand. I closed my fist around it and let it sink into my skin. A warm tingle spread through my body, like a hot cup of coffee on a cold day. I suppressed a shiver. "Honestly, I don't know what I am. These powers aren't mine."

"Only rumors of the Lost Sect speak of such abilities."

I took a deep breath and risked asking for help. "Atticus, I don't know what you did to become a Traiten, but I think there's more to you than just your crimes. I'm a prisoner here too, and I need help to figure out how to use this magic trapped inside me. Maybe we can help each other."

He lowered himself back into the chair across from me. "How?"

Atticus had been a Guardian. Surely, he had learned some of the things Silas could do with his magic. "Maybe I'm a descendent of this Lost Sect, or maybe not. The Brotherhood and the Council both want the magic trapped inside of me, which means I'm dead either way. I need to know how to use it to defend myself."

"You want to learn offensive magic conjuring?" His lips pursed, but to my great relief, he didn't look scared. He seemed... eager.

"Can you teach me?"

He considered me for a long moment. I held my breath in anticipation. With Silas's oath to me officially fulfilled, Atticus was my only hope of learning how to use my magic to escape and ultimately defend myself from both the Council and the Brotherhood. I didn't have a Plan C.

A mischievous glint lit his gaze. "If they catch us..."

I nodded. Some things were better left unsaid. If we were caught, the Council would kill us both.

Chapter Fifteen

The next morning, Atticus returned for my first secret lesson. After a full night's sleep, I'd managed to use the waterless disappointment they'd substituted for a shower, and I was finally clean from all the blood and filth. The combined sonic and magic pulses may have gotten me efficiently clean, but I missed the soothing steaminess of real water. Someone had left me undergarments, a soft brown tunic that fell to my knees, and a braided belt. I hadn't bothered to slip on the soft leather booties as I padded around barefoot on the thick rugs.

After my flurry of visitors the day before, it would be best to get an early start with Atticus. I purposefully didn't think about whether one of today's visitors would be Silas. Eventually, I would have to talk to him, but I had too many feelings I hadn't yet sorted through where he was concerned. To avoid all those visitors finding out what Atticus and I were doing, I suggested holding our crack-of-dawn lesson in the bedroom. Having a few rooms between us and the front door meant we would have time to hide any signs of our secret lesson before someone busted in. That was especially important if that someone was on the Council.

We sat facing each other cross-legged on the floor with a new tray of unusual food between us. The menu included a bowl of mushy stuff and more brown cheese.

Yawning, I pointed at the squares. "What's this?"

"A protein-based ferment," Atticus said and popped one into his mouth.

My stomach growled with hunger, but just thinking about eating it made me want to throw up. "So, what are we learning first?"

His mouth twisted in worry. "Guardians train for three anni before learning a single offensive spell."

I forced down a bite of unsweetened, chewy slop and planted my elbows on my knees. "I'm a quick learner." I had to be. Alaric wouldn't wait long before his offer became a demand.

Atticus's mischievous smile revealed his dimples.

"What do I need to know?"

"You must first harness the energy. Clear your mind and focus on the magic."

It was almost word for word what Silas had told me in the motel. The reminder of Silas brought back my intense confusion. He'd admitted that he'd used me to learn more about this Lost Sect, and we'd nearly had sex, even though he was married to this Aria person. But then he'd bargained so fiercely with the Council to save my life. But really, he shouldn't have promised to protect me in the first place if he couldn't keep his oath.

I blew out my breath and tried to clear my mind. I needed to put all those thoughts aside and focus. The most important thing was figuring out a way to save my own ass. I could sense the power all around me. It radiated from Atticus, the lighting spells embedded in the ceilings, and even the people farther away in the building. I could feel all of it; I just couldn't use it.

"You must first learn how to build the spell you want to conjure. We'll go over the base elements and conjure them layer upon layer until you've built to the entire spell. Once you have mastered that, you should be able to conjure it at will. We'll begin with the basic flare I showed you yester eve."

My leg started to fall asleep as I waited cross-legged for him to show me. I adjusted to a kneeling position and placed my palms flat on my knees. I was focused.

"You'll have to give me a command to access my magic and the sigil necessary to see the conjurings." His face stayed completely neutral. It must have bothered him that he couldn't even access his magic without permission, leaving him completely dependent on someone else's whims, not to mention the slavery part.

"Right. Do what you need with your magic thingy."

He gave me an amused grin before the Traiten marks on his wrists flared along with a second mark that matched the one Silas had used to check me for magic. A moment later, Atticus's aura flared red, and a small, glowing ball appeared in his palm.

"There are three layers to a basic conjuring. The energy orb has all three."

I could see multiple levels of patterns within the ball. But all layered together, it was difficult to see the individual patterns. The orb dimmed down to a single pattern of energy in his palm—a simple cross-hatched design.

"This is the base," he said.

"Got it. Show me the mid-layer."

"How did you know what it's called?"

I hadn't thought about it before I spoke. It had just come out. Marcel's memories must have been taking over. But I'd managed to keep my temper in check, and the memories were currently under control. My voice was a whisper when I spoke. "I don't know."

A pattern of interlocking circles appeared over the first layer, like a delicate chain surrounding the orb. It glowed brighter with the increased energy. "This is the mid-layer," Atticus explained. "And the third is the binding layer."

The pattern changed. It took me a second to understand that it was a three-dimensional weave of threads going through the other two layers. The third layer held the first two together. When it clicked in my brain, it felt as though I had known it forever. And I could add additional layers to grow the size and power of the spell.

"Got it," I said.

Atticus flinched in surprise. "Very well. Show me."

I reached for my magic, but it slipped away from me. I ground my teeth. I could do this if I could just grasp the power. Frustrated and hangry from the lack of decent food since our pit stop for burgers on the road several days ago, I reached into my pocket and pulled out Marcel's charm. I rubbed it between my fingers, searching for calm. Thankfully, Atticus didn't ask what it was. The metal warmed quickly between my fingers as I rubbed my thumb in tight circles over its etched surface.

"Take the orb from my hand," Atticus suggested.

The ball floated four feet away. I could feel the gently radiating power of it, warm and rich. I reached for it with my mind, determined to figure this out. The ball flew to me, and I held it between my hands. The power rolled between my fingers, tangible against my flesh before it sank into my palms and disappeared. I inhaled the rush of energy. Greater than a flash of adrenaline, the power of it energized my body. I wanted more.

Atticus's eyes were huge, but he stayed planted in his seat this time. Another orb flared in his palm. "I have an idea," he said. "Do it again, but don't absorb it. Hold it in your hand."

I pulled the power and resisted the urge to absorb it. Everything about it called to me. But I needed to learn control, or I was dead. I focused on Marcel and on the way he'd suffered. *He didn't die in vain.* I thought about Alaric trying to trick me into the Transference. *The Council will not steal my life.* I remembered Silas growling at me to control myself. *I would show them all.* I gritted my teeth and held the energy ball in my palm without absorbing it.

"Good. Can you do anything with it?" Atticus asked.

I pictured peeling back the layers of the orb. The ball split at the top and flowered open, each layer like a row of petals spreading across my palm.

"Five blighted hells," Atticus swore. "You can manipulate someone else's conjuring too?"

I was almost as surprised as he was. I focused on the orb in my hand and pictured a fourth layer sealing the others back up. A weave of tight, interlocking threads grew over the ball, expanding the size. I added another mid-layer and a third to bind it.

A six-layered orb glowed above my open hand, the size of a beach ball. The magic changed from red to white. If I did a seventh layer, it would need to be a secondary binding spell. *How do I know that?*

Maybe that was why I couldn't access any of the power inside of me. I had been going about it all wrong. Every time I'd been able to do something, I'd done it with someone else's power.

"What else can you show me?" I asked.

"I think you could do a shield at this rate. It might be just as—"

The door chimed, and I jumped, causing the power I held to sink into my palm. The influx of magic overwhelmed my senses. Like a sneeze, I couldn't control the shiver that trembled through my body. The dizzying combination of jumping too quickly to my feet and the rush of so much magic went straight to my head. My vision wavered, and I swayed on my feet. Tunnel vision set in, and I reached blindly toward the bed before I collapsed.

"Maeve?" Atticus caught me and lowered me to the bed, concerned touches fluttering across my forehead and pulse points.

"Well, that was a surprise," I noted.

The unexpected vertigo passed after a few deep breaths, and I pushed to sitting, still cradled in Atticus's arms.

Silas stood in the doorway, a white cloak draped from one shoulder. His gaze went from our awkward position to the rumpled bedding. His mouth clenched.

I pushed to my feet, tugging down the tunic, which had ridden up my thighs during my near-fainting spell. Silas's sudden arrival left me flustered. I was so angry with him but also strangely relieved to see him again. Honestly, I didn't know if I wanted to kiss him or hit him. Half of me was eager to see him, and the other half was annoyed at the way his presence made my heart beat faster. That made me one hundred percent confused.

Atticus jumped to his feet, and the blood drained from his face. His fist went over his heart as he bowed and stayed there. "Lord Commander."

"Don't salute me," Silas said with a snarl.

My mouth dropped open at his rudeness.

He stalked into the room, glaring at Atticus, his mouth twisted down. "Who assigned you here?"

Atticus straightened. "The Lord Magister, my lord."

"You're no longer assigned to Lady Maeve," he growled. "Leave."

The Traiten marks flared, and Atticus moved toward the door.

"Wait!" I exclaimed.

Atticus stopped and pivoted. His eyes bounced between Silas and me like a trapped animal.

Blood pounded through my veins, hot and fast. I couldn't lose the one person who could teach me how to use my magic. I pounced on Silas. "What is your problem? You're being a first-class asshole."

Surprise flashed across Silas's face before it settled back into anger. "He should have been sentenced to death for his betrayal. Do you even know what he did?"

"I don't care what he did! This Traiten sentence"—I waved in Atticus's direction—"is a disgusting abuse of power."

"Your Earthen governments imprison people for life! How is that different?"

"This is slavery!"

Silas scowled, his pulse pounding in his jaw. "Tell her what you did, Traiten," Silas said, his eyes still locked on me.

The bands on Atticus's wrists flared. "I am a traitor, who caused the deaths of innocents."

"Silas! That is so out of line." I didn't want Atticus to be forced to tell me his crimes. It was wrong to take away his free will.

"Tell her about Krittesh."

I flinched at the familiar name. Silas had told me about Krittesh—his first mission. There had been a lot of deaths, and they had been betrayed by a friend. Silas stared down Atticus, his jaw tight and his fists clenched at his sides. I had never seen him so furious.

Atticus lifted his head and locked his eyes on me. The unknown mark on his neck flared as he spoke. "The realm of Krittesh had endured many raids, losing entire villages in a single night. We swore to protect the remaining citizens, but I... accepted a bribe to leave the main gate unprotected." His voice wavered. "They invaded under cover of night, took everything of value, and killed everyone."

Silas's voice became a growl. "Tell her about the children, Traiten."

Atticus's eyes closed, but his mouth kept moving under Silas's command. "We found the bodies of the children." He swallowed and lowered his eyes back to his feet. "They were crucified and burned alive."

I clapped my hand over my mouth. A sick feeling spread through my chest.

Silas's face was rock hard. "The punishment is more than just."

"I accept responsibility," Atticus said.

My brain twisted in a confused jumble. This kind of total slavery was so wrong. But what he'd done... I stared at the two of them with open-mouthed shock. Silas had told me he'd had nightmares after Krittesh. I couldn't even wrap my brain around that kind of atrocity. I didn't want to.

That strange second sigil was still active on Atticus's neck. The complex pattern finally clicked in my brain; I had seen it before. I pointed at it and asked Silas, "Do you see that sigil?"

Silas scowled and narrowed his eyes.

"Look!" I insisted. "It's right there."

His aura flared brightly around him, and the mark that must let him see the patterns within spells glowed on his neck. "What sigil?"

"It shows up when he's talking about what he did. It's flat, and I didn't recognize it at first, but it's the same pattern you used in Earth. I think it's a compulsion spell."

Silas's head cocked to the side. "It's not possible to compel an Aeternal."

"Tell us again what you did," I commanded Atticus.

The Traiten bands lit and so did the mark on his neck. "I accepted a bribe to abandon my post." The whites of Atticus's eyes were completely visible.

"There! Did you see that?" I pointed. "It's just like the spell you used on the officer. Right?"

"Shite!" Silas swore. "It *is* a compulsion spell. How is that possible?"

"Does that mean someone is forcing him to lie about what happened?"

Atticus watched us both silently, nearly vibrating with tense energy.

"It shouldn't be possible to put a compulsion spell on an Aeternal. You can only do it to Mundanes who don't have magic." Silas stared at Atticus. "And I've never seen one permanently placed on someone. This is simply not possible."

"Clearly, it is totally possible," I said. "I think I can absorb the spell."

Both men stared at me in surprise.

"I think I can manipulate the energy, unravel it layer by layer." If I could control other people's powers, then I should be able to do this. I didn't know how, but I felt it in my bones. I swallowed down the panic that edged in with that realization—I could do this. The atrocity of the murders Atticus had described didn't match my gut instincts about the man standing in front of me. If someone had forced him to take the blame for crimes he didn't commit, I had to at least try.

Silas scowled. "We should confirm that it is a compulsion first. There are people who can—"

I put my hand on Silas's arm. "Someone did this to him on purpose. I'm guessing to cover up the truth about whatever really happened that night. He could be in danger if that person realizes we know about the compulsion. Whoever really caused those deaths needs to pay for their crimes."

Silas's mouth twisted. He stared silently for a long moment before his gaze returned to Atticus. "Take it slowly. And tell me what you're doing."

We all moved into the front sitting room, where I sat on the sofa. Atticus took the chair opposite me and sat on the very edge. His rigid stillness was a testament to how tense he was, but he still looked into my eyes eagerly. Silas stood a few feet back, watching us. I had no idea what I'd gotten myself into. There was a big chance I could hurt Atticus just like I'd hurt Titus when I pulled the magic from him. But despite all that, I was confident. I could do this.

I reached over and put my hand on Atticus's forearm. "Are you sure about this? It's your choice."

"I trust you, Maeve."

I smiled, truly touched by his faith in me.

Silas cleared his throat, his frown firmly in place. "What's your plan?"

"Atticus, can you tell us what you did again?"

"I am a traitor, who caused the deaths of innocents," he recited.

The incredibly complex sigil flared on his neck, and I examined it. Just like the orb, it had multiple layers to it. I tilted my head to the side, trying to decide where to start. "Keep talking. I need to tell the layers apart."

"I accepted a bribe to abandon my post..."

Silas moved closer. "The outermost layer is the element of control. It's represented with a diamond rune."

I placed the tips of my fingers on Atticus's neck and touched the sigil. I focused on drawing the energy away from the spell into individual threads.

The magic unraveled and snapped to me. "It's working!" Just like Titus's magic, the energy was off—wrong and oily feeling. The sigil shifted, revealing the layers underneath.

"This is bloody unusual," Silas said.

I snorted. *Understatement of the century.* "What's the next layer?"

"The ninth layer is the element of will. It's represented by a double chevron design."

"Can you draw it for me?"

He sat next to me on the sofa, and his warm thigh touched mine. I forced myself not to move away. He held his hand out for mine, and after a small hesitation, I gave it to him. He used the tip of his opposite forefinger to draw a shape on the center of my palm. As his finger traced along my flesh, I could see the design in my mind. I didn't know if it was magic or just the fact that I was hyper-aware of him.

Atticus continued talking. "I accept full responsibility for my crimes..."

I pulled on the threads of the ninth layer. They started to loosen and unravel. The energy absorbed into me and made my head fuzzy.

I pulled back.

"Is something wrong?" Silas asked.

Atticus's face lit with hope. I could push through a little nausea. I reached my fingers into my pocket to touch Marcel's charm, and I would have sworn I could feel a boost of power. The reassurance of its presence gave me the strength to keep going. My discomfort was nothing compared to the sacrifice Marcel had made.

Silas drew the next pattern on my palm. "Memory," he said.

I could see the circular pattern in the sigil. I placed my fingers back on Atticus's neck and called it to me.

With each layer, Atticus's aura seemed somehow better... cleaner. There wasn't a change in the color, but I could feel the subtle difference as I removed the dark magic conjuring.

"The binding layer is next. It's complex, as it holds the others together. There are three elements to a binding layer—"

"Base, mid-layer and seal," I whispered. *Just like the spell itself.* There was symmetry in magic that I instinctively understood.

Silas traced on my palm, and I could see the binding layer in my mind as a three-dimensional pattern. I searched for it within the sigil on Atticus's neck. It was complicated, weaving in and out of other layers, but once I found it, I tugged gently on the threads. The binding layer began to unravel.

I absorbed the magic, and my vision blurred. I closed my eyes. *I can do this.* "Next?" I whispered.

"There are six more layers," Silas said.

He drew the next one on my palm, and I absorbed it from Atticus. Each layer I took away made me feel worse. The energy of the sigil was dark and tainted. I remembered the warm sensation of Atticus's magic. Silas's magic was like a rushing river. This was like rotten milk; something was wrong with it. I was more and more confident that whatever had happened to Atticus had to do with the Brotherhood.

"Maeve? I'm not sure you're up for this," Silas said. "You should take a rest."

Atticus's Adam's apple bobbed, and his eyes were wide. I could tell it was taking a toll on him too.

I wiped sweat from my forehead. "Keep going. I don't know what will happen if we stop halfway."

"The last layer is the base." Silas drew the shape on my palm.

I opened my eyes and realized I was leaning against him. Atticus had repositioned himself on the sofa next to me. I didn't remember anyone moving.

I couldn't make myself sit upright. Without Silas's solid shoulder holding me up, I would have been slumped on the sofa. I took a deep breath and focused on the base layer, a two-strand weave of energy. I unraveled the threads of magic and took them away from Atticus.

"Done," I said, dropping my hand.

"Is it gone?" Atticus asked.

"Did you accept a bribe to abandon your post?" Silas asked him.

"No!" Atticus said immediately. He jumped up from the couch and whooped. Dimples popped out on each side of his giant, ecstatic grin. "Fratch, that feels good! I didn't accept a bribe, and I didn't betray my people!"

I smiled despite the sick feeling in my stomach.

"Who put the compulsion on you?" Silas asked.

He sat down just as suddenly, deflated. "My true memories of that night are fuzzy. I know I was attacked from behind. I believe it was from one of our own, or I would have sensed them slipping through our perimeter shield. When I awoke, the shield was down and the town was burning."

"Son of a shite-licking coward," Silas swore behind me. His chest rumbled against my back. "They left you just far enough outside the perimeter to make it appear as if you were escaping but close enough to be certain we found you."

"Yes," Atticus agreed. "The gold was planted on me. I was very confused when I woke up. And then I started confessing to things I hadn't done. It was a waking nightmare."

"You confessed almost eagerly," Silas agreed. "At the time, I couldn't understand your motivations at all—other than the gold. But I should have trusted your character well enough to know you wouldn't betray everything you stood for."

Atticus nodded, accepting his apology.

"The tainted magic belonged to the Brotherhood," I offered. "I'm sure of it." Just thinking about the disgusting feel of the tainted energy made my stomach swim. I pitched forward and vomited on the floor.

Chapter Sixteen

I wiped my mouth with the back of my hand as five floating discs the size of small plates swarmed the mess on the floor. Seconds later, they disappeared, leaving behind a spotless rug. The technological marvels saved me from an embarrassing cleanup effort, but the remnants of vomit still burned my nose and coated my throat. I felt terrible, and now I smelled like puke. *Awesome.*

"Is everything well, my lady?" Atticus asked.

"Don't make me compel you to call me Maeve," I threatened weakly. My voice was hoarse.

Atticus handed me a glass of water from the table, and I gulped it down. I didn't even have the energy to sit up from Silas's chest. The back of his hand brushed across the side of my neck, and I shivered.

"You've taken a fever," Silas said. "Atticus, can you call for a Healer?"

"Ah, you're being nice to my friend," I cooed.

"And now you're delirious," Silas said dryly, but his eyes tightened with worry.

Atticus moved toward the door.

"Wait!" I croaked. I pushed away from Silas despite my spinning head. "How will I explain what's wrong with me?" Another wave of nausea hit, and I placed my forehead into my palms and breathed through my nose.

"How can we help you?" Atticus asked.

I felt as though I'd been poisoned. I remembered the warm rush of Atticus's magic. Just thinking about it relieved a little of the sick feeling in my stomach.

"I think absorbing clean energy would help clear away the tainted magic from the compulsion spell."

Atticus's aura flared red. I was surprised to see that it was a brighter shade than before. With the compulsion in place, it had been a dark red, like the last minutes of a sunrise. Now it was stronger, more powerful. The spell had used some of his energy to power itself.

"I'll do it," Silas said. "As my Aegis, you already have access to my power. It should be easier."

If I didn't feel so awful, I would have been surprised by that bit of information.

Silas spoke over my head to Atticus. "Fetch a Healer in case one is needed."

Atticus moved toward the door again. "Yes, Lord Commander."

"Atticus," Silas called. "For the time being, don't change your behavior. We'll restore your standing, but I believe we'll have a better chance catching the traitor if they don't know your compulsion has been discovered. We have to be careful about who we bring in on this, but I promise you, we'll find the people responsible."

Atticus bowed again and left the suite.

The brilliant glow of Silas's magic lit the room. I debated over accepting his help. He had tricked me into trusting him because he believed I was part of the Lost Sect. He had tried to have sex with me when he was quite possibly married. Trusting him any longer would've been a mistake.

I shifted away from him.

"Maeve."

My stomach fluttered at the soft way he said my name.

His gray eyes were tight. "Let me help you."

The problem was, I needed his help even if I was mad at him. He extended his hand, palm up, and I placed my hand in his. His cool palm slid up my forearm until the sigil he'd branded me with rested over the matching one on his forearm. The symbols glowed, warm and soothing between our bare arms.

I gasped as his power flooded me. I remembered his magic feeling like a rush of cool water, but that comparison didn't capture the raw power that flowed through the shared Aegis bond. The essence of him flavored every part of his energy—strength, confidence, and pig-headed stubbornness. But there was also a softness tempering all that steel-hard resolve, something pure and loyal. The essence of Silas felt good.

His magic surrounded me and flooded my senses. I inhaled it and shivered as it cleared away the sickly wrongness of the Brotherhood's energy. Another tingling started, lower down.

Silas released his grip, and his hand slid to my upper arm, holding me close to him. He breathed heavily, his eyes dilated. I struggled to slow my own breathing, but my skin tingled with the aftereffects.

"How do you feel?" he asked, his voice like gravel.

I mentally shook myself. "Good. I'm good now." The tainted magic was completely gone. I felt strong, refreshed, and particularly interested in getting much closer to Silas. My eyes drifted to his lips. "That was…"

Silas nodded, his eyes on my mouth.

I bit my lip and tried to fight back the desire to kiss him. "Does that happen every time?" I whispered.

"I don't know," he said. We were dangerously close. "I've never shared power through a bonded sigil before."

"What about the bond-mating Elias mentioned?" The question came out accusatory before I had time to reconsider.

He released me and rubbed the back of his neck. "No. We don't share power. Not like that."

"You're lying again." My building desire cooled instantly as I realized I'd let him pull me in again.

He shifted in his seat before finally looking at me. "I'm not lying to you. Power sharing is only done during formal rituals. Yes, the bonded sigil we share is traditionally created during a mating ceremony, but..."

"That's the sigil you branded me with?" I stood up from the sofa. "A bonding sigil? I am *not* okay with some freaky mating ritual."

His expression went flat. "The Aegis is also a bond of protection. You haven't been subjected to a *freaky mating ritual*. I already have a bonded mate."

"Aria," I said.

It wasn't a question, but he nodded anyway. Her name had been burning holes in my brain. I had no reason to feel hurt over this information. He'd told me he didn't want a relationship with me, and I was perfectly happy being on my own, better actually. I wasn't okay with cheating. And I didn't need someone like Silas in my life—he was stubborn, complicated, and completely arrogant.

Words tumbled out before my brain could stop them. "Aria is the reason you're fine with sex with me but nothing *more*." My chest was painfully tight. "Do you love her?"

His eyes narrowed. "A mating bond is not like your Earthen marriages. It's an agreement between Houses, meant to produce an heir and further consolidate power. It doesn't matter who I love or who I have sex with as long as that requirement is fulfilled."

An arranged marriage was not a good excuse for trying to cheat on his wife—*with me*. I couldn't believe he was trying to justify his actions. "So you just get to have sex with anyone you want, then? Does she get the same sweet deal, or are we into double standards here?"

He was on his feet in a flash. "We barely speak to one another. Both you and she can have sex with whomever you want." His face grew dark and angular as he glared down at me. "But don't take a bloody Traiten into your bed. You clearly have your own double standards to examine."

My mouth dropped open. The accusation was so far off base, I didn't even know where to start. Mostly, I couldn't believe he had the audacity to try to tell me who I could and couldn't sleep with, not when he was married. "You're the one who tried to have sex with me!"

"You were just as interested!"

"You're married!"

"I told you, it's not—"

"Get out!"

He blinked, and his brow furrowed. "Come again?"

I pointed at the door. "You're a liar and a cheat. I don't want anything to do with you."

His face twitched, and I imagined that was about the same amount of reaction I would have gotten if I'd slapped him. My fingers itched to do just that. I took a deep breath and intentionally lowered my voice. I was dead serious. "Get. Out."

The door chimed, and we both looked up as the entrance dissolved away. Tessa rushed through the open frame. She slid to a stop and saluted with her fist over her heart. A man in a blue robe followed her in with Atticus close behind.

"The Traiten said you need a Healer." She stood between us warily. The tension in the air was hard to miss.

The Healer approached me. "Are you in need of assistance, my lady?"

My heart thundered angrily as I addressed the man. "It was a false alarm."

His brow scrunched in confusion.

"I'm fine," I said, allowing a growl of irritation into my voice.

With a glance at Silas, he said, "As you wish, my lady." He bowed and left quickly.

Smart man.

Silas's eyes burned with anger. "I'm pleased you're recovered, Lady Maeve. I bid you gods' day." He inclined his head at me then pivoted toward the door. "Traiten, come with me."

Atticus jumped and rushed to follow Silas out the door. Too late, I realized I had left Silas with the idea that I'd had sex with Atticus. Silas was furious with me, but I hoped he wouldn't take it out on Atticus. Silas deserved absolutely zero explanations from me, but I would have to straighten things out to keep my secret lessons going.

"Is all well?" Tessa asked when the room was empty and quiet once more.

I sighed. "Yeah. I'm fine."

"We heard yelling from outside."

I just wanted one drama-free minute in my life. "What did you hear exactly?"

"Just raised voices."

I chose to believe her. I couldn't take any more embarrassment. Having everyone know that Silas had tried to cheat on his wife with me was just about the last thing I needed to add to this mess. I moved to the dining room and eyed the food Atticus had brought that morning. My stomach rumbled. The squishy brown cheese was starting to look appetizing.

"Are you hungry?" I asked Tessa.

She picked up one of the purple vegetables and bit off a piece. "I didn't think anyone was brave enough to yell at him."

I picked up something green and lumpy that resembled a pickle. I bit into it and was surprised that it was sweet. "We have a habit of pissing each other off."

She chuckled. "You have the strangest expressions."

"Can I ask you a question?"

Tessa nodded hesitantly.

"You're a Guardian, right? But Silas isn't—or wasn't? I'm not sure I understand everything the Council said about him being a Prime and taking the Council seat or why he was a Guardian but he's not anymore."

She sighed and plopped onto the sofa with me, reaching for another square of protein. "That is a complex question."

"Ugh, you're not going to force me to trade questions like Silas, are you? Are all Aeternals so freaking difficult and secretive?"

Her face went blank with surprise, then she laughed. "No. Silas is a special case."

That brought on my own chuckle. I leaned my elbows on my knees. "Tell me about it. I spent three days with him, and we survived two attacks—well, three if you count the drunk bikers—and I barely know anything about him other than he doesn't trust anyone."

"There are few he can trust, true. But..." She picked up the second goblet from the tray and drank the amber liquid. "He trusts you."

"Me?" I barked out a laugh. "You have got that completely ass-backward."

"Did he not trade his freedom for your life?"

"I—No. He..." I had to stop and think about that. "He didn't want to join the Council. Honestly, I'm not sure I understand what happened."

"You are correct—Silas was a Commander." She picked up the glass of sparkling amber liquid and sipped from it. "He dedicated his life to the Guardians, and he fought hard to earn his rank. His family name did not help him; it hurt him. Our Lord Commander at that time disliked Silas's father. He made it twice as hard on

Silas, forcing him to prove he could make it on his own without his House's magic or influence. But Silas is a stubborn arse who never gives over."

I realized that she and Silas knew each other quite well, and her tone was fond. Silas had called her his friend, and I guessed she felt the same.

She continued. "So when Lord Alaric backed him into a corner, Silas resigned his commission and declared his bond-brother Prime of House Valeron in retaliation. It was a calculated move to strike back at Lord Alaric for..." She shrugged. "Well, he had his reasons. Like I said, he's stubborn, and he wanted his freedom. But he gave up that freedom in exchange for your life." She sighed and set the glass back on the coffee table. "The Council always gets what they want in the end."

Well, shit. That made me feel guilty. I'd been so mad at him for abandoning me, I hadn't thought about what he'd done to get the Council to back off their plan to drain my magic and kill me. A sudden shiver overtook me. If Silas hadn't intervened, I would be dead.

"Was the disagreement with Alaric about Lady Aria?"

Tessa jerked in surprise. "You're very perceptive."

"Aria's his daughter, isn't she?" It was an intuitive leap, but the blond hair from the woman in the vision and on Alaric made it an educated guess.

"Yes. And she and Silas are bond-mated."

"So that's why Alaric was upset about the Aegis bond Silas gave me. I don't understand why the bond with Aria made him resign his commission, though."

"It all fell apart with that gods-damned prophecy."

"What prophecy?"

Tessa didn't answer right away. I held my breath, hoping she wouldn't stop talking. I'd learned more about my mercurial protector in this one conversation than in the three days I'd spent traveling with him. Complicated feelings aside, since he was one of the few things currently standing between me and the Council, I really didn't feel bad about prying into his life. I reminded myself that it wasn't personal.

"There's no reason you shouldn't know, I suppose. Everyone in Aeterna does." She picked up the glass again but didn't drink. She just twisted it around in her hands. "Between Silas's family name, the way he took his first command, and the prophecy... well, suffice to say, he's infamous. Then the blasted prophecy surfaced shortly after our first assignment as Legati."

An anxious feeling started growing at the base of my spine. The Fate had quoted a piece of prophecy to us, and I had a bad feeling that whatever Tessa was about to tell me would be related to that. "What is the prophecy about?"

"No one really *knows* what a prophecy is about. There are entire Sects among our people who dedicate their time to deciphering a Fate's words. But his was somewhat obvious, although not highly specific." Her gaze shifted to a far-off look, and she quoted from memory.

"Fate forged by magic's light, the Lost Daughter becomes Eternal Might.

Marked twice, where once divided; the Chosen are bound as one, united.

Death's Fury will fight with force, together they reclaim the Earthen Source.

Death's Fate is set that hour, burning bright with a balance of power."

I shivered. Everything around us seemed to disappear for a moment, leaving only her voice and the prophecy. There was power behind her words. Magic. And I recognized some of those phrases.

The Fate spoke about "Death's Fate" right before she'd sent us to Aeterna.

A three-toned chime sounded, breaking the moment. I groaned. If I never heard that sound again, I would die happy. We walked to the front room and found Stephan standing on the other side. A friendly smile spread across his face, and a feeling of comfort washed over me.

Stephan was such an interesting counterpoint to Silas. They had a similar height and build, although Stephan's physique didn't reflect the hard, constant use obvious in Silas's more defined muscles. Stephan's chiseled jaw and high cheekbones—so like Silas's—were accented by blond hair and a dazzling smile. He was a damn fine-looking man, and so similar to Silas, yet completely opposite. It made my head spin.

His presence filled me with a sense of happiness and ease. Then I remembered he was an Empath who could project feelings onto me.

I scowled.

He laughed, and the comfort feeling let up. "Sorry. You're emanating some strong emotions. Just trying to help." He gave Tessa a small bow. "Second Legatis Tessa, a pleasure to see you again. Welcome home."

"Thank you, Lord Stephan," she said.

He held out a rolled leather case the size of a loaf of bread.

"What is this?" I took it and ran my fingers over the buttery-soft material. I unrolled it and found Ripper wrapped inside—cleaned, oiled, and in a new sheath. I ran my thumb over the perfect stitching along the seams. It was plain and sturdy and exactly right for Ripper. An over-designed sheath would have been ridiculous on a work-horse knife like the military-issued Ka-Bar. Nestled next to Ripper was the knife from the store Silas had dragged me into. The metal was now etched with the same elaborate symbol branded into my skin. His sigil.

I frowned at it.

"It's from my brother, with his gratitude for your help."

I barked out a harsh laugh. "Great timing. When did he ask you to deliver this?"

"I received it this morn. Why?"

"They are pissing off each other," Tessa said from behind me.

Stephan's head cocked to the side as he tried to decipher what she meant. I snorted softly and removed Ripper from the outer bundle. I would keep the new sheath because it was perfect for Ripper. I tossed the rest of it on the table. I didn't want presents from Silas.

Tessa leaned over the case and whistled in appreciation. "That is a beautiful knife."

The knife from the shop in Lower Aeterna was a work of amazing craftsmanship. I would have loved a knife like that under any other circumstances. On the streets, I could have pawned it for a month's worth of food. "Want it?"

She picked up the knife with wide eyes. "It has the sigil of House Valeron."

Stephan leaned over her shoulder, and she held it up for him.

"So it does." Stephan looked at me with an unusually serious expression, which reminded me instantly of Silas.

I let my confusion show on my face. "So?"

Tessa set the knife back down on the table. "I cannot accept it."

I ground my teeth and rolled the case back up. I held it out to Stephan. Obviously, there was extra meaning behind a gift like this. "Take it back to him, please."

"Can I change your mind?" He still had that thoughtful expression. I didn't like it at all.

I folded my arms across my chest. "Not gonna happen."

Stephan took the bundle from me, and the side of his mouth twisted into a grin. "It seems my bond-brother has finally met his match in stubbornness."

"Tell your bond-brother to leave me alone."

"You can tell him yourself." He smiled to take the sting out of his words.

"I'm not talking to him." I sounded like a stubborn six-year-old.

He shrugged. "As you wish. I came to request your company for the Exposition."

Tessa's mouth popped open.

"What's the Exposition?"

"It's the biggest event of the annis," she said.

"The Guardians like to show off their training and hard work—etcetera, etcetera—so we make a big festival out of it." Stephan's tone was roguish, and his eyes sparkled with humor. "It happens to be this evening, and I've found myself without a companion."

I suspected there were at least a dozen women who would break off their own arm to go with him.

"Will you accompany me?" he asked.

"Did Silas put you up to this?"

His lips twisted to the side. "I thought we weren't talking about him."

I laughed despite myself. Maybe it was the obvious differences between the brothers, or the subtle yet striking similarities, but I decided that I wouldn't mind spending time with Stephan Valeron. And it would be a good opportunity to see the city and perhaps find a way back to the Earthen portal facility once I figured out how to use my magic. "Fine. I'll go with you."

"Well, that's not the most enthusiastic response, but it's... What do Earthens say? It's a date."

Chapter Seventeen

With literally only hours of notice, Tessa brought in a full-length gown for me to wear to the Guardians' Exposition. The golden fabric had a full, draped skirt and two long bands of fabric, which she strategically wrapped around my breasts and shoulders. My back was completely bare, but the twisted strips of fabric tied around my waist and held the dress in place.

I wasn't against dressing up exactly, but I couldn't remember a time where I'd ever needed to be so... fancy. I felt like a Greek goddess. I pulled at the deep neckline and started to worry about agreeing to go to the Exposition with Stephan. It occurred to me that I might see Silas there, and the realization stopped me in my tracks until I very deliberately decided I didn't care. Silas was married, and I could go on dates with whomever I felt like. Plus, a trip outside the Council Centre was exactly what I needed to start coming up with an escape plan.

Tessa swatted at my hand. "You are perfection. Stop tugging."

"There's a lot of skin going on here. Why do you get to wear that?" I glared at her uniform. I would have been much more comfortable in what she was wearing. But at least they hadn't strapped me into high heels. A pair of gold leather sandals kept me on solid footing.

"I'm on duty." She wiggled her fingers at me. "You won't be out of place. Now hold still and let them finish your hair." The servants obediently swarmed me, pulling and twisting my long locks into something intricate with multiple braids.

"So... this Exposition is a big deal?" I asked Tessa.

"It's the end-of-level testing for combat weapons and determines the ranks for the Guardians."

The combat part sounded interesting. If Silas's swordsmanship was any indication of their training, this could actually be a lot of fun to watch. "Will there be a lot of people there?" I asked, eyeing the high slit in my skirt.

She laughed. "Yes. And you're going with Stephan Valeron. You better watch your back for claws."

Surprised, I jerked around and pulled my hair right out of the servants' hands. "What? Are you serious?"

She let out a chuckle. "I was speaking metaphorically. The Valeron brothers are like your Earthen celebrities. Stephan cuts his hair, and suddenly half of Upper Aeterna has the same style. Silas sneezes, and all the females faint." She motioned for me to turn back around and let the women finish my hair.

"Their family actually inspired a new naming convention—children bearing the same first letter as their House Prime. Silas and Stephan are named after their mother, Lady Sariah. Stephan thinks the mimicry is funny. He likes to see how far he can take it."

"I like that about him. He's so opposite of—" I course corrected around Silas's name. "He's not quite as intense as I would have expected."

"Yes. Silas finds it all very irritating."

Maybe Silas wouldn't be there after all if he didn't like public attention. A night away from Lord Asshole would be good for me. The whole event could be a nice escape from all my tangled feelings about him. I placed my fingertips on the hilt of my knife encased in its new sheath. After a moment's debate, I decided to leave it but picked up a thin gold chain one of the servants had brought to weave into my hair. I threaded it through the small hole at the top of Marcel's charm, clasped the chain around my neck, and let it fall just between my breasts.

The pressure of Marcel's memories, running from the Brotherhood, and the Council's politics were too much. One night away would definitely do me good.

An hour later, Stephan stood just outside the door. He wore a light-blue top that draped loosely over his broad chest. Wide pants matched the style of his shirt. His blond hair was loose around his shoulders. He looked good. Really good.

I bit my lip. The clingy dress with long slits up each thigh and a plunging neckline left little to the imagination. I wasn't usually self-conscious, but my brain had been so tied up around Silas, I hadn't considered what I was doing with his brother. I'd barely met the man, yet I had agreed to a date with him. Come to think of it, Stephan Valeron surely had his own motives for asking me to join him. I didn't know what he hoped to get out of our evening together—maybe it was just a date for him, as he'd said. The whole situation was so complex and confusing, and I only had pieces of the information I needed.

He bowed at the door and held out his hand. "My lady, you are radiant this evening."

I placed my hand in his and stepped out of the suite. Two Guardians stood on either side of my door, and Atticus waited across the hall, his eyes on the floor. When nobody tackled me back into the room, I relaxed and let Stephan lead me down the hall. Tessa, Atticus, and the Guardians fell into step behind us. We traveled outside and to the base of the mountain, where the air was fresh and fragrant. I inhaled the last rays of warmth from the setting sun. The evening sky was cloudless, bathed in shades of orange and red.

I had an unexpected pang of homesickness. Everything about this realm was similar to Earth, but still so foreign.

Two silver transport pods waited near the ports to the Lower City. Unlike the last time I was there—just yesterday—I realized there were very few people coming or going. Giant, flexible net-like screens stretched above us, affixed between buildings and poles when necessary, displaying information and pictures. The tele-nets showed a ranking board of competitions for the Exposition. The screens changed to an announcement about Silas's promotion to the Council. Our entourage squeezed into the first pod, and I ducked into the second to get away from Silas's face splashed across every screen. Stephan slid into the seat across from mine. The door materialized, and the transport moved forward smoothly.

"Lady Maeve?" Stephan grabbed my hand. "Is all well?"

I was completely unable to articulate the strange combination of feelings coursing through me. Stephan's gray eyes were so like Silas's, and the tightness in my chest thrummed again.

"I don't know what's going on between you and my brother, but you should know he's trying to help you. He's a good man."

The last thing I wanted at that moment was to hear what a *good* man Silas was. He was a *married* man—a married man who had kissed me, lied to me, and made me *feel* things for him. My emotions veered, and Stephan flinched.

"You must allow me to help—what's the Earthen expression? Mend fences. You're both distressed. Why are you angry with him?"

"I thought..." The hurt in my voice was too raw. I closed my mouth before I embarrassed myself. "It doesn't matter. I'm done with him."

Stephan's brows furrowed. "He's not trying to hurt you."

Like hell he isn't. "He's done nothing but manipulate and lie to me since I met him. Honestly, I don't know why I trusted him. I was stupid. I barely know him." Feelings for Silas were such a bad idea. "Dammit. It doesn't matter. He's married, end of story. I don't want to talk about this."

Stephan leaned back in his seat, and a knowing expression spread across his face. "It's a bonded mating. It's not like an Earthen marriage."

"Same difference." I folded my arms over my chest. If Stephan tried to give me the same excuses his brother had, I would lose my shit.

"His situation is complicated."

"That sounds like a Facebook status," I growled under my breath.

He wasn't deterred by the unfamiliar reference. "Are you familiar with the prophecy about my brother?"

I nodded, temporarily distracted from my anger by the prospect of learning more about the prophecy.

"It's about our House. The other half of that piece-of-shite prophecy is about Aria's House. She is the future Prime of House Certus—the firstborn and heir."

"Okay... What does that have to do with anything?"

"Lord Magister Alaric is responsible for interpreting prophecy. He is also Aria's father." He paused, letting that sink in. "The prophecy states '*The Lost Daughter becomes Eternal Might. The two are bound as one, united.*' That last part is a literal translation of our House's name: Valeron. And Aria was famously kidnapped as a young child by one of House Certus's rivals: the Lost Daughter. Alaric added that together and declared it the Fate's will that they become bond-mated. He forced them into it."

My mind twisted while I pieced together this messy puzzle. "Silas made it sound like this bonded thing was a mutual agreement."

"Most bonded matches are. In their case, it was not. However, once the Fate has spoken, there's not a lot the rest of us can do about it, especially when the weight of the Lord Magister is put behind it."

"Why would Alaric do that?"

"Because our family is older and more powerful than theirs. I know that sounds crass, but it's the truth." The angry expression twisting down his mouth and furrowing his brows seemed out of place on his face. "A quarter century ago, House Certus led a political rebellion, which they lost. The Council executed the whole lot of them, and only Alaric and his young daughter were absolved. Many suspected Alaric was involved, but there was never any proof. He's desperate to get back the standing his House used to have, and attaching themselves to our House would benefit him greatly."

Stephan resembled Silas more than ever when his expression slipped into a harsh scowl. "Silas had to accept the bonding, but he retaliated by ceding his birthright. He stepped down as Prime of our House and refused the Council seat he'd been groomed for, which naturally decreased Aria's standing as well. Alaric was—is—furious."

So many things were falling into place. Silas didn't want to be bonded to Alaric's daughter. He'd walked away from everything in protest. Then he'd brought me, branded with his sigil, in front of the Council, which had embarrassed Aria's father, a powerful Council Member. *Shit, what was Silas thinking?*

"In all honesty, Lady Aria has suffered the most from the situation. She's a social pariah in Upper Aeterna. She's a kind and gracious person, lovely in every way. She is also the sole heir to their entire familial power source and fortune. She would have been a desirable mate for literally anyone else. After the prophecy, she was bonded to someone who didn't want her, and they live separately." He blew out his breath and seemed to deflate in his seat. "Not that it's Silas's fault either. I understand why he's acted as he has. It's just a miserable situation."

With a pang of guilt, I realized I'd been too harsh on Silas. And I felt bad for this Aria person too. My feelings were even more confused than before.

"My brother has sacrificed much already," Stephan said. "I'd ask you to give him the opportunity to fix whatever he has done to offend you."

"I told him I never wanted to see him again," I admitted.

"I'm confident you can't get rid of him that easily."

A pang of loneliness hit me. I didn't know who I could trust and who was using me anymore. I believed that Stephan was trying to help, but he was also capable of manipulating my emotions. No one in this entire realm had my back.

Except Father Mike. He was the closest thing I had to a friend. Honestly, he was more like the family I never had. I wished he were around to give me advice. Silas had told him to return and report to the Council, but I just realized I'd never seen him in Aeterna. A sudden feeling of dread hit me—I didn't know if he'd made it to this realm. It was very possible the Brotherhood had found him first.

"I'm worried about a friend from Earth. He should be here, but I haven't seen him." An idea came to me, and a bit of hope blossomed inside the ball of anxiety. "Do you think you could find a Harvester named Michael Smithson? He was stationed in Boston."

Stephan nodded. "I'll make some inquiries."

The pods delivered us to a festival straight out of a gladiator tournament. Large open tents were spread across a vast field, with multicolored pennants strung between them. In the distance, a large arena towered over the field like a modernized version of a Greek coliseum. Magic surrounded the multi-level structure while transport pods zipped to and from the various open archways. The crowd pushed steadily in that direction, leading Atticus, Tessa, and the Guardians surrounding us toward the arena.

Magic was everywhere, filling the air with color. Auras in every combination of yellow, red, and blue flared around us. Silas had been right; a pure shade of magic was rare. Under temporary tents, vendors hawked food. Tele-nets hung between the stalls, displaying complicated scoring results and live feeds from the matches. The atmosphere was festive as we moved through the crowd, and I let myself enjoy the mood. I really needed a night off from worrying about people trying to kill me and plots for power grabs.

People kept recognizing Stephan, and he waved and greeted them cheerily, occasionally pausing to point out interesting wares from vendors' stalls, until we reached an elaborately carved port. A Guardian stood near it, his eyes locked on a tele-net floating above us. He jumped to attention when he saw us.

"My lady?" Stephan hooked my arm through his and led us onto the platform.

My stomach twisted before solid ground rematerialized under my feet. We landed in an enormous tent, and our entourage arrived a moment later. Tessa moved to the side of the pavilion with Atticus. At least a dozen other Guardians hovered along the sidelines with three times as many servants.

The enormous space included a large central area with dozens of private screened alcoves around the perimeter. The entire pavilion contained perhaps a hundred Aeternals socializing in the tent. The hum of conversation floated above the sounds of live music, peppered with bouts of laughter. People were in varying states of relaxation. Men were either bare-chested or dressed in tunics like Stephan. Equal proportions of women were draped in gowns like mine or far less, baring almost everything. There was so much flesh and so little fuss that after the initial shock, it was almost easy to dismiss it as the people ate, laughed, and lounged across the entire tent.

I recognized the Councilors scattered through the crowd. Nerves tensed in my stomach. Tessa told me this was the biggest social event of the year, and that meant I would probably have to deal with the Council. It was stupid of me to think I might get a night off. But I gathered up my mental energy and decided this could be a good opportunity. The conversation with Stephan had revealed how little I actually understood about the Council's motivations. I couldn't afford to make any more political mistakes. I needed allies on the Council who could help me convince the others that I was worth keeping around—until I found a way to get back to Earth.

A servant approached us, holding a silver platter with tall, thin glasses. Stephan picked up two flutes with bubbly amber liquid and passed one to me.

"It's called till," Stephan said. "Similar to Earthen wine."

I took a sip and was pleasantly surprised by the crisp, cool taste. It was way better than any wine I'd tried. Of course, I'd only had wine from a box, so what did I know? I hardly ever drank alcohol, but the till was delicious, and I took another sip as Stephan led me to one of the larger alcoves. Two servants appeared with food and more drinks. I waved away the brown cheese platter and took another sip of the sweet drink as I watched the people around us. Each person radiated a slightly different hue of power, creating a rainbow of flickering magic while they chatted and roamed the enclosed space in an ever-moving prism of color and sound.

I spotted Lord Councilor Elias talking with a small group of people. His white Council robe had been replaced by a short blue tunic that hung from one shoulder and draped off his back like a cloak. I needed powerful allies, and Elias was as powerful as they got. Preparing myself for some major ass-kissing, I waved at him. He broke off from his group, glass of till in hand. As he made his way over to us, I was struck again by how handsome he was. Honestly, he was beyond handsome. It was like seeing a celebrity up close and realizing he really was *that* good looking.

"Lady Maeve, what a pleasure to see you." He pressed his lips to the back of my hand. His thumb rubbed across my knuckles before he released me. "Lord Stephan, greetings."

"I was hoping to see you tonight," I said to Elias. "I wanted to talk."

"Indeed?" His eyebrows rose. "Lord Stephan, might I have a turnabout with Lady Maeve?"

Stephan gave him a tight smile. "If the lady wishes."

Elias wrapped my arm through his and led me toward the other side of the tent in a slow stroll. "Has your visit been pleasant, my lady?"

I took a deep breath to steady myself. "I'd hardly call it a visit. I'm a prisoner of the Council."

"Nonsense. You're welcome to go where you wish if you're properly escorted—for your safety. In fact, I shall arrange a tour of Aeterna for you."

"That would be great," I said with true enthusiasm. If I could get a better sense of the city, I could figure out how to get back to the portal when the time came.

"Upper Aeterna is quite safe, but we can't be too careful. Perhaps if Lord Silas were to accompany you..."

His tone was casual, but warning bells went off in my head. I didn't know what he was hinting at, and I really needed to avoid stepping into more problems. "I'm sure he's too busy with more important things."

Elias motioned to a servant against the wall, and she stepped forward with another glass of till. I took it and drained half of it in one swallow in a misguided attempt to calm my nerves. I made a mental note to slow down before I got drunk.

"I'd be happy to take you myself." Elias's eyes lingered on my revealing neckline. "I'd never be *too busy* for such a lovely creature as yourself."

My heart rate picked up. He made me nervous on so many levels, and I was way out of my league. "Don't you have a government to run?"

He laughed. "For you, my lady, I would be honored to step away from my duties. I find you... quite fascinating." He stepped closer and ran the tips of his fingers along the side of my neck. "Would you be interested in sex?"

Shock swallowed my tongue and rooted me to the ground. "Wow, uh. That's... wow."

"I've made you uncomfortable. I forget that Earthens are not as direct as Aeternals." He ran his hand slowly along my collarbone, following the length of my necklace downward.

I pulled back, uncomfortable with the direction of his caress, and his finger looped around my necklace. He pulled the pendant into his hand and furrowed his brows at the sigil on Marcel's charm.

"Sex is meant for physical pleasure," he said. "Yours and mine. I'm confident we would both enjoy it."

I opened my mouth, but no sounds came out. That was such a bad idea, I didn't even have words.

He released the charm, and it fell back against my overheated skin. "Would you consider joining me for the evening meal?" My stomach flipped as he shifted his body inches closer to mine. "I'd like to hear more about how you came to be entangled with the Brotherhood. How else could I be confident of your loyalties if we remain strangers?"

"Are you trying to seduce me or blackmail me?" I snapped my mouth shut and willed my brain to move faster than my tongue.

"The former. Although I'd hoped that would be more obvious."
His eyes crinkled handsomely. "Tonight, then? I'll send a servant to
escort you to my personal chambers."

"I'm not sure that..." I looked around. "I should probably talk
to Silas about..." *Shit. Think of something.*

"If you're seeking his permission first, you need not worry." He
leaned in and whispered conspiratorially. "I far outrank him."

"I don't need his permission," I said with a huff.

"Wonderful." He kissed the back of my hand and twisted on
his heel without another word.

I gaped at his back. I hadn't said yes, but somehow, I'd just let
the leader of the Aeternal Council corner me into a date. And he
had a lot more in mind than dinner. I'd tried to get Elias on my side,
not end up on my back.

This was bad on so many levels.

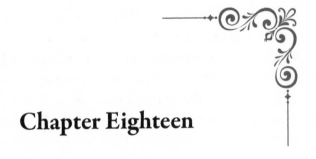

Chapter Eighteen

As Elias disappeared into the crowd, Lady Octavia, the Shifter Councilor, spotted me across the wide pavilion and made her way fluidly toward me. She moved with a graceful stride accentuated by a draped white dress that showed off her long legs and lean, muscular arms. Over the dress, a royal-blue swath of fabric was looped over one shoulder and draped across her body.

The narrowing of her eyes and her purposeful stride had me bracing myself. When she reached me, she didn't waste any time getting to her point. "Why did you come to Aeterna?"

"The Fate sent me—"

She cut me off with an impatient wave of her hand, sending golden bracelets tinkling on her arm. "I've heard Lord Silas's account. Let me be more to the point. I don't believe you're an innocent who stumbled into the Brotherhood's Transference. You're hiding who you are, and I want to know why. Whose side are you on, and why are you in our realm?"

I was so taken aback by her directness that I stopped to consider my response. There were a lot of sides to consider—the Brotherhood and the Council, of course. But I'd also learned about this Lost Sect who seemed to be interested in protecting Earth's magic. Then there was Marcel, who'd died trying to reach me, all for reasons I couldn't even begin to guess.

"If anyone had a way to get the magic out of me that didn't involve my untimely death, I'd be on *their* side," I said bluntly.

Her eyebrows rose at what she must have considered a confession of some kind. Of course, there was no way I would join up with a murderous group of criminals intent on killing innocent people to fuel their rebellion, but I continued on, letting the frustration of this ridiculous situation loose. "I don't care about the Brotherhood or your Council. Hell, if this Lost Sect of yours told me they'd get the magic out, I'd be their best friend. I don't know anything about your politics, and honestly, I don't care. I'm so far out of my depth here, I couldn't even begin to guess whose side I should choose. So I'm on *my* side, Lady Octavia. All I care about is staying alive."

She let out a loud laugh, tossing her head backward. "That is the first fully honest thing I've heard in ages. You're positively vibrating with sincerity."

My mouth twisted as I decided whether or not to push my luck. "Then I'd appreciate your honesty in return. The way I see it, if I prove that I can be valuable to the Council, I'm trapped here forever as your *guest*. But if I can't control this magic stuck inside me, you all are going to kill me and drain me dry."

Her eyebrows rose, but she didn't disagree.

"What I can't figure out," I continued, "is any possible way where I don't end up a slave or dead. So here's my question: How can I convince the Council to let me go?"

The whites of her eyes *shifted* to pools of gold. Her irises turned fully black, like a jaguar's, before they returned to a human shade of brown. "My people need what you have more than you need freedom. You want to survive? Prove yourself useful to someone more powerful than you. It's the way the world works."

Locking my knees in place, I forced myself not to step away from her. Instead, I looked pointedly around the room at the ostentatious wealth of food and people surrounding us. "Your people seem to be doing fine. You don't need me. I just want to go home and live my life."

"*These* people revel in excess." Her lip curled as she swept her gaze around the tent. "They don't know what it's like to live hand-to-mouth, serving others." She looked me right in the eye. "There will be sacrifices for the cause... and you would do well to remember that your life does not matter to anyone but you." She bared her perfectly human teeth in a smile that was most definitely predatory.

My hindbrain shivered in fear, telling my feet to start running, but I held her stare.

"Is all well?" Stephan's voice made me jump, and I found him standing behind me.

Lady Octavia frowned sharply at him. "We were just discussing the realities of life."

"Death is a reality of life," Ethan says angrily.

"I don't want to talk about this," I say.

"You can't just run away from your responsibilities!"

I spin around to confront him. With dark hair and high cheekbones, Ethan has boyish good looks that hold the promise of a handsome man, although his face is red and twisted in an angry scowl.

"You're safe here," he says more softly.

"None of us are safe, Ethan. She... she's dead." My breath hitches in my chest, stuck on the terrible pain balled inside me. "Murdered. I can't live like this anymore."

I blinked, coming back to the conversation with Stephan and Lady Octavia. That vision had been different—it wasn't full of torture and pain but seemed just as real. The heartbreak and pain of some kind of loss still burned, tightening in my chest.

"You're not scaring our guest, are you, Lady Octavia?" His carefully neutral expression reminded me of Silas, and my emotions veered again.

"I'm fine," I said absently, not wanting them to realize there was a lot more wrong with me than just wobbly emotions. Marcel's memories must have started going further back, and they weren't getting any happier. I grimaced. This was not a good sign for my mental stability.

A gong sounded across the room. I startled again, my hand going over my heart. I would have a stroke soon if I didn't settle down.

A man in a plain tunic stood in the center of the room. He stepped onto a low altar with two thick carved poles sticking into the air on either side of the stone slab. His voice carried across the room in a rich baritone. Stephan led me closer to the center of the crowd to listen as Lady Octavia headed in the opposite direction. Palpable excitement hung in the air.

"For a thousand anni," the man began, "the Original Houses have sustained us with their power and wisdom. Let each House bear the burden of their responsibility."

The gong sounded again, and three people moved forward, surrounding the low altar. I recognized Lady Octavia as she stepped out of the crowd, but the others had their backs to me. I peered around heads and shoulders and recognized the Fae representative, Lord Nuada.

"We honor the Original Houses, who were first to sacrifice for our people," the servant intoned.

The magics of those around the altar flared, and my head nearly jerked off my shoulders when I sensed a familiar rush of cool power through the Aegis bond. I twisted around the crowd until I confirmed that Silas was the last man standing at the altar. His golden flare accompanied the less intense red of Lady Octavia and blue of Lord Nuada.

A long, thin dagger appeared in each of their hands. They chanted something in an ancient language that refused translation in my brain and drew the blades across their palms. The knives sliced deep until blood welled, raising tendrils of power from the wounds. The individual threads wove together in a complex ring of magic between them. Heavy and powerful magic buzzed against my skin, calling to me. But I dug deep and resisted the urge to reach for it.

The servant continued his narration. "As the burden of leadership became greater, the Council was born."

Four more Councilors joined the circle. The Humans, Alaric and Elias, stood between Silas and Lady Treva, the final Fae representative. The Shifter representative, Lord Nero, stood by Lady Octavia, closing the circle. They each drew identical blades across their flesh and added their magic to the complex pattern of the conjuring growing between them. The power increased. It thrummed inside my chest until I had to clench my fists at my sides to resist the urge to pull it to me.

Beside me, Stephan laid his hand on my arm, probably sensing my struggle. I drew comfort from his steady presence and took a deep, calming breath as the magic continued to build.

"Thus, the Citizen Source was born of the few to provide for the many," the servant said.

A naked man walked into the center of the circle. He carried a thin beam across the back of his shoulders and wore a determined expression on his face. He stepped onto the low platform and slid the pole into place, bracing it against the two vertical ones, forming a frame with himself in the middle. He clasped the pole above his head with both hands then closed his eyes. His face rose to the ceiling like a supplicant in prayer as the magic of the Council enveloped him.

My eyes locked on the Traiten bands around his wrists. They were dormant, not glowing with any magical compulsion.

The gong sounded.

The people around me recited in unison, "We sustain the Council and their leadership."

Seven knives flashed. The Traiten twisted on the poles. Blood stained his flesh, dripping down his chest and legs onto the altar.

I gasped, and magic pounded against my skull. Power flowed from the Traiten's wounds and back into the Council's circle.

Elias slashed the man's chest, and more magic flowed. Lady Treva cut shallowly across his stomach. Lord Nero drew his blade down the length of the man's arm. Silas cut across his back. The man twisted with each wound but made no more than grunts of pain as they bled him. His hands gripped the pole above him, the Traiten bands seemingly dormant. The full power of the Council pounded through my veins in time with the blood pouring from the Traiten's body. My stomach lurched, and I covered my mouth to keep from crying out.

Stephan gripped my shoulders firmly. Whether he was holding me up or holding me back, I couldn't tell.

Blood flowed as they cut the Traiten again and again. They made dozens of cuts, and with each wound, his magic poured into their spell.

The pounding in my head grew stronger, the magic called to me, and bile rose in my throat. No one made a sound of surprise or revulsion. No one tried to help.

The man was a mess of blood and mangled flesh. A strangled noise escaped my throat—I had to do something.

I stare down at the gash in my thigh. My pants are soaked in blood, and it's not stopping.

"It's a flesh wound." An older man with sandy-blond hair hands me a long length of bandage. "Wrap it up. The lesson isn't over."

"But..." My leg throbs with pain. I grimace as I wrap the bandage tightly around my leg.

"Hurry up. In real life, you have to fight through the pain or die."
He tosses a dagger from his right hand to his left, nods at the knife on
the ground in front of me, and settles into an attack stance.

Stephan pulled me around to face him with a concerned furrow of his brow. On every side of us, the crowd pulsed with eager
anticipation, their attention locked on the gruesome scene at the
altar. I focused my anger and shock on Stephan, and he took it with
perfect understanding.

I moved to do something—anything. But Stephan shook his
head and glanced toward the altar. Silas stepped onto the low stone
platform, reached around the man's neck from behind, and drew
the blade sharply under his chin. The man's head twisted with the
force then dropped limply to the side. His legs gave, and he folded
into the pool of his own blood, splashing crimson over Silas's legs.

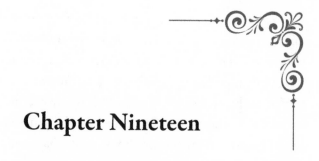

Chapter Nineteen

The Council's spell flared with the power of the man's life. I could feel the pure jolt of energy as it was absorbed into their conjuring and disappeared. The only thing left was the mutilated corpse at their feet.

Silas dropped his knife on the altar and stepped down with a defiant glare, accompanied by disappointed murmurs from the crowd.

Tears of rage and disgust burned my eyes as each Councilor stepped forward and placed his or her palms into the blood. They mixed their magic with the Traiten's and soaked up the last of his life. The Council had killed him to fuel their power, and they'd done it for entertainment.

The gong chimed for the fourth time. The crowd flowed to other entertainments, and the buzz of social conversation returned to the room. Music started somewhere in the background.

I stared at the dead man discarded on the altar.

Stephan pulled me into one of the smaller alcoves, sliding the lattice screen closed behind him. It wasn't soundproofed, but it provided as much privacy as possible given the circumstances. "Are you well?" he asked in a low voice.

Angry tears spilled from my eyes. I couldn't come up with the words to express the horror of what I'd just seen. "No one tried to help him. They murdered him, and no one did anything!"

"The Council makes a spectacle out of providing for the citizens. I'm sorry you had to see that."

"*That's* how they fuel the Citizen Source?" I demanded. "How could Silas be part of that? They just murdered that man in the most gruesome, painful way possible."

"The pain he endured was nothing compared to what it could have been. Silas ended that Traiten's life as a mercy."

A disgusted guffaw slipped from my mouth. "Maybe Silas spared him more pain, but not before he participated in that disgusting, barbaric ritual."

"That Traiten volunteered for death to restore his House's honor."

"A slave can't say no!" But even as I said it, I remembered that the Traiten bands hadn't glowed with magic when he'd walked up to that altar. I wasn't naïve enough to think the Council wouldn't have forced him into "volunteering" for his own death, but he hadn't been forced by magic.

"I'm not defending the Council's methods, but they have served justice this day." His intent gray eyes held mine. "We must pick our battles. Change is not fast."

Bile burned in my throat, turning my words sour. "Things need to change faster."

Stephan released me and straightened. He handed me another glass of till from a nearby golden platter. "Come, let's get you some fresh air. It's time for the finals."

Silas, the Councilors, and the entire bloody mess had disappeared by the time I'd gathered myself enough to follow Stephan back through the tent and outside to the arena. The sun shone down on us, but I shivered despite the heat. We walked through an arbor-lined path and onto the ground level. Cool, fresh air calmed my overheated skin as he led us to a private, shaded seating area. We sat close to the field, separated from the arena by only a transparent, magical barrier.

Around the circular stadium, the spectator seating rose into the air at impossible angles. I could clearly see the cross-hatched threads of magic supporting the bleachers, but the sheer height of the colosseum stunned me. I craned my neck to the top, where large tele-nets floated above the center of the field, relaying close-ups of the action on the field.

The arena's field was a maze of barriers and debris that resembled the aftermath of an explosion. In the very center, a large clearing featured a floating orb that glowed atop a four-foot pedestal. I drained the last sip from my flute, and before it left my lips, a servant handed me another. Stephan finished greeting the people around us just as two contestants entered from opposite ends of the maze: a man with caramel-colored skin and a shaved head, and a tall woman with short, dark hair. I squinted at them.

"Is that Tessa?" My vision seemed blurry. I put down my half-empty glass and waved off the servant who instantly tried to replace it. "She didn't tell me she was competing!"

Stephan smirked. "Guardians are a reticent lot. If they give you three words in a row about themselves, you have a friend for life."

A flare shot across the sky, sending the contestants racing into the maze from opposite ends. The man navigated cautiously, expecting attacks at every turn, while Tessa ran quickly on her end. She zipped around corners and dodged magical booby traps, looping steadily toward the center, while her opponent lagged on his own side of the arena.

A fourth turn led Tessa into a dead end. She tried to double back, but a mass of thick vines shot from the ground and wound around her legs. She fell hard on her knees with the vines up to her thighs and slithering higher. Tessa conjured a knife and hacked at them, but every time she managed to cut one loose, another snaked upward. Her waist became entangled by the thick gray appendages, and judging by her grimace, they were squeezing her.

"Come on," I whispered at Tessa, who was still struggling on the ground.

The walls in the central clearing began to compress, closing off the maze from where the glowing orb and victory waited.

The man broke into a run, barely avoiding a whip-like flare of magic before he slid into the central clearing just as the walls closed. The crowd cheered, and he raised his fist in victory.

Tessa was locked out.

She flipped onto her stomach, and magic flared around her. A wave of energy burst outward, burning the vines to greenish-gray ash. She pushed to her feet, soaked in sweat. Tessa backed away from the dead-end path and ran at the vine-covered wall then scaled her way to the top of the fifteen-foot maze.

I held my breath. She wasn't giving up!

She stood and ran on the top of the wall, flying over the uneven, narrow path at a reckless speed that spurred renewed excitement from the onlookers. Tessa approached a ninety-degree turn without slowing, but instead of following the path, she leapt across the six-foot gap to the next ring of the maze and raced on.

The crowd cheered wildly, and I rose to my feet with them.

Tessa's opponent spotted her on the wall across the clearing from him. His face twisted in disbelief before he spun and ran for the center of the field to reach the orb.

From the wall, Tessa conjured a glowing disk and flung it at the man. He threw himself out of its path just before it slammed to the ground at his heels. Dirt exploded and rained down, obscuring him from view.

The crowd went wild, and I jumped up and down, cheering for Tessa along with them.

Tessa dropped into the clearing and ran after the man. Two steps in, the dirt boiled beneath their feet. Like an ocean full of tentacles, pustules grew and breached the surface at random. Within a few seconds, they burst and sent a plume of steam and boiling dirt high into the air.

Caught in the middle of the minefield, both contestants twisted around the explosive pockets, trying to reach the orb fifty yards away. Tessa threw magic at her opponent's feet. The man dodged and jumped right into one of the large bubbles. It burst around him, and he was caught in the explosion of superheated earth.

The crowd sucked in its collective breath.

Tessa ran toward the orb, throwing magic in front of her from both hands, popping the superheated bubbles before she reached them to clear a path to the finish. She reached the pedestal, grabbed the orb, and held it over her head in victory.

"She did it!" Stephan cheered. We both whistled and yelled with the crowd.

The Healers rushed in and took the man off the field. He was alive but covered in painful-looking red blisters. Guilt hit me for enjoying a sport that resulted in such painful and unnecessary injuries. But at least the man wasn't a Traiten. He'd participated of his own free will. My anger returned for the man the Council had murdered. I collapsed back in my seat, emotionally exhausted.

"You needn't have feared for Tessa," Stephan said. "She is quite capable. She did well."

A crew of servants flooded the field and worked quickly to prepare the arena for the next challenge. I wondered if they were ever given days off. Even holidays were working days for them.

There was so much I didn't understand about their culture, but some things were just wrong. Slavery was wrong. Taking away free will was wrong. Murdering people to fuel your city's magical power was not an acceptable alternative to a humane punishment for crime. The memory of the man's death—knives slicing into him over and over, bleeding him to death—made me so angry, I felt nauseated.

I couldn't believe Silas was a part of that.

Slaves cleared the arena into a single stage for the awards. People crowded into the standing-room spaces between the seats and the stage, but our area remained unobstructed. Hundreds of spectators stood shoulder to shoulder around the perimeter fencing, waiting to cheer on their friends, family, and favorites.

The members of the Aeternal Council were now conspicuously seated on a raised section above the stage, displaying their white robes and a wealth of ornate jewelry, as they oversaw the awards.

My stomach twisted as Silas stepped onto the stage in ceremonial armor, a crimson cloak draped off one shoulder. I couldn't tell his mood from his neutral expression, but I knew he didn't like all the attention. The Traiten's blood was gone, but the crimson cloak reminded me of what I had seen earlier, and sickness twisted in my stomach. A golden breastplate covered Silas's chest, and he wore a matching pair of boots with shin plates. His sword hung in a scabbard on his left hip. The cloak flowed behind him as he walked to the center of the stage with long, confident strides.

A dozen people followed Silas onto the stage, all dressed in similar armor. Commander Corin and Tessa were the only ones I recognized as the competitors filed in front of the stage, dressed in plain black uniforms, and organized themselves into three groups.

When they were situated, blue-green power flared from a woman on the stage. Her voice carried throughout the arena. "Harker of House Pontius, come forward."

A man moved onto the stage and saluted her.

"You have demonstrated skill in your weapon, and bravery in your heart. With blood and sweat and skill, you have earned the rank of Centurion!"

They clasped forearms, raising a cheer from the Guardians.

She called up the rest of her group, and each person received the same recognition. The next two groups advanced individually to Second or First Legatis respectively. Finally, Silas stepped forward. I balled my fists as his larger-than-life face projected onto the screens above the arena. His aura lit with brilliant golden power, and his voice carried across the arena. "Second Legatis Tessa d'Vente, step forward."

Tessa moved to the front and saluted Silas with a fist over her heart.

"You have demonstrated skill in your weapon, and bravery in your heart," Silas said. "With blood and sweat and skill, you have surpassed every rank of the Guardians. For your victory in battle and your loyalty to Aeterna, you now join the elite ranks of the Commanders."

The Guardians cheered wildly, whistling and stomping their feet on the ground.

Tessa grasped forearms with Silas. He leaned down and said something in her ear, and they thumped each other on the back. She grasped arms with each of the people on the stage before she faced the crowd and pumped her fists in the air.

We cheered louder, and my heart swelled for Tessa.

"Congratulations to our Guardians," Silas announced. "They have brought honor to their Houses this day and joy to the heart of Aeterna!"

The cheering turned into a chant from the crowd. The chant continued until everyone picked it up, repeating the words in unison. Silas frowned.

"What's going on?" I asked Stephan.

"Advancing through the Guardian ranks can also happen through a challenge. The challenger chooses a Commander to replace in a fight to the death. It's a barbaric practice, but the crowds love it."

I frowned. Bloodlust for entertainment was quite the thing around here. My anger from earlier came back full force.

Silas held up his hand, and the crowd quieted. He pulled his sword from its scabbard. His aura flared golden, and he twisted the blade in the same lazy pattern I'd seen in Boston, warming up his muscles. An amplified projection of him floated on the tele-net above the arena, and his voice rang out. "If there is a challenger among you, let them step forward." His feral smile crossed his face, surely dissuading anyone who might have been tempted to try their magic against his.

"Do I have a challenger?"

The crowd went silent. Silas scowled as he spun slowly around the arena. He turned full circle. No one would challenge him. His magic disappeared as he replaced the sword at his hip.

The crowd sighed.

The Guardians dispersed, and Silas walked to the back of the stage, where he spoke to the Councilors seated there. I recognized the light hair and hawkish features of Lord Magister Alaric. Next to him sat a beautiful blond woman.

She stretched her hand over the railing, and Silas took it. He placed a kiss on the back of her hand. Shock wove through every nerve in my body. It was the sad woman from the vision in the Fate's temple. In real life, she wore a smile that made her even more stunning. A crimson dress was draped loosely over her tall figure, and her long hair fell in an elaborate braid over her shoulder. She looked radiant as she stood and smiled down at Silas. *Aria.*

Her hand gently cupped her stomach for a second before she lowered it to her side. If I hadn't been staring so intently, I would have missed it. The gentle curve of her stomach was barely more than a bump.

Aria was pregnant.

"I challenge you!" I yelled.

Everyone stared at me. My challenge echoed across a thousand pairs of lips until I caught a glimpse of myself on the tele-nets above. My face was flushed, and my eyes were flashing. I didn't care.

Silas—and the Council—had mutilated and murdered that Traiten. They enslaved people and killed them. And there he stood, not even hours later, with a woman he supposedly didn't love, yet she was smiling and pregnant. They were happy. *No. Just no.*

Stephan whispered furiously, tugging at my arm, but I ignored him.

Silas and I locked gazes across the arena. His eyes narrowed, and his mouth twisted into the condescending grimace I hated.

I marched toward him. The magic barrier melted away in front of me when I strode onto the field and headed straight for Silas.

The announcer's voice rang out across the arena. "A challenger!"

The crowd roared in delight.

Silas stalked halfway across the arena and met me in the middle. "What are you doing?" he demanded.

"Challenging you," I responded, using the voice I reserved for idiots.

"You're making a mistake," he said with an angry hiss in his voice. "A very *public* mistake."

I dropped my voice to a furious whisper that only he could hear. "You are an arrogant, insufferable murderer—and your *wife* is *pregnant*, you cheating bastard!"

I clenched my fists at my sides so I wouldn't start punching him. I hadn't meant to just blurt my accusations at him like that, and challenging the Lord Commander of the Guardians in front of half of Aeterna was possibly the stupidest thing I had ever done, but I was raging mad. Someone needed to pay for the injustice of everything that had happened today, and I couldn't stand by and do nothing any longer.

Chapter Twenty

"Out!" Silas snapped.

The few people still in the reception pavilion rushed for the exit. Everyone fled his wrath as I planted myself firmly in front of him and prepared to take down the dragon. I didn't even care that he had stormed off the field and left all of Aeterna wondering what the hell was going on. I followed him. He wasn't getting off the hook this time.

He paced the floor in front of me with a half dozen long, angry strides before he spun and paced back again. His magic flared around us in the pattern I recognized from the Council's privacy spell. "Explain yourself," he demanded.

"Explain *myself*?" My voice rose in outraged disbelief. "You have got to be kidding me! I just watched you murder a man, Silas! I'm sorry, but I won't just sit there and do nothing while you go around being all happy with your *pregnant wife*. Not after what I saw."

He bared his teeth. "That man was a Traiten."

My fists were balled at my sides again. "Murder is always wrong, Silas! Slavery is wrong!"

"Exactly. He robbed and murdered three people! He deserved to die."

"He—" My righteous anger stuttered. The Traiten was another criminal, of course. A murderer. "I didn't know that."

"You don't know a lot of things. And yet you continuously pass judgment," Silas said with a scowl. "He was sentenced to death or life as a Traiten. He chose to die in a way that would restore his family's honor."

"But the Council bled him for his magic!"

"Yes," Silas said, his face hard.

"They stole his life energy, just like the Brotherhood."

"That man deserved to die. The Council used his death for the greater good of the citizens. The world is better off than when he was breathing, and that is the honor he's restored to his family. It's our *duty* to enforce law and punishment."

The way the Council chose to enforce their laws was barbaric. But I started to wonder if the world wasn't better off without someone who had murdered three people. Still, I didn't want to let Silas off the hook quite yet, not when he'd lied to me and tried to have sex with me while he was married. "What about your *wife*? You've clearly been doing more than 'barely speaking' with Aria."

"How did you know?" he asked.

"Know what? That you're a cheater?" The till had made my tongue even sharper than normal. At the moment, I didn't care what he said about bond-mates and power agreements and all that. He'd made a promise to someone else and then tried to have sex with me. That made him a cheating bastard.

He ran his hand over his face. "How did you know about the pregnancy, Maeve?"

A little flutter hit my stomach when he said my name. I punched it down with both fists. "She cradled her stomach." Looking back, it wasn't a whole lot to go on, but Silas had just confirmed my suspicions.

He continued to pace, mumbling something I couldn't make out. Something was wrong with the way he was acting. I'd expected his anger. And I was prepared for him to tell me it wasn't any of my business. But something different emanated from him, and it felt strangely like fear. He seemed overwhelmed, almost nervous. Silas was usually so confident. The uncertainty I could sense from him made me pause. Then I reminded myself that he was a terrible person and I didn't care.

Aria rushed into the tent with Stephan right on her heels. Silas stopped pacing as they passed through the privacy spell.

"Silas?" Aria reached for him, her face tentative and... scared?

He stepped away from her and resumed pacing. "She knows about the pregnancy."

Aria and Stephan wore matching expressions of surprise. Stephan shifted on his feet.

I could feel his anxiety. I had gotten into the middle of something I did not understand at all, and confusion tempered my anger.

"How?" Aria whispered, her hand flitting to her stomach protectively.

I nodded at her hand, and she dropped it immediately as understanding crossed her face. She leaned into Stephan, who wrapped his arm around her, and it finally hit me. Aria and Silas had never wanted to be together, but...

"Oh my God." I stared at Stephan in shock. "It's yours."

Stephan nodded, a mixture of fear and protectiveness in his face. He cared about Aria. It had been obvious in the way he'd talked about her. But I hadn't realized the kind of love he had for her was romantic and that Aria felt the same way about him. Silas still paced the floor, his shoulders tense. I'd misunderstood—again.

"Silas has agreed to claim the child as his own," Aria said quietly. Her eyes were wide and watery, reminding me of the vision of her in the Fate's temple.

Silas stopped pacing and frowned. His eyes were dark with the weight of too much responsibility. That look on his normally confident face hurt me in a way I hadn't anticipated. Right on the heels of his pain, my anger surfaced. This time, I directed my ire at Stephan.

"So, Silas is what, your cover story? You get your happy ending together while he plays out the shitty-ass prophecy and pretends to be Aria's baby daddy? How could you do this to your own brother?"

I was so angry, I accessed my power without thinking. The room glowed in shades of white. The pattern of each of their lives was written in the magic all around me and pulsing in time with my rage. Aria and Stephan flinched and stared at my aura. Their matching expressions of surprise and fear didn't stop the rage burning through me.

"Enough." Silas put his hand on my shoulder. "You don't need to defend me. I gave them my blessing a long time ago. I love Stephan too much to make him suffer through a *shitty-ass prophecy* with me." His lips twisted upward at my terminology. "And Aria too. We don't all need to suffer. If anything, it is I who owes them an apology. With Stephan as Prime of our House, we'd planned to petition Lord Alaric to absolve the bond-mating and allow Aria and Stephan to be together."

"But then you took back the Council seat to save my life." I released my magic. The energy faded away, returning the world to everyday colors. "This is my fault."

"Lord Alaric will not agree to absolving the mating bond now that Silas is Prime to House Valeron," Stephan said.

Silas frowned at his brother. "I failed you."

Stephan laid his hand on Silas's shoulder. "We'll find another way."

The brothers nodded at each other in solidarity.

Aria took shelter under Stephan's arm, and something heavy settled in my heart. This whole situation was just too much misery for one family, and I'd made it worse.

"This arrangement works for us," Silas continued. "Aria and Stephan get their happy ending, as you called it, while we fulfill our obligation to the prophecy. The pregnancy is new, and we haven't figured out all the details yet."

"What about you?" I asked him.

His brows drew together in confusion.

I finally understood why he pushed me away. He was protecting his family, allowing Aria and Stephan to be together, even if it was in secret. "You've made the best out of this situation for everyone else, and I respect the hell out of that. But don't you want *more...* for yourself?"

"You seem to be under the impression that I'm not happy," he said with a frown.

I searched his face for any hint of his feelings and found nothing. His expression was completely blank.

"I need you to keep what you know to yourself," he said.

My gut tightened into a nauseous ball as I agreed. I would keep their secret because it was the right thing to do, especially after Silas had traded away their collective freedom to save my life. But it hurt that he still didn't want me in his life. He'd told me multiple times he wasn't interested in more. I just hadn't realized until now that he wasn't interested in more with *me.* Yet I kept naively inserting myself into their lives.

Stephan cleared his throat. "We'll leave you two to discuss—"

"No, you stay," I said. "I'm leaving."

I exited the pavilion quickly, leaving them to their private business and vowing to be done with the whole family. All I did was make a mess of things I didn't understand.

I was so wrapped up in my own thoughts that I didn't pay attention to the crowd outside.

"The challenger!" the announcer roared as my feet stepped outside the pavilion. The crowd cheered as my face, all splotchy and red, appeared bigger than life on the tele-net above the arena.

A thousand sets of eyes weighed on my shoulders. My hot temper had gotten me into trouble again, and now my furious anger was gone. I felt deflated, and I'd completely forgotten about the stupidity of my challenge.

The crowd started cheering when Silas strode out of the tent behind me. He grasped me by the upper arm and dragged me into the arena with him. Then he released me at the edge of the clearing and strode to the very center, ensuring all eyes were on him.

He faced Alaric, Elias, and the other Councilors standing near their seats. "I won't fight someone who has no training." His voice echoed around the now-silent arena.

The crowd murmured, trying to figure out exactly what was going on.

"I withdraw my challenge," I said loudly.

Murmuring continued as everyone tried to make sense of the situation.

Up on the raised pavilion, the Aeternal Council conferred together. Alaric was the only one not whispering in someone's ear as he glared at me, his aura lit with golden power.

The air around me thickened into a blurry fog. I squinted at it until the mist straightened into a distinct pattern and a portal opened ten feet in front of me.

I dove out of the way as a Rakken leapt out, barely managing to avoid a full collision. I rolled to my feet just in time to see a cascade of energy shiver down around me. All the air rushed out of my lungs. I was trapped inside a twenty-foot dome of magic with three Rakken and a portal.

The first Rakken—a giant, scarred monstrosity with an ugly, hairless hide—lifted his head and sniffed the air. One of his ears was a torn, deformed stump. Ugly twisted his head to the side, and slitted eyes fell on me. The beast's nostrils flared wide, and his jaw hinged open to let loose a blood-chilling shriek.

I slapped my hands over my ears and tried to hold my brain inside my skull as the noise reverberated against the dome of magic trapping us together.

Fear and confusion tangled in my head. Silas had said the Brotherhood couldn't attack me in Aeterna, but the snarling Rakken in front of me proved otherwise. Another shriek sounded outside the dome, and I noticed two more Rakken loose in the crowd. Screams cascaded across the arena, setting off mass panic. On the ground level, the elite and powerful citizens of Upper Aeterna skimmed out of danger, leaving the coveted arena-side seats empty. Everyone else shoved each other and rushed for the exits.

All the Rakken took up the howling, and the deafening noise echoed off the dome, freezing my brain as pure, primal fear slithered down my spine. I was trapped and weaponless.

Ugly stalked forward. He was less than ten feet away—an easy leap for a Rakken.

Outside the dome, Silas threw a wave of blinding gold magic at the loose Rakken. The animals dodged, and the energy slammed into the shield with an audible boom, fracturing into veins of magic that crackled across the surface.

All three Rakken inside the dome paused to assess the potential threat.

Guardians flooded the field and began attacking the Rakken and the shield alongside Silas, smashing even more magic into the dome. Their efforts lit up the barrier with every blast, but the shield held.

Ugly focused his attention back on me with a very human snicker on his demonic face. The other two Rakken flanked him. The one on my left darted forward. I twisted away from him, and they all shifted with me. Lefty darted forward again and snapped his jaws in the air just shy of my face. I stumbled backward, and they adjusted with me again. The Rakken surrounded me, leaving no escape other than the portal five feet to my right. Its dark, opaque surface rippled ominously, giving no clue what could be on the other side.

I pushed my back flat against the shield, and dark power sizzled along my flesh. It sank into me, and I jumped back instinctively. The tainted magic had the same bitter taste as Atticus's compulsion sigil, which shouldn't have been a surprise considering the Brotherhood had conjured this spell. If I tried to absorb the magic out of the dome, I would probably end up puking my guts out while the Rakken ate me.

All three Rakken stalked forward with their teeth bared. Ugly crouched. His lean muscles were tight along his forelimbs, and his long claws dug into the earth as he prepared to pounce like a giant cat. I glanced at the portal. I couldn't go through that doorway and straight into Titus's arms. I just needed to figure out how to stay alive until Silas broke through the barrier between us. I wished fervently for Ripper. Even a small knife was better than no knife when faced with three innards-eating demon dogs.

The Guardians took care of the loose Rakken and concentrated their efforts on pounding the shield from the outside. Every blast of energy sizzled across the surface, weakening it. It shivered with each impact but held my rescue outside the barrier.

"Maeve!" Silas yelled, his magic causing thunderous impacts every few seconds. "Don't go through that portal!"

No shit. For once, I fully intended to do what Silas told me.

Lefty lunged at me, but I had no more ground to give. He snapped a double row of teeth inches from my leg. If I had Ripper, I could have stabbed him in the eye. He was so close, I could smell his rancid, meaty breath.

But he didn't bite me. *He could have bitten me.*

They were trying to herd me into the portal! They needed me alive and on the other side of that doorway. My chances of living through this were looking up.

Lefty pulled back, and his head twisted to the side. He seemed confused.

"Screw you!" I screamed in his face and kicked him like a toddler having a tantrum, swinging my foot right up under his jaw.

His mouth smacked shut from the impact. My sandal-clad toes crunched, and pain radiated up my foot.

Lefty growled and swiped a massive paw at me.

My head slammed against the shield. Air whooshed out of my lungs as magic sizzled over my body and pain flamed across my back. His claws had shredded my right shoulder.

Lefty stood over me, and his nostrils flared as he inhaled the scent of my blood. Every shred of human intelligence I'd seen in his eyes fled. He opened his maw. His lips were pulled back, exposing killing teeth and dripping saliva in long, wobbly strings.

He was going to eat me, orders be damned.

Ugly slammed into Lefty, pushing him away from me. Lefty snapped back, and the two grappled. Ugly apparently remembered they weren't supposed to kill me; they were supposed to herd me through that portal to Titus. And apparently, Titus needed me alive to get their magic back.

Righty jumped into the fight, and I couldn't tell if he was for or against keeping me alive.

As the animals fought each other, my mind raced for a way out of this mess. I had no weapon and no way to reliably access Marcel's magic. Silas was trapped on the outside of the shield, and regardless of which Rakken won their argument, I was dead.

Lefty got a hold of Ugly's throat, ripped it out, and yowled in triumph. The foul smell of Rakken blood hit me just as Lefty leapt over his dead leader and skidded to a stop in front of me. Righty circled around and joined him.

I swore in frustration. They were going to *eat* me. I glanced at the portal. Going through that meant certain death and giving Titus the magic Marcel had died to keep out of his hands. I glanced around for any other salvation, but all I could focus on were the two Rakken covered in the blood of their leader. I tried to decide if being ripped to shreds by animals was better than the torture Marcel had endured.

Wrapping my fingers around Marcel's charm hanging from my neck, I willed it to give me strength. I was out of options. I had only one way to defend myself. I had to absorb the power from the Brotherhood's shield. The thought made me want to curl up and die on the spot. Absorbing their tainted magic was going to hurt. I pushed my entire backside against the shield and opened myself to the power that fueled it. Blackness flowed through me, but I took it all and let it overpower me.

Lefty leapt.

The last of the shield's power wavered a split second before it shivered and collapsed. I crashed to the ground with it. Pain and nausea coursed through my body, and I convulsed with the tide of dark magic.

A wave of golden energy flared through the sky above me, and like a giant blade, it crashed into Lefty, slicing clean through the beast. His front half fell at my feet, claws still reaching.

Magic twisted the beast back to man. Two charred halves of mangled, naked flesh lay at my feet, causing my stomach to rise up into my throat.

My vision blurred as more flashes of magic surrounded me. Howls pierced my ears.

Hazy figures raced toward me. I clutched my head. I was drowning in the tainted power—thick black magic. It was a million times worse than the spell I'd absorbed from Atticus. My lungs filled with ink, and it clawed up my throat, choking me. I fought it but wasn't strong enough to resist. The dark energy pulled me into unconsciousness.

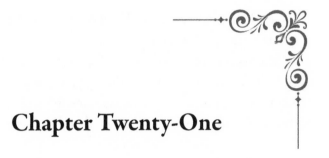

Chapter Twenty-One

Someone was strangling me.

I gasped and pushed my long, tangled hair off my face. My racing heart calmed as I sat up in a soft, warm bed, covered by a thick blanket. I was in a room I had never seen before.

Bright sunlight shone through a window, reflecting off the dark-red walls and creating a warm, cocooned space.

Outside, tall buildings blocked the view, giving me no clue where I was. On the wall opposite the bed, a small shelf held a collection of toys. I stared at a short wooden sword, blinking while my mind caught up. This was a child's room in someone's home.

The elegant gold dress I'd worn to the Exposition hung off my shoulders, shredded and covered in dried blood and dirt. I twisted to look at my shoulder and felt no pain. I must have been healed after I passed out. But Marcel's charm still hung around my neck. I rubbed my thumb across its raised surface as I tried to reconstruct exactly what had happened.

A single chime sounded on the other side of the wall.

"May I enter?" a muffled male voice asked.

"Atticus?" *What the hell is going on?*

The door disappeared, and Atticus entered the room with a slight bow. He was wearing a plain brown shirt and loose pants—which could have fit two of me inside—wrapped around his tree-trunk legs. "Are you well?"

I was fine. Great, actually. I'd begun to recognize the post-healing buzz of energy. "What happened?"

"After you were attacked, you required a Healer." He nodded at my torn dress. "When you didn't regain consciousness after the wounds were healed, the Lord Commander realized you'd absorbed the tainted magic of the shield and that you needed clean energy."

I nodded. *Where is Silas?*

"He made quite the scene transferring power to you. Unfortunately, the Council had not evacuated with the rest of the citizens. Lord Magister Alaric was... upset."

I bit my lip. Silas was incapable of keeping a low profile. He just had to flaunt the fact that we had a bond by sharing power with me in front of all of Aeterna, all while refusing to give Alaric's daughter the same benefits. Bad idea if he wanted to keep Alaric on his good side. Now Alaric would hate me even more.

My fuzzy memories were starting to return. "I saw you rush on the field during the attack. What if someone saw you and realized the compulsion was lifted?"

"I owe you my life, Maeve. I'd take the risk a thousand times over." At my frustrated sigh, he added, "If anyone bothered to pay attention to the actions of a Traiten, they'd simply assume I'd been ordered to assist. I assure you, my actions held little risk."

I sighed. I wouldn't call fending off Rakken low-risk, but it wasn't worth arguing about. "Where am I?"

"You're in my familial home in Lower Aeterna, my lady," he replied softly. "You slept through the night and most of this day." Atticus sat on the edge of my bed. "The Lord Commander wishes that you remain hidden here until he can figure out who is helping the Brotherhood. He believes there may be a traitor within the Council."

"A traitor? Why does he think that?"

"He's long suspected it. We believe the Brotherhood is recruiting citizens from Lower Aeterna with someone on the Council helping to transport them to Earth."

I remembered something I'd seen just before the attack. "Alaric used his magic to make the shield! I saw his flare right when it happened."

Atticus quirked his head to the side. "He couldn't have made that shield without being noticed."

The shield had been made from the tainted energy of the Brotherhood's spell. Alaric's flare had been pure golden—no dark edges from stolen life magic. "Damn it. You're right. Could Alaric have been doing something else to help the Brotherhood?"

"It's possible, but it would be hard to prove. We don't know who the traitor is, and while Lord Silas works on that, you're best off hiding here."

"No one knows where I am?"

"No one except my family and the Lord Commander," he replied. "No one will think to search for you in Lower Aeterna."

I would have to miss my date with Elias. Equal parts relief and frustration hit me. It would have been good to find out more about him and maybe remove him from the suspected list of traitors. But that was ludicrous because Elias wanted to get me in his bed, not tell me his deepest secrets. And I was not going down *that* path. Staying out of sight would probably be good for a few days.

"I'm surprised Silas sent me here. He thinks we're sleeping together."

The blood drained from his face. "I need you to correct that impression with the Lord Commander."

I glared at him. "He doesn't have any say in who I have sex with."

"Don't take offense," he pleaded with his palms up in a placating gesture. "I simply mean that Lord Alaric is using me to sow the seeds of discord, and it would not help the situation if Lord Silas believes we are having sexual relations."

Confusion made my brow furrow. "What do you mean? How is Alaric using you?"

"Silas and I advanced through all five levels of training together and had our first assignments together as greenies. Lord Alaric assigned me as your Traiten as an intentional thorn in his side, likely in response to him bonding with another whilst denying Lady Aria the Valeron sigil."

Atticus was amazingly perceptive, and I was stupid for not realizing it on my own. The way Silas had reacted when he'd seen Atticus in my quarters was exactly what Alaric wanted. The political tension between the other Councilors and Silas was more complicated than I could hope to understand on my own. With Atticus's insights into the situation and his willingness to help me without an agenda, I felt as though I could trust his assessment of the situation. I was grateful to have him on my side.

So I was in hiding while Silas found the traitor on the Council. I could've done worse. A guest in Atticus's house was a solid upgrade from prisoner of the Council. "Got any edible food around here? I'm starving."

As if I had summoned her with magic, a woman appeared in the doorway with an armful of clothes and food. Her long dark hair was swept back into a simple ponytail, and she wore a brown tunic and leggings. As with all the magic users I'd seen in Aeterna, it was impossible to tell her age.

"Lady Maeve, this is my mother, Junia," Atticus said.

The woman set the clothes and a tray of food down on the bed next to me and pulled me into a hug. "Thank you for returning my son to me."

After a moment of surprised hesitation, I hugged her back. When she pulled back, tears shimmered on her cheeks. Real suffering pulled at the corners of her eyes.

I didn't know what to say. "It's nice to meet you, Lady Junia."

"Just Junia," she said softly. "We're not an Upper House."

"Right. Sorry."

"You are welcome here, Lady Maeve. We are honored to offer our hospitality to you, meager as it may be."

"No, this is great." I picked up the stack of clothes she had given me. The wardrobe I'd been given by the Council was entirely made of soft, flowing fabric. The basic tunic and leggings Junia offered were plain brown cotton. Stiff and thick, the clothing had a utilitarian feel that spoke of hard work, reminding me of jeans. I missed my jeans.

"Thank you," I said. "Please call me Maeve. I'm not really a lady; I'm just a girl from Earth with no family." I said it to lighten the mood, but Atticus and his mother gaped at me as if I'd just told them I kidnapped puppies for a living. I cleared my throat awkwardly.

Junia offered me food, and I gratefully picked up one of the baked, stuffed buns she'd brought. It was an immense relief to find something edible in this realm. Before she left, Junia pulled me into another hug and kissed my cheek.

"I think we should talk to the families of the missing citizens," I told Atticus when we were alone. We had to find a connection between them if we were going to figure out what the Brotherhood was up to. My gut told me the missing people were the key.

Atticus paused with a piece of bread halfway to his mouth. "I'm not sure going into public is a good idea. After what happened at the Exposition, you could be recognized. Your white flare is notable."

"I promise not to access my magic. No one will even look twice at me. I swear." In his mother's clothing, I was already dressed for the part. "I can't just sit here."

"The Lord Commander ordered it."

I gave him my hard stare. "The *Lord Commander* needs to realize I'm not one of his minions. He doesn't get to make choices for me. I'll go by myself if you're scared of him." Channeling one of Silas's most irritating expressions, I raised a single eyebrow in challenge.

A wry grin lit Atticus's face. "I suspect you're very likely to get yourself in trouble. It appears I have no choice but to go along and protect you."

I grinned back. "How can we get the names of the families?"

"It shouldn't be hard to cross-reference who lives in each House with their current resource allotment." At my confused expression, he explained that each month, Lower Houses were given an allotment of resources, such as food, based on the number of daily assignments they completed. "If the allotment has decreased recently without a corresponding decrease in their House headcount, we just might have our missing people."

"How do you know all that?" I asked, sincerely impressed.

He shrugged. "I've learned to stay two steps ahead to make even."

He didn't sound bitter, just resigned to the facts of life. I wondered if I would have the same outlook if I had gone through everything he had. He'd had to fight to become a Guardian, then they'd made him a slave for something he didn't do. If I were him, I would've been angry as hell. I couldn't help but wonder how different his life would have been if he were from Upper Aeterna.

"But those records are kept by the Council," he said. "We'll need Lord Silas to get them."

I frowned. "That's going to take a while. Isn't there anything we can do today?" Hiding in the Lower City was a great opportunity to find out more about the Brotherhood, and I didn't want to waste it. Plus, a trip through Lower Aeterna could help me plan an escape route when the time came.

"I do know two families with missing sons. I believe they haven't reported it—they were too afraid of the consequences. The second shift just ended; we can probably find them at home."

We set out on foot in search of the families Atticus had identified. As we walked, I noticed that the difference between Upper and Lower Aeterna was stark. The buildings were, for the most part, in need of repairs. Each red-stone structure rose ten or more levels, stacked with individual living quarters. It appeared that each generation had added additional units on top of the deteriorating bottom floors. Haphazard streets wound through an endless maze of neighborhoods, and tele-nets hung at intersections of major pathways, displaying reminders about energy rationing.

No one wore finely crafted, lightweight tunics, robes, or capes. The clothing of Lower Aeternals would best be described as utilitarian and serviceable. Self-consciously, I adjusted the decorative headscarf Atticus had suggested I wear to disguise my recognizable auburn hair. The elaborate wrapping had seemed ridiculous at first, but I was relieved to see several other people wearing something similar as we traveled through the streets of Lower Aeterna.

Atticus and I went to the first address together, a tall building squeezed between two others. An older woman answered the unit on the fourth floor, confirmed she was a relative of our first missing person, Maxim, and invited us in. It was impossible to tell her exact age, but the wariness in her movements made me suspect she'd lived a long time and seen too much hardship.

Armed with the information on where Maxim had been assigned, we told her we worked at the same farm and were concerned because we hadn't seen him recently. As we sat inside her threadbare sitting room, she served us tea and told us everything she could think of that might help us find her grandson. The way she talked about him made it obvious how loved he was.

Pretty quickly, a story started to emerge of an angry young man who wanted more than his society would give him. I understood wanting more, especially when surrounded by so much wealth just out of reach. It reminded me of the people living on the streets of Boston—sleeping in the shadows of grand brownstone buildings on elegantly cobbled streets. So much opportunity was in front of them, but it was completely out of reach. Compared to the opulence of Upper Aeterna, this family had nothing.

Everything the woman told us made me think Maxim was a perfect candidate to join the Brotherhood. He didn't want to be a farmer like his parents. He wanted to be a Harvester, but his family didn't have the standing to qualify for the training. They couldn't even get him an apprenticeship within the merchant's guild. In the end, he didn't have any good options. It was a classic radicalization story: unfulfilled life, no future, no options. Someone like him would have definitely found the Brotherhood appealing.

"He's not the only one," the grandmother whispered over her cup of tea.

"What do you mean?" I asked.

"A handful of us have reported our missing family members, but the Council accused them of being traitors." Her shoulders lifted in a defeated shrug. "Most of the missing are not reported. There are more every month. I've heard of at least a dozen in the past fortnight."

"Can you tell us who they are?" I asked.

The woman's face pinched, and she clammed up. She didn't want to betray anyone else's secrets. Eventually, we excused ourselves to visit the other House Atticus knew about. By the time we traveled across the city, it had gotten dark. A man answered the door of the seventh-floor unit, dressed in a brown servant's uniform. I immediately noticed the public sigil visible to me on both sides of his neck. He was a Barren, born without magic.

"We're looking for Cato," Atticus said.

"I am Castor. Cato is my bond-brother." His eyes went wide. "Are you Atticus?"

Atticus tensed. "Do I know you?"

"No, but you're the one everyone's talking about," he said with a quick glance up and down the street behind us. "The Traiten the Council set up."

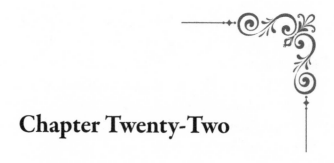

Chapter Twenty-Two

"How do you know about Atticus?" My voice had risen too high, and I tried to control my growing panic. If word was out about Atticus's compulsion, then whoever had betrayed them at Krittesh had already discovered that we'd removed their spell. They would've covered their tracks, and we would have no way to clear Atticus's name.

We sat on a tatami-style mat in the front room of his house, and Castor's voice took on a reverent tone, full of awe. "They didn't want to let you train with the Guardians, but you fought for it and earned it. People are saying that after Krittesh, the Council punished you for crimes you didn't commit. They're using you as an example to keep us all in line."

I was relieved that he didn't know about the compulsion. According to this man, Atticus was some kind of local hero—a success story who had been punished for daring to fly too high. He gazed at Atticus with star-struck admiration. Suddenly, he jumped up and rushed out of the room. Atticus glanced at me with alarm, but Castor returned quickly and handed a small, portable console to him. "Here."

Atticus's eyes went wide before he swallowed and handed it to me. It was a picture of Atticus in a Guardian's uniform. He had shorter hair, and his bright brown eyes were young and eager. Superimposed over the image was the symbol of the Traiten drawn in red, and it was dripping like blood. Underneath his picture were the words "Remember Atticus."

Castor's brow furrowed in anger, and his voice rose. "The Council needs to be held responsible for their actions against you, against all of us. We're going to change things."

This man was a perfect candidate for the Brotherhood, and he seemed to be in the loop with a group of like-minded people. We needed to get inside information about what they were doing because I would bet a lifetime supply of hamburgers that they were connected to the Brotherhood. We needed to be on the inside. "You're right, but how? There's nothing we can do."

"We're having a meeting in two days to talk about change," Castor said. "Will you come?"

We left Castor's house with the information we needed about the Brotherhood's secret recruiting meeting. Things were looking up, and I couldn't wait to get back to Atticus's house so we could talk about our next steps. We navigated the dark streets, which were busy with people ending their work shifts. As we turned a corner, I ran straight into someone, almost knocking him off his feet before I recognized him.

Oh shit.

Lord Alaric grunted as he stumbled backward. "What in all five hells—" His face twisted from anger to open surprise. "Lady Maeve?"

The man he'd been talking with slipped into the shadows right as I noticed him. I got the vague impression that he was male from his height, and he had short, light hair. He wore dark clothing. It could have been a Guardian's uniform, but I wasn't sure.

"Lady Maeve! What are you doing in the Lower City?" Alaric's voice held an accusing tone, and he craned his head past me as if expecting a troupe of guards to be in tow.

I froze, unable to come up with a good excuse.

Atticus stepped in smoothly. "Lord Silas thought it best if she remained hidden given the recent attack on her person."

"Yes, that's what happened. I'm supposed to stay hidden."

"Then what are you doing on the streets, at nightfall no less? And with only this Traiten to guard you? No, no, this won't do. Traiten, take Lady Maeve back to the Council Centre. She'll be much safer where we can protect her."

"But I'm supposed to stay here. Silas wants—"

"I will accompany you back myself," Alaric interrupted. He gave Atticus an impatient glare. "Traiten?"

Silas had removed the Traiten compulsion, but Atticus snapped to attention as if the bands were still on him and put his hand on my shoulder. I thanked my lucky stars that regular Aeternals couldn't see the magic sigils that were no longer around his wrists. "My lady, if you'll come with me? We'll return directly."

Damn it. I had no choice but to go back to the Council Centre. I'd just blown the little freedom I had. I gritted my teeth and allowed them to lead me back to my prison.

The three of us traveled quickly in relative silence to the nearest set of ports. Alaric guided us to the base of the mountain and up the ridiculously long stairs before returning me to my rooms. He instructed Atticus to wait outside then joined me—without an invitation—inside my suite.

"Have you considered my proposal?" he asked as we stood awkwardly inside the first room.

It took me a minute to recall what he was talking about. "You want me to transfer my powers to you?"

He inclined his head graciously. "For the good of our citizens."

I just barely refrained from rolling my eyes. "Right. The thing is, I don't know how to do that."

His gaze narrowed. "Think carefully before you turn me down. I am a powerful ally and an even more dangerous enemy."

"I already told you I'm happy to cooperate. But I inherited this magic from someone else, and I don't know how to do anything with it." Inspiration struck, and I added, "Is there anyone who can teach me?"

He wrinkled his nose. "Our knowledge on this subject is somewhat limited."

I smiled sweetly at him, pleased with my stalling tactic. "If you can find someone to teach me, I'm willing to try."

He pursed his lips. I got the distinct impression that he wasn't fooled by my stalling. "Very well. I will make inquiries. But when I find the proper tutor, you will attempt the transfer?"

"If I transfer the power to you, I can go back to my old life? No strings attached?"

He smiled, but it wasn't friendly. "That is our agreement."

"Then you have a deal."

"My lady." Alaric bowed as he activated the doorway. "I'll take my leave of you and bid you God's eve. I have a few things I wish to discuss with the Lord Commander about safety protocols."

Out in the hall, Atticus grimaced at that last statement just before Alaric whirled on his heel and left. The doorway rematerialized behind him, locking me once more inside the suite. I wandered back to the middle room and found a tray of completely unappetizing vegetables and a decanter of warm till waiting on the large circular table.

I plopped into one of the high-backed chairs and released a heavy sigh. I'd ruined my hiding spot by running into Alaric, and Silas would definitely hear about it. I should've been worried about that, but I couldn't muster up the energy. Alaric had agreed to find someone who could teach me, which was a long shot, but it bought me at least a few days before he decided to force the Transference ritual. All in all, I'd done fine.

As my anxiety settled, I realized I had never asked Alaric why he was in the Lower City or who he was meeting with. He'd been surprised to see me there, so he hadn't been out searching for me. I had no idea if it was normal for a Councilor to be out in Lower Aeterna at night, but his reaction had seemed suspicious, as had the mysterious man who'd disappeared so quickly.

I remembered Alaric glowing with energy at the Exposition just before the Rakken attacked. Given the history between him and Silas—and how Silas had used me to embarrass Alaric in front of the Council—I definitely couldn't trust Alaric to be on my side. Not even if I fulfilled my end of the deal and figured out how to give him Marcel's powers.

I made my way over to the bathroom, showered, and changed clothes. At least the day hadn't been a total loss since I'd found an important lead to the Brotherhood. Just when I'd settled back into the front room with my tangled thoughts, the door chimed.

Silas stormed into the room. His jaw was clenched, and his face was flushed with anger. He wore loose linen pants and a sleeveless tunic that left his broad chest mostly exposed. The striking blue color perfectly set off his steel-gray eyes and olive complexion.

"What the fratching hells were you doing out in the Lower City?" he demanded.

I blinked and tried to ignore the way his sculpted body lit flames inside me. He looked like a Greek god, one that was currently very, very angry with me.

Atticus trailed him in, and judging by the color on his cheeks, he'd already received his own chewing out.

"Don't I get a hello? Or a 'Hey—kick-ass job taking out those Rakken. Glad you're still alive'?"

Atticus grimaced.

I had no idea why I insisted on infuriating Silas every chance I got. It was like a mental illness.

Silas's glower got hotter. "First, you publicly challenge me in front of all of Aeterna, making yourself quite possibly the most recognizable person in the entire realm. Then you traipse around the Lower City, practically begging the Brotherhood to kill you. It's a fratching miracle you're still alive!" His voice rose as his anger grew. "You were supposed to be *hiding*. Can you not stay out of trouble for one gods-damned day?"

I was tempted to point out that I'd been in disguise but wisely decided Silas wouldn't react well to that observation. And considering Alaric had recognized me immediately, Silas might have a small point about getting myself into trouble. But it had been worth it.

"I took a calculated risk." There. That sounded appropriately tactical. "And it paid off. We found out when the Brotherhood's next recruiting meeting is."

Silas's glare didn't relax even a fraction. "When?"

"Two days," Atticus offered behind him. "We know the location as well."

"That is... something," he said begrudgingly.

I continued, encouraged. "And Atticus knows a way to figure out who the rest of the recruits are. We just need access to the Council's records."

Atticus shared his theory about comparing resource allocations for each House to their headcount. We just needed Silas's access to get their names from the Council's database. By the time Atticus had finished, Silas's angry stance had unclenched a little.

Silas's magic flared, and a console appeared in his hand. He tapped on it for a minute before he shared the bad news. "The records are restricted."

"Even to Councilors?" I asked.

"Yes. I convinced Elias there might be a traitor on the Council, but I didn't realize he'd restrict *all* the records. He's the only one with full access. It's just as well until we figure out how the Brotherhood are getting their new recruits out of Aeterna."

"Then we need Elias to get the information?" Atticus confirmed.

"Wait," I said. "What makes you think Elias *isn't* the traitor?"

Silas shook his head. "The two positions—Leader of the Aeternal Council and Leader of the Rebellion—are completely at odds. Why would he be one if he is already the other?"

"I don't know," I mused. "But I don't trust any of them. Elias is a slippery snake who clearly has his own agenda. Lady Octavia threatened to sacrifice me for the cause. She sounded a lot like the people we met today in Lower Aeterna, actually. And don't forget Alaric. I have no idea where his politics land him, but he hates me on principle. And he's been acting really suspicious."

I told them about Alaric's flare of magic just before the attack at the Expo, the man I saw Alaric meeting with in the Lower City, and finally his offer to take Marcel's magic off my hands in return for my freedom. I also brought Silas up to speed on the way the Brotherhood had used Atticus's sentence as fuel for a rebellion. "We can't trust anyone, even Elias," I concluded.

"Agreed," Silas said. "This information, as well as the search for Atticus's attacker, needs to stay only with those we trust. I have a few I trust within the Guardians—as well as Corin, Tessa, and Stephan. No one else until we figure out how it's all tied together."

"It's too bad we don't have a way to access those records," Atticus said as his shoulders slumped.

An idea hit me, but Silas really, really wasn't going to like it.

I cleared my throat. "I still have my date with Elias..."

"Come again?" Silas asked.

"I sorta agreed to have dinner with Elias. Tonight, at his private residence." Both men twitched, and I rushed to point out all the benefits of my plan before they got a chance to shoot it down. "If you show me what I need to do, I could access his console and get us that information without involving anyone else. Elias will never know."

"No," Silas said.

"I'm not sure that's entirely wise," Atticus said at the same time.

They had matching expressions of male concern. It was pretty easy to read the cause between the lines.

"I'm not going to let him seduce me. I'm not stupid."

Silas literally rolled his eyes. "Your poor judgment aside, he is very much going to seduce you. He'll do whatever he can to learn your true identity."

Because according to Silas, there was no other reason to want to sleep with me. "Unless you're offering to step up to the plate, *you* don't get to be annoyed every time someone else wants to have sex with me." The words just came out before I could stop them. My brain couldn't move faster than my mouth when he was around. It was definitely a disorder of some kind.

"Being annoyed at your sexual escapades is apparently a full-time occupation," Silas griped back.

"For the last time, Silas, I didn't have sex with Atticus! And you have no say in who I *do* sleep with."

Both men shifted uncomfortably, avoiding eye contact.

Okay, maybe I'd overreacted a tiny bit, but I didn't appreciate his commentary. If he wanted to be involved in my sex life, I'd already given him an embarrassingly obvious invitation. I'd made it pretty damn clear how I felt, and he was the one pushing me away. He didn't get to have opinions from the sidelines.

I took a deep breath and tried to be logical. "There's nothing to be worried about. I'll go on this date, find a way to spend some alone time with Elias's personal console, and get our list of potential defectors."

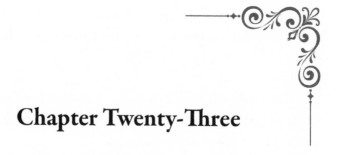

Chapter Twenty-Three

ater that evening, Elias's servant arrived and took me to Elias's
suite at the City Centre instead of his personal residence.
When I realized where she was taking me, I almost backed out right
then. Silas's intel had been about locating the consoles at House
Marius, including the layout of the rooms. I'd planned to use the re-
stroom adjacent to the study as an excuse to slip in and get what I
needed. Silas had even given me a small device that had been preprogrammed to find and transfer the right records from Elias's console.

Now I had no idea if any of that would work. I didn't even
know if Elias kept a console at his suites in the Council Centre. But
I couldn't just give up. I had to try, even if that meant I had to go in
completely unprepared.

I smoothed down the fitted, knee-length tunic with damp
palms as I followed the servant—surrounded by my handful of
guards—across what seemed like the entire length of the Council
Centre to Elias's suites.

Elias's personal quarters were huge, at least five times the size of
the space they'd put me in. Floor-to-ceiling windows made up the
entire city-facing wall. I took in the amazing view as Elias poured
us glasses of till.

"I never tire of the view," he said, handing me a fluted crystal
goblet.

He wore a loose shirt and linen pants in an olive-green color that complemented his complexion and set off his brown eyes. The man was handsome, powerful, manipulative, and knew how to dress in style. I was so far out of my depth, it wasn't even funny.

"I guess being Lord Councilor has its perks."

He chuckled softly. "Some. Although I must admit I don't spend much time here. I prefer the comforts of House Marius."

"Oh? Work doesn't keep you here late very often?" I took another glance around, hoping to see a console lying out somewhere. No such luck.

He sighed. "Only when my duties keep me, like this evening."

I gestured to the various buildings built out from the cliff face. "Is your house up there somewhere?"

He took the opportunity to position himself behind me and adjust my pointing hand. "Yes, just there," he said in my ear. His hand trailed along my bare arm.

I took a sip of till and moved to set it on the nearest surface, creating distance between us. I needed to avoid sexual tension at all costs. And I needed a reason to explore and find one of his consoles with access to the database. "Would you give me a tour of your suites?"

His brow crinkled in amused confusion. "A tour?"

"Oh, is that not a thing here? In Earth, people show each other their homes. It's a way to get to know someone on a date. I can see how you live your life, the things you treasure, what you do in your spare time."

He unleashed the full wattage of his celebrity smile. "It would be my pleasure."

He offered me his arm, and I curled my hand around his bicep while he led me through the open living space, pointing out art and items he'd collected. Along the way, he maneuvered his arm around my waist, stroking my bare shoulders at times with his free hand, and keeping his body close to mine.

There were no consoles or work stations in sight.

We moved through the various rooms including a formal dining room, a sitting room, a well-equipped exercise room, and a small art gallery, until finally he led me through a hallway lined with closed doors. "These are the bedrooms—"

"What about an office?" I hoped the edge of panic didn't show in my voice. "You must do so much, leading the Council. I'd love to see where you work."

He frowned. "I have a separate office located near the Council's chambers."

Damn it. The whole night would be a waste if I couldn't get my hands on a nonrestricted console. "I thought someone as important as you would be working all the time." *God, I was laying it on thick.* "Don't you have a space where you work here?"

He smiled, apparently pleased at the compliment, and opened one of the doors. "This is my personal library."

The room was lined with bookshelves, and just like the other rooms on this side of the suite, it had an entire wall of windows. A cushioned bench ran the entire length of the wall, complete with pillows. The three other walls were lined with built-in bookshelves, and in each corner sat a pair of comfortable armchairs. In the center of the room sat an impressively large wooden desk.

Various papers, files, and other items lay across the top of the desk. A small, portable console sat on top of a stack of papers. *Bingo.* My fingers itched to pick it up and run, but I forced myself to casually scan the bookshelves nearby. I ran my fingers along a row of book spines. "Wow, there must be thousands of books in here."

He hummed as he came up behind me, and his hand glided over my hip. "You like books?" His voice was low and seductive.

"It's an impressive collection." I twisted free of his wandering hands and used the motion to reach inside my bra and palm the electronic storage device Silas had given me. I flashed him the flirtiest expression I could muster as I made my way around to the desk and scanned the surface. "So, this is where you work."

He came up behind me again, trapping me between him and the desk.

Holding my fingertip over the device, I activated the preprogrammed transfer function. I twisted around in Elias's arms and plastered a smile on my face. His hands traveled to the sides of my neck, stroking the sensitive skin as he pressed closer to me.

"Have you learned enough about me?" His eyes lowered to my lips. "Is my nest feathered enough to impress the lady bird?"

I forced the smile to stay on my face. "It's all very impressive."

He pushed closer, forcing me to sit back on the desk. My hand landed on top of the console, and the file transfer device vibrated slightly under my palm as it connected.

The console's screen lit up, and Elias glanced down at it.

Shit. I stretched up and kissed him.

Elias kissed me back, pushing himself between my legs and forcing them around his hips.

The transfer device was supposed to vibrate a second time when it finished. Silas said it would take only a few minutes. But with Elias's hands and mouth all over me, a few minutes seemed like an eternity.

His hand smoothly brushed the hair off my shoulders and gripped the back of my neck. The other hand pulled me closer. He tilted my head, and his lips moved over mine.

I had to admit, he was a damn fine kisser. Any female with a pulse would find him attractive and sexually magnetic. The kiss distracted me enough that I didn't notice his free hand until it slipped inside the neckline of my tunic and fondled my breast.

The device vibrated under my hand, and I jerked back with a small gasp. "You said something about dinner?"

His expression was amused and slightly irritated. "Am I making you uncomfortable?"

"No. It's just that you *did* promise me dinner on this date, and I'm hoping you're a man of your word."

"So I did." To my utter relief, Elias pulled back and held out his hand.

No doubt he was confident in his ability to get me into his bed after feeding me, but I would deal with that problem when we got there. I discreetly adjusted my clothing, using the motion to slip the device back inside my bra as he led me to the dining room.

We ate a meal full of foreign, although high-quality and not altogether unpleasant, food while Elias lobbed insinuations at me. I did my best to gracefully dodge them without being rude. He also had a fair number of questions about my background, my family, and my knowledge of magic. I answered those questions honestly. There was nothing to hide about my true background or identity. If I could get Elias to believe that I was just a nobody Mundane before all of this had happened, I would have a powerful ally on my side. And I needed one because I was quickly racking up enemies. I hadn't forgotten the Council would be perfectly willing to sacrifice my life in order to get at Marcel's magic.

After the meal ended and servants had cleared the table, Elias offered me another glass of bubbly till and a seat on a comfortable settee in the adjacent sitting room. A roaring fireplace dominated one wall of the cozy room. I wasn't sure if it was real fire or magic, but the crackling warmth created quite the romantic setting.

He sat on the small couch, his thigh touching mine from knee to hip, and gathered my free hand in his. "I've quite enjoyed getting to know you, Lady Maeve. Your company is so refreshing."

"Really? I've never had anyone say *that* before."

His eyes crinkled with humor. "You say what is on your mind without intrigue or insinuation. It's been ages since I had a conversation without at least two subtexts to work through simultaneously."

"I'm glad you feel that way," I said, truly relieved. "I'm not very good at all your politics."

"I've noticed." He laughed, and his fingers skimmed deliberately along the outside of my thigh. "You are truly a pleasure." He took the glass from my hand and set it on the table nearest us. "Speaking of pleasure..." He lowered his head to my neck and ran his lips lightly over the skin just below my ear.

For a hot minute, I was tempted to just go with it. Sex with Elias would—no doubt—be enjoyable. He was skilled at this game of seduction, and if his kissing were any indication, he would be great in bed. My pent-up sexual tension could definitely use a release. It would be a great distraction from everything.

And that was the problem. I was emotionally aware enough to know that sex with Elias wouldn't be just a pleasurable distraction. It would be about politics and the possibility of gaining a powerful ally. But more importantly, it would be about getting over my hurt feelings about Silas.

I leaned back with a sigh. "I'm sorry, Elias, but I'm not going to have sex with you tonight."

"Are you not pleased with my attentions?" He shifted, hovering over me. I had to lean back into the sofa to keep some space between us. "I believe I've been pretty transparent about my desires, but yours—I must admit—are a mystery."

A shiver of fear ran down my spine. He was bigger and stronger than me, and we were alone in his private quarters. Even if I screamed, I suspected the servants I'd seen throughout the evening wouldn't come running. I might be out of options if he didn't back down.

"Your, uh, *attention* is tempting. But it's all a little fast. For an Earthen, I mean. Sex on the first date is considered... trashy."

"Really?" His head tilted to the side. "Trashy. What an interesting word. It has such a depth of meaning. Well, *my lady*, I would not want you to be construed as trashy when you are so clearly anything but." He stood and offered me his hand.

I almost sighed in relief as I rose to my feet with as much grace as the Queen of England. "Thank you for a lovely dinner."

After an exchange of pleasantries that included lots of hints about future liaisons, Elias had a servant escort me back to my suite, accompanied of course by my personal gaggle of Guardians.

When I was safely deposited back into my suite, I wasn't surprised to find Silas waiting for me.

He looked me up and down, and I didn't like the way his gaze lingered on my hair and neck. I patted both self-consciously, wondering if it looked as though I'd made out with Elias. I dropped my hands and decided it didn't matter what Silas thought. He didn't get a vote.

And the new set of tingles his presence caused needed to shut the hell up.

"Here." I held out the transfer device, but he didn't move to take it.

"Did you—"

I glared at him. If he asked if I had sex with Elias, there was no force in either of our realms that would stop me from slapping him.

He cleared his throat. "Did he harm you?"

"No." I tossed the device at Silas, and he caught it with one hand. "I had a perfectly enjoyable evening, and now I want to go to bed."

One of his damn eyebrows rose.

"Alone." I walked past Silas and into the bedroom. I didn't stop until I'd reached the bathroom door and sealed it shut behind me.

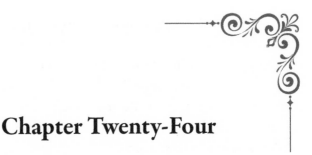

Chapter Twenty-Four

The next morning, Tessa showed up unexpectedly at my suite. Her previously short hair fell past her shoulders in a soft brown wave that covered her pointed Fae ears.

I stared at it in confusion. "What happened to your hair?"

"Silas asked me to track down the missing people on your list, so I'm blending in. Short hair is for Guardians." She brushed a hand through it. "Combat and all that."

I examined her new locks. "Is it a wig?"

She laughed. "No, I did a simple conjuring to lengthen hair. And I've changed my eye color as well." She blinked at me with baby-blue irises.

"Oh," I said like an idiot.

Dressed in a basic green tunic and leggings, she looked like any other person in Lower Aeterna. Without her lavender eyes and short hair, no one would recognize her as the Fae Guardian who'd won the tournament just yesterday.

I invited her in, and she clasped forearms with Atticus before the three of us sat in the front room together.

"Silas told me about the compulsion," Tessa said to Atticus. "I'm pleased to learn of your redemption. I hated seeing you as a Traiten, even when I believed you were guilty."

"Congratulations on your promotion, Commander. Your win was well fought."

"Wait, did you guys know each other before?" I asked.

"We trained to become Guardians together."

I toyed with the long necklace attacked to Marcel's charm as I remembered my earlier suspicions about Silas and Titus knowing each other. "Did you know Titus too? I don't know his family name. He's the leader of the Brotherhood."

They both shifted on their feet and had lots of places they needed to look all of a sudden.

"Look, I know Silas knows him, and it seemed personal."

Atticus finally looked at me. "He was a Guardian."

"Atticus!" Tessa said with a hiss.

"She's just going to go around asking questions if we don't tell her what she wants to know."

"That's right. I won't ask questions if I already have the answers." I put on my best Girl Scout smile and tried to appear trustworthy and innocent. I would've offered them cookies if I thought it would help.

"Titus Trivalent," Tessa said finally. "House Trivalent was solidly lower class before gaining enough power to demand entrance into the Upper City, roles within the Sects, all of it. Social standing here is multi-generational. That kind of change in a single generation is notable. It made them famous all over Lower Aeterna. Then came Titus with a strong flare and a cruel streak. He joined the Guardian training program the same year as us."

Atticus picked up her story. "He got a reputation for fighting dirty. He hurt people unnecessarily. Killed another trainee during a practice exercise. They tried to kick him out, but his House claimed discrimination."

"It went all the way to the Council," Tessa said. "Silas was the ranking witness at the incident, and he testified against him. Titus was lucky he wasn't required to offer a penance."

"What's a penance?" I asked.

Atticus whistled between his teeth. "It's something you offer when—What's the Earthen saying? When the shit hits the fan?"

I laughed and held out my fist. "Five points for correct use of Earthen swearing."

He bumped my fist.

"Owing a blood debt to another House can be manky shite." His lip curled. "Too bad in hindsight, actually."

"They definitely didn't run him to the post with nothing more than an expulsion from the training program," Tessa agreed.

"So, Titus is leading the Brotherhood, but the Council is trying to keep it quiet," I summarized. "And from what I saw yesterday, half of Aeterna is probably tripping over themselves for a chance to join them."

Tessa and Atticus gave me matching looks of surprise.

"What? They have no other options. They can serve the Upper Houses for the rest of their lives without any hope of improving their situation or take option B—join the Brotherhood for a better life."

"We're not supposed to talk about any of that," Tessa said slowly.

"It's an open secret, though," Atticus said to her. "Titus, the Brotherhood, the unrest in the Lower City—it's a pot about to boil over."

"Why not just reveal what Titus is up to?" I asked. "He's killing people and absorbing their powers. No one would follow that monster."

"It's tricky," Tessa said. "In the Lower City, Titus is a hero, a true rags-to-riches story. The Council is afraid if the citizens discover his role in the rebellion, people might follow him, regardless of his actions."

We all chewed that over until Tessa said, "I almost forgot! I come bearing gifts." Her blue-gray magic flared, and she produced

Ripper along with some kind of intricate new sheath with two long straps. "It's a thigh holster," she explained. "Your knife is a bit large for concealment, but Silas said you're attached to it." She frowned as though she couldn't figure out why.

A small thrill of excitement coursed through me. Getting Ripper back was like having a little piece of me returned. I threaded the leather straps through the custom-modified holster and secured it around my upper thigh. I rose and went through a few experimental movements. The holster seemed to work well, despite holding a larger-than-normal knife.

Tessa's face sobered. "Also, I came with a message from Lord Stephan." Her eyes swept over me. I had the feeling she was about to deliver bad news, and my own eyes narrowed in response. "He apologizes that he couldn't deliver it in person."

My whole body went stiff, and I dropped back into my chair.

"Your friend Michael Smithson never made it to Aeterna," she revealed. "We can't find him."

My heart thudded with growing fear. There was only one reason Father Mike wouldn't have returned to Aeterna to find me like he'd promised—he'd been captured by the Brotherhood. He might already be dead.

Tessa leaned forward and put her hand on my knee. "Silas already sent Guardians to search for him back in Boston."

"I led the Brotherhood right to him!" Until now, I'd been doing a good job of holding it together, but this was too much. "They'll torture him and kill him, just like they did to Marcel! What if Titus already killed him?" I dropped my head into my hands as tears flooded my eyes.

"We don't know that your friend is dead," Atticus said softly, placing his palm on my shoulder.

"The Brotherhood has him. That's why there's no sign of him. If he's still alive, it's so they can torture him for information." Guilt twisted in my stomach. I had no doubt what Titus would do to him—I'd lived through Marcel's memories. "I should have killed Titus when I had the chance." Conviction washed over me. "I'm going to kill him."

My anguish compressed into something solid. Titus would pay for taking Father Mike. He would pay for Marcel. And he would pay for ruining my perfectly normal life. I would do whatever it took to take down the Brotherhood, starting with him.

Tessa gave me an unexpected hug. "I'm sorry I must leave you with this news. I must return to the Lower City during the changing of the next shift if I'm to blend in."

"Before you go, is there anyone on your list named Marcel?" I asked.

She pursed her lips. "Who is Marcel?"

"He's the man who transferred the power from the Brotherhood to me." *The man whose memories are always on the verge of taking control of my mind.* "Other than that, I have no idea who he was."

"We'll find something," she said with an encouraging grin. "This is a good lead, Maeve. We're doing all the right things. It just takes time."

The knot in my stomach twisted. "Let me know what you find out about Father Mike."

She agreed and left. Atticus wrapped his arm around my shoulder and pulled me into his side. I stiffened at the unfamiliar affection, but he patted my shoulder until I relaxed. The moment of comfort brought on a fresh round of tears. I was so exhausted and emotionally wrung-out. It was nice to have a minute to acknowledge how hard everything was.

After a minute of my tears soaking his shoulder, he said, "Silas will find your friend."

I sat up, wiping my eyes on my sleeve. Even if Father Mike were alive, I had no idea how Silas would be able to find him. Silas and the Council had been trying to track down Titus for so long. My hopes plummeted.

Atticus lowered his head until we were eye level. "If you give up on hope, what do you have left? Be strong, Maeve."

That was almost exactly what Father Mike had said to me when we parted in Boston. I managed a watery smile. I would be strong for Father Mike.

Atticus and I ate breakfast together, and he talked me through a few more basic exercises with my magic. I wasn't making much progress, but I was still determined to learn how to defend myself. The magic was so far away, and it was hard to access it on demand. Just as we finished our lesson and our meal, the door chimed again. I'd ceased being surprised by all my visitors until I saw who walked through.

Lady Aria paused inside the open doorway. Dressed in a golden top with fluttering sleeves, the expertly draped fabric hid any sign of her pregnancy. A delicately pleated skirt skimmed the floor, and her blond hair fell in elaborate braids down her back. She looked just like a freaking fairy princess. It wasn't fair for any one person to be that beautiful. Even knowing she was in love with Stephan, I felt a twinge of insecurity.

"Lady Maeve?" Her voice rose, uncertain.

Atticus moved discreetly to the side, out of her line of sight. I tried to act casual as I rose to greet her, but I had no idea what she wanted or how she felt about me. When it came down to it, I was a threat to her secret life. She had just as many reasons to hate me as her father.

"Lady Aria." I tried to keep the nerves out of my voice.

Her eyes raked from my head to my feet.

I braced myself.

"I am pleased to see you," she said sweetly. "I'd like to show you around the City Centre on market day. Perhaps some shopping?"

"What? Why?" I cringed at my own harsh tone and softened my voice. "I mean, I'm not allowed to leave. I'm a prisoner of the Council."

"Nonsense. I received express permission from my father. If we're properly escorted"—she glanced over her shoulder to a knot of Guardians waiting in the hall—"we may travel within the Upper City freely."

My brain churned with anxiety. For all I knew, she was planning to stab me as soon as she got me alone. I stared at her, unable to get past her shocking presence. She locked gazes with me and pushed her shoulders back a fraction, lifting her chin as though steeling herself. She was nervous too.

"Would you please join me?" she asked.

It was the first time anyone from this realm had ever said please. I'd seriously thought it was a word that didn't exist in Aeterna.

I nodded despite myself. "Okay."

"Lady Maeve," Atticus interjected, "you should check with the Lord Commander first."

Aria's shoulders straightened. "I have my personal guard with me. She will be safe."

"Lord Valeron wishes her to remain here," Atticus said with a frown.

Aria's unexpected backbone impressed me. But I also wasn't going to be foolish and run off without letting anyone know where I was going. "Traiten, please inform the Lord Commander of where we've gone and that he doesn't need to be worried about us."

Aria nodded in approval, and Atticus bowed his head, not quite concealing his grimace of disapproval.

Two sleek silver pods hovered outside, ready to transport us. Three large men in fitted Guardian uniforms stood at attention until we were safely seated inside.

As soon as our butts touched down, she said, "I want to talk to you about what Silas said at the Exposition."

I tried not to grimace. She sure didn't waste any time.

"Silas made it clear that your family is none of my business," I said.

"He has feelings for you."

I let out a harsh laugh. This was just too much. He'd made it clear that I only complicated his life. One minute, he was hot; and the next, cold. He knotted up my insides. And talking about it with his pregnant wife—*bond-mate, whatever*—was not a good idea.

"I'd like to know if you feel the same for him."

"Nothing is happening between us. We're not even on speaking terms."

"Why not?" she asked softly.

Mentally, I'd been prepared for her to confront me about Silas and tell me to back off. Reassuring her would be easy because I didn't want to be tangled up in their mess. There were so many reasons Silas and I were not going to happen. But this was not what I had expected at all.

"Besides the obvious?" I waved my hand at her perfect face, her immaculate clothing, and her belly, then I sighed. "To start with, we disagree whether I should do whatever he says without question." I frowned, realizing he acted like that because everyone around him actually did do whatever he said. *Damn, what a head trip.*

"You're both strong-minded," she corrected.

"We drive each other crazy."

"He took you under his personal protection and became your Aegis. That's... unheard of."

"The bond thing? He did that to manipulate me."

She shook her head. "Giving you his sigil was an act of trust. You have access to his familial source and are tied to him directly. He's personally responsible for your actions and your safety."

"Why are you defending him?" I huffed. "Your father almost had kittens when he found out Silas gave the Valeron sigil to me."

"My father used the Fate's prophecy as leverage to push Silas into the bonding. Consequently, Silas drew his boundary at sharing the Valeron power source with me. They'll never see eye to eye on it, but I understand why he's acted as he has."

"Silas is stubborn," I argued.

"He is. But he has shown me, and Stephan, incredible kindness." She cradled her stomach again, reminding me of everything she had to lose.

"What do you want from me?" I finally demanded. I couldn't wrap my brain around what she meant by this strange pep talk. Stephan had also been pushing me at Silas, and I just didn't get it. They had nothing to gain from my interference in their lives. Plus, Silas didn't want me involved in his life. He'd made that very clear.

"Silas and I tried to find a suitable way to make our arrangement work. Eventually, he spent his time away from Aeterna, doing the Council's bidding, and I lived my life here." Aria's hands twisted in her lap, and her eyes lowered. "I didn't intend to fall in love with Stephan. I know how despicable I must seem."

The pod shot straight up like an elevator, and my stomach dropped. I didn't know the details of everything that had happened between the three of them, but she was just as stuck as the rest of them and trying to make the best of a bad situation.

I squeezed the bridge of my nose. "It isn't my place to judge you."

"Silas has sacrificed everything. I won't let him sacrifice his own happiness." Her mouth narrowed into a determined line. "And *you* make him happy."

I snorted. Mostly, I pissed him off. A lot. And he'd told me very clearly that he didn't want a relationship with me. But her words made me wonder. Silas had played the role of protector for so long, I wondered if he was still trying to protect his family by denying himself anything that would further complicate their already impossible situation. That might explain the roller coaster of emotions he'd put me through. And possibly, despite everything, he had the same confused feelings I did. "What are you saying exactly?"

"I'm asking you not to give up on him."

"I already screwed up your plans once. Wouldn't this put you all at greater risk? What if Alaric found out?"

"It is a risk. My father could disinherit me and enact sanctions against House Valeron." Her gentle, refined features tightened. "But it's also the right thing to do. I have found my happiness, and Silas deserves his as well."

The pod slid to a stop, but she made no move to get out.

"I'll think about what you said," I told her, careful not to promise anything. I had a lot to think about. I couldn't believe Silas's wife—or whatever she was—had asked me to be in a relationship with him. It wasn't a traditional marriage, and obviously, she was in love with Stephan, but this was all too crazy to believe.

She placed her hand on mine. "That's all I'm asking." The door opened, and she slid gracefully from the pod, while I scrambled after her.

The guards flanked us as I emerged into the bright Aeternal sun and took in the crazy bustle of the City Centre on market day. We were in the circular courtyard of the central portal, directly above the streets of Lower Aeterna. It was a world of difference. Well-dressed men and women strolled the streets, leisurely examining the goods of the market.

Dozens of merchants lined the open space. Among the familiar sights and smells of a street market, I saw just as much unknown magic and technology. Tele-nets hung between the booths, advertising their goods. The vendors toward the center had their own ports, which must've linked back to their permanent shops. Servants bustled through them, carrying baskets of inventory.

"I understand you did not bring any clothing of your own from Earth," Aria said. "Men never think of such things. May I take you to my tailor? It's the official reason for our trip this day."

I examined my own clothing. I'd changed into a pair of wide-legged pants and a long tunic to cover the new thigh holster holding Ripper. It was quite baggy, and the colors didn't match. Next to Aria, I was pretty much a hot mess.

"Could your tailor make me some long tunics with slits up to about here?" I held my hand at my hip. "And some matching leggings?" Now that I had the thigh holster, I could wear it over the tighter-fitting pants, and the slit would still allow easy access.

Aria inclined her head and looped her arm through mine. I let her lead me, trying not to be jealous of her innate elegance. Everything about her was ridiculously graceful.

As we walked arm in arm, a child ran right into my legs. The little boy gazed up at me with big brown eyes. He couldn't have been more than five or six.

He held out a necklace. "This is for you." At the end of a long, braided cord hung a round pendant the size of a golf ball. I took it and examined the intricate carvings on the piece. Something about the design pulled at my memory.

"What is this?" I asked, but the boy had already run off.

The pendant flared with magic.

"Drop it!" Aria yelled.

Pressure sucked at the air. My insides wrenched a moment before everything disappeared.

I landed in a new location, clutching my stomach with one hand and the pendant with the other while my body tried to reorient itself.

Titus sneered down at me. "Hello, kitten."

Chapter Twenty-Five

Titus backhanded me. Pain exploded across my face, and I fell onto the floor.

Rough hands lifted me again. Blood dripped from my mouth, which throbbed in time with the pounding in my ears. Two men zip-tied my wrists and ankles to a chair as I tried to clear my vision.

I'd been pulled—skimmed—from the courtyard to a nondescript room. Another chair sat on the opposite side of the room, facing me. My stomach sank. "Aria!"

Aria was bound to her own chair, and her terrified gaze was locked on me. I groaned, realizing the spell that had pulled me there had swept up Aria with it. I had been beyond stupid for accepting the pendant on the street.

Four generic white walls, a door, and several people were in the small room. I saw no windows. Other than the vague impression that we were in a house, I had no idea where we were.

I reached for my magic but felt nothing. That was when I noticed a new pendant around my neck. Marcel's memories flashed over me along with a swell of panic. Titus had used the same pendant to block his magic before he'd tortured and killed him.

Aria whimpered, "Maeve!"

My head was still spinning, but I noted the same pendant hanging around her neck.

"Silence her," Titus commanded.

The shorter man, a stocky brunette, stuffed a cloth in Aria's mouth and slapped a piece of silver duct tape on top. Aria's eyes were wide with panic.

"Get the others ready. Quickly," Titus ordered.

The man rushed out of the room. We were left with Titus and the last of his minions, a lanky man with an obnoxious smirk.

Titus held Marcel's charm in one hand and twirled Ripper with the other.

My heart hammered wildly, sending my head spinning.

"I'm asking nicely just this once. Tell me where your people are," Titus said.

"That wasn't a question," I replied automatically. My mind spun furiously. Titus believed me to be part of the Lost Sect, and I didn't know how to convince him otherwise.

Titus's minion smashed his fist into my face.

My head jerked to the side, and pain exploded along my cheekbone. Fire flamed along the entire left side of my face.

Aria screamed behind her gag.

Titus grabbed my face. My vision swam, and my whole world was pain. Someone had stuffed straw in my head. No, something sharper—needles. Needles were stabbing my brain.

"You can tell me, or I can let Remus loose on you." He jerked his head at the other man. "He likes to get creative."

"I'm going to kill you," I warned Titus. I tried to turn the pain into a glare. But every jagged breath stabbed like shards of glass in my head. With my hands bound and blood dripping out of my mouth, I was as threatening as a stuffed bunny.

Titus stepped back, and Remus smirked as he stepped into view again.

My new friend Remus hit me in the stomach. Another blow landed, and I doubled over the pain, gasping and choking. *Air. I need air.*

Someone cried out. I didn't know if it was me or Aria.

"Stop!" I gasped. "I'll... tell you everything I know."

The blows paused, and I struggled for breath. My brain wouldn't move fast enough. Titus kept asking questions I didn't have answers to. But I would've said anything to make the pain stop.

Remus's smile lit up his eyes.

Disgusted anger grew thick in my chest. The sick bastard was enjoying this. I needed to stall until I had a plan, but I had no way to answer Titus's questions. I tried the truth one more time. "I'm not part of the Lost Sect."

"Tell me how to find them." Titus's eyes lit with what I could only describe as manic fervor. "Tell me now!"

Remus backhanded me on the other side of my face. The force wrenched my head to the side. My vision blurred, and I couldn't see out of my right eye anymore. It wouldn't open. Moaning, I let my head flop on my neck. Everything hurt. I had to find a way to make them stop. I needed a plan before they beat me to death. I needed *time.*

I took a deep breath and carefully raised my head. It hurt like hell. My words slurred with pain. "Before I tell you anything, you have to release Father Mike."

"Who is Father Mike?"

"He—you—" The pain in every part of my head made my brain move slowly. "You don't have him?"

"This Father Mike was the man sheltering you in Boston? I did not realize how much he meant to you, or we would have tried harder to kill him." Titus bared his teeth at me and shifted the nails on one of his hands into claws. He dug them into my shoulder, and I screamed. "Rest assured, after you are dead, I will find everyone you love—including this Father Mike—and I will do everything I can to make their deaths painful and slow. He can be first."

Despite the pain, a wave of relief washed over me. Father Mike was alive, and the Brotherhood didn't have him! He must have escaped and gone into hiding.

Titus released my shoulder and pulled Ripper from my thigh holster. He looked at the knife thoughtfully before he turned and held Ripper's blade to Aria's throat. "Perhaps a similar motivation would suffice?"

Pale and wide-eyed, Aria froze. She whimpered as Titus pushed the blade against her porcelain skin. A thin red line of blood dripped down her throat. Titus shifted his grip, grabbed a fistful of her long hair, and prepared to drag the blade across her neck.

Aria's nostrils flared in silent terror, her whimpers buried behind the gag. Her eyes never left mine. She was begging me to do something.

"Wait! I'll tell you where they are! Just let her go—she's pregnant!"

Titus released her with a satisfied smirk.

"You know you're a sociopath, right?" I asked as my mind raced. I had to give him something believable. But my mind was drawing a complete blank.

I tensed as Remus moved to hit me. Titus held his hand up, and Remus backed off with a disappointed grunt. Titus's eyes narrowed. He took a step back and tapped the knife hilt against his chin again.

"Why are you doing this?" I demanded. "We never did *anything* to you!"

It was apparently the right thing to say. His mouth twisted at the edges. "You have no idea what your people have done! *We* are the backbone of Aeterna, and we're done supporting *them*"—he pointed Ripper at Aria—"with our sweat and blood. It's time for our army to rise up and vindicate the martyrs of our cause!"

"Then why do you need me? You have your army!"

He snorted angrily. "As usual, Silas fratched everything up, not even realizing what he'd done. We got a small spark of discord over a Traiten instead of a martyr for our cause. But don't worry, kitten, our army grows every day. The Council's short-sighted energy rationing sees to it."

He was talking about Atticus! They had intended to kill him when they set him up, and Titus had no idea we'd discovered the compulsion that had led to Atticus's false confession.

"If you have what you need, why chase me across Earth for the tiny bit of magic Marcel stole? I'm nothing compared to your big plans."

"The magic he stole? You really don't know, do you?" Titus leaned in so close, I could see flecks of gray in his ice-blue eyes. "Your people were very clever. But you can't hide in plain sight anymore. Everything I need to know is in here." He tapped Ripper's handle on my temple.

I flinched back. "What are you talking about?"

"I'll break the binding for you—crack you open like an egg and get the location of your Sect," he said. "And when I track down the last of your people, I will control *all* their abilities and Earth's Source. Not even the Council can stop me with that kind of power."

My brow scrunched in confusion. "Why are you telling me all this?"

"You have two options, kitten. We can do the Transference, and believe me, it will be very painful for you. Or you can tell me where they are now, and I'll make your death quick."

I laughed without humor. I couldn't help it. "Has anyone ever gone for the 'your death will be quick' option? I mean seriously?"

"We're wasting time," Titus growled. "We'll have to risk the unbinding. I'll return when we're ready."

He squatted in front of Aria. "Good gods, what an unexpected gift you are, my lady. Delivering the body of Silas's mate and unborn child to him will truly be a pleasure."

He handed Remus my knife and the pendant. "The blonde is yours. Have fun."

My entire body clenched in horror as I realized what I'd done.

Remus followed Titus to the door and locked it behind him. He spun back to us, and a grin spread across his face. Circling behind Aria, he flipped her long hair with his fingers.

Her chin quivered, and her nostrils flared in sheer terror.

He licked his lips.

"Remus," I said, drawing his attention away from her. "You're a sick bastard." Nothing like insulting the creeper right out of the gate, but begging would only encourage him.

The sound of his chuckle sent shivers down my spine. "You've got quite a mouth on you."

"I think you broke my cheekbone," I grunted. I would be lucky if that was all the damage he did. The pain was threatening to push me over the edge of consciousness. I'd never been so miserable in my life. Every movement hurt, but I had to push it aside. I couldn't break now.

Remus crouched in front of Aria. She cringed as he picked up a strand of her hair between his fingers.

"Do you remember me?" he whispered.

Tears streamed down her face. She tried to speak, but the gag muffled her words.

"If we had more time, I'd work you over nice and slow." A strangled sob escaped her, and Remus laughed again. "Even though we'll be rushed, I'm still going to enjoy this." He slid his hand under her skirt, pushing the delicate fabric up her thigh.

I was helpless, tied to the chair, without magic. Memories from Marcel's last days threatened to overwhelm me. I fought them back. I couldn't afford to black out. We weren't going to die like this.

Remus's aura flared, filling the room with dark-amber energy, a shade just shy of orange and tinted to black at the edges with stolen life. He was Human and Shifter, I guessed. He used Ripper to slice into his palm then wiped the flat of the bloody knife on Aria's cheek.

She whimpered again.

"Shhh," he whispered. He drew the edge of the blade lightly down her neck to her collarbone. Crimson liquid welled from the shallow cut. His palm followed the same path, mixing their blood.

Aria trembled in her chair. Her head rocked violently back and forth until he took a fistful of her hair and held her in place.

"Remus!" I yelled, but he didn't pay any attention to me. "Wait! You don't want to do this!"

Dark energy built around him. A pattern grew out of the magic—sharp edges and intersecting angles, skewed like a spiderweb and black like death.

I reached for my magic again, mentally clawing against the magical block, but there was nothing.

Aria's whole body convulsed. She screamed behind the gag in a long, high-pitched wail of pain. Magic drained from her to Remus.

"Stop!" I yanked against my restraints. The sharp plastic dug into my skin, strong and unyielding. The chair jumped and clattered on the floor with my frantic movements as I tried to free myself.

Aria jerked in the chair, spasming and screaming as he dragged life from her.

Remus's magic burned darker.

"Stop! She's rich—her family can pay you! Remus!" My screams turned into sobs. "You're killing her!"

Aria's screaming stopped, and she slumped forward, her head dropping to her chest.

Remus stepped back, and the threads of the conjuring disappeared. "You're right," he panted. "I want her alive. I'm not done with her yet." He used Ripper to slice through the zip ties binding her wrists and ankles before pushing her unconscious body to the floor. Her head banged against the hard tile with a sickening thud.

"Aria!"

Blood was smeared along one side of her face and neck, and her skin was pale. She was so still, I couldn't tell if she was dead or alive.

Chapter Twenty-Six

Remus knelt over Aria and pushed her skirt up to her waist.

"Get away from her!" I jerked in my chair, straining against the zip ties. I couldn't let this happen. "You're not even man enough for a conscious woman? You psychotic, ugly troll!" I screamed words at him, anything to make him stop. "You're weak! Pathetic! A tiny worm with a tiny dick!"

He twisted and flicked the knife in front of my face. "When they're done with you, you'll be begging me to kill you."

Relieved and equally terrified, I spat blood in his face. Turning his anger onto me was my only weapon.

He lunged at me and grabbed me by the throat, choking me. I gagged against his grip.

"Teeny... weeny... cock," I choked out.

He released me just as suddenly as he had attacked. I heaved in air, gasping around the pain in my throat.

"You want a ride first, bitch?" He slid the knife under the neck of my tunic and ripped it open in a single violent jerk. With another flick of the knife, the fabric of my bra was severed.

His lips curled into a leer as he stared at my bare flesh.

I channeled my inner Silas and glared at him with complete disdain. "Is that it? You're going to strip me into submission?"

He backhanded me again.

My broken cheekbone crunched. Fire seared my brain, and my vision flickered black. Gasping, I focused on getting air into my lungs for several breaths.

Remus moved behind me and cut the ties at my ankles. He grabbed a fistful of my hair and yanked my head backward until I stared up at him. "I'm going to cut out your nasty tongue, but first I want to hear you scream."

Nausea and pain threatened to pull me under. I couldn't pass out.

He sliced through the ties around my wrists and yanked me to the ground by my hair. Before I could do more than flail, he kicked me in the side.

I screamed and crumpled. *Broken rib.* Tears flooded my eyes as I gasped for air. Pain radiated through my chest with every movement.

Remus crawled on top of me, pinning me on my back. Panic clawed at my chest when he pinned my arms at my sides and tore away the ripped pieces of my tunic. His hands were all over my body. He clawed and groped my exposed skin. He ripped my pants off and started on my underwear. When he reached for his zipper, I jerked one arm free, sending a searing jolt down my entire left side. Fighting through the pain, I tore the magic-blocking pendant off my neck. It clinked on the ground next to me.

He stared at it.

Magic surged through me.

Understanding lit Remus's face a second before his skin lit up from the inside. Thousands of pinpricks of energy flew from every pore of his body, obeying my call. He jerked in surprise, and a high-pitched, frantic scream tore from his lips. Writhing in pain, his body convulsed over me. His eyes bulged until I could see only the whites, before he fell to the ground. Dead.

The energy felt like a jolt of electricity straight into my blood. The power of an entire life's worth of magic flooded me with tainted energy. I rocked on the ground, frozen under the terrible weight of it.

For several minutes, every nerve ending in my body throbbed with pain. I lay there, unable to move. My stomach twisted, and all I could do was draw ragged breaths. Finally, when the wave of nausea lessened, I blinked and looked around. Aria lay ten feet away, her eyes locked on me in terror.

Careful of my bruised and broken body, I scooted slowly along the floor. I collected Marcel's charm and Ripper, both of which were lying on the ground near my tattered clothing. Flames ripped down my side as I cut away Aria's restraints, gasping for breath with each movement.

Her breathing was fast and shallow as she pulled the pendant from her neck and threw it against the wall. The gag followed. "Thank the gods," she sobbed. Her magic flared, and I was horrified to see it had gone from a strong blue to a pale, almost colorless gray.

I gasped. "Your flare."

Her eyes locked on my face and went wide. "Gods bless us! He was trying to kill us!"

"We need t'get outta here." My words slurred with agony. My jaw must've been broken. I glanced at the locked door. We could try to fight our way out and make a run for it, but I was not in any shape for that. I was still recovering from the side effects of absorbing Remus's energy, and it still burned. I could feel the power of it tainting me. Aria would've been useless in a fight, and on top of that, I didn't know where we were.

The doorknob jiggled. "Remus, playtime's over," Titus's amused voice called from the other side.

Aria's already pale face went white, completely drained of any color.

"You have to skim us," I whispered.

When Aria's fear transformed immediately into determination, I could have kissed her. She grabbed my wrist and closed her eyes. The energy bent around us like a dome, creating the shimmering outline of a skimming spell. I could see the pattern as the familiar conjuring built, but we didn't budge.

"Remus!" Titus called.

"I can't skim us both," she whispered. "I don't have enough power."

I released her hand. "Go."

"I'm not leaving you here!"

Banging sounded from the other side of the door. "Remus! Unlock the gods-damned door," Titus demanded.

"I'm right behind you," I lied. I gripped Marcel's pendant for comfort. If only I'd learned something useful with my magic. I couldn't control it for shit.

Aria shook her head frantically.

The door crashed open. Titus pushed into the room with four men flanking him. They froze in the entryway, surprised to find Aria and me huddled on the ground.

Titus lunged.

I had no idea what I did when I reached for Aria's conjuring and forced my magic into it. Connected to the magic in my moment of panic, I sensed Silas. Like a beacon in a storm, his presence radiated through me and lit the way to safety. Unbelievable pressure squeezed my brain as I shoved all the power I had taken from Remus into the layers of Aria's spell. It solidified and glowed white.

The air shifted around us, and the room disappeared.

We landed on the cold stone floor of the Council's Centre.

I gripped my head before it imploded. Too late, I remembered that no one should've been able to skim into the Council Centre. I had just used Aria's spell to force my way through some serious magic with the weight of two people. My vision swam as six shocked Council members stared down at us, plus Silas, who had risen to his feet.

Aria cried out, and everything went black.

THE FLOOR UNDER MY back was cold and hard. I stared up at an ornate ceiling of soaring arches and fancy architecture that I might have appreciated in a different life. Complex magic danced in the air. It made me dizzy. I squeezed my eyes shut, took a deep breath, and inhaled the clean, crisp smell of Silas.

A white cloak was wrapped around my body, holding back the full chill of the stone beneath me. I no longer felt the burning pain of my broken rib, or my jaw, or anything else that Remus had broken. I was already healed. *Simple joys.*

"Your powers may not ever be as they were before, but you are not barren," a voice to my left said. "And the fetus is not in distress."

I turned my head toward the sound. Aria sat cross-legged on the ground five feet away from me, surrounded by a knot of people. A green-robed Healer knelt in front of her with the pleased expression of someone delivering good news.

Alaric knelt in front of her, holding her hand. "You're with child?" His eyes were wide in surprise.

Aria looked at Silas in alarm. He stood between us in the middle of the chamber floor, his arms folded across his chest.

Alaric turned to Silas. "Do you claim the child?"

"I do," Silas said levelly. His face gave nothing away.

Alaric pulled his daughter into a hug. Over his shoulder, Aria's eyes landed on me.

"Maeve!" Aria gasped. She disentangled herself and came toward me. "You're awake!"

I was relieved to see that she seemed fine. Even the blood on her neck had been cleaned.

I tried to push off the floor and landed back on my elbows with my head spinning. A Healer I hadn't noticed hovering over me took the opportunity to list the many injuries I'd just had healed. Her clinical tone still managed to drip with disapproval. I was right about the broken rib, jaw, and cheekbone. But I'd missed the orbital socket, silly me. Aria held my hand while the Healer methodically sprayed a cool mist over my skin, wiped me clean, and left. Once again, I owed my life to magic.

"Titus did this?" Silas asked me, his jaw clenched in anger.

"And a man named Remus," I said. "They tried to take back the stolen magic."

Aria's brows furrowed at my slightly altered version of events, but I shook my head at her. I needed time to figure out all the things Titus had said, and I didn't want the entire Council—possible traitor included—to know everything.

"It was Remus of House Trivalent, Father," Aria said.

The name seemed familiar, but I couldn't remember where I'd heard it.

Alaric's head snapped up.

"He recognized me," Aria continued. "He drained my power and tried to rape me. I'd be dead if Lady Maeve had not risked her life to stop him. She drew his attention away…"

The familiar name finally clicked. Titus was a Trivalent. Atticus had said the whole family was bad news; they must have been related. My stomach twisted.

I pulled Silas's cloak tighter around me. "They couldn't have taken us out of this realm without a dedicated portal, right?" I asked the room in general.

"That's correct," Alaric confirmed. "A talisman would not be capable of skimming you from this realm."

"Then they're here in Aeterna. At least five of them. Well, four now. Remus is dead." *May he rest in hell.* Silas raised his eyebrows but didn't press me. My rage was still fresh, and I had no guilt about killing the sicko before he murdered Aria and me.

"Lord Magister," Elias said, his voice loud and accusatory as he addressed Alaric. "How did Magister Remus get his magic back?"

"It's not possible," Alaric replied, his face flushed.

Elias's eyes narrowed. "After his conviction, you advocated for Remus's sentence to be commuted to exile. You were responsible for stripping his powers. Now your former Acting Magister has joined the Brotherhood, and his magic is intact. Given the history of your family's treachery—"

"That is wildly out of line!" Alaric practically shouted. "I was proven innocent of anything to do with their rebellion. And my own daughter was in danger today!"

"And yet Lady Aria is unharmed," Elias said, sweeping his hand toward Aria. "Why is that, do you suppose?"

Everyone in the room went deathly quiet as they absorbed Elias's accusations.

Aria took a half step forward as though she might contest the accusations against her father. Silas grabbed her hand, holding her in place as Alaric sputtered his own protests. The ties to Remus were the hard evidence we'd been searching for. Alaric had lied about carrying out Remus's sentencing and set him loose in Earth with the Brotherhood. He was the traitor on the Council, helping them fuel their rebellion.

Alaric's protests of innocence were drowned out by the other Councilors' angry murmurs as they came to the same conclusion I had.

Elias motioned for the Guardians stationed around the room. "Lord Alaric will be detained until a trial can be held."

Three Guardians formed another net-like spell that settled over Alaric, blocking his magic. They grabbed him by his forearms and dragged him out of the room as he yelled excuses the whole way. Riotous arguments broke out as the Councilors discussed Alaric and his treachery. No doubt everything he'd ever done or said would be analyzed in the light of his betrayal.

Aria opened her mouth, but no sound came out. Silas laid a hand on her shoulder and whispered in her ear. She delicately wiped tears away with her sleeve.

"You scared the ever-living shite out of me," Silas said quietly, kneeling next to me. I tried to get a read on his expression, but as usual, it was impossible.

Elias talked with Nuada and Lady Nero, but he kept looking in my direction. He ran his fingers over his lips as he watched Silas and me. Embarrassed, I pushed to my feet on unsteady legs. Silas steadied me with a hand on my waist. I still couldn't read his strange expression. He was upset—angry at me, no doubt. A potent combination of relief and anger seared across my awareness, and for a moment, I thought I'd sensed it from Silas. I really needed to get some sleep.

"I'm fine." I said, pulling away from him. Too many eyes were on us, and I didn't want him to feel responsible for me. He needed to take care of Aria. I adjusted Silas's giant cloak and tried to untangle it from my legs. In my own realm, I hadn't needed recovery time after being healed, but I would kill for a nap right now. I was so tempted to find the nearest soft surface and crash. The room started spinning, and I swayed on my feet.

Silas swept me up in his arms like a child.

"What are you doing?"

"You need to rest," Aria said beside him.

"I'm taking you somewhere you can sleep," Silas said.

"I can walk."

He ignored me and announced he was leaving. No one objected, but Elias stared after us as we left the Council Centre with Silas carrying me in his arms.

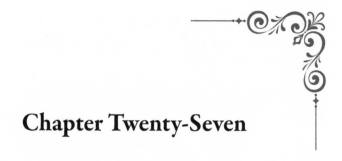

Chapter Twenty-Seven

I squirmed in Silas's arms as we traveled through the hallways of the Council Centre. "Put me down. This is ridiculous."

His grip tightened. "You were just beaten almost to death, fought off a rapist, and then broke through a level-five conjuring. Can you not accept help just once?"

"I'm fine." I cast a sideways glance at Aria, but she seemed fine on her own two feet. I folded my arms across my chest, refusing to loop my arm over Silas's neck.

"You're disoriented, nearly naked, and one of your feet is unshod."

I glanced down at my feet. He was right; I had lost one of my soft-soled shoes. *Huh.*

He carried me all the way to the port at the base of the mountain. I could feel people staring. I should have insisted I was fine, but the still-dizzy part of me was a tiny bit relieved. And he smelled amazing, like soap and lemongrass. I recognized the post-healing side effect of amorous feelings flaring inside me, but I couldn't bring myself to care. Forgetting my pride, I let my head rest against Silas's solid chest and inhaled his delicious scent.

We traveled through the port and emerged into a grand foyer. The pressure sent my head spinning again. A large golden shield with two crossed swords hung on one wall of the spacious room. Two large beasts with horns and claws holding a circle of ivy between them were etched into the crest. Inside the ivy was the sigil of his House. An inscription in a curling script ran under the crest.

"House of Valeron, the Eternal Might," Silas translated for me. "Be welcome in my familial home, Lady Maeve."

He set me gently on my feet, and Aria immediately wrapped her arm around my waist. It was ridiculous to lean on a pregnant woman for support, but she wouldn't let go. Silas placed one palm against a wall, and it melted into a doorway. We walked into the most opulent hall I had ever seen. I stared at the vaulted ceilings of a room the length of three basketball courts.

Dappled sunlight filtered through an entire ceiling of colored glass soaring stories above us, creating a domed courtyard. In the center of the hall, the Valeron sigil was set into the floor in what appeared to be sparkling gems. Archways lined the walls with a half dozen hallways connecting to other parts of the building. The house must be enormous.

"It's ostentatious," Silas said, rubbing the back of his neck. "We use it for receptions and official functions."

I had no words. The room was beautiful and ornate, and holy hell—Silas's family was loaded.

Stephan exploded out of one of the doorways, and Aria released me to rush to him. I caught my breath as his empathic side projected an overwhelming mix of emotions. His worry and relief mixed together into a potent ball in my stomach. Silas's arm replaced Aria's around my waist as the two lovers touched foreheads tenderly. Stephan placed his hands gently over her stomach, and love flared between them, his and hers.

Silas's grip tightened around my waist.

The sudden burst of emotions I felt cut off abruptly when Stephan gained control again. "Thank you for bringing her home," he said to me. "I am in your debt."

I gave him a watery smile, unable to speak around the lump in my throat. The two returned back up the hall, wrapped around each other.

"Can you walk?" Silas asked me.

I nodded, and Silas released his hold on me. My legs were shaky, but I was determined to make it under my own power. I was so tired. The emotional and physical trauma was too much. I wouldn't admit it, but I was grateful Silas stayed close as he led the way through a long, richly decorated hallway, past half a dozen doors until we reached a bedroom.

The furniture in the room was heavy and masculine. A thick blanket, the same rich green color as the drapes, covered a four-poster bed. The floor-to-ceiling window on the opposite side of the room framed a dark sky and a balcony beyond it. I wondered if it was a real window or another magic-infused illusion like at the Council Centre.

"You can sleep here."

The blanket was tossed back from where someone had slept on the giant bed. Several sheathed swords leaned against the wall, and a stack of books with titles in foreign languages lay on a round side table. Two portable consoles rested next to the books.

"Is this your room?" I asked.

"Yes. Officially, it's a servant's quarters. The Prime suite is occupied by my brother and Aria." He gripped the back of his neck and flashed me an awkward grin. "The guest suites are on the other side of the house. I thought you'd appreciate a shorter walk considering your condition. You can't skim within the house, so..." He looked around the room self-consciously. "I can wake someone to set up a different room if you'd prefer?"

It was a rare peek into his life. I could ask for another room, but this bed was so close. And it probably smelled like him. I glanced at the window. If it wasn't a complete illusion, it was the middle of the night.

"No, this is good." I didn't know if he planned on sleeping in the bed with me. My brain was too exhausted to contemplate how I felt about that possibility. I really needed to sleep.

Silas indicated a closed door on the side of the room. "There's a cleansing room behind there. Do you want to wash?"

My skin was free of blood from the Healer, and I was so, so tired. "I just want to sleep. Can I borrow a shirt?"

Silas rifled through a closet and came out with a black top. He turned his back as I slid out of his cloak and into the shirt. It fell to my thighs. I slipped into his bed and groaned in pleasure. As I suspected, the bed was sinfully comfortable. I closed my eyes at the luxury that seemed unimaginable after the day I'd just had.

The lights dimmed, and I opened my eyes to see Silas standing by the door. Panic hit when I realized he was leaving. I didn't want to be alone. I opened my mouth and said the first thing that came to mind. "The Brotherhood knew where I would be today. They were waiting for me."

Silas's face darkened, and his jaw flexed. "I want to bring Remus back from the dead and kill him again."

A shiver ran down my spine. "Can you do that?"

"No. But right now I'm tempted to try." He moved back into the room, and the pressure in my chest let up.

"I don't feel guilty exactly, but it wasn't a pleasant way to die." I closed my eyes, remembering all the people I had drained of magic. They'd all been trying to kill me, but the body count was adding up.

"He was sentenced to die for his previous attacks before Alaric used his influence to have him exiled. You did both our realms a favor."

The knowledge that Remus had hurt other people made me sick. Everything that had happened today threatened to overwhelm me.

"Stephan and I owe you a personal debt for saving Aria. She is... fragile."

I remembered the way she had confronted me about my feelings for Silas, and her refusal to leave me behind today. She was refined and soft-spoken, but she wasn't fragile. "She's stronger than you think."

"I only mean that she's not a fighter," he corrected. "She sees good in everyone and wants to fix all their problems. We were always a poor match that way." He ran a hand across his stubbled chin and sighed. "Who else knew you were going to the City Centre today?"

"You and Atticus, obviously. Aria's guards. Anyone who saw us leaving. It's a long list. But Alaric is the one who cleared the way for me to be there. He could have easily arranged the ambush."

"I'll follow up with each one, see who they talked to. If we can link them to Alaric, the Council will have an easier time with his conviction."

"What are they going to do with Alaric?"

"If the Council can gather enough evidence, we will vote for execution." He studied my face and sat on the edge of the bed. "What he's done is inexcusable. Think of all the lives the Brotherhood has destroyed."

"I know he hates me, but I can't believe he would do that to his own daughter."

"Alaric proved a long time ago that he only cares about himself. He would do anything for more power." Silas's jaw clenched. "He will pay for what he's done."

"I don't understand how Titus and Remus got into Aeterna undetected." I scanned the room, feeling as if Titus could be anywhere, lurking in the corners.

"The portal to and from Earth is secure," Silas said. "Everyone must be authorized and logged upon entry and departure."

"Could they have someone who is covering up their tracks?"

Silas hummed in agreement. "I'll review the records myself tomorrow."

"You need to keep this quiet until you figure out who's helping them. You don't want to scare the traitors off before we have a chance to question them."

He gave me a half scowl. "I'm aware of how to do my job."

"Can the Council keep Alaric's imprisonment quiet?" I asked.

One of Silas's eyebrows rose. "The Council has been keeping this quiet for half a decade."

Right. "I want to help you get the proof you need."

"You've been attacked twice. You need to stay here where you're protected. House Valeron is secure, and our people can be trusted."

"But I can tell if someone is using the Brotherhood's power," I argued. "And you can keep me safe while we do it. Win-win."

He frowned but then nodded. "I can live with that."

"Did we just make a compromise?"

A shadow of a smile lifted the corners of his lips. "I can't believe it either."

I tried to hide a yawn and failed.

Silas stood as though he were going to leave then paused. His magic flared gently around him. "I almost forgot. You dropped these when you landed in the Council's chambers." He held out Ripper and Marcel's charm.

Tears welled up in my eyes, and I had to look away. "Stay with me, Silas." My tone bordered on pleading.

He froze, his face buried in shadows, making it impossible to guess what he was thinking.

"I don't..." He cleared his throat. "I'm not sure that's a good idea. Sleep well, Maeve."

I WOKE UP IN A SWEAT, my heart pounding. Remus had terrorized my dreams. The sky outside was still dark, but my brain brimmed with too much turmoil to sleep. Intent on a shower, I got out of bed and padded on heavy legs to the bathroom. A dim light glowed when I walked in, but it took me several minutes to gather the courage to look in the mirror. I had been healed but was still surprised that I looked normal.

Random bits of horror popped into my head as I stared at my reflection. *The crazed look in Titus's eyes. Remus's rough hands on my body. Aria unconscious on the ground.*

I shook myself out of my daze and tried to figure out how to work the shower. I couldn't see a showerhead, but a panel of buttons looked promising. I stripped off my clothes and started pushing things at random. A pulse of air washed over me. Another sonic-magic shower. I sighed. I really missed the steamy comfort of hot water. The pulse carried the crisp scent of soap, which smelled like Silas. After I was done, my skin was clean, but my mind still hadn't slowed. With a sigh of disappointment, I slipped back into his T-shirt.

I returned to the bedroom and found Silas waiting for me near the bed. He was in the same clothes from earlier, and his hair was sticking out as though he'd been running his hands through it. "I... felt your fear through the bond and came to check on you."

Confused, I blinked at him. He could *feel* things through the Aegis bond? My expression must have given away my surprise because he hurried to add, "I can only sense strong emotions: fear, pain. I would have mentioned it earlier—I forget you don't know certain things. Don't lose your temper."

His obvious fear over ticking me off cooled my anger before it had a chance to really get started. "That seems... intrusive. And totally one-sided, I might add."

"You could feel the same from me. If you prefer, I can show you how to block everything."

"...should block everything."

"Are there any side effects?" a man asks. He's outside my immediate scope of vision. His voice is distant but familiar.

"Just the intended ones. She'll be groggy for a few days, but she should be fine to travel immediately." A thin-haired man with light-brown hair leans in and pats my arm in a fatherly gesture that brings tears to my eyes. "I'm so sorry, Mae. We're all so sorry."

"I'm ready," I respond.

The vision had come on so fast, I froze in place for a moment. But this one had been different—it wasn't Marcel's memory. "Something happened to me," I said to Silas. "But I can't remember..."

I blinked, and Silas stood in front of me with a murderous expression. "He's not going to hurt you again."

He misunderstood the cause of my distress, but my throat tightened with unexpected emotion. Maybe I wasn't alone in this. Silas cared what happened to me, and I wasn't expecting the warm feeling that brought. My entire life, I'd lived on my own, looking out for myself, and I was fine with that. Being alone had made me tough, independent. And I liked that about myself. But Silas's concern made my heart ache in a way that was both incredibly comforting and painful at the same time.

Silas pulled me into his arms and tucked my head under his chin. "You're safe now."

I leaned into his chest and held my breath as I listened to his steady heartbeat. The dark cocooned us, creating a space for whispered truths. "I've been having more visions. I thought they were Marcel's memories, but..."

His hand moved to the back of my head and stroked my hair.

"There's more to it than just Marcel's memories." I wasn't sure how to explain it. "I feel like I'm starting to remember things from my past, but it's not really *my* past. I can't explain it. I feel like I'm losing my mind."

He buried his face in my hair, and I leaned into his chest.

"Titus didn't want just my magic. He was after my memories. He wanted to do something called an 'unbinding,' but I think he wasn't sure it would work. He thinks something locked in my head can lead to this Lost Sect, and he's planning on stealing their powers." I took a deep breath and admitted the thing I'd been worried about. "Silas, I think I did something to my memories."

He pulled back with a concerned frown. "Whatever is happening, we'll figure it out. Tessa is an expert on archaic conjurings. Maybe she can tell us something about this unbinding spell Titus mentioned."

"I just want to forget everything for tonight," I whispered. "Titus, Remus... the Council. Everything bad. I know that makes me a total coward."

His arms tightened slightly around me. "You're the strongest, most brave woman I know."

I smiled at the respect in his voice. "Wait, did you just give me a compliment?"

"You seem to be suffering from a skewed understanding of my opinion about you."

His lips were so close, and his body was pressed against mine.

"What *is* your opinion about me?" I whispered back. "Honestly, you confuse the hell out of me."

His eyes dropped to my lips. A struggle played out on his face, and he shook his head slowly. "Maeve..."

I pulled back, not wanting to hear the rejection that was about to follow. His life was complicated, and I had vowed not to insert myself into it. "Never mind. Forget it." I tried to untangle myself from his hold. "I know you don't want me to—"

"*Wanting* you is not the problem."

His mouth closed over mine so suddenly that I froze for a moment before I kissed him back. My whole body ached to be closer. I leaned into him and wrapped my arms around his shoulders. His hands pulled me tighter against him. Our mouths moved together, hungry for each other.

Kissing Silas was like all the best things about magic. Warm tingles slid across my skin, and happiness pooled in my soul. He was warmth and strength, and I couldn't get enough.

When we pulled apart, he rested his forehead against mine and cupped my neck with his hand. "Gods, I know I shouldn't drag you into my life." His thumb stroked along my jaw. "But I can't seem to let you go."

My heartbeat stuttered for an entirely new reason as I searched for the right words. "I know your life is complicated." This moment was a tipping point. Saying the wrong thing would push him away. But I didn't know what I could say to overcome his obsession with keeping me safe from his messy life. "I don't care about any of that. I just want *you*. Just tell me you want me too, and we can figure out the rest of it together."

He stepped back from my embrace, holding my hands. "I won't tie you to me while I drown, no matter what I want."

"What do you really want, Silas?" I let my confusion and irritation show in my voice. He kept jerking me around—kissing me like that then telling me we couldn't be anything more.

His mouth drew into a hard line, and he released his grip on me.

Frustration got the better of me. "Just tell me what you want, dammit! No more mind games."

"What I want doesn't matter. I never wanted any of this to happen. My life is such a fratching mess. You know I'm bonded with Aria, and I've claimed her child as my own. I can't recognize you publicly."

"When are you going to get it through your head? I don't care about any of that!"

He grabbed my hands again and squeezed them painfully hard between his. "Maeve, you don't understand. You'd inherit all of my enemies, but you wouldn't have my name to protect you. If I'm bonded to someone else, you'd be little more than a—a concubine to House Valeron, an interloper between mine and Aria's rightful bond."

"Screw everyone else! I don't care what they think about me."

"You deserve so much better. I can't do that to you."

I was cold all over as we looked at each other. That was it, then. I wanted him, but the price was too high for him. Even though I would've been the one paying that price, he wouldn't let me into his life. I couldn't let him into my heart if he didn't want me in his.

I wrapped my arms around myself. "I can't keep doing this with you."

"And I won't ask it of you." Pain reflected in his eyes before the blank mask slid into place, widening the distance between us.

He left without another word. I had no tears to cry over him, just a burning pain in my heart.

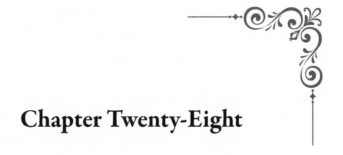

Chapter Twenty-Eight

I awoke alone the next morning. The sun streamed through the window, catching dust particles floating in the air like flecks of shimmering magic. With the cover of darkness gone, I felt like an intruder in Silas's personal space. Every inch of this room reminded me of its owner—the books on the table, the weapons displayed on the wall, even the smell of him in the bedsheets.

I had to get out of there. I couldn't stay in this house with Silas. My heart couldn't take it. In the bathroom, I found a neat stack of clothes sitting on the counter. I suspected the finely embroidered tunic and leggings were Aria's, but it didn't bother me. Pausing, I considered my feelings about Aria, but I decided there was no reason to be jealous of her. My heart had burned itself out over Silas.

Ripper sat neatly on top of the folded clothing in the new thigh holster. Silas's doing, no doubt. I very deliberately didn't let myself feel anything about that. I changed into the new outfit, twisted my hair into a braid, strapped the knife on my thigh, and tugged the long tunic down to cover it. I lingered in the room alone, dreading seeing Silas. My feelings were raw, but I needed to focus on bringing Titus and Alaric down. I needed to chill out, or being around Silas would burn me from the inside out.

Cold thoughts, Maeve. Cold like ice.

Resolved, I followed my nose toward the smell of breakfast. It was possible I'd been hit hard enough to get a concussion, but I could swear I smelled bacon. I stopped in the doorway of a large dining room. My attention was immediately drawn to Silas. His back was to me as he talked to a servant holding a silver tray.

A painful thump of my heart sent my stomach into a tailspin, and I turned away.

Stephan, Aria, Tessa, and Atticus were gathered at a long table in the center of the room, chatting casually. Empty plates and several servants clearing away dishes suggested they had already enjoyed a big breakfast. Apparently not one to pass up an opportunity to eat, Atticus shoveled food into his mouth from what I had to assume was his second or third helping. The man could eat.

I frowned in disappointment at the roots and grains on his plate. There was a vast array of food, but no bacon.

Tessa saw me and jumped up to bury me in a python-sized hug. "Gods curse our eyes; you gave us a scare, Earthen."

She released me, and everyone took a turn, doubling the number of hugs I had received in my entire life. Except Silas, of course. He'd disappeared somewhere. I tried to feel relieved about that, but my stomach was still in knots.

"This is literally everyone I like in this realm," I said, making them laugh. "What are you all doing here?"

"They banged on the door until we let them in," Silas groused behind me.

His voice made me jump, and the heavy feeling in my stomach doubled down without warning. Stephan caught my gaze, and his brows lifted in a question.

Damn Empath. I gave a slight shake of my head, and Stephan stayed quiet, although a small frown played across his face. I prayed no one else noticed the tension between Silas and me. I couldn't deal with explaining my feelings at the moment.

Aria chuckled lightly at Silas's grumpy complaint and reassured Tessa and Atticus they were more than welcome. When I made it to the table, Silas set a plate of food in front of me, and my mouth watered at the sight of eggs and bacon. The smell was heavenly. I hadn't seen any drool-worthy food for *weeks*.

"Grease and salt for the Earthen," Silas said. He sat and draped his arm around the back of Aria's chair.

"Where did you get bacon?" I was determined to act normal, but I couldn't quite meet his eyes.

Atticus reached over to snag a piece off my plate, but I slapped his hand away. Everyone laughed, and I caught a rare smile from Silas.

"I have ways," Silas hinted.

Stephan snorted. "He sent someone to an Earthen *grocery store.*"

My heart thumped in surprise. I bit my lip and reminded myself that Silas didn't want me in his life. I needed to move on. *Cold like ice.*

As I ate, Aria and I relayed snippets of what we'd learned from Titus during the abduction. Tessa shared that her time spent in Lower Aeterna had been useless. She hadn't been able to get anyone to talk to her about the possible defectors.

Eventually, Silas got down to business, and we discussed the reason everyone had gathered at House Valeron this morning. "Maeve and I are going to dig into the arrival records at the portal facility. Tessa, I need you to keep searching in Lower Aeterna for more missing people. Take Atticus. Whoever put the compulsion on him was with the Brotherhood, and they're using him as a lightning rod for their cause. Having him there might get more people to open up. We need to know what the Brotherhood is planning next."

Tessa rose from the table. "On assignment together, like old times."

"What about the Brotherhood's recruiting meeting?" I asked.

"Visiting those families was reckless," Silas growled. "And irresponsible."

He was hyper-focused on the wrong point, as usual.

I narrowed my eyes. "It's our best lead."

His eyebrows rose in an all-too-familiar irritated expression. "You will not attend this meeting."

"I can attend alone," Atticus quickly offered.

I glared at them both. "They'll get suspicious," I argued.

"You're too recognizable," Silas continued. "You'll ruin your *best lead* and get yourself killed. Listen to me for once. It's too dangerous."

I bit my lip. His eyes flicked to my mouth. The damn butterflies woke up in my stomach.

Ice, goddammit!

Silas swiped his hand across his face, and his expression softened. "Please, Maeve."

They were the magic words; he actually said please. As much as I hated to admit it, he was right. I was too recognizable to the Brotherhood. Getting myself captured at one of their meetings would be idiotic. I nodded, and his shoulders relaxed.

"Atticus can infiltrate this group and report back on their movements," Silas said. "We'll come up with a plan."

THE FAE CENTURION MANNING the portal facility was terrified of Silas. I couldn't blame him, especially since Silas was in a really foul mood. I'd already tried to convince him that I should question the man alone, but he didn't buy it. The tension between us made us both irritable, and Silas released his temper on everyone in our path. *So much for being inconspicuous.*

The poor Guardian guided us to the central control room, where he accessed the portal logs through a handheld interface and, with shaking fingers, projected them onto a vertical console. "Is this what you needed, Lord Commander?"

Silas and I squinted at a very long list of names, dates, and other information I had no idea how to decipher. With Silas laying on the menace, I decided to be extra nice to the Centurion.

"All these people traveled to Earth?"

"Yes, my lady."

"You can call me Maeve. You've been so helpful, Centurion..."

"Lysander." His eyes flitted between Silas and me, and I knew without looking that Silas was scowling at him.

I shifted to the side, blocking him from Lysander's view. "Could you show me the arrival and departure records side by side?"

As we leaned in to scan the names of each of the records, the smell of Silas's soap invaded my nose. I could practically feel the heat of his body against my skin, so I shifted away from him.

"Why doesn't that entry have an arrival name logged?" Silas asked, pointing.

Lysander tapped the screen and swallowed. "I don't know, my lord. It must be an error."

"Are there any other records that don't have a name logged?" I asked gently before Silas could berate him.

Lysander pulled up three entry records and an equal number of departures over the past month. The last no-name record was an arrival on the day before I was kidnapped. When I asked him to check farther back, he found at least twenty entries and same-day departures that hadn't logged names.

We were onto a pattern. I started to get excited.

"That's a big oversight, Centurion Lysander," Silas said with menace.

Lysander started stammering possible explanations.

Silas's default mode was intimidation, which was only going to terrify the man and bury the information we really needed. Giving Silas an icy look, I tried to tell him silently that he needed to back off. It was the first time we'd maintained any significant eye contact since the night before, and I didn't like the way it made me burn inside.

Antarctica, glaciers, polar ice caps.

Silas folded his arms across his chest and glared back.

Silently, I told him to stop being an idiot. He was going to ruin our chances of finding anything out if he didn't back down.

He scowled.

I returned the scowl and raised him some lifted eyebrows. Finally, he huffed and stepped back, accepting defeat.

"Lysander, is there a way to see the person on duty when each of these incidents happened?" I asked gently.

He tapped around on the console then glanced at Silas. His Adam's apple bobbed as he swallowed nervously. "I'm sorry, but that information seems to be missing as well."

Silas harrumphed behind me.

Damn.

"That's okay. It's not your fault," I assured Lysander. He exhaled in relief as we all considered the information.

"Someone could have accessed the system and erased the information," Lysander volunteered, his eyes rising to me hopefully.

"Can *anyone* do that?" I asked.

Silas started pacing.

"Only members of the Council could erase the records, Lady Maeve."

Alaric could have done it, but it wasn't quite the proof we needed. I chewed on the inside of my cheek as Lysander looked over my shoulder to watch Silas pacing. The man looked terrified—as if

Silas might conjure up a sword and run him through at any second. Actually, he might not have been that far off.

"Can you see *when* they were altered?" I asked.

As he worked on it, Silas continued to stalk, and I resisted the urge to tell him to stop. Since we didn't know who had made the alterations, we couldn't tie it back to Alaric. If we could figure out the day the records were altered, maybe we could retrace Alaric's steps and establish an anti-alibi. Or we could interview the people who had been on duty those days. It was a long shot, but it might work.

"Got it. The records were altered on three separate occasions." Lysander beamed at me—a broad, pleased grin that would never have happened with intimidation. "The Guardian on duty each time was Legatis Landas of House Crispin."

"Landas?" I asked Silas. "As in the jerk-wad who escorted us to the Council Centre?"

Silas spoke to Lysander in a measured, level tone that scared the shit out of me. "Fetch Legatis Landas and bring him to me."

Lysander jumped out of his seat and ran for the door.

"What are you going to say to Landas?" I asked as soon as we were alone.

He scowled. "I'm going to tear apart that sodding mongrel until he squeals like the shite-licking coward he is."

"I don't know half the words you just said, but I'm gonna go out on a limb and guess that you're angry."

He gave me a glare that could have melted flesh.

In my super-patient voice, I pointed out the obvious. "We need Landas to lead us to whoever's been helping the Brotherhood. It's gotta be someone on the Council."

"We already know who it is—everything points back to Alaric!"

"You really think he had Aria kidnapped?" I snapped. Silas was in full rage mode, which put the responsibility on me to think rationally. *God help us.*

"Who else has a better motivation?" Silas demanded.

"Putting your personal issues with Alaric aside," I said carefully, "he wouldn't sacrifice his link to your House. Aria is his ticket to returning his House's standing in Upper Aeterna. And she almost died, Silas. Titus was going to kill her."

Silas's lip curled into a snarl.

"If you confront Landas, we'll lose the only lead we have. We need to follow him and see who he's working for."

"We know who he's working for," he said, but his voice drifted as he started to think about it. He'd begun to doubt too.

My mind was spinning through all the possibilities, when a realization came to me. "Titus had at least four people with him in Aeterna, and a dozen helped attack us in Earth. Plus, all the Rakken we killed in Alaska, and five more at the Exposition..."

Silas's brows scrunched. "What are you implying?"

"There aren't enough errors logged to get all of the rebels from Aeterna to Earth." I chewed on the inside of my lip as I put the pieces together. "Let's say they're sneaking people out of Lower Aeterna to join their cause. This facility is monitored, and every alteration of the log requires Alaric—or whoever is supporting Titus—to personally alter the records. That's a big risk. By my count, they've moved several dozen people to Earth, but there's only a few altered entries here. A second portal is the only thing that makes sense."

Silas stared at me as he digested my theory.

"It could be wherever he took Aria and me. I think we were in someone's house. Probably in Lower Aeterna."

Silas started to respond, but the door opened, cutting off his reply. Legatis Landas stepped inside. Dressed in a Guardian uniform with his dark hair still bound in a topknot, he no longer wore the smug expression I'd last seen on his face. His round brown eyes flicked between us before they steadied on Silas and he dropped into a salute.

Silas's voice was quiet. "Unfortunately for you, I still remember your name, Landas."

I swore under my breath. Silas was pissed, and he was not going to back off. We really needed to know who this guy worked for, not nail him to the wall.

Landas's nostrils flared as he asked, "Is something wrong, Lord Commander?"

"We have a number of missing data logs, and each time this occurred, you were the officer on duty. Why is that?"

Landas rocked back on his feet. I could practically see his mind spinning. "I was running a diagnostic test, my lord. I—I may have caused some errors in the data."

"You didn't alter the records?"

His eyes went very wide. "No, my lord."

Silas's eyes narrowed. "Did you report the errors?"

"No, my lord. I didn't think it was important enough. I can fill in the missing data by hand."

Silas stepped closer to him. The Legatis's wide eyes flicked to me. I gave him my hard stare. He wouldn't get any help from me.

"Do you know how I earned my first command?" Silas asked.

Landas's face drained of color.

Silas leaned in, inches from his face. "I do not abide traitors."

Landas went stiff, and the terror in his face made me very curious what Silas was talking about. He'd told me about Krittesh—maybe there was more to that story.

Silas narrowed his eyes, considering the man. "Finish your test. If you find out someone is altering the records, I want you to come to me. No one else. Do you understand?"

Landas's head jerked. He blinked rapidly then stammered, "Yes, my lord."

"Leave us."

Landas saluted and fled the room.

"Great work," I snarked at Silas. "Pushing him got you nowhere. You should have listened to me. We could have followed him back to whoever he's working with."

"Right now, he isn't sure if we know what he's done or if we believed his story. He's scared, and he'll want reassurance from whomever he's working with. Now we'll see who he runs to."

It was a bold move. Silas used intimidation like a precision weapon. Grudgingly, I had to admit it might work. I just hoped he hadn't tipped our hand.

"If they have access to a second portal," Silas said, returning to my theory, "it would take an enormous amount of energy to power. But it's not in Lower Aeterna. Alaric must be diverting power to it, which would be very difficult to do with the current energy rationing in the Lower City. I suspect it's in Upper Aeterna, and somewhere private, or they'd be noticed. A home would work."

"Do you think the second portal is the reason for the energy rationing? It takes a lot of magic, right? They could be diverting power to the portal instead of into the Citizen Source."

"That's... clever." The corners of his mouth twisted down. "We'll search for a hidden portal at the Magister Training Compound, where Alaric trains his people. Then we'll sweep lower Aeterna and start asking questions. It's time to get these fratchers scared and running."

Fear and anger were building in the Lower City. The city was drenched in gasoline, and Silas was about to throw a match on it. I just hoped the whole thing didn't blow up in our faces.

Chapter Twenty-Nine

That evening, I sat on the open-air balcony at House Valeron with Tessa and Atticus. We'd just ended the latest installment of my crash course in magic. Between the two of them, I had learned a lot about how to use the power locked inside me. Today we'd practiced pulling magic from objects. I still couldn't directly access my magic, but I'd learned how to kick-start it through absorbing energy from someone else's conjuring or an object that had power. Just a little bit was enough to allow me to start a spell, then I could pull the energy into a conjuring. Once I had mastered that, they taught me the basic spell for marking and calling objects. I was thrilled to finally have a way to magic up Ripper whenever I needed.

Sunlight filtered through the manicured vines draped on the arbor above us. A warm breeze blew the scent of flowers through the air. But a heavy weight settled in my chest. Atticus had eagerly agreed to the undercover mission to infiltrate the Brotherhood and was excited about the recruiting meeting the following day.

"Are you sure you want to do this?" I asked him. "They tried to make you a martyr to fuel their rebellion. They know who you are."

"Silas has arranged for my sentence to be publicly retracted thanks to my efforts to save you during the Exposition. They have no reason to suspect I know of the compulsion, and as of tomorrow morning, I'll be more famous than ever in Lower Aeterna. How could they turn me away?"

"It's dangerous."

He grinned. "No shit."

I gave him a fist bump. "Another five points for excellent use of Earthen swearing."

Tessa picked a leaf from the groomed bush nearest us and twirled it between her fingers. It fluttered from front to back, one side green, the other gold. "I've been wondering—do you think Marcel transferred *all* of his memories to you? Could you really find the Lost Sect?"

"I don't know," I admitted. "I've been trying to avoid reliving them. I almost lose control every time one sneaks up on me."

"Maybe if you access the memories in a controlled environment," Tessa said, "it won't be so traumatic. The Lost Sect may be the only ones who can truly help you control Marcel's abilities. Maybe they even have a way to remove them without killing you."

"I don't know," I said. "I blacked out and killed seven Rakken last time the visions took over too deeply."

Tessa whistled between her teeth, and the leaf fluttered to the ground. "You're more dangerous than you appear, my Earthen friend."

"You just need a way to stay calm and not get caught up in reliving those memories," Atticus said.

His words sparked an idea. "That's brilliant!" I was so happy, I leaned over and kissed him on the cheek.

He started in surprise.

"I know exactly what I need to do."

MY THOUGHTS DRIFTED as a feeling of intense calm emanated from Stephan and washed over me. I wanted to curl up in the overstuffed armchair, but unfortunately, he'd insisted on involving Silas, and I had more of an audience than I'd anticipated.

"I think you're putting her to sleep," Silas said.

I let my head flop toward his voice, struggling to keep my eyes open. With Stephan's emotional intervention, it hurt a lot less to be around Silas. All the jagged edges were dulled.

"Is... kinda like bein' drunk," I slurred.

Stephan released my hands, and the warm fuzzies let up a bit. "You're quite entertaining when you're drunk."

Silas scowled, which I found inexplicably hilarious. "So serious all the time," I said with a big, exaggerated frown.

Stephan chuckled, spurring me on. I attempted my best "exasperated Silas" expression, complete with one raised eyebrow. "Look at me! I'm Lord Commander Silas the Scowly. Fear me, mortals!"

Stephan howled with laughter, and I giggled. I never giggled.

I couldn't remember what had been so funny a second ago. "What's wrong with me?"

Silas folded his arms over his chest. "Gods' curses, Stephan, that's enough."

My emotions leveled out, and I realized what I had said. "Stephan! What the hell?"

"Best we're getting all the problems sorted now, yes?" His eyes were wide and innocent. I didn't buy it.

"I can't believe I said that." I snuck a peek at Silas. His mouth was set in a thin line, and his shoulders were stiff.

My mortification dimmed to a low simmer as Stephan worked his calming magic.

"We're going to do a test before we try this for real." Stephan glanced at Silas.

"Are you sure she's calm?" Silas asked.

"What's going on?" My heart rate started to pick up, and then I felt fine. *Totally chill.*

Silas rubbed the back of his neck, and I narrowed my eyes. I recognized that expression. "What did you do?"

"We found something you need to know while searching for your Father Mike."

"What? What happened to him?" My panic spiked then calmed right back down. *Like a magic Valium.* I nodded appreciatively at Stephan. I should bottle that stuff and sell it on the street.

"We don't know what happened yet." Silas's voice was gentle, and his concerned tone made my insides twist despite being under Stephan's influence. "We found some papers in Michael Smithson's personal residence behind a concealment spell—paperwork for your passport and a few other identities for him. They were hidden with these."

He handed me two printed photographs. The first was a picture of an auburn-haired woman and a young girl with two long braids. They were holding hands and smiling in front of a circus tent. The second photo showed the same people, but they were older, laughing together in someone's house. A birthday cake with the number eighteen sat on the table in front of them. I stared at the teenager in the photo in complete shock. It was undeniably me.

"What is this?" I demanded.

"I believe that's you and your mother. The resemblance is striking."

The woman had the same hair color as me, and the same eyes. I'd never seen her before in my life. My heart lurched into my throat before another wave of calm passed over me.

"No," I said. "No. There's no way. I don't know this woman. I don't remember this at all."

"Titus mentioned an unbinding spell," Silas said gently. "I think Michael Smithson took you from your people and placed you under a memory binding so you wouldn't remember."

"Father Mike would never..." I shook my head, thinking of my surrogate father figure. He'd rescued me off the streets and given me a second chance when I was just fourteen. But the girl in that photo was me. And she was clearly turning eighteen alongside a woman who looked like her mother.

"He's been hiding you," Silas continued. "It explains your memories, your abilities, and why he didn't return to Aeterna after I found you both in Boston."

"Why? What could Father Mike possibly gain from kidnapping me and making me forget my family? And before you ask, he never did a thing to hurt or abuse me in any way."

"I'm not certain yet," Silas responded. "I know you don't want to believe this—but Michael Smithson could have taken you for access to your unique abilities, or perhaps for leverage against your Sect."

My entire world started to slide sideways. Father Mike was the person I'd considered my adopted family. He'd been nothing but kind and loving to me. I stared down at the photograph of the teenage me with the woman I didn't remember except in glimpses of shattered memory.

The memories that were surfacing were not just Marcel's—they were mine. The things I could do weren't just because of him—I had those abilities. I was part of the Lost Sect, and I didn't even remember it. The evidence was right in front of me, and now I knew the truth—Michael Smithson had taken me from my real family.

He'd lied about everything. Everything I believed about my life was made up, and the realization staggered me. I didn't know who I was. I couldn't trust anything I remembered.

I needed time to process the realization, but it reminded me of another lie that still stung. "Why did you lie to me about the Lost Sect?" I asked Silas. "If you believed I was one of them all the way back in Earth, why didn't you tell me?"

"When I met you, I didn't know who you were or what your allegiance was. Titus wanted you alive, which led me to believe you were one of the Lost Sect, and I hoped you would lead me to them," he said. "It was never personal."

"It got personal."

Stephan walked to the far end of the room, giving us the illusion of privacy, and my emotional dampening let up a little.

Silas crouched next to me, and my heart rate picked up. "I know you think I'm despicable, but it was never my intention to hurt you."

"I don't think you're despicable, Silas." My fingers reached for the strong line of his jaw, wanting more than anything to touch him. "It's not your fault I started to feel... the way I feel. I know you don't want me to, but I can't help it. I'm trying to accept that you don't want the same things."

He captured my fingers in his own. "You know what I want? I want someone who loves me for me, not my family name. Someone I could raise a child with, not a bond-mate to sire an obligatory heir between Houses. Someone who challenges me, and infuriates me, and never takes any orders—no matter how frustrated that makes me." The corners of his mouth lifted, and his eyes crinkled. He kissed the backs of my hands, and the gesture was unbearably sad. "You made me want all those things—all the things you deserve to have and I can't give you. Loving you hurts too much."

"You love me?" For the first time, I could consciously feel the strength of his emotions through the Aegis bond we shared: desire, fear, longing, and love. It was all there in a confused knot as tangled as my own feelings.

"Gods, I tried not to."

"Don't push me away," I pleaded.

"I don't want to."

"See, I knew you two could work it out," Stephan interrupted with a grin.

My fingers slipped from Silas's grip. I'd forgotten about the Empath. This whole scene had been thanks to Stephan's interference with our emotions.

Stephan ignored our glares. "I won't apologize. You both need to stop denying your feelings."

My raw emotions skipped right into embarrassed anger. "We're not puppets! You can't just make us feel whatever you want."

"I didn't make you feel anything. I simply amplified what you were already projecting."

"Stephan," Silas growled, rising from the ground.

Stephan pointed his finger at his brother, and his carefree expression slipped into a determined scowl that I associated more with Silas. "You bury your feelings as a coping mechanism from growing up with an Empath and an overbearing father who withheld his approval."

He pointed at me. "You're afraid your feelings make you weak, so you avoid them. Not to mention, all the emotions you're denying every single time you're around my brother."

Silas rubbed the back of his neck, and I flushed. But neither of us argued. Apparently, I couldn't muster up the anger Stephan's actions deserved because he was right. I should have been upset at his gross violation of our feelings, but he'd forced our guards down, and I finally had a glimpse into what Silas felt. It was good to know he was just as lost as I was.

Maybe Stephan was right, and I was afraid of my feelings. But I didn't know what to do about that now. We'd both admitted our true feelings, but there still seemed to be no way to meet in the middle. True to Stephan's accusation, I decided to stick with what I could handle at the moment and changed the subject.

"So... We still need to find the memories Titus was after. They could answer a lot of questions, including what happened with

Michael Smithson." I took a deep breath. "Will you still help me, Stephan?"

Stephan returned to his seat across from me, thankfully allowing us to move forward from the previously painful conversation. "I'm ready," he said.

"Let's do this." I pushed everything else to the back of my mind, closed my eyes, and let the barrage of memories lurking in the corners of my mind flood over me.

The memories came too fast.

Pain. So much pain.

Titus sneers down at me, and blood drips from his hands. "Tell me, Marcel. We can end this now."

Pressure seemed to build behind my closed eyes. I had to push through Marcel's last memories, but it hurt too much. I whimpered and struggled for a full breath until a warm hand squeezed mine, filling me with calm. The Empath was using his powers for good.

Grounded in Stephan's solid grip, I worked through the memories before Marcel was captured. He was in Boston, searching for something. I recognized the places I saw—the shelter, one of the restaurants where I worked, the hospital.

My mind was pulled deeper into the visions. The memories danced like shadows, flitting by too quickly before the next one pushed in. They blurred in my mind until the memory sort of skipped, and it wasn't one of Marcel's memories anymore. It was mine.

The woman stands outside, her back to me as I peer through the wooden barn slats. Her arms rise, palms out in front of her as if she is holding back an invisible force. White magic flares around her. I feel the strength of it in my chest, humming with power. Beyond her, I see a wall of men and snarling beasts—Rakken.

"Mom!" I scream.

A rough hand grabs my arm, and I twist around in surprise. Marcel. His face is younger than I expect, a teenager with shaggy hair.

"We have to go!" he shouts over the piercing howls of the Rakken.

I twist to look back over my shoulder. "She needs me! I can help!"

"No! She's buying us time!" He pulls me behind him, and I crane my neck to keep my mom in sight even as Marcel pulls me away. "Run!"

The last thing I see before I am dragged away is the Rakken and a blaze of white magic from outside.

My heart lurched, filling my chest with painful tightness. I pulled back from the memories with tears trailing down my cheeks. When I opened them, I was surprised to see Silas holding my hand. Stephan's emotional dampening let up, and the full weight of what I'd learned settled over me.

Silas searched my face, his grip strong. "What did you see?"

"I saw..." I tried to sort out all the snippets. There was too much emotion to deal with as I tried to process everything I'd learned. I took a deep, steadying breath. "Marcel searched for me in Boston. He thought I could help them." I swallowed thickly.

Silas's brow furrowed in concern.

"I think I'm experiencing his memories *and* mine. I just had another memory of my own. I think I just saw our mother die," I whispered. "Marcel was my brother."

Surprise flashed across Silas's and Stephan's faces.

I took a shuddering breath, and Silas rubbed his thumb across my knuckles.

I pulled my hand away. I could only deal with so much emotional drama at one time. "Thank you for helping me," I said, my voice too tight. I stood.

They both rose with similar expressions of concern.

"Maeve?" The soft way Silas said my name tugged at my emotions, and more tears pooled in my eyes.

I wrapped my arms around myself. I'd just found out I had a brother who was murdered trying to save me, and a family I didn't remember because I'd been taken by a person I had trusted completely. I had no idea who I was anymore, and I didn't want an audience for the breakdown I was about to have. "I need a minute alone."

Chapter Thirty

The scent of night-blooming flowers floated on the air as I leaned against the balcony railing overlooking Aeterna. The sweet, musky smell was a sharp contrast to the anxious anticipation pooling in my gut.

It had been two days since my realization about my true past, and I had spent it trying to come to terms. Marcel was my brother, and that meant I was part of the Lost Sect, just like Titus had said. I didn't remember anything about my family or my abilities because the person I'd seen as my father figure had kidnapped me and stolen my memories. To add to my anxiety, last night had been the Brotherhood's secret recruitment meeting.

"Atticus has been transported to Earth," Silas said, striding onto the balcony. He stripped off his white Councilor's robe and tossed it on the back of one of the outdoor loveseats.

I forced my feet into action and moved to the loveseat. We suspected Atticus would get recruited, and probably even that night, but I still questioned the decision to put him in danger. I tucked my feet under me on the small sofa and gazed into the darkening sky. Aria and Stephan sat quietly on the other sofa, curled into each other. Atticus was our only lead toward finding out the Brotherhood's plans. But now that his undercover mission was a reality, dread weighed on me.

"So he's in?" I asked, biting my lip. The day before, Atticus's sentence had been publicly lifted, thanks to his heroic efforts to save my life at the Exposition. The news had spread through the Lower City like wildfire. Titus's original plan had been to make him into a martyr for their cause, but a living hero was better than nothing. Pardoning Atticus had been a guaranteed way to get him into the Brotherhood.

"Yes. We already got our first communication from him." Silas set a small red rock down on the table in front of me. It was the pre-assigned symbol for a successful insertion into the Brotherhood.

The communication system was my idea. Just like the Guardians conjured weapons by marking them with a sigil and pulling them with magic, Atticus had a small satchel that could transfer everyday objects with a tiny amount of magic to the coordinating one we had. Each one had a preassigned meaning. It was sort of like uploading and downloading documents from the internet.

Silas took up my abandoned spot and leaned against the railing overlooking the city. "But no unusual activity was logged at the portal."

We'd been expecting that, but at least it confirmed our theory that the Brotherhood had a second portal. "We need to find the other portal," I said, stating the obvious.

The corners of Silas's mouth pulled down. "Short of sweeping Aeterna with Guardians, I've done everything I can. We'll have to wait until Atticus can send us a more detailed message."

"What about that Landas fellow?" Stephan asked.

"Nothing," Silas said. "No deviations from his assignments at the Guardian compound or the Council Centre."

"He's lying low after you scared him," I accused. "I told you to back off."

"Or perhaps he's able to access the portal from one of those places," Stephan suggested.

Silas frowned. "Both are secure. I would know about a portal at either location. The Council has to clear all access points, and they're extremely paranoid about anything they can't control."

Aria cleared her throat. "My father had a portal in his personal chambers before Earth was closed. Could they be using one like that?"

"A private portal?" Silas asked, shocked. "Why didn't you tell us this earlier? This could be the proof we need of Alaric's involvement with the Brotherhood."

Aria's hands twisted in her lap.

Stephan threw a scowl at his brother. Silas started pacing in long, quick strides that carried him down the length of the narrow balcony and back again.

Aria gave me a sad smile. "We used to take trips to Earth for chocolates when I was a child."

Stephan wrapped his arm around her shoulders. No matter how miserable her life had been since the prophecy and the arranged bonding, she loved her father. She had Stephan, so maybe she wasn't as unhappy as she could have been. But still, her feelings had to be complicated.

"I'm surprised the Council didn't find it when they searched his office." Silas's brow furrowed. "Unless..." He paused, his eyes narrowing. "Alaric must be diverting power to cloak it—even the flare. Gods, that would take an enormous amount of magic."

"But Alaric controls the allocation of all energy resources," Stephan said. "He could figure out a way to divert enough magic for a second portal with anyone suspecting."

"That's what Maeve suggested," Silas said in agreement. "It might be tied to the energy rationing. If he's cloaking it, we'd have to literally stand in front of it when it was activated. There's no way we'll find it on our own."

"Does it only take a big power boost to activate a portal? Or is there like a magic password or something?" I earned confused looks from all of them. "How much magic would it take to activate a portal?"

A grin spread across Silas's face as he caught up with my idea.

A FEW HOURS LATER, I followed Silas through the port and emerged at the mountain's base below the Council Centre. I barely had to pause as the world reoriented around me. My lessons with Atticus and Tessa were paying off.

I followed Silas up the double set of stairs and deep into the mountainside. The guards stationed sporadically throughout the Council Centre hallways saluted Silas as we passed. Some glanced at me, but just as Silas had said, no one questioned a Councilor being there in the middle of the night, even with a guest. We'd debated bringing Aria and Stephan but decided it would attract too much attention.

We walked quickly through the giant, empty main chamber, our footsteps echoing off the stone floor. I scanned the empty seats, remembering my first day in Aeterna when I'd stood in front of the Council with my life spinning out of control. We reached the wall behind the raised sun platform. Silas paused in front of a sealed door and held his hand in front of a scanner. The door chirped and melted away.

"Was that a spell? I didn't see a flare."

"Latent identification," he said.

Right. I didn't know which was more confusing: advanced magic or advanced technology.

We passed chamber doors decorated with the same symbols carved into the backs of the Council chairs, one for each Councilor. Silas greeted Lady Treva as we walked by. She gave me a curious glance but didn't say anything as she continued past us.

We paused outside Alaric's door. Finding the second portal was our only lead. Proving that Alaric had one would be the solid evidence we needed to help convict Alaric as the traitor on the Council. If my plan didn't work, or if the second portal wasn't there, we would have to wait days to hear back from Atticus. And that was assuming the Brotherhood had allowed the new recruits to see where the second portal was as they'd transported them to Earth. I somehow suspected Titus wasn't that trusting.

The raised depiction in the center of Alaric's office door held a triangle with weaving lines wrapped around each of the three sides—the symbol for magical energy, reflecting Alaric's stewardship over energy distribution and the training of magic users. Atticus had taught me a lot about the Council.

I pulled Ripper from my thigh holster.

Silas raised an eyebrow.

I shrugged. "I'm not taking any chances."

"I'm pleased to see you taking your safety seriously for once."

I rolled my eyes, and Silas activated the door with a little chuckle. He tapped a panel inside, and the door materialized behind us.

"No locks?" I asked.

"Not for Councilors. Our offices remain accessible as a symbol of our trust and unity." He snorted. "*And* Alaric's additional security was already neutralized when the Council swept his chambers."

Shelves overflowing with random objects lined the walls. I could've spent hours examining all the things in the room. Most of his collection seemed to be household items from Earth except that each one glowed with pale-magic power. My eyes snagged on a glowing toaster and a TV remote that both radiated faint, clear energy.

In contrast to the clutter of the rest of the office, Alaric's desk held only one item—a small opaque crystal resting on a three-pronged stand. I picked it up and jumped when an image appeared in my mind. A little girl ran with a gleeful smile, her long blond hair swirling behind her. *Aria.* A warm feeling of fatherly pride spread through my chest.

"That's a memory catcher," Silas said behind me.

I set the stone back on its stand, and the feelings faded with the hologram. I still didn't understand how Alaric could risk his own daughter to set me up. Maybe he hadn't intended for her to be swept up in the skimming spell. "Do you think these"—I gestured around the room—"knickknacks are going to be a problem?"

"The Magistry neutralized them. They shouldn't have enough residual power to do anything. But we should be careful. Don't stand too near."

I moved to the center of the room. Each of the magic-powered objects had a small presence in my mind, creating an outline of the room I could have seen with my eyes closed.

Silas's magic flared next to me. "I am ready."

"Here goes nothing," I whispered.

I imagined Silas's magic funneling to me, out through my hands, and back into the room. The energy began to respond, and I shivered in pleasure. I hadn't taken very much through our bond, but it was hard to let it go again. I focused and pushed it outward. Once I kick-started my power by absorbing his, I kept the flow going from my own magic, just as I'd practiced with Atticus and Tessa. The objects closest to me glowed brighter. I pushed the power farther, lighting up items along the way.

Terrified I would take too much, I carefully drew more of Silas's magic by pulling a small stream through our shared bond. I held all the building magic inside until the pressure became uncomfortable.

With Silas watching closely, I threw my palms out and pushed all of our combined magic into the room.

The blast of magic sent an entire wall of knickknacks vibrating. The clattering noise grew louder as I funneled the entire burst of energy into the small office.

The air in front of us shimmered and formed an iridescent doorway.

I stared wide-eyed, almost not believing my plan had worked. We'd found the second portal.

The surface flickered. I cocked my head to the side, trying to figure out what it was doing.

"Shite!" Silas pushed me out of the way.

I fell to the floor in a heap just as magic surged over my head and flexed back.

A man walked through.

Legatis Landas froze mid-step with his mouth open in surprise. We stared at each other. Silas tackled him from behind, and Landas fell to the ground with a surprised yelp. Silas's magic flooded the room, forming a multilayered matrix of energy before it solidified into a pattern more complex than anything I had seen before. There were at least five layers that settled over Landas in a net-like spell.

Pinned facedown, Landas struggled against Silas's hold without success.

"Get something to tie him up," Silas said with a grunt.

I scanned the room, spinning in a full circle.

"Hurry!"

"It's not like this is the Home Depot!" My eyes landed on an old lamp. I grabbed it off the shelf and held it out to Silas.

He raised an eyebrow. *Damn his judgy eyebrows straight to hell.*

"Use the cord."

The lamp clanged on the floor as Silas looped the long cord around Landas's hands, binding them with efficient movements.

"What did you conjure?" I asked as Silas sat Landas up, still locked in an unbreakable hold.

"I blocked his magic."

No wonder the layers were so complicated. I wondered if that was the same spell the Brotherhood had used to make the necklaces that held Aria and me. A remembered shiver of terror flashed over me, but I pushed it down. We were going to stop the Brotherhood from hurting anyone again, and Landas was the first one on the list.

"You're going to tell us everything you know, you manky arsehole," Silas demanded.

Landas scowled but kept silent.

"I could get it out of him," Silas said with a sideways glance at me.

I grimaced. There had to be a better option than beating him. "What about a compulsion?"

Landas lost his smug expression. Real fear burned in his eyes.

"You can't put a compulsion on someone with magic."

"But the Brotherhood did it to Atticus," I said. "Maybe there's something different about their magic?"

"It's worth a try." Silas's power wove through the air, forming the layers of the conjuring. He tried for several minutes, but each time the last layer finished, it sort of slid off of Landas. "Gods dammit! It's not working." He adjusted his hold on Landas. "It's just not possible to compel Aeternals."

But Atticus had been compelled by someone with the Brotherhood's stolen powers, and Silas had put a compulsion on that Mundane officer. "Could it be something about their magic being different—like Humans to Shifters?"

Landas tried to rein in his growing terror and failed miserably. His eyes flicked between us. We were onto something.

Silas's eyes lit up. "Not races. Differentiated power *sources*."

"That's how the Brotherhood put the compulsion on Atticus!" I said. "By using the stolen life magic as a completely different source from Atticus's magic!"

Landas struggled against Silas's hold.

"Does the Lost Sect use Earth's Source?" I asked. Maybe *I* had access to that source.

"Let's find out," Silas replied in sync with my thoughts.

With Silas still holding him from behind, I crouched in front of Landas. "I don't know how to do it."

Landas slammed his head forward and tried to head-butt me. I fell back on my rear, narrowly dodging his attack.

Silas punched him hard across the chin with a solid hit that made my teeth ache. Landas slumped to the ground and stayed there, groaning.

I remembered firsthand how much that hurt. "Was that really necessary?"

Silas shrugged and shook out his hand. "It was satisfying."

Silas told me how to build the compulsion, layer by layer. I had already seen and unraveled each of the layers on Atticus's, so I was able to build the conjuring quickly. The layers solidified and covered Landas. This time, it stuck to him.

I had a moment of conflicted emotion about forcing him to follow our commands but decided it was different than what the Brotherhood had done to Atticus. It was only active as long as I held it—it wasn't permanent. We weren't going to make him confess to crimes he hadn't committed or make him our slave. All we needed was the truth, then we would let him go to face the consequences of his actions.

"Tell me who you're working with on the Council," Silas demanded.

The door pinged open. Hunched over Landas, I froze in complete surprise. Elias stood in the doorway, flanked by Guardians, and glowing a vibrant yellow. He took in the room and Legatis Landas tied up on the ground.

"What's going on here?" Elias demanded.

"This man is part of the Brotherhood," Silas said. "He's going to tell us who he's working with on the Council."

Elias narrowed his eyes at me. "You're using compulsion."

"We realized that Maeve could—" Silas paused, his brows drawn together. "How did you know that a compulsion spell was possible on an Aeternal?"

My entire body tensed. "And how can you see what we're doing?"

Elias's eyes flicked between Landas and us before his mouth pursed.

Silas slowly unfurled from his crouch as he stood and faced Elias. His eyes stayed locked on the Councilor. "Landas, who are you working with on the Council?"

"Lord Elias," Landas responded blankly.

Elias's magic flared. With a flick of his hand, the Guardians fell to the ground. I couldn't tell whether they were unconscious or dead before a wave of energy slashed through the chamber. Silas dove in front of me, blocking it with a wall of his own magic. He rolled to his feet just as Elias flung another attack at us.

Silas and I dove to the ground. I landed next to Landas just as the compulsion spell around him crumbled. He picked up the heavy, antique lamp between his tied hands and swung it like a baseball bat at my head. I dodged and slashed at him with Ripper, drawing blood from a shallow cut to his forearm. He scrambled behind the desk.

Elias lobbed magic through the small office. Knickknacks shattered with deafening sounds all around us. A wooden shelf exploded to my left. Splinters flew at my face, and I threw myself on the ground again. *Too close.*

Landas reemerged from behind the desk with his hands untied. He ran at me, and I popped back onto my feet, preparing to fight him off.

"Down!" Silas yelled.

I dropped like a good soldier and covered my head with my arms. Silas's magic flashed, sending a wave of power toward our enemies.

Elias threw up a shield and blocked Silas's assault. He backed into the desk, where Landas once again crouched under cover. Silas followed them both with his sword clutched in his hand, blood dripping from a gash on his other arm.

Elias grabbed Landas, twisted, and spun him into the sword's path. The blade slid into the Legatis's chest. He didn't even have time to react. His body went limp, and he slumped over the sword with a surprised grunt.

Elias kicked the Legatis's body forward, knocking Silas off-balance. He fell backward and landed on the ground, pinned under Landas's dead weight.

Energy swirled around Elias. A snarl twisted his handsome face with animalistic fury as he intentionally sliced his palm on the blade still sticking out of Landas's back and grabbed Silas's wounded arm. Their blood connected, magic flared, and Elias pulled the magic from Silas.

Silas cried out, and his whole body convulsed.

"No!" I screamed. I pushed to my feet, gripping Ripper. I reached for my magic, but I couldn't grab hold. The energy drained in streams from Silas. Elias's aura flared brighter, a harsh golden brilliance surrounding him.

I threw my knife at Elias's chest. He flinched away at the last second, and it caught him in the shoulder. He stumbled backward and tripped over a busted toaster oven. He fell. His head smacked the edge of the desk, and he crumpled to the floor.

I helped roll Landas's dead weight off Silas, and he pushed shakily to his knees.

"Silas! Your magic!" His aura had faded from a brilliant golden color to a sickly pale yellow. The wrongness of the color made my insides twist.

A fresh group of Guardians rushed into the room.

"Help!" Elias groaned from the floor, grasping his bloody head. "They're trying to kill me!"

"Seize Elias!" Silas commanded.

The Guardians stood frozen between the Lord Councilor and their new Lord Commander.

Elias pushed himself up along the desk, my knife sticking out of his shoulder. "Lord Silas is working with the Brotherhood!" Elias's voice was a perfect mixture of horror and anger.

"No, wait. Elias is the traitor!" I yelled.

"They killed the Guardians!" Elias countered.

Covered in Landas's blood, Elias pointed toward Silas's sword still sticking out of the Legatis's chest.

The guards' faces hardened as they took in the sight of that plus the bodies of dead Guardians littering the floor.

Silas pulled the sword out of Landas's chest with a wet sucking sound that made me cringe. He wobbled as he pushed himself to his feet and raised his sword. His magic flared that sickly pale yellow color as he faced down the four men approaching us. We weren't going to be able to fight our way out of this mess. If we surrendered, it would be our word against Elias's, and there was a whole lot of bloody evidence against us.

"Lay down your weapons," Silas commanded. But the guards didn't stop. The visible evidence against us was too damning. Silas snarled as the guards advanced.

I grabbed the first thing I could reach—Alaric's memory catcher. I pulled energy from it to kick-start my powers and pushed magic toward the hidden portal. It flared, and everyone dove, avoiding the burst of magic that flexed into the room.

The portal was our only escape route. "Come on!" I yelled at Silas.

With a feral snarl on his face, Silas spun back toward Elias, who had worked his way over by the door and to safety behind the Guardians. The Guardians moved in unison, like the well-trained unit they were, throwing a wave of energy at us. I threw my hands over my face, but the expected blast never came.

Silas held a shield between us and the wave of searing magic.

The guards on the other side blurred behind the incredible heat as Silas strained to hold it back.

"Silas!"

His shield cracked around us, unraveling. We backed toward the portal.

"Go! I'll hold the shield!" he yelled.

"Hurry!" I yelled as I jumped through the portal.

Chapter Thirty-One

I landed hard, stumbling face-first onto the dusty plywood floor. The memory catcher rolled out of my grip and landed in a strip of sun streaming from a huge window framed in industrial black metal. I grabbed the drained crystal and twisted around to stare at my portal. All that remained was an old brick wall embedded with the stone outline of a gate.

The portal was closed. I was alone, and Silas was nowhere to be seen.

The realization clicked—Silas had never planned on following me through the portal. I scrambled to my feet and placed my hands on the brickwork. I had to get back there. Silas wasn't going to be able to hold that shield on his own. I tried to access my power, but nothing happened. I was too frantic, and I had no one else to absorb magic from to kick-start my own. Even the memory crystal was drained.

I pounded on the brick wall with both fists. "Dammit! You stupid, stubborn idiot!"

He was going to get himself killed. I took a deep, unsteady breath. There was nothing I could do for him now. I had to trust that he would be okay, because the alternative was unacceptable. In the meantime, I had no idea where I was. Panic flared. I'd just traveled through the Brotherhood's portal, which meant some of them could be there. I had to get out quickly. Judging from my view out the window, I was on an upper floor. The building had structural, exposed brick walls and a thin layer of dust. An attic. The room had a random assortment of mismatched furniture that had to have been acquired from the streets on trash day. I inhaled the sweet smell of fortune cookies.

I swore at my own stupidity. It made sense that the Brotherhood's portal was where they'd kept Marcel, back near Boston. I was an idiot for not thinking of that earlier.

A narrow set of winding stairs led to the only exit from the floor. I pocketed the crystal and crept down them, expecting an attack at any moment. The staircase groaned, and I froze. My own breathing was loud in my ears as I inched down the last five steps and emerged on the main floor of the factory. I escaped through the empty storefront without issue. Outside, in the early morning sun, it was cold without a jacket and only a thin tunic for cover. The change in temperature was a surprise. The warm, moderate weather of Aeterna had not prepared me for the crisp fall air of Boston. I wrapped my arms around myself as my mind spun in circles.

I needed to get away from there before the Brotherhood found me. But I had nowhere to go and no money to get there. I ached to head to the shelter and pretend that Father Mike would be there to comfort me. The pain of his betrayal stabbed me again. Instead, I forced myself in the direction of Davis Square and the bus station.

Ten minutes later, I slid through the back doors of an overcrowded bus of morning commuters. The driver either didn't notice me avoiding the fare or didn't care. I crouched low in my seat as we rumbled through Boston. I got off a dozen stops later, a random choice that landed me in Copley Square, an upscale urban area in Boston's Back Bay.

Wandering through the streets, surrounded by a mix of historic brick buildings and modern skyscrapers, I still had no idea what to do. I found an out-of-the-way spot where I wouldn't have to worry about people passing by—especially at such an early hour—and slumped on a green metal bench. I was out of options. I had no resources and no plans.

My fingers clenched around Marcel's charm as my thoughts returned to Silas. The stubborn idiot was either dead or imprisoned. I rubbed the arm branded with his House sigil. Fear curled up my spine. Silas could be dead. I closed my eyes and tried to sense him through our bond but felt nothing. I didn't know if I was too far away or if that meant he was dead. I shook off the terrible possibility. He was too damn stubborn to die. I had to believe he would be okay and focus on keeping my own butt safe. Silas would insist on it.

There was really only one option left. I needed to find the Lost Sect. If I were one of their descendents, maybe they would help me. At the very least, they probably wouldn't kill me and steal my magic. At least, I hoped not. And if they had the same abilities, maybe they could teach me how to use the magic stuck inside me, and I could figure out a way to rescue Silas.

But the Council and the Brotherhood had both tried to find the Lost Sect and had failed for decades. All I knew for sure was that they were here in Earth. As I thought, my leg bounced up and down as if I'd thrown back a six-pack of energy drinks.

I froze when I realized I unconsciously sensed power in my surroundings, as though the air itself was full of magic. I closed my eyes, opened my mind, and inhaled the energy all around me. Magic was everywhere. When I realized this, my powers expanded, flaring around me. Now that I was calm, accessing my magic seemed easy. It required almost no effort, like breathing. I didn't know whether to laugh or cry at the realization. This had to be the difference between the Aeternal and Earthen sources. My ability to put the compulsion on Landas had confirmed my connection to the Earthen source. Here in Earth, I was closer to my magic than ever before.

Marcel's charm pulsed in my palm. I grasped it tighter and sensed the faintest of pulls. If Marcel was one of the Lost Sect, maybe I could use his—

Pressure twisted my stomach.

Two men skimmed in front of me, clad in leather and carrying swords. The closest one grabbed me by the shoulders. A familiar pulling sensation started to form. He tried to skim off with me.

I grabbed a head full of brown hair and slammed my knee into his face. He cried out, grasping his bleeding nose. I twisted out of the other man's reach and jumped off the bench. I pushed energy into Marcel's charm, praying it would do what I believed it would. The familiar sensation of skimming pulled me through the air. The bus stop fell away.

HORSE-DRAWN BUGGIES rolled along a gravel road, and wood-framed buildings lined both sides of a dirt street down the center of what appeared to be a small town. Men and women walking on the street stopped mid-step to stare at me.

I spun in a circle, trying to process the new location. *Did I just time travel?* I was definitely still in Earth, but the town surrounding me completely lacked any modern technology from what I could see. The people weren't dressed in Amish clothing, though—I saw jeans and T-shirts all around.

Someone yelled. Magic flared all around me. An entire arsenal of personal weapons appeared, flashing threateningly toward me from every man and woman in view.

I held up my palms and looked around in awe. Every flare glowed white like mine.

A netlike spell sprang over me with the same complex magical tapestry Silas had conjured on Landas, blocking my magic until I could barely even feel the energy around me. As if I'd lost my sense of smell, everything dulled.

I resisted the urge to fight back as two men grabbed me by the shoulders. Without a word of explanation, they marched me through the town with my arms pinned to my sides. I'd found the Lost Sect, now I needed to talk them into helping me. "I need to talk to someone in charge! I'm one of you. Hey! I said I need to talk to your leader."

They didn't answer as they frog-marched me forward. A crowd of people followed us, murmuring and whispering. I fell silent and waited to see where they were taking me.

The buildings we passed were basic—mostly single-story structures with barn-shaped roofs. Two buildings rose higher than the others—a large bell tower and a barn-shaped hall with a flat-roofed square extension. It was either their Town Hall, their school, or their church. Maybe it was all three. As they marched me down the gravel road, the crowd trailing us grew, their auras lit with white magic.

I tried to take in everything. Equal parts excitement and nervousness rushed me. I'd found the Lost Sect. But as usual, I didn't have a good plan. I had no idea how to talk them into helping me. If they were anything like the Council, they would want something in return for their help. But I had nothing to offer and no backup plan.

The men pulled me inside the tall Town Hall building, leaving the crowd outside. The large, open room had exposed wooden beams in the high ceiling, but the space was dominated by a stone table with six sectioned pieces placed together in a large, wide circle. Plain wooden chairs sat in rows of circles around the stone table, creating rings of seating for at least a hundred.

Three people sat at the stone table. A lean, fit man with receding sand-colored hair stood with a stiffness in his stance that made me think he might have been favoring an old injury. The second man had olive skin and small, square glasses. They both wore basic T-shirts and jeans and appeared to be in their late thirties. The latter man frowned as he looked me over.

The third person, a woman, wore a white button-up shirt tucked into a high-waisted black skirt that flowed to her ankles. Her auburn hair was swept into a bun at the nape of her neck.

My attention froze on her, and my brain stopped working. It was the woman from the photographs.

Her keen gaze took me in. "Maeve?"

I flinched. "Who are you?"

"Let her go."

The men released me, and I shook out my numb arms as the magic-blocking spell around me melted away.

"How much do you remember?" the woman asked.

I opened my mouth and closed it again. Memories twisted in my brain, but I pushed them down, afraid of losing control. This woman was triggering some serious confusion. I stared harder, trying to decide if she was the person in the photograph—the woman Silas had guessed was my mother.

"I'm Deanna." Her eyes drifted over my features, and her mouth dropped into a small frown. "This is Casius." She pointed to the man at her side. "And Thomas." She indicated the man with glasses, who scrunched his face in confusion.

She addressed the men without turning away from me. "It's her, right? I'm not losing my mind?"

"Definitely her," said the man she'd called Casius.

"Do you know who I am?" I asked.

"Maeve." She rolled my name the same way Silas did.

I brushed away a pang of anxiety. I had to trust that he was okay. There was nothing more I could do to help Silas.

"Gods, I haven't said that name in ages. Your mother always loved that name."

Images of the auburn-haired woman from my memory surfaced, bringing along a sharp ache in my chest. There was so much I didn't understand. "You know my mother? Who are you?"

Deanna cocked her head to the side, and her mouth pursed. "Your mother was my twin sister. I'm your aunt."

My brain started prickling. The hair and her features were so like my own. It was like looking into a fun-house mirror—the parts were different, but they were all there. I swallowed around a dry throat. "I don't remember you."

Her eyes narrowed, suspicious. "Then how did you find us?"

I held up Marcel's charm, still on the chain around my neck. "I channeled power into this."

"We don't make homing spells. It's too dangerous if it falls into the wrong hands." She leaned in to examine the charm without touching it. "Thomas?"

The older man leaned forward, pushing his glasses up his nose as he too looked at Marcel's charm without touching it. "It's been imbued with magic from our source. It's not a homing spell exactly, but you must have followed it back to us through accessing your own magic. It's quite clever, actually. Only one of our own would have been able to use it."

"Where did you get it?" Deanna asked.

"I found it, and it brought me here." My answer was vague, but I didn't dare give her more information. Even if she was my aunt, I didn't know if I could trust her yet.

She pursed her lips, thinking, before she spoke again. "You don't remember anything else?"

"Honestly, something is wrong with my memories. I think I was taken from my real family, and it had something to do with your people here."

"You weren't taken; you left us six years ago."

A dull throbbing started behind my eyes.

She nodded at my arm. "Your magic and memories were bound after your mother died."

Her words felt like a weight, slowly crushing me. I considered the interlocking triangles inked onto my skin. *Holy hells.* The tattoo wasn't a tattoo at all; it was a magic-blocking spell.

"May I?" She reached for my forearm, and power flared around her.

I nodded then flinched as she touched the tip of her finger to the tattoo, but no pain followed. The mark flooded with energy until she pulled her finger away, and the glow faded. "The binding is still partially active," she concluded. "We can help you unbind the rest, and your memories should return. If it wasn't intentional, do you know what caused the binding to begin breaking down?"

I paused, unsure if I should tell her about the power Marcel had stolen from the Brotherhood and that they were chasing me. I didn't want to scare her off before I figured out what had really happened to me. I needed their help. "I think Marcel, my, uh, brother, did it. He transferred a lot of power to me when he died."

Deanna's face tightened, and she sat down. Moisture pooled in her blue-green eyes. "I'm so sorry, Mae. He left several months ago. I didn't know what he was planning, or I would have tried to stop him from leaving."

The emotion in her voice made me feel guilty for breaking the news to her like that. She was his aunt, after all. "I'm sorry. I don't really remember him—other than his final moments. I have this whole other set of memories, and neither seems completely real." She seemed to really care about what had happened to me, so I swallowed and decided to go for the big ask. "Will you help me remember?"

She reached toward me but pulled back without touching me. "Of course we will. We're family. After your mother was murdered, your father agreed to help you forget. He didn't think you were safe here anymore, and he wanted you to have a chance at a normal life." She shook her head as though she didn't agree. "He hid you among the Mundanes."

Blurry feelings and half-remembered recollections started to click into place in my brain. "You mean Michael Smithson—Father Mike?"

She nodded. "Your father."

My memories started bleeding at the edges. "How is that possible? I..."

My father reaches for our hands, his eyes puffy and bloodshot. "It's for the best," he says.

I glance at Marcel next to me. He stares back at our father with a hard face. "Mom always said we're stronger together—"

"Marcel." My father sighs, his face tight with a weary expression. "Come with us. It's not safe here anymore."

My feelings are so raw that I'm numb. I don't want to feel this way anymore. I can't keep running and waiting for them to find us. I can't do it anymore. I just want to forget.

Marcel pushes back from the table and lurches to his feet. The chair screeches across the wood floor. "Then leave! Run away and hide. But don't pretend it's what's best for all of us!"

The memory slammed me into one of the wooden chairs lining the aisle. Tears burned behind my eyes. I couldn't believe I'd ever doubted him. Even without my memories, Father Mike had always been my family. He'd always loved me and taken care of me.

"Where is he?" Deanna asked, glancing toward the door as though expecting him to walk in. "I would have thought Michael would come with you or at least send word."

The tears spilled over. "If he's not here, then the Brotherhood has him. Titus promised to kill him."

Deanna's face drained of color. She stood from her chair before she changed her mind and sat back down again. "I didn't know. I'm so sorry." Her lips tightened into a thin white line. "We've all lost so much."

We sat in silence. I couldn't wrap my brain around how everything I'd learned about my past was possible. My whole life was made up, and now that I'd finally gotten some answers, I'd already lost an entire family I didn't remember. I'd chosen to walk away from the painful memories six years ago, and I wasn't sure if I was ready to get them back. I had so much to figure out.

Finally, I found at least one concrete question I could ask. "What does that mean exactly? That you bound my magic? And what did that have to do with my mother's death?"

"We'd established a remote farm in northern Idaho. Every few years, the Council would send a patrol of Guardians, and we'd have to hide for a few months or relocate if they got too close. But for the most part, we lived undisturbed." Deanna swept her long black skirt to the side and sat back in her chair. "Until the Brotherhood. Six years ago, they found us, and Delilah—your mother—sacrificed herself so the rest of us could escape. She was our strongest, the Anchor of our Circle.

"After she was killed, we realized the Brotherhood had found a way to trace our magic. They were hunting us, absorbing our powers and with them our ability to access Earth's Source. We were a risk to the very thing we had sworn to protect."

She reached over and squeezed my hand. The gesture felt familiar and foreign at the same time.

"The Sect fractured," she continued. "Some chose to hide in remote locations like this farm, shielded by magic-dampening spells;

others moved to heavily populated areas, hoping to blend in. Some even gave up their magic and became like the Mundanes."

At that, Thomas and Casius shared a look, and I realized there was a lot more to that story. It sounded as though their entire community had fallen apart.

"Your father bound your magic in order to hide you and erased the traumatic memory of your mother's murder. He thought you could live a normal life. We... disagreed. You were so young, and the trauma was so fresh. You just needed time to heal." She leaned toward me and rested her hand on my arm. "You begged him to help you forget. In the end, it was not my decision, so we helped him do it. We bound your memories and your magic, and you both left. I've regretted it every day since."

The sharp pain in my chest grew, like a fist squeezing my heart. It became hard to breathe. *I had a mother. Delilah. Father Mike was Michael, my father. My brother, Marcel, and my aunt, Deanna.* Faces and names and memories flitted around the edges of my consciousness.

It was too much. I stood and paced the aisle between chairs. Casius had to sit down to avoid being bowled over. Silas's stress management habits had rubbed off on me.

The random thought sent another pang of fear through my chest. I could lose Silas too. He could already be dead.

Thomas cleared his throat. "I've never heard of this happening before, that one person could undo a binding spell—even partially. It should require a direct connection to a source."

I finally pieced it all together. "Marcel used the Brotherhood's magic to do it." What I'd seen in the flashes, and in my own tattered memories, formed the picture I'd been avoiding. "I believe he came to Boston to bring me home, but they found him first. Titus tortured him to give up the location of the Sect, but he wouldn't, so they tried to do a Transference to steal his abilities and his memories." I swallowed hard. I had no memories of Marcel as my brother, but the memories of his torture were terrible. "Marcel found me, magically I mean. We connected just before they killed him."

Thomas scooted forward in his chair, his expression intent. "He linked with you during a Transference?"

I remembered the very first vision I'd had and the wave of crushing magic that I'd believed to be a panic attack. We were connected at the moment Titus slit Marcel's throat—the exact moment at which he'd performed the Transference. "Yes. I'm positive. He used their magic to break the binding on my magic. I have the Brotherhood's magic that he stole during the botched spell, and they're trying to kill me to get it back."

Casius tapped his fingers on his thigh. "I didn't even know that was possible."

Tears filled Deanna's eyes. "He was a fine young man. I'm so sorry, Mae."

The familiar use of my nickname—the name Father Mike called me—was like a stab to my heart. I didn't remember them yet, but I couldn't deny that these people were my family—a family I'd forgotten because of the Brotherhood. My hate for Titus made me physically hurt. I added Elias to that list; he'd betrayed his people and mine. They both had to be stopped. My pain hardened into anger. I wouldn't let all the sacrifices be for nothing. I would hunt them both down and kill them.

"Marcel fought the Brotherhood until the very end," I said. "I'm going to stop them. They're going to pay for Marcel, for Father M—my father. For my mother. For everyone."

I locked gazes with Deanna, Casius, and Thomas. Their expressions reflected my sadness and anger.

"Will you help me stop them?"

Determination spread over each of their faces. "We're stronger together," Deanna said. "It's time to fight back."

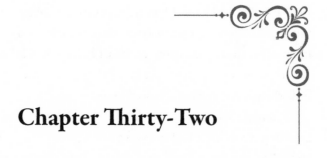

Chapter Thirty-Two

Magic flowed over the circular stone table in the middle of the large hall. At each section, one of the six leaders of the Sect stood in front of a carved magic symbol. They called themselves the Circle. I stood between Deanna and Casius. Thomas stood to Casius's left, and the other three Circle members—Tamara, Jason, and Leah—took the remaining positions.

Beyond the Circle, the rest of the Sect gathered, watching. Deanna told me they always included everyone in major decisions. Each person got a vote, and the room was packed with hundreds of people. The rows of chairs were filled, and more people stood behind those, watching.

I had expected some debate about the decision to fight, but there was none after Deanna showed them my flare. She expected me to take my mother's role of Anchor to the Circle, which would allow them to access the full power of the source and give them the opportunity to finally fight back against the Brotherhood.

It didn't escape my awareness that this was the very thing my father had tried to shield me from. Everyone in the room had lost someone to the Brotherhood. They were all done running. Now they were mostly concerned with making sure my magic actually worked. *No pressure.*

"Linking to the source should take care of the remainder of the binding," Deanna said. "Afterward, your memories should return fully. Go ahead and access your magic, and I'll show you how to join the Circle."

Everyone stared at me. It had been almost easy to access my magic since I'd returned to Earth, but all those eyes on me were making me doubt my ability to do it again. The stress of potential failure made it hard to focus. They were about to find out I knew absolutely nothing about magic. I cleared my throat. "I usually have to absorb someone else's power. I can't consistently do anything with my own magic."

"We call that drafting," Thomas said. "It's the most energy-efficient way to start a spell, but you don't have to do it that way every time. You should be able to access your own magic with the proper mindset."

"But I couldn't even access my power unless I took it from someone else. While I was in Aeterna, I tried —"

"Ah," Deanna said. "You were too far from your source. Try again. I believe you'll find the process a lot easier."

Her words confirmed my realization that being closer to my own source would help. I didn't need to take energy from other people to kick-start my own magic. I cleared my mind and opened my myself to the energy around me. Now that I understood it was my own magic, and I was calm and close to my own source, magic flared brightly around me. I sighed in relief.

Deanna laid her hand on my shoulder. "Good. Now imagine the magic as a physical form outside of you. Most people start with a sphere."

I formed the layers of an orb in my palms, grateful for my lessons with Atticus and Tessa so I didn't look like a complete idiot. The power flowed from me, pliant and responsive. It grew brighter in my palms.

"Now we'll exchange power to form the connection," Deanna said.

"Won't using this much magic alert the Brotherhood?" Titus had followed Silas's flare to our location in Alaska, and we were already channeling a lot more magic than anything I'd seen outside of Aeterna.

"No," Thomas said. "The shield dampens our magic. We're safe."

The ball of magic flew out of my hand to Jason, who was sitting across from me. I flinched in surprise.

He added his own power to it, growing the size, before it zipped to Leah. This time, though, Jason seemed to keep one of the threads in his hands, leaving a thin trail of magic connecting him and Leah. Casius took the orb next, and another silken thread of magic connected him to Leah. Soon, the entire Circle had passed the magic from one person to another, in a spiderweb of shared energy, until it returned to me.

Deanna leaned in, presumably to explain how to keep part of the magic for myself before it moved on, but I'd been watching closely. I nodded at Jason. He called the magic to himself, completing the full Circle, and I was ready. The smallest white thread stayed in my hands, connecting me to the Circle.

"Within the Circle," Deanna said, "you are the Focus, which means you'll be closest to the magic. We need as much as possible to flow through you in order to break the remainder of the binding spell. Because we share a blood bond, I will be your Anchor."

"I don't know what any of that means," I whispered.

"You don't remember," Deanna corrected. "But you will. Trust yourself and your training. We've done this before."

She had the same expression I'd often seen from Father Mike—my father. Pride. Love. Family.

I could do this even if I didn't remember how.

"We're aligned in order of power." She pointed around the Circle, and I realized that the flares receded on my left and right equally from the strong, bright flares of Casius and Deanna then faded into the softer, less intense flares of Leah and Jason, who stood across from me. *From strongest to weakest.*

"Wouldn't it be better to have only the most powerful magic users?" I asked, noting that there were stronger flares among the onlookers.

"The strongest users typically sit closest to the Anchor, to absorb more of the..." She searched for the right word. "Impact. But since we all draw from Earth's Source, the strength of the flare doesn't matter. That's also why we all flare white regardless of heritage. It's about balance. You'll see."

The magic built from person to person, creating an intricate, layered pattern that thrummed in my chest and head. The magic was stronger than anything I'd experienced before. We were connected to it as a part of us. It was perfectly balanced.

The net of energy lifted from each individual, high above our heads, weaving and growing. The flare was so pure, I could see the strands of color layered within it. Shades of blue, yellow, and red refracted like a prism. Just like the Council's powers, the combined magic created a white flare within our spell. Earth's Source was a perfectly balanced combination of all the different types of power from all the people living on the planet. The ring flexed and grew, forming an arc around us, connecting each of us to each other and the source. It was absolutely breathtaking.

"Can you feel it?" Deanna asked. "That is the life energy of an entire planet. It flows through all of us."

The feeling was like nothing I could describe. It was pure magic. It was energy and life, every life on the planet—all the realms, even Mundanes. It was all in there, and it was a part of me.

"This is why we couldn't let the Council drain Earth." Casius said quietly. "We've dedicated our lives to protecting it."

"Let's start the unbinding," Thomas said.

Deanna reached for my hand. When I placed my palm against hers, the power of the source pulsed inside my brain. I gasped as the walls in my mind fell away and the last of the binding shattered. Memories flooded back.

The smell of pine and earth as Marcel and I played in the woods together, building a secret fort between the trees.

My mother's words of encouragement as I practiced deconstructing the layers of a conjuring. The warmth and strength of her white magic filling the room and boosting my own fledgling powers.

Endless hours of weapons training with Casius.

My first kiss with a boy named Ethan.

My parents, happy and holding hands as we walked through a field ripe with stalks of tall grain.

The day my mother was murdered.

The pain of my mother's murder was so fresh. I actually grasped my chest. She died protecting me, Marcel, and our entire Sect. The anguish of her death felt like a jagged, burning hole in my chest. I couldn't breathe.

I had a different life than the one I'd thought I lived. In my real life, I had a family. We'd been happy before the Brotherhood. Fresh pain burned through me. The memories of Marcel's torture and murder were transferred with his attempt to unbind the spell hiding me, but the rest were mine. I had fought the old memories so hard that I'd pushed them down and repressed my own mind. Now, six years later, the binding was broken, and I was a different person entirely.

I opened my eyes and saw everything for the first time.

THE NEXT MORNING, I walked alongside my aunt Deanna through a field that was tall with a nearly ripe harvest of corn. She'd outfitted me in a plain brown shirt and a pair of too-short jeans. Size issues aside, I was glad to be back in denim.

I'd spent the evening remembering and reliving my own memories, but my memories of the Sect ended before they had come to this town. It was a strange homecoming. My entire understanding of who I was had shifted literally overnight. Even though the people in the town welcomed me like family, I still felt like an outsider. And the memories hurt. I had a lot of loss to deal with at once.

My anxious feelings weren't alleviated by the fact that the Circle had already turned down my request for help. They wouldn't create a portal back to Aeterna. I was frustrated, but I had to admit they had good reasons. Even with their magic-dampening shield to protect the town from being discovered, the Sect couldn't create a spell of that size without being found. I'd brought up the possibility of just getting a message to Aeterna—maybe to Stephan or Aria—but they didn't want to risk the Council finding out about them. Thomas had informed me that the dampening shield would make it impossible for magic of any kind to get out, so I couldn't do anything without their approval. Non-magical Mundanes could walk right through, but anything magic would get stopped. So I had no way on my own to communicate with anyone in Aeterna.

I'd tried connecting again to Silas through our bond, but I suspected the distance was too great, or maybe the shield blocked it. Either way, a growing knot of worry built in my stomach, but I didn't know what to do to help him. I'd even considered returning to the Brotherhood's portal in Boston, but without the Sect's help, it was too risky.

I finally forced myself to be brutally logical. If Silas was dead, there was nothing I could do about it. If the Council believed Elias, they would search for the proof they needed to vote on Silas's execution. And there wouldn't be any. They would give the search at least a few days, just as they had for Alaric. My best shot at freeing Silas would be to bring the Council the real traitors.

"What is all this?" I waved my hand in the air, indicating the miles of farmland surrounding us.

"We're considered a progressive branch of the Amish community." Deanna lifted her chin toward the translucent dome of energy stretched across the entire town, blocking any sign of our magic. It covered the entire town like a giant, delicate bubble, protecting us from discovery. "If only they knew just how 'progressive' we are."

The field opened to a large clearing, which revealed a row of wooden practice targets stretched in a line down the center. For several minutes, we watched Casius training a group of older teens, his lean frame standing tall and stiff as he instructed them.

He caught sight of us and trotted over, favoring his injured leg. "Do you remember any of your training?" he asked me.

I conjured Ripper into my hand. By the time I was fifteen, I had spent hundreds of hours training with him. Maybe even thousands. Every member of our Sect had since we were old enough to handle a weapon. As magic absorbers, we couldn't use our energy offensively, making physical weapons a necessity. Casius honed that necessity into an art.

The memories of living on the street and getting into knife fights were created by my own mind as a connection to my extensive training, but my skills were really the result of years of hard work. Silas was right—I had been trained in hand-to-hand combat. Even without my memories, my instincts had served me well against the Brotherhood.

I flipped Ripper in my palm and spun toward the targets twenty yards away. The knife flashed and landed in the center. *Bullseye.* "I remember."

The right half of Casius's mouth lifted. "We missed you, Mae."

The nickname made my lips curve up. These people were skilled and brave. But they had been on the run for years, and from what my aunt had told me, they'd hidden since my mother's murder. With the Brotherhood recruiting from Lower Aeterna, and Shifters going into Rakken mode—choosing to spend their time in their animal form until they lost their humanity—the Sect had no chance against the Brotherhood.

My spirits plummeted. Titus would expect them to be running or hiding. He wouldn't expect us to bring the fight to him. "We need something more magically offensive."

"Our magic doesn't work that way," Casius said. "Manipulating the energy into a conjuring is one thing, but pushing pure energy outward into anything offensive is counter to our abilities."

I wouldn't have questioned that belief before I lost my memories. "It's counter to our *instincts*, but it's not impossible. When I didn't know who I was, I absorbed the Brotherhood's magic and turned it against them. Several times."

"How?" Deanna asked, her eyes wide.

"I'll show you. I need someone to conjure up a really big energy ball."

Deanna called two teenagers over to us. Together, they built up a ball of magic the size of a watermelon. When the final binding layer was in place, I pulled it to me and focused hard not to absorb it, just as I had done in practice with Atticus and again with the tainted power from the Brotherhood. With the pure magic of my people at my fingertips, it was twice as hard.

With gritted teeth, I took control of the ball of magic, spun with it, and flung it into the target down the field. The target exploded into shards of wood and hay.

"That's brilliant!" Casius whooped.

We practiced conjuring and throwing the sizzling energy in teams. Not everyone could resist the urge to absorb the magic. I paired the fastest producers with the few who had success redirecting. Before long, a few had even come up with variations of the technique.

Joseph, a father of three young girls, became quite good at throwing smaller, more accurate orbs. Jason, the third male from the Sect's Circle, came up with a way to work in teams. Two people conjured small amounts of power and took turns feeding it to a third, who flung it at the desired target. As a team, they were able to move twice as fast with less strain on everyone.

We didn't stop practicing until the sun had set and we were all bone tired. That night, I sat with the Circle after the kids were long gone to bed and many of the spectators had drifted off for the night. The conversation moved to strategy, and the ideas were all over the place.

"We have to catch the Brotherhood off guard," I finally said. "We have to take the fight to them." I explained about Titus's recruiting efforts in Aeterna and how Atticus was already with them somewhere in Earth. He could tell us how the Brotherhood was taking the new recruits to Earth via our communication system. "I just need a way to talk with him."

An hour later, with the Circle in agreement on a strategy, I followed Thomas to an outbuilding shaped like a small barn. He placed his palm on the corner post. His magic flared, and a doorway opened. Light shimmered overhead as we hurried inside the barn. The door sealed behind us.

Thomas sat at a workbench situated under a window, and I paused in front of a bookcase full of strange items. Each shelf was labeled in neat, square handwriting. Runes, herbs, parchment, metals... the items were endless. Another shelf was dedicated entirely to different types of crystals. Thomas's expertise in all things magical was impressive, and he'd already started tutoring several promising students, including Tamara, one of the leaders of the Circle.

Thomas motioned me over to his desk, and I leaned over the moonlit surface. He pulled out a small wooden box and a woodburning pen with a metal tip. He plugged the tool into a wall outlet. It heated slowly, giving off a burnt smell.

I'd already explained the communication system to him, including the unique sigils linking Atticus's satchel to Silas's coordinating one in order to upload and download messages. Thomas pushed a piece of carbon paper and a pencil toward me. "Can you draw the symbols?"

It took me a few tries before I was confident I had drawn them correctly.

Thomas placed my drawing over the box's lid and began chanting. Magic flowed around him as he used the woodburning pen to burn the mark into the wood. When he finished, he pulled the paper away and channeled his magic into the sigil. The symbol for Atticus's satchel glowed brightly before it faded to black. Thomas rubbed his thumb over the symbol and handed it to me. "If I've understood your system correctly, this box should connect to your friend's satchel." He pushed his square glasses up his nose and leveled a knowing look at me. "It won't connect to your contact in Aeterna."

I swallowed back my disappointment, but I couldn't pretend as if the idea hadn't occurred to me.

"I'm sorry, Mae. It's just too dangerous."

I placed my pencil in the box and focused on the sigil. The energy clicked into place and tingled with the familiar desire for more. I sensed the pencil disappear, and I released the magic link.

"What does the pencil mean?"

"We set up a system of communication that wouldn't be obvious. The first object could be anything. It means we want an update, but we need to know that it's all clear."

Atticus would assume the message came from Silas, but I didn't want to take the risk of a written note until we confirmed it had worked.

"And now?" he asked.

"Now we wait."

IT TOOK ATTICUS UNTIL the next morning to send his response. As I sat at breakfast with Deanna, the box flared with magic, and I opened it eagerly. A small folded piece of paper sat inside.

Atticus had scribbled in pencil, "You missed the check-in. New orders?"

It had been two days since I'd left Aeterna, and Silas and Atticus checked in every other day. That meant Silas hadn't connected with Atticus after I left. He'd been taken captive... or worse. Dread crept up my spine, but I needed to focus on one problem at a time. Getting information from Atticus would help us stop Titus, and stopping Titus might be the only way to prove Elias's treachery and save Silas.

"Elias is a traitor. Found second portal. Silas captured. Where are you?" I wrote. I thought for a few seconds and added, "Eat this note." Not my most clever thinking, but it would get him all the information he needed and hopefully wouldn't leave him with an incriminating message the Brotherhood could find.

The box glowed a minute later, and I retrieved his message and read it out loud for Deanna and Casius.

"Maeve? Brotherhood followed your flare to Lost Sect. Attack at Blood Moon."

Deanna and Casius exchanged glances, their eyes wide.

My stomach dropped with sudden despair. I'd been so eager to escape the men who had attacked me at the bus stop, I hadn't even thought about them following my flare. I'd led the Brotherhood straight to the Lost Sect. Marcel had been tortured for their location, and I had given it away with my carelessness.

Sick guilt twisted my stomach. "They must have followed me when I skimmed here from Boston. I'm so sorry."

Deanna laid a hand on my shoulder. "It was an honest mistake."

Her instant forgiveness did little to soothe my guilt. I was an idiot. We weren't ready yet. We'd planned to take the fight to them with a surprise attack, but they were coming to us. We hadn't had enough time to train. The Rakken were going to tear us apart.

Deanna leaned over my shoulder. "It says the attack will be at the Blood Moon."

"What's the Blood Moon?" I asked.

The deep creases in her brow drew deeper. "It's the convergence of the Autumnal Equinox, a full eclipse and a harvest moon," she said. "All three haven't happened for a hundred years."

I had a vague memory that the Equinox had to do with the moon being near the equator, and it happened sometime in September. But the rest of it was lost on me.

"If you're going to do something with a lot of power," Casius added, his voice distant with stress, "you try to align it with an astrological event. The bigger the event, the more potent the magic."

"When is it?" I asked.

Their expressions were pinched. Deanna grimaced. "Tomorrow night."

"We're not ready for this," Casius said. "We need to run while there's still time. We have families and children here."

Casius was right; we weren't ready. But we couldn't keep running and waiting for them to find us. We were as strong as we were ever going to be, and I couldn't afford to wait any longer. I needed to help Silas, and Atticus couldn't stay undercover forever. It was now or never.

"If Titus knows where we are, he'll have people watching us," I said. "They'll just follow us wherever we run. They think we don't know about the attack. We can build up our defenses here and attack from behind our shield. We still have the element of surprise on our side."

Casius chewed on his lip. "You're suggesting a counterattack."

Deanna raised her eyes to the ceiling in thought. "We can quietly evacuate the families. We'll have the defenses of the town and the advantage of surprise. And we have Mae as our Anchor, giving us the full power of the Circle. I agree with Maeve. We stay and fight."

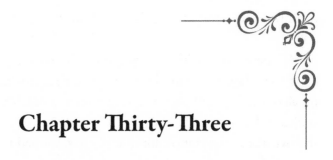

Chapter Thirty-Three

Two hundred pairs of eyes were glued to the horizon and the giant bloodred moon. It loomed over us and cast a bright light over the grim faces around me. It was the night of the Equinox.

Over the past twenty-three hours, a steady stream of people had left on foot from an underground tunnel that connected the Town Hall to a hidden exit miles away from the town. They left in small groups, without using magic. Casius had had the foresight to build the tunnel when they'd first settled in the town. Families had said hasty, fearful goodbyes and fled, leaving behind only those who could fight.

We'd been busy organizing ourselves and reinforcing our shield. Each person who remained in the town was assigned to a group with a specific responsibility during the attack. Thomas led the first and largest group, which was focused on maintaining the town's shield, our primary defense. They were camped out within the bell tower and were also in charge of our alert system. If everything went to hell and the shield collapsed, they would be in charge of the cut-and-run signal.

The second group included those who'd excelled in the offensive training to engage the Brotherhood on the ground. Casius led them, dividing them into four subgroups stationed around the town. They planned to stay behind the shield. If it came down to hand-to-hand combat, my group would have already failed miserably.

We were tasked with diverting as much magic as possible from the Brotherhood. I'd already warned everyone not to absorb too much of the Brotherhood's magic at once and risk becoming incapacitated from the tainted energy. I hoped they would remember that when the temptation hit. Simply put, we had to drain their magic before they broke through our shield, but we would have to be careful about it.

The thirty-five people in my group stationed ourselves on the roof of the Town Hall, which gave us enough height to survey the entire town. We had no idea where the attack would come from, and the visual clarity would help. We were joined by Deanna, the other five members of the Circle, and a handful of people who had enough power to skim and convey information between all of the groups stationed throughout the town.

Crouched in our positions, every person bristled with weapons and grim determination. In addition to Ripper strapped to my thigh, I had a second knife and four small throwing blades in a custom Rambo-style holster. I rolled my shoulders, shifting the straps crossed over my back. We were as prepared as we could be while we waited.

I chewed on the inside of my cheek as I watched the giant red moon. It was aptly named. The color of it was ominous, truly the color of blood. I tried not to think of it as a bad sign, but blood would be spilled. I had talked my people into fighting, when all they knew was years of running, and there was a very real possibility I was about to get us all killed. I puffed out the air trapped in my cheeks and pushed back my doubts. It was too late to turn back.

I peeked over the roof's ledge and trained my eyes on the town's perimeter, expecting the Brotherhood to skim into sight at any second. Around us in every direction, golden-headed grain waved in the cool night breeze, rippling like an ocean tide. Nothing had broken the still night. We would need to implement shifts soon. There was no use staying up all night and exhausting ourselves before the Brotherhood showed.

A bell rang out from the church spire.

One toll: South.

I twisted and found a portal shimmering into existence several hundred yards south of the town. Voices called out as everyone spotted it. The now-rippling surface reflected the red moon like blood in water. I held my breath at the unexpected sight.

The red surface shimmered, and a pack of Rakken bounded out of the portal. Silently, they dropped into the cornfield and disappeared between the tall stalks.

The air grew thick with silence as we waited for them to reemerge.

The first beast flew out of the field and slammed headfirst into the shield at the town's southern border. It shrieked, and the dome flickered, sending ripples of energy crackling across the surface.

The rest of the pack reached the shield and attacked with their powerful, razor-sharp claws. The heavy impacts were audible, even from our hiding spot on the rooftop, and sent energy sizzling across the shield with each blow.

The fighters on the ground conjured waves of high-energy magic at the Rakken. Thomas had managed an impressive modification to the shield, essentially reversing it to allow our magic to escape outward while still keeping anything magical from getting in. He was a freaking genius. Moving in pairs, our fighters lobbed their magic at the beasts. One fell with an ear-splitting screech, and the other Rakken retreated into the grain.

I let out a relieved breath. The shield had held.

I turned to my assigned communicator, a young man named Justin, who was just barely out of his teenage years. He grimaced as he watched the field.

"When the Rakken attack again, tell our people to draw the energy away from them. Remind them not to absorb it if possible."

He shook out of his stupor, nodded with determined bravado, and skimmed to the ground to relay my instructions.

The bell tolled twice. *East*. I pivoted, searching for the cause. A second portal opened and spewed black insects the size of cats. Thousands of them swarmed over a harvested field like a slow, dark wave flowing toward the town. Jerky movements on spiky limbs caught the moonlight, which reflected off their hard, shiny shells. Each shell segmented, sliding like overlapping plates of armor across their backs. Serrated pincers longer than their torsos extended on each side of their heads, dripping thick yellow mucus.

The large, twitching mass of insects spread into a neighboring field. The slime that dripped off their foot-long pincers was some kind of acid, melting and setting fire to everything it touched. Flames consumed the dry stalks, and smoke and fire spread behind the insects through the fields.

On the ground, the closest offensive team conjured a ball of energy the size of a small horse and blasted it at the horde. It slammed against their hard shells. The energy unwound and fizzled across their backs, skittering harmlessly across the group like strands of white lightning. The creatures didn't even slow.

I had once heard that a cockroach could survive a nuclear blast. I swore in frustration.

The fighters on the ground switched tactics and attempted absorbing the magic from the creatures. I couldn't tell if any of them fell; the swarm was too thick to identify individuals.

The front line inched to the town's perimeter, jerking and clicking and hissing. The shield would have to withstand another attack.

We waited anxiously for the slow-moving tide to hit the barrier. The shield didn't even flicker as they went right through it. *What the hell?*

An alarmed cry rose from the people on the ground. They scrambled back as the insects swarmed past our primary defense. A man on the ground disappeared under a sea of black before our people broke and scattered. They clutched at blistered limbs and melted clothing, trying to get away from a scorching wave of heat riding with the swarm.

I watched in horror as several people were swallowed under the assault in mere seconds.

"The bugs aren't magic!" I yelled. The shield kept out foreign magic of any kind, but a regular person could to walk right through—or a nasty, acid-dripping creature transported from another realm.

The heat surrounding the horde forced our people to dodge forward and back with barely any time to make contact, cutting down one or two at a time before retreating. It wasn't enough. The giant, flaming cockroaches skittered across the field closest to the town, lighting everything in their path on fire. There was nothing we could do from where we were.

Their hard shells deflected our magic assault and a good portion of our weapons. The mindless insects didn't react or try to avoid the blows. As soon as an insect fell, ten more swarmed over its carcass.

"Redirect them!" Casius yelled. "Fall back and create barriers. Turn the group to the field!"

The message was relayed, and the fighters engaged them with swords and machetes, while others retreated in a disjointed effort to create barriers. Casius swore and started relaying more detailed orders through several messengers at once, trying to organize the efforts on the ground.

Screeches from the south drew my attention. The Rakken had taken up a new tactic, rushing forward and taking turns as they clawed at the shield then ran back for cover. Our people pummeled them with magic, but the beasts were smart as men and quick as animals, dodging the random attacks. The shield wavered with every contact, and I wasn't sure how long it would hold. I didn't have much time to worry about it before the insects reached the first line of buildings. Acid hit the side of a wooden house, and it burst into flames. Within minutes, two neighboring buildings caught fire.

In all our planning, we'd never anticipated this kind of attack. We'd planned for the Brotherhood and the Rakken, but the nonmagical insects from some hellish realm were going to burn the town down around our ears.

"Tell Tamara's group to put out the flames," I directed a messenger.

"Thomas, get that portal closed!" Deanna yelled.

Good idea. We didn't want any more unexpected surprises coming through.

The bell tolled three times. I swore and scanned the horizon for the new threat. A portal on the northwest side appeared in the sky, creating a third bloodred pool of liquid hell. It tossed out five flaming creatures flying on jagged, leathery wings. Each one was the size of a minivan and burned red with energy. They looked like prehistoric birds on fire. The firebirds swooped high into the air, arched, and dove at our shield. Moonlight filtered through the thin skin of their wings, illuminating red skin and veins, turning the air crimson around us.

Holy hell.

They tore at the shield with their claws, and the magic flickered.

Our defenders cast magic at the firebirds. One of them snatched a ball of energy right out of the air, and it disappeared in its claws. A second one swooped down at the top of the shield, raking its claws along the dome. The whole thing dimmed.

"They're absorbing the magic!" I yelled. "Pull the energy from them before the next attack!" With my group, I focused on absorbing energy from the firebirds before they broke through the shield. The birds were too far away. They were only exposed to our abilities when they dove toward the shield to steal its power. We had only seconds before they rose high in the air on strong, powerful wings, once again out of our range.

I grimaced and swore. We couldn't catch a break.

The screeching of the Rakken stopped, and my ears rang with the lack of sound. I turned back to the east to check on the beasts. They were tearing up the ground, digging a tunnel under the shield.

"How far down does the shield go?" I demanded.

"About five feet," Thomas said, his attention also locked on Rakken. "We never thought about this possibility."

Damn it. We should have extended the shield. We just hadn't had enough time to think of everything.

"Focus on the Rakken!" I directed my group.

We absorbed the demonic beasts' energy, spreading the disgusting magic between us to minimize the effect, and together we took out two Rakken before the rest of the pack tunneled underground. They slipped in faster than I could count them. A half dozen, maybe, were headed under the shield and into our town. Three different threats from three different portals. Dozens of buildings burned as the horde of insects followed the fighters through town. The firebirds ripped at our shield from above, and the Rakken were digging under it.

I couldn't believe the hell the Brotherhood had just rained down on us. Powering three portals would take an insane amount of energy, even with the help of a Blood Moon. And Titus was still out there, waiting for his turn. I focused myself. We had to deal with the problems we knew about, starting with the Rakken about to break into our town.

I scanned our rooftop until I found my aunt overlooking the south side. "Deanna! You have to get the people off the ground before the Rakken break through!"

"Everyone to the rooftops!" Deanna commanded, projecting her voice with magic.

The message spread, and people rushed for the buildings. Those with enough power to skim escaped to the highest rooftops. Everyone else ran for the lower structures, clambering up the sides or running inside the houses.

"Higher!" I screamed at the people. "Get to the roofs!"

My voice was lost in the noise of attack.

The Rakken clawed their way under the shield and bounded into the town. Inhumanly shrill screams rattled my bones. Four monsters chased after a group of people racing for our building. It was a matter of seconds before they would be overrun.

There wasn't any time to draw out their life magic or conjure an energy ball and redirect it at the Rakken. I skimmed down to the ground and loosed three of my throwing knives into the face of the closest Rakken. One lodged in its left eye, catching the monster by surprise. It stumbled and fell to the ground. The other Rakken leapt over their fallen comrade, and I dodged out of the way before they ran me down.

My messenger, Justin, skimmed next to me with weapons in hand. He attacked a Rakken with a broad machete, but the blows didn't even slow it down. An almost casual swipe of the beast's claws ripped Justin's stomach open. I raced toward him with Ripper, but the Rakken tore him apart before he even hit the ground.

The rest of the demons caught the group of fleeing people, and the sounds of screams and tearing flesh carried over their inhuman howls. Five people were dead in a matter of seconds. Blood and gore soaked into the ground as the Rakken feasted, completely ignoring me a dozen paces away.

Up the street, three Rakken screeched as they scaled the outside of a two-story building, where a half dozen people had sought refuge on top of a low balcony. Claws sank into the side of the building as the monsters scrambled up the vertical face. The people were trapped. Judging by the intensity of their flares, they didn't have enough power to skim on their own. Some prepared to jump and make a run for it.

A knot tightened in my gut. I had to do something. I skimmed to the low roof just as the first Rakken clawed its way over the top. It snarled and opened its giant maw like a snake, unhinging its jaw, revealing razor-sharp teeth.

The woman nearest me screamed.

I held out my hands. "We're skimming to the Town Hall!"

I had no idea if I needed physical contact, but it was how I'd taken Aria through the protective barrier of the Council Centre. We didn't have time for a consultation. Six pairs of hands gripped me.

I gritted my teeth and pulled the magic from all the Rakken around me—the three on the roof and the ones down on the street closest to us. The magic obeyed my call, crashing into me with a wave of sick, dark energy. I resisted the urge to absorb the power and redirected the magic into a skimming spell.

The rooftop shifted and fell away. The group of us landed on the Town Hall in a heap, and I barely caught myself before I faceplanted. Carrying that many people took a huge amount of energy. My lungs were on fire, as if I'd just run a marathon.

Excited cheers and whoops greeted us. People clapped me on the back, knocking the remaining breath out of me.

"You're crazy!" Deanna yelled with a huge smile. "I've never seen anyone do that."

I sat down on the roof, draping my arms over my knees, determined not to move for as long as possible. The people I rescued hugged their neighbors. A small victory, but it was worth it. Nothing else had gone right for us since that first portal had opened. We needed to regroup and take out the Rakken. We couldn't let them or the fire bugs force us outside of our shield into the arms of the Brotherhood.

I took stock of our situation. The entire eastern side of the town had caught fire from the insects' slow and steady crawl. Thick black smoke blew over us, but our people had managed to build barriers from mounds of dirt, redirecting the mindless bugs away from the Town Hall.

People around me coughed and covered their faces. The Rakken howled again. I shuddered, too tired to see what destruction they were causing on the streets below. The firebirds above the shield cast a red pall over everything as they absorbed magic out of our dimming shield. Our situation couldn't get much worse.

The shield flashed and disappeared.

The firebirds swooped down and sprayed flames from their beaks. Their entire path lit with flames, creating a monster-sized runway of destruction across the town. A row of fire flamed down the length of the rooftop as they dove toward us, their strong wings beating down powerful blasts of air. I scrambled to my feet and threw myself out of the path of destruction.

People raced to put out the flames, pounding them out with magic and clothing. If our building caught fire, it would go up just as fast as all the other wood-framed structures. Then we would be forced down to the ground with the Rakken.

The church bell rang out twice, and every head snapped to the eastern horizon. Figures appeared one by one at the town's perimeter, surrounded by dark, tainted magic. I stared at them in numbed disbelief. The shield was down, and the Brotherhood had shown up to finish the job.

The pressure shifted on the roof. I froze at the familiar sensation, unable to react fast enough as two dozen unknown men dressed in leather armor skimmed among us.

One of the men grabbed the shoulders of the woman I had just saved from the other rooftop. Her eyes went wide, and her mouth popped open in silent surprise before they both disappeared.

"No!" I lunged but grabbed only air.

Yells of dismay rang around us as twenty-four of our friends and loved ones disappeared with the attackers.

"Get the shield back up!" I screamed.

Thomas's group formed a conjuring circle and began chanting. Deanna swiped her palm in an arc through the air. The pattern of her magic faded into a soft, opaque shimmer, and I peered into a magnified view of the land in front of us. My heart skipped a beat when I saw a familiar head of blond hair. Titus stood on the horizon, clothed in leather armor, blood dripping from his clawed left hand. He was enveloped by the threads of a Transference spell. On the ground at his feet lay a twisted heap of bodies. The horror dawned on me slowly—they were all dead, drained of magic.

Hatred flared white-hot inside me. I would kill Titus. I would do it with my bare hands if I had to, but he was not going to leave there alive.

"That's Titus," I said to Deanna.

Her lip curled in anger. "They're too far. We can't pull his magic."

"Time for offensive measures," Casius said.

"Focus on that man!" she ordered, pointing with her finger.

Rage filled us for our murdered people and for the decade of terror caused by the Brotherhood. Working in teams, we barreled magic at our enemies.

A domed shield materialized above the Brotherhood, blocking our assault. The energy kept flying at them as if our rage were a physical, tangible thing pummeling their defenses.

Dark magic swirled around them as they stayed safe inside their bubble while our barrage whaled uselessly against their defenses. Whatever they'd built was larger than any conjuring I had seen before. Finally, I recognized the hatched, short waves of the energy. But the spell was so large, I almost didn't believe what my eyes were seeing.

"It's a Transference!" I yelled. A spell that large could suck the magic out of us as a group, and if they managed to get enough of our magic, they would have access to Earth's Source just as Titus had planned.

"Gods save us," Casius whispered. "That's a *super* conjuring. The power needed to fuel that..." His voice trailed off in terrified awe. In addition to the Blood Moon, we all knew where that power had come from—stolen lives.

"Get that shield up now!" Deanna commanded. The Transference continued building, even though it was already massive.

"We have to pull the energy away from them." I couldn't absorb that much tainted magic. Just thinking about it made me feel sick.

"Can you redirect it?" Deanna asked.

"It's too much," I said. Even if I could manage a conjuring big enough to redirect that much power, the size of their spell would leave me incapacitated afterward. "I need the full Circle."

She put a hand on my shoulder, and we shared a moment of silent understanding. "We have to run."

I ground my teeth. Titus was right there, and this was the best chance I'd had at stopping him. But I couldn't do it alone. I itched to skim down there and bury my knife in his heart. But if I did that, the Brotherhood would most likely capture me, drain my magic, and further fuel their own power. If they absorbed the power I had locked inside of me, it might just give them enough to access Earth's Source. Our entire cause would be lost.

The firebirds flew over us again, and fifty desperate people threw magic at them before they had a second chance to crisp us. Two of the prehistoric birds fell out of the sky with roars of death. The other three banked abruptly and veered off.

"We'll get our people in the tunnel," Deanna said. "Some of us will stay behind and provide cover from the roof."

I stared at her. Anyone staying behind would be sacrificing themselves. It couldn't end like that. We had fought too damn hard and lost too much.

"Maeve can't be captured, or they'll have enough power to finish us all," she continued. "Get her to the tunnels at all costs. Casius and I—"

"Look!" I yelled, pointing farther out to the east.

Beyond the Brotherhood, more men appeared in a flare of multi-hued magic—shades of red, yellow, and blue. They stood two and three deep, spanning an entire field of grain.

Deanna adjust the magnified view and swore. "The godsdamned Guardians found us." Her voice lowered to a hoarse whisper. "We're all dead."

A wall of magic pulsed from their front ranks, and two-thirds of them transformed into snarling beasts. The front lines were comprised entirely of Shifters.

Like the Rakken, they had some resemblance to Earthen animals, but each beast was more foreign than familiar. A cross between a bison and a bear—but twice the size of either—anchored the center of their front line. Wolflike creatures with elongated front legs and pointed tusks lined up on either side of him. Flanking them, catlike Shifters with too-long snouts—no doubt full of teeth—coiled on lean muscles, ready to chase down anything that escaped. Every single one of them was a dangerous predator.

A chorus of shiver-inducing howls went up from the Guardians. I took it all in, slack-jawed with awe.

Behind the Shifters, the ones still in human form glowed with shades of blue and yellow power, adding their magic to the mix. I swiped my hand across the magnifier, searching the ranks of the Guardians. There had to be at least two hundred of them. But I found what I was looking for, right in the center rear. My heart skipped a beat. *Silas.* He was alive, leading the rescue with his sword at his hip.

I laughed with utter relief. *He really was too damn stubborn to die.*

His magic flared a pale yellow around him, but he was otherwise unharmed. Next to him stood a group of Commanders, including Tessa. I nearly skipped with joy at the familiar faces coming to our rescue.

With the arrival of the Guardians, the Brotherhood hadn't moved, and their Transference spell hadn't grown either. They stayed behind their shield, waiting. Titus's blond head wasn't visible because he was surrounded by his men, but I bared my teeth in feral joy as I imagined his reaction at that moment. They wouldn't be crushing us just yet.

The Guardians' lines of men and beasts merged into three distinct wedge shapes. The bison-bear was at the center of the middle group, and the wolves and feline creatures created the flanking formations. Those still in human shape stood nearest Silas while magic formed around them. I had no idea what they were preparing to do, but I knew their attack would include brute force and magic.

Silas raised his hand, and the Guardians surged forward, completely silent and in formation. A blast of magic slammed forward from the group, sending the hair on my arms straight up. The Guardians' energy wave crackled across the surface of the Brotherhood's shield, shuddering the entire dome. A moment later, the front lines of the Guardians' Shifters slammed into the shield, ripping and tearing at it.

"Why aren't they fighting back?" I wasn't an expert by any means, but the Brotherhood should have been putting their efforts into a counteroffensive. They couldn't have just been waiting out the larger and more powerful force. They had to be up to something.

"Time to go!" Deanna yelled. "Let them fight it out. We're not sticking around to see who gets to us first."

"Wait! The Guardians are here to help us. That's Silas leading them!"

"Silas?" Her face drained of color as she peered into the viewer. "As in Commander Silas *Valeron?*"

I didn't correct the title. It wouldn't have helped to tell her that Silas had been upgraded to Lord Commander and now sat on the Aeternal Council. "He's here to help us," I insisted.

Deanna's brow furrowed.

"He took me in as his Aegis when the Brotherhood found me in Boston. He saved my life more than once! He's here to help us."

Deanna looked horrified at that news. Every member of the Circle stared at me with an open mouth or furrowed brows. With my memories now recovered, it wasn't hard to understand their shock. I'd grown up on stories of the Guardians' raids and even a few about Death's Fury. Before the Brotherhood, the Guardians and the Aeternal Council were the stuff of our nightmares.

"Deanna, you have to trust me."

"We still have time to run," Thomas said.

The sounds of battle raged around us. The town was in flames. Death was at our doorstep, but hope still grew inside me. "If we run now, the Brotherhood will never stop chasing us." I tried to infuse confidence into my voice. "We have a chance to end this for good."

Everyone looked to Deanna. She considered each of them in turn, and I waited, surprised at my own confidence.

"What's the plan?" Deanna asked me.

Every gaze locked on my face. They were putting their lives in my hands. The pressure of leading these people threatened to overwhelm me. I pushed down my fear and hardened it into resolve. We were done running, done being hunted and killed off one by one. We would never run again. We would fight or die.

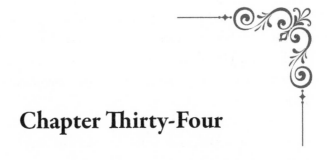

Chapter Thirty-Four

With each minute, the Guardians weakened the shield and pushed the Brotherhood toward the town. But Titus still wasn't fighting back. It didn't make any sense. I couldn't figure out what Titus was planning as he let them slowly chip away at their shield and their resources.

If they got too close to us, my people could drain their powers. Or if the dome fell first, the Guardians would crush them. No matter how much magic Titus had stolen, the Brotherhood couldn't compete with the Guardians in direct combat. They were outnumbered and out-trained.

Either way, the Guardians' assault gave us the time we needed to get our own shield back up. The reassuring glow of energy cascaded around our building, and I exhaled in relief. Everyone still alive had been collected and brought to our rooftop, and we were as secure as we could be.

On the field, Titus's shield flickered violently. I bit my lip, waiting for it to fall. After several minutes, I swore under my breath. With the aid of the Blood Moon and the stolen lives of our people, the Brotherhood had magic resources out of proportion to their small numbers. But it was only a matter of time until the Guardians broke them. They couldn't hold out forever.

A slow fog rolled along the ground toward the town, and I caught my breath. Within it, the layers of a conjuring built. The Transference was back. *Shit.* It suddenly made sense to me why Titus hadn't fought back. They'd been focused on building the Transference. Titus must have realized, as I did, that they would never beat back the Guardians without more power. He was simply holding off the attack long enough to steal our magic and gain access to Earth's Source.

The Guardians had bought us the time we needed to regroup, but the Brotherhood still stood between us and our rescue. Our shield wasn't as strong as the one they'd already destroyed, and they still had a pretty good chance of smoking us out if the fire made it to our building. We were running out of time.

"We can't wait any longer, Mae," Deanna said, eyeing the same fog. "Are you ready?"

I took a deep breath. "We have to take down their shield."

I scanned the battlefield as Deanna and Thomas organized the Circle. Accessing my power, I built a tiny flare in my palm, and the members of the Circle took their places around me.

The flare flew from my hand to Leah. Her power pulled toward Deanna and then Jason and onward through every person in the Circle until it returned to me and we each held a thread connecting us to the group. Just like I had done when we'd broken the last of my binding, I opened myself to the energy. The magic spun and grew. The patterns floated in the air, layer upon layer, building into a prism of refracted color inside the white glow of our magic. Every nerve in my body pulsed with energy. The combined power lifted over our heads and completed the Circle.

The magic was pure ecstasy, and I lost awareness of everything else. I closed my eyes and shivered with pleasure. Deanna said I would feel when it was time to stop absorbing the massive power of the Earthen Source, that the pressure would be too much. But with my connection to the Circle, I barely noticed any pressure. They were an extension of my magic, making my boundaries feel nonexistent.

Power radiated out of me in white streaks of energy. With the binding gone and my own memories restored, all fear of losing control slipped away. I was one with the magic inside me. It was time to do what I'd been born for.

I acted as the Focus again, reaching for the Brotherhood's shield. Their magic was dark, its energy pulsing like an oozing sore. With the power of the Circle behind me, and the Guardians pushing them closer every minute, the Brotherhood's magic was finally accessible, even at a distance. Just as I had with Atticus's compulsion spell, I grabbed threads of magic from the Brotherhood's shield and unraveled it layer by layer. The increased energy hit me in a rush of nausea. I gasped as it flowed over me, but the Circle flexed, absorbing the tainted death magic. Groans of revulsion echoed through each of us until the stolen life energy was absorbed into the source, cleansing the magic.

I bared my teeth in grim determination and growled, "I'm coming for you, Titus."

The weight of unclean magic filled me with a steady ache. The discomfort grew again to pain. There was too much bad magic for even the Circle to absorb. The Brotherhood's shield had dimmed but wasn't completely gone. The Guardians continued to assault it from the opposite side, but the steady growth of the Transference hadn't slowed.

A heavy knot settled in my gut. Beside me, Deanna swayed on her feet. She reached out and grasped my hand. I grunted with the strain. Sweat coated my forehead. Across from me, Tamara passed out, her aura cutting off as she fell to the floor. The pressure increased on each of us. Thomas swayed and fell to her left. Others rushed to help them.

I took more energy into myself and tried to bear the additional burden. We were in a fight against every single person channeling power into the Brotherhood's shield. The weight of it crushed me, but I couldn't give in. I wouldn't let Titus win.

I gritted my teeth and raised my hands, visualizing my fingers ripping into their shield and tearing apart the threads of magic. Sweat formed on my skin as I pulled as hard as I could. Their shield shimmered like a bubble of magic. It flexed and stretched until the threads of power twisted so far apart, it popped. The shield came crashing down.

An enormous wave of tainted magic crashed into us—the backlash from the Brotherhood's shield. The Circle helped spread out the poisonous black magic, but Leah and Jason passed out. Deanna curled over and vomited on the spot. I barely managed to hang on to the contents in my own stomach.

"It's down!" Casius panted.

I dropped the connection to the Circle. Cheers erupted from the rooftop. The enormous pressure in my mind receded, and Deanna and I leaned against each other in relief.

On the field below, the Guardians rushed the now-defenseless Brotherhood. With a roar, the front lines collided in a mess of magic, steel, and claws. The bison-bear plowed through men and Rakken, sending bodies flying around him. With a second toss of his head, the bison-bear's giant horns speared a Rakken through the chest, lifted him off the ground, and threw him into the air. Titus and his men scattered, completely unable to form a unified defense.

"Mae?" Casius laid a hand on my shoulder. His shirt was soaked with sweat.

"I'm okay," I gasped. I felt as if I'd run a marathon then crawled through a desert for funsies. But I would be fine.

The noise of the battle rang in my ears, a cacophony of violence. The lines of the two groups folded and blurred until I couldn't tell friend from enemy. I also couldn't tell who was winning. I scanned for Silas, worried about him fighting with drained magic. The battle below was chaos, but I spotted him thick in the fray, sword in hand, before I lost sight of him again.

As we watched, a group splintered from the rear ranks of the Brotherhood and hid amid the tall stalks of grain. After a few minutes, the threads of another conjuring started to take shape. Another Transference.

You've got to be kidding me. I swore under my breath. Every part of me was exhausted, mentally and physically. The heat from the burning buildings drenched me in sweat and smoke. I was sore and tired, but it still wasn't over. We weren't safe yet.

Taking a deep breath, I gritted my teeth and reached for the threads of the Brotherhood's Transference.

Nothing happened.

Alarm ripped through me. Without the Circle, I was too far away to absorb the magic. We had maxed out our abilities. The other four members were just regaining consciousness. Leah hadn't moved, although two people were trying to wake her. The knot of anxiety in my stomach grew into a bubble of fear.

"The Transference!" I yelled hoarsely. "We can't stop it without the Circle."

Casius pushed to his feet and joined Deanna and me, his face haggard. "We need to focus on the people. Dead men can't conjure."

It was hard to tell who was conjuring the Transference and who was fighting. Everything was mixed together. "I can absorb their life energy, but I need to be on the ground."

Deanna and Casius looked at each other in silent communion. "I'm going with you," she finally said.

Before I could object, she called out six names. Each person stepped forward silently, and I recognized some of the faces from the training sessions. They were capable fighters, good with close combat. We were all exhausted, covered in grime and sweat, but they stood tall as Deanna explained the need to get me closer to the fight. I stood a little straighter, gathering strength from their trust. It was up to me to make sure this wasn't a suicide mission.

"Okay," I said. "Let's do this."

We skimmed into a field of grain, between the Rakken fighting the Guardians and the group creating the new spell. Everything was chaos, and our arrival went unnoticed as expected. We crept to the edge of the field on all fours over the dry, hard stalks that had been crushed to the ground from the previous season's harvest. They poked at my skin as I stretched my mind to the Transference and followed the tendrils of magic back to the individual conjurers. Six men stood in a tight knot, connected together by magic. A ring of another half dozen men stood guard, protecting them from physical attack.

I gasped when I spotted Atticus among the guards. A long, jagged line ran down the side of his face. It looked like a cut from a knife—red and puckered—and it was only an inch from his left eye. His magic was a shade of red tinged in black. I stared in horror. Atticus had absorbed energy from someone. *What did they make you do?*

I had intended to pull the magic from the men fueling the Transference spell, but I needed to avoid grabbing Atticus's power along with them. *Somehow.* I'd never tried anything like this. I focused on the others until each person became a small flare of energy in my mind. Taking a deep breath, I focused on the tendrils of magic connecting the men to the Transference.

Not Atticus. Not Atticus. I tried to narrow my focus away from him, then I yanked the magic away.

Screams tore through the air as most of the men around Atticus fell.

The power snapped to me, and I gasped. I tried to release it outward, but the combined weight of so much raw power kicked me in the gut. Panting, I stopped a second before I drained them of everything. I almost blacked out. My whole body convulsed as I gasped.

I forced my eyes open, stared at the unconscious men on the ground, and released my grip on their magic. I wouldn't kill people if I didn't have to.

The Transference spell shrank but didn't disappear. Some of the conjurers were still conscious, and the determined bastards kept working.

A large group of Guardians broke into the field between us and the Brotherhood. Chaos exploded. The Brotherhood scattered, and the Guardians pursued. Trampling, screaming, and fighting surrounded us.

"We need to skim out of here." Deanna's eyes scanned in all directions. "It's too risky on the ground like this. We have to get behind the shield."

"The Transference is only stalled," I replied. "I have to finish this before they pick it up again."

A man crashed through the grain and emerged just to my left. Deanna's curved scimitar sliced through his neck, splashing hot blood across my face.

Another person appeared. Two from our group lunged at her.

"Wait!" I recognized Tessa a second before she was attacked. Layered with leather armor and weapons, she carried two blades in her hands. Both were bloody. My people pulled up short, their weapons raised, but Deanna shifted her body between Tessa and me.

Tessa lowered her weapons, her eyes locked on my anxious guards. "The Lord Commander requests that you return to the safety of the rooftop."

I snorted. That didn't sound like Silas. "What did he actually say?"

Tessa grinned. "There was more swearing. Less asking."

"*That* sounds like Silas. I'm almost done stopping the Transference for good."

"It's safer on the roof," she said.

I shook my head. I couldn't reach the rest of their conjurers from the roof.

"I already tried talking sense into her," Deanna said, stepping back. And just like that, they were on the same team.

Tessa stepped inside our circle and glanced at the dead man on the ground. "This is not a defensible position," she said calmly.

She sounded just like Silas. Soon, she would be threatening to throw me over her shoulder and drag me to safety. So I gave her the same response I would have given him. I ignored her.

I closed my eyes and focused. I could feel the Brotherhood's conjuring as it built again less than fifty yards in front of me. It was slower, but someone was still channeling power into it. I took a deep breath and followed the threads of power back to three men. I couldn't see them since they were hiding in the field like we were, but I could sense their magic.

Presumably none of them were Atticus. I hoped he'd been able to find a way back to the Guardians, but I wouldn't take all their magic, just in case. I pulled the energy out of the conjurers and inhaled through my teeth as they fell. I shuddered and folded over myself as I released the dark magic, confident I hadn't killed anyone.

The fog fizzled and shrank. They didn't have enough conscious men left to feed it any more power. I couldn't see Atticus anywhere. I hoped he'd taken the opportunity to escape in the chaos of the battle.

"Done," I said. "Let's go."

Now that the Transference was down and I had drained most of the Brotherhood, the cleanup could be done by the Guardians. My group gathered into a tight knot, ready to skim back to the roof.

I spun back to Tessa. "Is Silas..." I didn't even know where to start. I wanted to ask if he was okay, if the Council had captured Elias, if his magic would return. I had so many questions. "What happened with Elias?"

Tessa's nose wrinkled, and her mouth dropped at the corners. "He fled. Along with several Councilors. There will be a lot to figure out after this."

"How did you know where to find us?" I asked.

"Maeve, you really should return to—"

A voice echoed across the field, amplified by magic. "Maeve O'Neill will surrender, or her people die."

Titus!

Silently, our group snuck our way back to the edge of the field. Half a football field away, the remainder of the Brotherhood had regrouped around Titus. They faced the town with a new, smaller shield protecting them from the remains of the battle happening at their back.

In front of Titus, a knot of people knelt in the dirt, hands tied behind their backs. *My people.* They each wore a pendant around their necks that blocked magic. I recognized some of them from the ambush on the roof, including Joseph, the father of three young girls, whose accuracy with the conjured energy had impressed me. My gaze snagged on a familiar face, and my heart stopped.

My father knelt in the dirt next to Titus. Bruises and a nasty split lip disfigured his face. Titus gripped his shoulder and pulled him to his feet. I bit down hard on my knuckles to keep from crying out.

"Come out, kitten," Titus called. "I have someone who wants to say hello!"

I rose from my crouch. Tessa yanked my arm, pulling me back to the ground. "What are you doing?"

"That's my father!" I cursed myself for telling Titus about Father Mike.

At my side, Deanna swore quietly. Each captive had two members of the Brotherhood flanking him—seven captives and fourteen members of the Brotherhood, plus Titus. Even with reduced numbers, they held the upper hand.

I flipped Ripper over in my hand and weighed the odds of stabbing Titus in the face then skimming out with my father. Deanna squeezed my arm.

"I can't just sit here!" I hissed.

"He's cornered and gambling on your emotions," Tessa said.

"He's going to kill them!"

Deanna looked as ill as I felt. "Michael would not want you to sacrifice yourself for him."

"One minute left, Maeve!" Titus called out. "Are you really going to let your *father* die?"

My heart raced in my chest. I couldn't breathe. Every second was an eternity of weighing what I should do. I couldn't let him kill those people. I had just gotten my father back, and I couldn't lose him like this.

Tessa dropped her hand on my shoulder, holding me in place. "They have a shield. You'll never get to him."

"Maeve, no," Deanna ordered. "If they get your powers, we're all dead."

"Time's up!" Titus called. He motioned to a group of his men. They dragged four prisoners to the front, and I stared in confusion as Titus moved away from my father.

As I watched in indecision and horror, Titus slit Joseph's throat then drew the blade across his own palm. Titus's magic flared. Joseph jerked and twisted silently, his body lit up from the inside. Titus's battle cry carried across the field as he absorbed the magic. Joseph collapsed to the ground, dead.

Titus's men slit the throats of three more prisoners in quick succession as I stared, powerless to help. Titus mixed his blood with theirs and stole their magic, and I couldn't do anything but watch as his aura flared from red to white. He had finally absorbed enough of the powers of my people. He could access Earth's Source. And now his magic was as powerful as my own.

He turned back toward my father.

Murderous rage pounded through my veins. I would kill Titus. He needed to die. *Now.*

I opened myself to the source and skimmed straight for Titus. I slammed into the shield surrounding the Brotherhood, but I didn't even feel the pain of impact. Losing critical seconds, I tore at it with my hands and pulled with my mind, tearing through layers of magic. My screams of rage joined the sounds of battle around us.

Deanna skimmed next to me and pushed her palms into the dome. The threads unraveled twice as fast between us.

Tessa and the rest of our guards arrived at my side. Pressure pulled at my gut as our people skimmed down and joined the battle on the ground. Fury and magic flashed stronger than the clash of steel around us.

I forced the magic of Titus's shield to bend around my will until an opening ripped through the barrier.

Titus's eyes and aura overflowed with white power. He bared his teeth at me as he strode forward, his hands shifting into clawed appendages.

"Hold it open!" Deanna yelled. She ducked through the opening and skimmed to my father's side.

His head jerked up in surprise. "Deanna?" His eyes caught mine. "Maeve!"

A wave of power exploded from Titus. It rode across the open air, a shimmering crest of white energy as destructive as it was beautiful. Everything inside the shield burned in its wake.

It slammed into my father and Deanna.

I screamed.

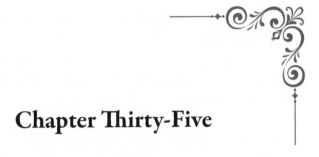

Chapter Thirty-Five

The shield crumbled under the combined power of my people. Bursts of pressurized magic overlapped until it was impossible to tell each arrival apart from the next. Everyone was on the field. Weapons clashed. Growls and shrieks pierced my ears. Magic flowed around us in a wild riot of power as people and beasts fought.

None of that mattered as I watched my father crumple to the ground.

I ran to his side. His familiar features, lost to my memory for so long, were bruised and misshapen. Slack. The memories of Father Mike, my mentor and friend, and those of my father blurred together—two people who were one. His face was a part of both my lives.

Deanna lay on the ground next to him, clutching his shoulder, her mouth distorted into a grimace. Her easy smile would never grace it again. My father and my aunt were dead.

"No, no, no!" I shook my head furiously. Tears welled in my eyes.

Rage took over. I found Titus standing in the center of the chaos. His head thrust backward, and his eyes closed as his arms rose from his sides. Everyone lay dead around him, while the magic he stole flew to him in a violent maelstrom of power, raising the hairs on my neck and arms.

Titus raised his hands above his head and opened his eyes. An enormous pulse of energy blasted from him upward into the sky.

The strength of it knocked me backward. I stumbled and landed on my butt, gawking at the sky above us. A Transference spell the size of a house shimmered above the death and carnage on the field.

His conjuring was three times bigger than the portals combined. I had never seen anything so massive. The patterns of energy twisted and moved from the outer edges to the inner, circling around the spell's center point. The power of it rippled in the air, linking Titus and the conjuring in a tapestry of magic threads that shone white with stolen life.

He had the power of my people, and now he would take the life magic from every single person on the field, maybe more.

I scrambled to my hands and knees. Rage and hatred powered me. Titus's face rose to the sky as he poured more magic into his creation, oblivious to the world around him.

I skimmed and stabbed Ripper between his ribs.

Titus's eyes flew open. He grabbed both my arms and bared his teeth, digging his clawed hands deep into my flesh.

I screamed and lost my grip on Ripper. The energy around Titus shifted, and his new abilities sucked at my magic, trying to absorb it.

I fought back. The energy crashed between us, pulled by our powers and our wills, while the Transference floundered above. My hair whipped in the wind as we grappled for control. He snarled, the knife still sticking out of his chest. I screamed my rage back.

Magic flared, and Atticus appeared next to us. He thrust his sword straight through Titus's stomach.

Titus's eyes flew wide in surprise, and he screamed in agony.

Atticus pulled his sword free.

Blood poured from the wound as Titus released me and grabbed Atticus by the neck. Every cell in Atticus's body lit up from the inside as Titus ripped the life energy from him.

"Atticus!" I grabbed the hand locked around his neck.

White magic flared around the three of us as Titus and I fought for control of Atticus's life. Caught between our powers, he became the ultimate fulcrum of our battle. It took all my concentration to protect him as he choked and flailed.

Titus thrust his free hand into the sky, and more energy poured into his super Transference. It flared above us and grew, sucking mine and Atticus's magic into itself.

Titus laughed, high-pitched and manic.

Atticus gasped against Titus's grasp. "Close it!"

No. I couldn't lose focus. I had to keep Atticus alive.

"Maeve," he said with a choked breath.

The whites of his eyes had burst with red spots. The jagged scar down his face throbbed a bruised purple color.

"Please…" His eyes locked on the super conjuring above us.

It was the worst choice I could make and the only one I had left. Releasing my hold on Atticus's life was the only way to stop Titus and save everyone. I knew I would never forgive myself as I let go.

Atticus screamed in agony, an involuntary cry of pain that cut straight through my heart before he folded to the ground.

His life energy snapped to Titus.

Titus inhaled through his teeth and closed his eyes. He froze—just as I knew he would—caught in the moment of absorbing Atticus's magic.

I slammed my palm into Titus's chest and grabbed the power inside of him. That magic did not belong to him. His eyes bulged, and he screamed, high and curdled. He jerked in my grasp, clawing at my arms and shoulders, but it was too late.

I took it all without mercy. I reclaimed every life he had stolen. I did it for Atticus and Deanna and my father. I did it for all of us.

Titus's eyes rolled back in his head, and he collapsed on me. I shuddered as the dark magic coursed through me, and I fell to my knees, holding him in my arms.

When the wave of nausea finally passed, I still burned from the inside out. I pushed Titus's body away. It tumbled to the ground next to Atticus.

The battle still raged, but the sounds of violence and death barely registered as I stared at Atticus's lifeless body. I looked at Titus next to him and felt nothing. I was completely numb.

The Transference spell pulled at my magic, drawing my attention upward to the swirling vortex, which had grown big enough that it pulled in the energy all around us. It was self-sustaining, and it would continue to pull in power and grow, consuming all of Earth's magic energy.

The power of hundreds of stolen lives had been poured into the creation of that Transference spell.

The Fate had said my moments would be full of death. Its saccharine voice filled my mind.

"Fate forged by magic's light, the Lost Daughter becomes Eternal Might.

Marked twice, where once divided; the Chosen are bound as one, united."

I was a member of the Lost Sect, a daughter. I held out my bared forearms that were marked twice—once with the symbol of my people and again with Silas's sigil. We were bound as one and united.

The prophecy was about me. This was *my* destiny.

The Transference above me threatened everyone I loved and my entire planet. With every life in Earth balanced against my own, the choice was clear. What I was about to do would end me.

I reached toward the source. Without a Circle or an Anchor, I was connected to too much power. A single person couldn't control the energy contained within the source. It pulsed with the essence of everyone I had lost: Atticus, my parents, Deanna, Marcel. The force of it overtook me, burning through every cell in my body. I became one with the magic, transcending individuality, time, and all the realms within our planet.

It claimed me, and I screamed in agony until I broke. I was no longer my own; I was something bigger.

I thrust my arms to the sky. Pure energy soared before it arched back down to Earth, trapping the super conjuring inside a giant dome of my magic. No one else had to die with me.

I took my last breath and pulled the tainted energy away from the conjuring. It pooled in my gut like a cancer.

I willed myself to take more.

The pressure spread to my lungs and grew spikes. I raised my arms and commanded it to obey my call. The magic squeezed my brain, and I staggered under the weight. My vision went dark around the edges, but the Transference still pulled against my magic. Sweat soaked my back as I strained to absorb the tainted super conjuring.

Desperate fear flashed through me. I wasn't strong enough.

"Maeve!" Silas pushed through the chaos on the field until he reached my shield. His leather armor was covered in blood, and his sword gleamed more crimson than silver.

We locked gazes through the shimmering wall of magic separating us. There was so much left unfinished between us. Even filled with the agony of the source's full power, my heart found room for the pain of losing him. There was no going back, and there wasn't time to say goodbye.

Silas's face drained of color. "Maeve! Don't do this alone!"

"The Chosen join as one, united." I didn't know if the voice coming from me was mine or that of the Fate.

Silas's eyes were dilated. He dropped his sword on the ground and pressed his palms against the barrier between us.

A renewed sense of destiny hit me. The prophecy wasn't just about me; we were supposed to do this together. The tiniest flicker of hope sparked as I realized that together, we had a chance.

I reached for him. My shield parted around my arm like falling water. Silas and I had been heading for this moment from the beginning. The inevitability should have bothered me, but it was strangely comforting. We grasped forearms. The overlapping triangle sigil of my House met the interlocking circles of his, and I pulled him through the barrier and into our fate.

Through the Aegis bond, I could feel his presence more clearly than ever before. For once, I wasn't confused about his emotions. The bloodlust of battle pounded through his veins, and so did the fear of losing me. His love for me surrounded it all.

I sent him back all the love in my heart.

If we continued down this path, we might both die. Maybe it was our destiny from the beginning—like stars going supernova. A collision course set by fate a million years before the explosion. There was no going back after this. We would burn brightest together.

"Do it," he said.

I reached through him and channeled the legendary power of House of Valeron. His source, although distant, was a well of power that sizzled in my mind—cool, crisp, and strong. Careful not to deplete his already reduced magic, I dragged the energy through him. It rushed to me like a waterfall, purifying the taint of the dark magic I had already absorbed.

Every muscle in his body strained against the force of my draw against his source. His teeth gritted, and his fingers tightened around my arm, digging into my already bloody flesh. The marks of power on his skin glowed just as they had in the Fate's temple, turning his aura back to a brilliant gold.

I wrapped my magic around him, forming the same conjuring as our Aegis bond. He flinched when the energy sank into him. He was now branded with my sigil. I could feel it. We were united, joined as one, just as the prophecy said we would be.

Death's Fury will fight with force, together they reclaim the Earthen Source.

Death's Fate is set that hour, burning bright with a balance of power."

Our magics were perfectly complemented. Where my power absorbed, his acted. Where his was frenzied, mine was harmonious. I was no longer buried under the compulsive need for more. I was balanced with the super conjuring above us, Silas, the Guardians, my people, and the core of energy within the Earth.

I released the combined energy into the air above us, pouring the strength of our powers into the sky. Our magic slammed into Titus's conjuring. A brilliant explosion lit the space above us. Like water pulled backward into the ocean, the spell collapsed on itself. The threads of the Transference spell reversed, and an inferno of magic power shot from the center and slammed outward.

Silas and I braced each other against the backlash of crushing magic. I funneled everything I could back into the source, but the flare of power that burst from us tore down the shield I'd constructed and splashed onto the battlefield.

People were tossed backward from the physical force as the magic backlashed over everything.

"Death's Fate is set this hour."

Silas pulled me into his arms, and we sank to our knees, leaning on each other, too exhausted to stand on our own. We'd survived.

Dark smoke billowed in the air from the burning town, obscuring the sunrise and the destruction around us. Behind the town's shield, demons prowled the streets. On the field, the wounded cried out for help. The dead covered the ground, shrouded in gray ash. The air was thick with it.

Silas pulled back and scanned my face. "Are you hurt?"

Death and magic saturated my skin. "I'm alive," I whispered. "And so are you."

He flashed his cheeky, boyish grin. "I told you I'm hard to kill."

"You're too stubborn to die."

He laughed. "I like that."

"Me too," I said. Then I kissed him. Our lips connected, and for one blissful moment, the world's problems didn't matter.

BY THE TIME SILAS AND I returned to the center of the battlefield, the remaining Brotherhood were gathered in a small knot, watched by exhausted Guardians. The last firebird had been killed, and even though the insect horde had burned everything to the ground, our people had finally managed to contain them.

My gaze traveled over the bodies, and my heart clenched. I walked numbly to my father and knelt at his side. Memories of a happy childhood flooded me. They pushed uncomfortably against the false memories of growing up alone on the streets. Silas placed his hand on my shoulder, and I laid my hand on top of his. The pain was too much to bear alone.

"The last of the Brotherhood is broken," Acting Commander Corin announced behind us in a solemn baritone. "Victory is ours."

The lump in my throat made it too difficult to speak. Titus was dead. The Brotherhood was gone. *But at what cost?*

Tears fell onto my father's face and streaked through the ash on his skin. I remembered the man I had known as Father Mike. My father. *He died because of me.*

I needed to remember him as he had been, not as the broken body before me with his hands bound behind his back. I tried to loosen the rope with numb fingers that were slick with blood, sweat, and ash. Silas eased my hands away and cut through the rope. Black and purple bruises ringed my father's wrists. I positioned his arms over his chest and forced myself to look away. I closed Deanna's eyes with my fingertips. Her auburn hair, flecked with ash, fanned around her like a halo.

She died because of me.

A few feet away lay the battered, scarred body of Atticus, my friend. *Because of me.*

I had convinced the entire Sect to stay and fight. So many had died. *It was all because of me.*

"The price was too high," I said.

Chapter Thirty-Six

The battlefield was slick with mud and blood. Conjured rain put out the burning buildings and forced the remaining ashes to the earth. The town was a complete loss. The Guardians spent the final hours of sunlight hunting down the last of the Rakken and scorching the insects. My people gathered our dead.

Each body was shrouded and carried to one of five funeral pyres, placed side by side in their final resting places. Two hundred of my people had stood and fought, and almost half had lost their lives. The Circle had lost Deanna, Thomas, and Leah. Families had been torn apart. Our physical wounds were treated by Aeterna's Healers, but no one would leave without scars.

The Blood Moon rose, a faded version of the night before, while the living stood in the trampled fields to honor and release the dead. Casius recited their names as the sun set behind the pyres. When it touched the horizon, a flare set the bodies alight. The heat burned against my skin.

Silas stood with his head bowed and hands clasped in front of him, flanked by his commanders, including Tessa and Corin. Their bloody armor was gone, replaced by black fatigues. With dark hair and clothing, Silas was indistinguishable against the night, just like the first time I'd seen him.

The Guardians hadn't been without casualties. Out of three hundred who had fought, sixteen bodies had been returned to Aeterna along with the members of the Brotherhood who'd surrendered. The Brotherhood's dead were burned on the field, and Atticus's body would be given to his family.

Silas and I locked gazes across the flames. Fire flickered over his features, casting shadows. I didn't know how he could stand to see so much death all the time. The Fate had called him Death's Fury. I didn't know how he could deal with the pain of it.

We stood until the last pyre burned out. As the sky darkened, everyone drifted off one by one to the field of tents set up by the Guardians. I watched the embers until it became too dark to see anything else. The smell of fire and death overwhelmed my senses, while the names of the dead looped through my mind. I recognized too many of them.

"Maeve."

I blinked away unshed tears and glanced over my shoulder. Silas stood behind me, his face cloaked in shadow. Silently, he moved closer, and we stood together for a long time.

"It doesn't feel like we won," I finally whispered. A lot of people had died because of me. Nausea twisted in my stomach again. "How can you handle this... this—" My voice broke.

"Leading people into battle is easy." He moved toward me, and I could finally see his face. His eyes were kind but tight with his own memories. "Regardless if you win or lose, it's what comes afterward that haunts you."

"So many people died because of me," I said.

He pushed up the sleeve of his left arm and showed me the three raised scars running parallel across his forearm. They were thin and long, like deep slices from a knife. "Commanders receive a mark for every loss. We bear the consequences of our actions for the rest of our lives."

Slowly, I ran the tip of my finger over the scars. It seemed fitting to have a physical reminder of the loss.

"You never forget," he said. "But just like cuts from a blade, the pain fades with time."

Once again, my life had spun out of control, and he was the only person on the planet who understood what I was going through. "Thank you," I whispered. It was hard for him to show vulnerability. He was letting me see a side of himself he kept private.

He rolled the sleeve of his shirt down and rubbed the back of his neck. "I owe you an apology. There's so much to say; I'm not sure where to start."

A knot tightened in my stomach. I was exhausted and numb, and I wasn't ready for this conversation.

"What happened with Elias?" I interrupted.

Silas ran his hand over his face, and the weight of responsibility showed in his expression. "Walk with me?"

We walked away from the ashes and into a field of young grain that stretched out to the horizon, untouched by the destruction around us. The Blood Moon hovered above, so large and full that it seemed I could reach out and touch it. The red color seemed fitting. *Blood. So much blood.*

The heat from the fire seeped away, and I wrapped my arms around myself in the chilly night air.

"Are you cold?" Silas's magic flared around us, and I froze, my temporary chill forgotten. The strength of his magic had grown even more brilliant than before. His aura had been pure gold, but now his flare bled white at the edges—just like my powers and the combined powers of the Council.

"That's... new," Silas said levelly.

When I'd first encountered the Aeternal Council, I had believed the white flare was a sign of the strength of a person's powers. But with my memories restored and my experience with the source, I knew it was a sign of how balanced someone's magic was. Perhaps the Council's combined flare was white because they carefully balanced the purest types of magic between Human, Shifter, and Fae. My magic was white because I could directly access Earth's Source, where all life was magically tied and balanced. *"Burning bright with a balance of power,"* I quoted. "I think I changed the balance of your power when I bonded you to my source."

He stared at me with a completely blank expression.

"You're freaked out."

His face unfroze, and he barked out a laugh. "I suppose I shouldn't be surprised. You have completely turned my life inside out in every possible way."

He started walking again, and I forced my feet to move after him. His energy felt like a warm blanket wrapped around my shoulders. The feel of it was different, more familiar, like an extension of my own power. I pushed the liquid, crystalline patterns of his conjuring with my mind. It danced in the air, shimmering as we walked.

"Elias is gone. His accomplices fled with him," he said, answering my earlier question.

"How did you get out of Alaric's chambers?"

"When my shield gave out, they captured me and took me to the Council." He shrugged, dismissing the details. "Elias claimed I was the traitor and pushed for execution."

Only Silas would sound so casual as he talked about being captured and almost executed. My heart clenched. He stood right in front of me, but I found it hard to breathe.

"I'm surprised Elias didn't try to kill you."

Silas's feral smile slipped through. "He *tried.* But the Guardians were witnesses, and they wouldn't attempt to kill me without the approval of the full Council, no matter what Elias ordered."

"How did you convince the Council you were innocent?"

"Elias was overconfident," he continued. "The Council was reluctant to take action with no more proof than his word against mine." He released his magic, and the soft shimmer faded, replaced by moonlight. "Stephan and Aria worked behind the scenes. Unlike me, they're both brilliant at learning secrets, making friends, understanding alliances. Stephan's sodding brilliant at politics. He was able to convince the right people to wait for actual evidence of my supposed betrayal."

We paused in the middle of the field, surrounded by thigh-high grain and blanketed in moonlight. I ran my fingers over the sprouted tops, shocked that something so fragile had survived the destruction.

"I gave the Council your list of missing persons from Lower Aeterna, and we found concrete evidence that connected Landas to the Brotherhood."

"How? We didn't have anything on him the whole time we had him followed!"

"He is the bonded child to House Crispin. But we had his father's house searched as well, and Aria identified the room where Titus held you. We found blood." He grimaced, and his gaze slid toward me, gauging my reaction.

I nodded, relieved that particular piece of the puzzle was resolved. After everything I'd been through, the kidnapping and beating I'd endured seemed like a long time ago.

"Your note was the final evidence," Silas said.

"My note?"

"Atticus didn't eat your note." Silas snorted in amusement. "He sent it to our message box with his own information about the attack against your Sect. Stephan brought it to the Council, and with the evidence piling up, Elias ran." He grimaced in distaste. "As did the Fae Councilors, Lord Nuada and Lady Treva."

"That's how Elias found us in Alaric's office!" I suddenly remembered that we'd seen Lady Treva on our way there. "They've been working together."

"We believe they've been working together for years, diverting Aeterna's resources and blocking even the most basic functions within the Council. With the traitors revealed, Alaric's name was cleared as well. We're still piecing together the connections between all of them."

"Thank God for Stephan," I said.

Silas hummed in agreement. "He's a good man."

"He said the same thing about you." *Back when I tried to convince myself I didn't have feelings for Silas.*

He rubbed the back of his neck again. "I'm afraid I haven't been living up to that reputation. Not with you at least."

My heart skipped a beat.

The tips of his fingers grazed my arm. "I'm sorry I was such a jack's ass to you."

I shook my head at his ridiculous swearing, but my heart was beating too fast.

"I want you to understand why I hurt you, and to apologize. I was afraid you'd be in danger if anyone realized how I felt." He sighed. "If I'm being fully honest, I didn't want to have feelings for you."

"That's really..." I searched for the right word. "Stupid."

One side of his mouth curled briefly. "It hurt you more than protected you, and for that, I'm sorry. You were in danger regardless of my feelings. On top of that, I did a piss-poor job of pretending I didn't care. I don't think I fooled anyone but myself." Both of his hands stroked slowly along my arms, sending tingles across my flesh. "I was fine with my life as it was before you flipped the whole world upside down. Wanting more is torture."

The moonlight glowed on his face, reflecting from his earnest gray eyes. His thumbs stroked my shoulders, and electricity fluttered low in my belly.

"What about your mating bond with Aria? You're still stuck in a miserable situation because of the prophecy."

"The prophecy was about you. Us. And that makes my whole fucking life finally make sense. Alaric can enact all the sanctions he wants. I don't care."

I opened my mouth to award points for his correct use of Earthen swearing and closed it again. Pain cut deep, like shards of glass. Atticus wouldn't be collecting any more points from me.

Silas searched my face. "Say something."

So much had changed since I had asked him for more. My memories had been restored. I remembered everything I had lost, everything my people had sacrificed to protect Earth from the Council, the Brotherhood, all of it. I was a different person.

"You can't break the bond-mating without Alaric's blessing," I said. And we both knew Alaric would never allow that.

"Let's leave everything behind," he said. "Tonight. Pick a place, and we'll disappear—Earth, Aeterna. Hells, we'll find a new realm no one has heard of." His eyes burned with intensity. "Don't you want more?"

I rubbed my palm over the building pain in my chest. "Wanting has never been our problem, Silas."

He slipped his fingers between mine. "Tell me what you want."

My heart squeezed in my chest. I loved him. I couldn't deny it. I loved him like a desperate idiot, even when I had thought he didn't want me in his life. But there was too much standing in our way.

"What about Aria and Stephan?" I asked. Silas had claimed the baby as his own, and my heart clenched. "You have to make things right for them."

"I don't know," he breathed. He pulled me against his chest and pressed his cheek against my temple. His arms gripped me so tight, as if he could hold us together before the world pulled us apart.

"They deserve so much more." I placed my hand on his chest, over his heart. It beat under my palm, strong and steady. "So many people are counting on us."

"What happened to 'screw everyone else'?"

"Half the Aeternal Council just defected. And Elias is still out there."

His jaw flexed against my temple as I continued.

"Lower Aeterna is a powder keg about to blow, and your government just fell apart. I know you hate the way the Council manipulated you, but you're a part of it now. And after all you've done to give Stephan and Aria a life together, you can't abandon them." I sighed. With my memories restored, the weight of responsibility sat on my shoulders. "Without me, the Circle can't access the full power of the Earthen Source. They need my help to recover from centuries of hiding and all our losses fighting the Brotherhood. We're scattered across Earth, and I have to help bring them home. I just don't know how the two of us fit in with all of that."

"I won't give up that easily," he said.

I ran the tips of my fingers across his stubborn, determined jawline. I was tearing out my own heart. Neither of us could live with ourselves if we ran away from everyone counting on us. But our lives couldn't overlap in two different realms with the Council and the Circle between us.

Crunching footsteps alerted us to someone's approach. I stepped away from Silas, and both of us flared with magic as Tessa appeared a few yards away.

"The Circle is waiting for you," she said, her eyes locked on Silas's new flare.

I took another step away from Silas. He reached for me, but I shook my head. For once, his expression was completely unguarded, and his pained expression matched the feelings shared through our bond.

"I'm sorry," I whispered.

I skimmed to the ring of tents before he could talk me out of my decision. A shimmering dome extended across the site, blocking outside magic from entering, including Silas and the Guardians. Casius waited just inside the boundary.

I paused before I walked through, wiping the moisture from my eyes and gathering myself. I couldn't deal with the pain of my impossible feelings for Silas right then. I simply didn't have room for more emotions. The Circle was waiting, ready to start working on everything that had to be dealt with. I had to push down my feelings until I could accept the pain of letting Silas go.

A few minutes later, Silas, Tessa, and Acting Commander Corin walked up to the dome. Casius extended his hand to each, granting them access through the barrier.

I turned away from Silas's burning gaze, but the emotions raging through our bond were full of pain.

Polar ice caps. Antarctica. Cold like ice.

"Thank you for welcoming us, Lord Casius," Silas said. His voice was stiff.

"Just Casius. We aren't formal here." He motioned toward me. "You can thank Maeve for convincing us to hear you out. I can't promise anything, but we owe you our lives today." He shook his head as if he couldn't believe the words coming out of his mouth.

While Casius led us through the encampment, Silas's stare weighed on my back the entire way, but I couldn't meet his gaze. Tents circled campfires burning brightly into the night sky as we passed huddled groups of exhausted survivors. Their whispers followed us as we wound our way to the center, where the Circle waited.

My guilt flamed higher. The Sect had stayed to fight because I'd asked them to. I'd told them we could win this. And now so many were gone. We weren't celebrating a victory; we were mourning our losses.

The three remaining members of the Circle gathered around a large fire, sitting in what would have been a circle if not for the obvious gaps. I sat next to Casius, and the empty spot on my right was like a fireball in my heart.

Silas stood on the edge, with Tessa and Corin a few feet behind him. "I recognize your losses this day," Silas said to the Circle. "Your dead are remembered."

"They remain in our hearts," a soft chorus of voices responded.

Casius, Jason, and Tamara stared openly at Silas, Tessa, and Corin. I couldn't blame them for being nervous. They'd been running from the Guardians for generations. Even I had grown up fearing them and hearing tales of terror before the Brotherhood. If I'd had those memories when I had met Silas, I would have run the other direction and never stopped. It had taken a lot of convincing to get my people to agree to broker a deal with the Lord Commander of the Guardians.

"I'm here to discuss your Sect's return to Aeterna," Silas announced.

Angry murmurs rippled through the Circle.

Tamara stared at Silas with furrowed brows and a raised chin. "We're not going back to Aeterna."

Silas bristled. "An arrangement needs to be reached—"

"Our home is here," Jason said firmly.

"You have nothing left here," Silas countered. "The Council will take care of you."

I gritted my teeth. He was going about this all wrong. His approach wouldn't work, and we didn't have time to waste. "Silas, please sit down." I pointed at the ground next to me.

Eyes popped around the Circle as he sat without argument to my right, crossing his long legs on the ground.

"We're all on the same side here," I said. "You all saw what happened today. The Guardians risked their lives to stop the Brotherhood, and they lost people too." I paused so the Circle would think about my words, then I locked up my feelings and forced myself to meet Silas's gaze. "Your dead are remembered."

"They remain in our hearts," he murmured, and we locked gazes.

His eyes flickered in the firelight. The gravity between us was undeniable, drawing us together. But there was so much standing between us. I swallowed hard and looked away.

I turned my attention back to the Circle. "We refused to run from the Brotherhood today, and I refuse to run and hide from the Council any longer. It's time to take back control of our lives."

Casius nodded in silent agreement.

"Silas can help us find a way to live our lives in peace." I held each of my people's gazes before I spoke to Silas again. "My people will not leave Earth. This is our home. You need to accept that so we can move forward. It's time for a new arrangement between our people."

WE TALKED LONG INTO the night and finally agreed to a plan, which Silas would present to the Council. The Lost Sect would not return to Aeterna. The Council would leave us in peace in return for access to a portion of the Earth's energy, which we would harvest and transfer to them. We would no longer need to run. All our people who were still in hiding could return, and we would be free to live our lives without fearing the Aeternal Council.

"I have one more condition," Silas announced. "I want Maeve to return with me to Aeterna and present the plan to the Council."

I stared at him in shock.

Casius was the first to object. "No. We can't agree to that. She's too valuable to our Sect, and the Council could use her as leverage."

"Maeve is the perfect intermediary," Silas disagreed. "She helped to flush out Elias as a traitor within the Council, and she killed Titus. She will be respected as a leader within your Sect. As such, she can present your terms with the greatest chance of success. And if she presents your conditions, then I remain neutral. I can influence the Council from within."

I had very mixed feelings about this plan. On one hand, being around Silas would only cause more pain. But his proposal did make sense for all the reasons he'd just shared. And a tiny part of me hoped it might give us the time we needed to figure out how to make our stars align.

Casius tapped his fingers on his thigh as he thought. "If the Council were to harm her—"

"She is under my protection," Silas said. His face went hard. "I gave an Aegis oath to protect her, and no one will dare harm her."

"I think she's proven capable of protecting herself today," Tessa murmured.

I nodded at her in solidarity. Finally, someone appreciated my mad skills.

Casius's fingers started tapping again. "Maeve?"

I looked at Silas. He had presented the plan as the best option for my Sect, but he was also bargaining for himself. For us. Once again, our fate hung in the balance. But this time, I had the power to choose which way it would tip.

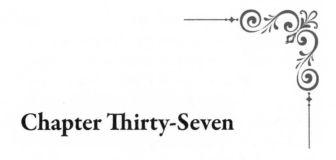

Chapter Thirty-Seven

Atticus's body lay atop a rough-hewn stone altar, shrouded in white linen. I fought back tears as I watched his family beside the flower-strewn altar. They stood in a large group, discreetly wiping their eyes. His parents held each other, and tears dripped freely from his mother's chin. I remembered the tears in her eyes when she had thanked me for freeing Atticus from the compulsion spell. Now her son was dead.

The Council chamber was packed to the point of claustrophobia. Atticus had been absolved of his Traiten sentence, but Silas had seen to it that he was restored to his title of Guardian posthumously. Atticus was being buried as a hero. And that meant that everyone who had any social status had shown up for the funeral, and so had most of Lower Aeterna. Everyone knew Atticus's name.

The crowd was tense as Silas stood behind the altar in full dress uniform, golden armor gleaming over his chest. Six other Guardians stood behind him, decked out in ceremonial armor, including Tessa, who once again sported short hair, and Corin, the imposing Acting Commander of the Guardians.

Silas had spent the past two days meeting with each of the families of his fallen Guardians and attending Council meetings, some of which I'd attended as we negotiated our treaty. Between all of that, I hadn't been alone with him at all. Other than negotiations, we hadn't talked since I'd turned down his offer to leave everything behind.

Our time had run out. We still hadn't found a way to make everything work, and I was more convinced than ever that our responsibilities would keep us apart. It was tearing my heart open, but I didn't know how to fix it.

What was left of the Council stood with their own families to the side of the great chamber, opposite Atticus's family. Their white robes made it easy to count how few remained—only the Shifter representatives, Lord Nero, and Lady Octavia, along with the Human ones, Lord Alaric, and Silas. Elias's treachery had gone deeper than anyone could have suspected. Everyone had been surprised when the Fae Councilors, Lord Nuada and Lady Treva, had fled with him. The Council still hadn't unraveled the full extent of their treachery, but we knew that Elias had engineered the energy shortage by diverting power to the Brotherhood, preying on the lower-class citizens, and gridlocking the Council for years.

Alaric stood with his arm around Aria as she delicately wiped tears away. The small swell of her belly was unmistakable now. My heart clenched again, thinking about her child—Silas's named heir.

Alaric nodded at me. When I'd returned to Aeterna, I wasn't convinced I could trust him, but he had been cleared of any connection with the Brotherhood or Elias. He had also been instrumental in getting my proposal approved by the Council. With Silas and Alaric on the same side, the rest of the Council had fallen in line with less argument than I would have thought possible. The Council was reeling and desperate to restore their power. Bringing additional energy into Aeterna through a deal with the Lost Sect would go a long way toward stabilizing their government again.

Surrounded by the small entourage of people Casius had insisted on sending with me, I watched a stranger eulogize Atticus. Stephan stood at my side as the man talked about our friend as though he were a different person. If he said the word "sacrifice" one more time, I was going to scream. There was no remembrance of the vitality and humor that had defined Atticus, or the dedication it had taken to get into the Guardian training program, or the ridiculous amount of food he could put away.

Angry murmurs echoed through the crowd. There was also no mention of the way the Council had falsely imprisoned him because of his class or the reason he'd become the unwilling symbol of the rebellion.

This funeral was not what Atticus deserved. I locked eyes with Silas and shook my head. Although his blank mask was firmly in place, his hands clenched and unclenched at his sides almost convulsively. He stepped around the speaker and walked off the stage to Atticus's family. The man stopped mid-sentence to watch what Silas was doing.

My stomach twisted as more whispers spread through the crowd of people.

Silas bowed his head in front of Atticus's parents. "I offer penance for the death of Second Legatis Atticus of House Fervatis." His voice carried across the silent room, and surprised whispers echoed back through the crowd. I watched with them, just as confused and anxious.

Energy flashed around Silas, and the crowd gasped. The purity and strength of his magic had already been legendary, and as I'd suspected, his new white flare didn't go unnoticed.

A small dagger appeared in his hand. He held the knife out, hilt first, to Atticus's father.

The man took the dagger with shaking hands. Silas pushed up the sleeve of his shirt. Atticus's father drew the blade deeply across Silas's forearm, carving a fourth mark.

I covered my mouth and watched blood pour from the gash. Silas held his arm out to Junia, Atticus's mother. She ran her thumb over the wound and licked it, ingesting Silas's blood. Atticus's father did the same, then he took Junia in his arms, and the sound of her weeping brought tears to my eyes.

Silas faced the crowd. "Atticus was a good man. His sacrifice *was* great, and there's no doubt that his actions were the turning point of the battle for Earth." He exhaled sharply and rubbed his hand over his face. "Death in battle is not glorious, and it's certainly not easy for those left behind."

Silas and I locked gazes. Through our bond, I sensed the shift in him from my spot in the crowd. He let his guard down in public, giving a rare glimpse of the man I had fallen in love with. "Atticus was more than just his sacrifice. He was a son." Silas nodded at Atticus's family. "And a friend. We failed him—*I failed him*—and still he was loyal. He fought his entire life for the same opportunities others are born into, and ultimately, he gave his life for them."

The people around me started whispering again. From the lower Houses, angry murmurs rose, joined by fresh confusion.

"In his honor, enrollment into the Guardians will be opened to everyone, regardless of House standing. There is a place for every skill and ability. And I will push the Council to do the same for all Sects. I've asked the Council to commit to a representative from Lower Aeterna among our number. It's time to bridge the divide between Upper and Lower Aeterna. I won't leave our people behind any longer."

Cheering erupted from the Lower Houses, although I couldn't help but notice that not everyone was thrilled with Silas's proclamation. The Council members had clearly not been expecting Silas's announcement, which publicly pressured them to add equal representation. And many around me were not going to be satisfied with a few minor changes. What Silas had just done was a step in the right direction, and my heart was a little lighter knowing Atticus would approve, but there was still a long way to go.

SAYING GOODBYE WAS hard. Tessa, Aria, and Stephan were strangers whose lives were now entwined with mine, and each of them was dear to me. I would miss them terribly. I'd already sent my entourage through the shimmering gate as I said goodbye.

I hugged Tessa first. We had spent the night mourning Atticus and making plans to stay in touch. She had become someone I respected and trusted—a true friend. She had her responsibilities with the Guardians, and I would be in Earth, but we promised to visit as often as possible.

There would be opportunities to see Tessa again soon. Silas's announcement at the funeral, and my deal with the Council, had already caused a lot of change, not the least of which was reopening access to Earth. My people, officially known among the Aeternals as the Earthen Sect of Harvesters, would integrate with the Aeternal Harvesters to control the flow of energy and people to and from Earth. Our Sect would benefit from the additional trade and the right to live our lives out from underneath the will of the Aeternal Council.

I hugged Aria. "Send word when that baby comes," I said, releasing her. "I'll be here in a jiffy. With presents."

Her eyes lit up. "Chocolate?"

I laughed. "You bet."

Stephan gathered my hand in his and kissed the back of it. "Lady Maeve, it has truly been my pleasure and honor." His eyes crinkled handsomely as he grinned. That was as close to a "thank you" as a Fae would get, even a half-blooded one. I gave him another hug.

My eyes slid to Silas, and butterflies twisted in my stomach. He looked as if he hadn't slept in days. He scowled at the floor, his arms folded over his chest. The Council needed his advice and his vote at every turn as they tried to recover the stability of their government.

He had barely managed to make it in time to say goodbye. I could imagine how much he hated it all.

His eyes lifted to mine, full of fire. The butterflies reacted violently.

"Fare you well," Stephan said, ushering the others from the room.

Silas and I were finally alone, and every part of me ached to throw myself into his arms and never leave.

"Nothing has changed." I choked on the words and couldn't meet his gaze. I didn't know what else to say. A confused knot of emotions roiled in my stomach as I chose my people over my heart. It was the right thing to do, the responsible thing.

He closed the distance between us in three long strides and cupped my face between his palms.

I wrapped my arms around myself to keep from folding into him.

"I won't give up that easily," he said quietly. "I need you in my life, Maeve O'Neill of Earth."

I loved him so desperately. Leaving him behind hurt so hard and felt so wrong.

Slowly, he closed the distance between us until our lips connected. I leaned into him, hungry for his touch, even though it scorched my heart. Tears slipped from my eyes. He lowered his forehead to mine and stroked my tears away with his thumbs. I closed my eyes and wanted nothing more than to stay in his arms forever. But reality was too crushing.

"This hurts too much."

"Say the word," he whispered. "We can leave it all behind."

He would never forgive me if I asked him to do that. And I couldn't be that selfish. "I love you, Silas. But I can't ask you to walk away from your life here. It's not who you are. And I can't abandon my people, either."

He held me closer. "We can figure out a way," he promised. "There can't be two more stubborn people in any realm of Earth."

We held each other as I breathed in his scent and savored the taste of him on my tongue. I couldn't do it. I couldn't give him up. Just like the Fate's prophecy had said, we were bound together. "We have to find a way," I said.

Hope flared through our shared bond, his and mine. He kissed me again, and this time, it was filled with the fire of fierce determination.

"We will," Silas promised. "Soon."

Slowly, we pulled apart. We had overcome so much already. There was still a long way to go, but we would find a way to make it work together.

"Soon," I vowed.

I turned and walked through the portal to Earth, leaving my heart behind in Aeterna.

Acknowledgements

Writing a book takes a village, and I couldn't have done it without mine. First, I'd like to thank my children and my husband. It wasn't always easy for them, but they sacrificed endless hours of my time and attention while my side project turned into something bigger. I'd also like to thank my 'guysies'. You know who you are. Each of you supported me, listened to me, and cheered me on when I decided to write a book like a crazy person. Your kindness over many years and miles has brought me to tears more than once. Thanks to family, friends, and coworkers (and basically anyone who talked to me for more than five minutes) for listening to me and for giving me the courage to stretch myself.

A big thank you to the writer community at large. Countless authors took time to read, to critique, and to give advice while they shared their journey with me, for which I am endlessly grateful. (Even the guy who said he'd rather pull out his own fingernails than read the first draft of my opening chapter twice. He wasn't very nice, but he wasn't wrong.) And a special thanks to my editing team whose detailed input and creativity made this story shine.

And last, thank you to my readers. Thank you for trusting me with your time and your imagination. Thank you for joining me on the best part of this journey.

About the Author

B.P. Donigan was born and raised in Alaska. She left to attend college in rural Idaho, graduated from not-so-rural Utah, and finally moved to very-not-rural Boston, where she lived and worked for ten years.

After paying her dues to extreme winters, she resides now in sunny California, with her two kids, two dogs, and one amazing husband. Like any good superhero, she spends her days building her cover story behind a desk and her nights saving the world (on paper, at least).

Read more at https://bpdonigan.com/.

About the Publisher

Dear Reader,

We hope you enjoyed this book. Please consider leaving a review on your favorite book site.

Visit https://RedAdeptPublishing.com to see our entire catalogue.

Don't forget to subscribe to our monthly newsletter to be notified of future releases and special sales.